THE CALL OF THE RIFT

CREST

JAE WALLER

Published by ECW Press
665 Gerrard Street East
Toronto, Ontario, Canada M4M 1Y2
416-694-3348 / info@ecwpress.com

Editor: Jennifer Albert
Cover design: Erik Mohr/Made by Emblem
Cover illustration: © Simon Carr/
www.scarrindustries.com
Maps: Tiffany Munro/
www.feedthemultiverse.com
Author photo: © Rob Masson

LIBRARY AND ARCHIVES CANADA CATALOGUING IN PUBLICATION

Title: Crest / Jae Waller.

Names: Waller, Jae, author.

Series: Waller, Jae. Call of the rift ; bk. 3.

Description: Series statement: The call of the rift

Identifiers: Canadiana (print) 20200403397 | Canadiana (ebook) 20200403419

ISBN 978-1-77041-458-7 (HARDCOVER)
ISBN 978-1-77305-651-7 (EPUB)
ISBN 978-1-77305-652-4 (PDF)
ISBN 978-1-77305-653-1 (KINDLE)

Classification: LCC PS8645.A46783 C74 2021 | DDC C813/.6—dc23

The publication of *The Call of the Rift: Crest* has been generously supported by the Canada Council for the Arts and is funded in part by the Government of Canada. *Nous remercions le Conseil des arts du Canada de son soutien. Ce livre est financé en partie par le gouvernement du Canada.* We acknowledge the support of the Ontario Arts Council (OAC), an agency of the Government of Ontario, which last year funded 1,965 individual artists and 1,152 organizations in 197 communities across Ontario for a total of $51.9 million. We also acknowledge the contribution of the Government of Ontario through the Ontario Book Publishing Tax Credit, and through Ontario Creates for the marketing of this book.

Canada Council for the Arts

Conseil des Arts du Canada

Canada

PRINTED AND BOUND IN CANADA

PRINTING: FRIESENS 5 4 3 2 1

For Kathleen

"A mother is not a person to lean on,
but a person to make leaning unnecessary."
— Dorothy Canfield Fisher

Beru Territory
Nokun Bel
Haka Territory
Ferryhouse
Koreba Iren
Nordmur
Thúnveldt
Hafenaast
Caladsten
Gåmelheå
Rin Territory
Tamun Dael
Kotula Huin
Aeti Ginu
Tamu Territory
Bitaiya Iren
Arèt Ocean
Nordfyskår
Algard Island
Sordfyskår
Holmgar
Marijka
Caladheå
Ile vi Goyero
Toel Ginu
Copra Bay
Ile vi Dévoye
Yeva Iren
Innisburren
Gallnach Territory
LEGEND:
Town/Village
RIVER/FOREST
Territory
Area Name
Kateiko Rin's Travels
in Anwen Bel and Surrounding Lands
CIRCA 620-630

Sanctuary Villages
Vunfjel
Kotula Iren
Turquoise Mountains
Nyhemur
Anwen Bel
Oberu Iren
Nettle Ginu
Se Ji Ainu
Sky Bridge
Dúnravn Pass
Tømmbrind Creek
N. Iyun Bel
Crieknaast
Roannveldt
Iyo Territory
Ingdanrad
The Crux
To Brånnheå
N
Stengar
S. Iyun Bel
Rutnaast
Eremur
Burren Inlet
Kae Territory
Yula Territory
Laca vi Miero
Ukan Bel
Hårengar
T. Munro 2017

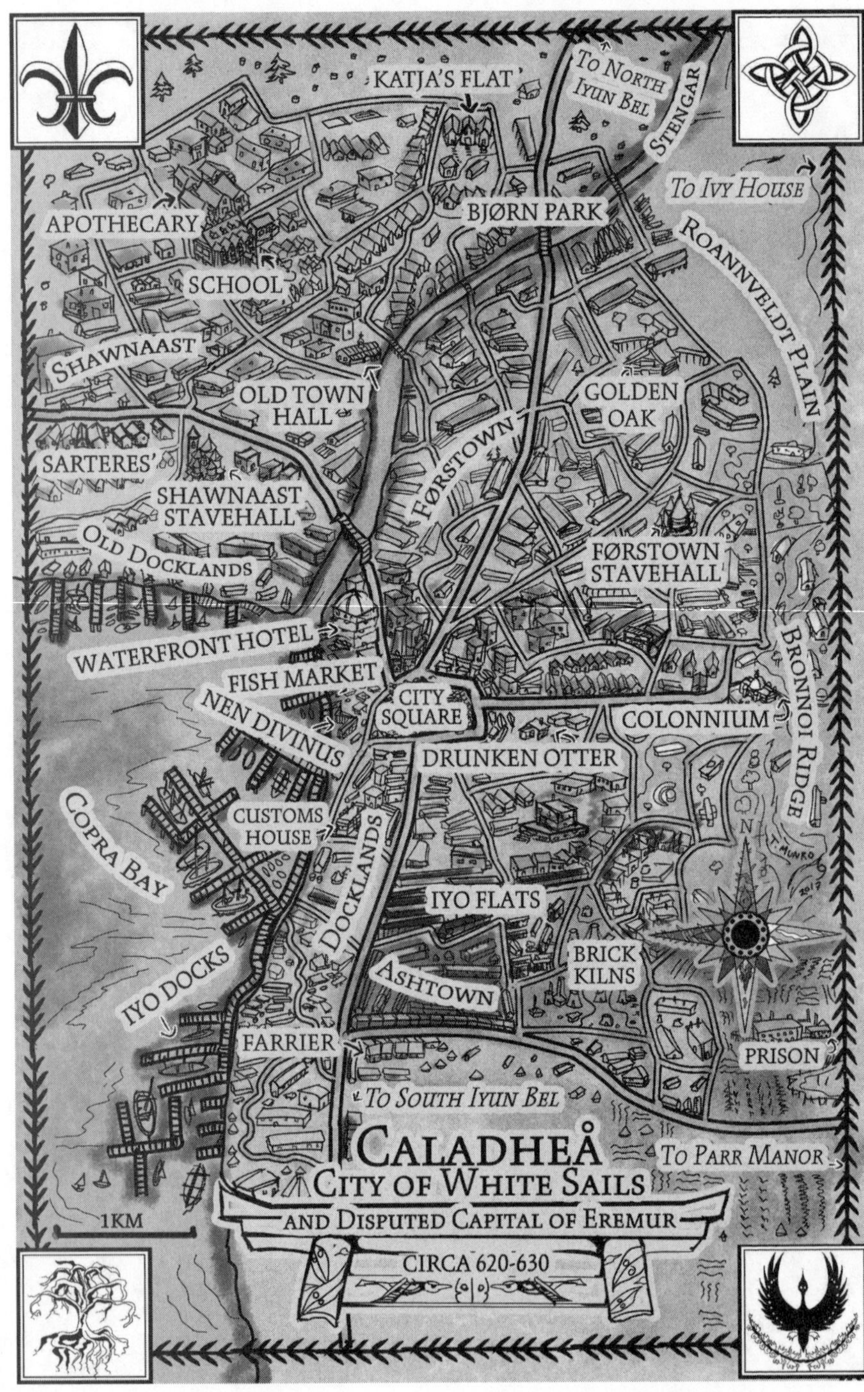
KATJA'S FLAT
To North Iyun Bel
Stengar
To Ivy House
Bjørn Park
Apothecary
School
Roannveldt Plain
Shawnaast
Old Town Hall
Golden Oak
Førstown
Sarteres'
Shawnaast Stavehall
Old Docklands
Førstown Stavehall
Waterfront Hotel
Bronnoi Ridge
Fish Market
City Square
Nen Divinus
Colonnium
Drunken Otter
Copra Bay
Customs House
Docklands
T. Munro 2017
N
Iyo Flats
Brick Kilns
Iyo Docks
Ashtown
Farrier
Prison
To South Iyun Bel
Caladheå
City of White Sails
To Parr Manor
1KM
and Disputed Capital of Eremur
Circa 620-630

1.

THE RIVER

"Ooh, how about this, Kako?" Nili thrust a scrap of amber cloth at me. "If I embroider that in white, you'll look all shimmery."

"You'd lose me on the lake." I waved at the sun-struck cove where we lounged with our friends, cooking breakfast and preparing for the day's work. Shafts of golden light cut through puffy clouds and glittered in the morning mist. Cottonwoods with yellowing leaves shaded the beach, dripping dew into puddles with tiny *plinks*.

I went on sharpening my fish knife. Every autumn Nili sewed me new shirts and leggings, and every autumn we argued about it. She insisted that bright berry dyes would complement my colouring — brown hair, brown eyes, tanned skin. I wanted something dark for tromping around the muddy rainforest.

After I refused her fifth choice, Nili shoved swatches back into her fabric bag. "I don't know why I care," she huffed. "You'll outgrow them anyway."

"Sorry. Should I stop wearing clothes?"

"*That'll* get Canoe Boy's attention." She snickered. "Are the duck potatoes done? I'm starving."

I knocked a bundle of singed leaves from our campfire. While Nili grew up learning textiles from her mother, my mother had spent years teaching me to sense and control water. Closing my eyes in meditation, I slipped my mind through the leaves to the small roots inside the bundle, measuring the water temperature and the amount of steam. I peeled the charred leaves back with my knife to reveal small steaming roots. "Perfect—"

Cheering interrupted me. Several boys were spitting squash seeds onto a tarp, competing to get one furthest. Onarem, an axe-jawed leatherworker, raised his fists over his head and called for anyone brave enough to challenge him.

Nili stood up. "Ai, bludgehead!"

She popped a seed in her mouth and spat. It soared over the tarp and plunked into the lake. Onarem gaped. Nili kissed another seed and spat it at his bare chest. Laughter rippled through the onlookers.

As we ate, an ochre-red canoe slid into the cove. Its high prow was carved into a kinaru, the long-necked water bird that was our tribe's sacred crest. I peered at the paddler and swore. If I'd known Rokiud was home from summer travels, I'd at least have brushed my hair.

"*Yan taku*," Nili breathed as he landed. "I forgot how lush Canoe Boy is."

I pushed her jaw shut. Like every boy in our tribe, the Rinjouyen, Rokiud went shirtless to show his tattoos, which included crossed paddles on his chest for being a canoe carver. He'd razored off his hair, leaving a thin black layer like leaf fuzz. It highlighted the sharp angles of his face.

Onarem punched his arm in greeting. Rokiud swiped at his head. Onarem tackled Rokiud and they rolled head over boot, shouting joyfully and trying to pin each other in the shallows.

Nili elbowed me. "Go say hi."

"I'm done wasting time on Rokiud," I said, picking soot from my fingernails. "I have things to do. Training for my water-calling test, working my trapline—"

She looked at me like I was made of stupid. "You passed every practice test, and it's not trapping season yet. C'mon." She pulled me to the shore and beamed at Onarem. "Kateiko and I wanna go fishing by the old smokehouses. Can you take us?"

Onarem scrambled up, dripping. "Uh, my canoe's only got two seats—"

"Riiight," Nili sighed. "Guess we gotta ask someone with a bigger boat."

"Nei, hang on," he stammered. "Rokiud, why don't you bring Kateiko? We'll all go."

Rokiud grinned at me, shaking droplets off his head. "Do your water-caller thing and we've got a deal."

My stomach flip-flopped. I seeped my mind into the fibres of his breeches to dry them, acutely aware of his muscular legs. I tossed my fishing gear into his canoe's bow, then stopped when I noticed gouges in the hull. The carved kinaru's bill had broken off. "What happened?"

"I went over a waterfall and hit some rocks," Rokiud said. "No big deal. I resined over the damage, so it hasn't rotted."

He's the rotten one, my mother would say. For years the elders had refused to initiate him as a carver — first for skipping lessons, then sneaking off to river-race, then stealing his father's war canoe to race again. The day they were finally going to evaluate his work, he'd found crude symbols painted on his hull, probably a prank by another kid. I'd made new paint from ground ochre, helped Rokiud cover the symbols, and dried the paint just before the elders arrived.

His proud look while getting his carver tattoo had been the most beautiful thing I'd ever seen. Then, before I worked up the nerve to say anything, we'd separated for summer. My family had canoed to an alpine village of itherans, the foreigners who'd settled around our land. In the high pastures, busy trading my furs for goat wool, I'd tried to forget about Rokiud. Here, eye level with his radiant smile, my resolve melted like honey in sunlight.

I dropped onto the bow seat and grabbed a paddle. Rokiud leapt into the stern and pushed off. We glided from the cove onto the lake proper, framed by steep valley walls dense with forest. Tendrils of mist parted around us. Nili and Onarem followed in his boat, her laughter carrying across the turquoise water.

All along the beach, canvas tents hung from huge conifer trees. The canoes at my family's campsite were gone. Everyone must've left for the day. My father had jokingly moaned that I'd grown up enough to avoid my parents, but they didn't mind as long as I gathered my share of food. I wondered if I could keep it secret that I was going fishing with Rokiud — then a voice hollered my name.

Fendul, a lanky older boy wearing a sheathed sword, walked out from the woods. "Where are you headed?" he called.

I raised my fishing net. "To catch bears."

He looked unamused. "Remember to stay off the downriver branch of Kotula Iren. It's not safe these days."

"The river I canoed every summer to get to the ocean until your father banned anyone from going?" Rokiud said. "You think I'd forget?"

Fendul rubbed the lines tattooed around his arm, a marker that he was our okoreni, the second-in-command of the Rin-jouyen. "If you knew what's going on out there—"

"Let's go," I interrupted. Fendul and I lived in the same plank house at our permanent settlement. I got enough lectures from him.

We pushed off again. Rokiud's bitterness radiated like smoke. Earlier this year Fendul's father, our current leader, had declared the war-torn coast too dangerous to visit — for everyone except Fendul's family, who'd travelled there on some diplomatic whatever. All I knew was itherans kept fighting over land that wasn't theirs to begin with.

"Where'd you go instead this summer?" I asked Rokiud.

"A new village up north," he said. "Some itherans fled the coast and settled in the high mountains. It'll be rough come winter, but I guess they plan to stay, 'cause they hired me and my brothers to build log cabins. Waste of our skills." He shook his head. "Anyway, how was your trip? Did you . . . y'know?"

I winced. Coming of age was the most sacred rite in the Rinjouyen. Our ancestral spirits gifted us an animal body, our attuned form, that we could change into at will. Rokiud had attuned at twelve and most of our friends at thirteen. I was well into fourteen and still waiting. *Surely soon*, my parents whispered when they thought I was asleep.

Most people kept their attuned form private, but Rokiud had boasted that he got the form of a blackfin whale, sleek and deadly. Other kids dared him to prove it, so he transformed in the lake and capsized their canoes. He was only a year older than me, but ever since then, there'd been a gulf between us. I stowed my paddle and started untangling my net so I didn't need to meet his eyes.

"Wait," Rokiud said. "Let's go down the river and see if the salmon run started."

"Fendul just said—"

"Piss on that. You think I attuned by doing what I was told?"

My insides lurched. "You'd break the rules to help me?"

He shrugged. "I owe you for the canoe paint. Couldn't have passed my carving apprenticeship without it."

Refusal pressed on my tongue, but Fendul's warning seemed ridiculous. The coastal skirmishes were thirty leagues away. "I'll go if Nili comes," I said. If the boys did something dumb, she and I could take one canoe and go home.

Rokiud flashed that honey-melting grin. "Ai," he called to Nili and Onarem. "Wanna look for salmon?"

Nili looked to me. When I nodded, she called back, "Sure."

We paddled past the old crumbling smokehouses where we'd planned to fish, then past our sacred tree, an immense rioden with sprawling branches and mossy bark. Finally we rounded a forested point. Rumbling signalled Kotula Iren ahead. It'd rained overnight and the current ran high and fast, beckoning with promise. My future was out there in the unknown.

Our canoes hit white froth and careened onto the river. We glided around bends, slicing through patches of floating leaves. The rush was intoxicating. I knew that this sense of freedom was the real reason Rokiud suggested coming. It was too early for salmon. I'd have to return to the lake to catch enough fish to dodge my parents' ire, but I would've gladly ridden the river forever.

Then Rokiud said, "What's that ahead?"

In the distance, a speck floated on the water, growing larger. It shifted on the left, right, left. Someone was paddling a canoe upriver toward us, but the motion was weirdly off pace.

"Let's go back," Onarem said. "I didn't sign up for getting caught."

"Nei, wait," I said. "Are they in trouble?"

"*Kaid*," Rokiud swore. "They will be if they lose to the current. There's rapids further down."

Something yanked in my gut. This felt like a test from our ancestral spirits. A brave person would help, but a responsible person would obey the rules and turn back. Maybe I hadn't attuned yet because I didn't know which I was. I thought of the gouge in Rokiud's canoe, imagining the stranger's craft hitting a boulder.

"Fuck the rules," I said. "We're going to rescue them."

Onarem dropped his protests when Nili told him to shut up. We paddled hard and soon neared the stray boat. Its prow was uncarved and tall enough to handle ocean swells. A man was slumped inside, clutching a paddle that dragged uselessly through foaming water. I grabbed at his canoe and missed. The current yanked it out of reach.

We'd nearly caught up again when the canoe disappeared around a bend. We rounded it, too, and hit rapids coursing through a ravine. Echoes roared off the rock walls. The stray canoe spun this way and that. Whitecapped waves struck its hull, rocking the man's limp form.

"I'm going for it," Rokiud yelled over the thunder of water. "Gonna need your help, Kateiko." He yanked off his boots, dove into the river, and swam toward the stray canoe.

I kept paddling as I dropped my mind into the current, struggling to restrain it. Nili tossed Rokiud a rope. He looped it around the stray canoe's prow. She hauled it in while Onarem kept them afloat, but rapids kept pulling the crafts in opposite directions. I called on as much water as I could, sweat running into my eyes, and guided all three canoes forward until the ravine widened to reedy banks.

Nili and Onarem tumbled ashore and pulled in the stray canoe. With a last surge of strength, I ran Rokiud's canoe aground. The boys lifted the stranger and eased him onto the mud. He sagged, breathing shallowly, gripping his paddle like it was fused to his hands. One leg of his breeches was rolled up, exposing a sticky poultice over a crusted wound. I choked at the stench of infection.

Rokiud drew his fish knife and sliced open the man's sleeve. Underneath was a kinaru tattoo. The man was Rin like us, yet I'd never seen his face. Neither had my friends, judging by their confused looks. I reached for his sleeve to tear it further and check his family crest.

"Stand back," a voice commanded.

I whirled. Fendul stood on the riverbank. Birds landed around him and shifted to their human forms — an owl and falcon to Rin warriors, a black-billed swan to my dark-haired, tattooed mother. Rokiud and I backed up, hands raised.

My mother drew forward as if she were in a dream. She dropped to her knees and stroked the man's hair. My eyes widened. No one in our confederacy would do that to a stranger. Touching someone's hair, one of the sacred parts of the body along with the heart and blood, was an intimate act saved for relatives and loved ones.

"Yotolein?" she breathed.

Before I could find words, Nili bent over the man's canoe, pulled back a tarp, and yelped. Huddled in a pool of river water were two shaking children.

2.

STRANGERS

I'd heard stories here and there about my mother's missing brother. Yotolein had been scourge of the rainforest, ambushing other kids with mud cakes and sneaking off to swim rivers. But while his sisters grew up, Yotolein grew angry. At eighteen he ran away. For several years, people from coastal jouyen mentioned seeing him, but when that stopped, everyone figured his blood was in the earth for good.

He had no tattoos for fatherhood, so we didn't know who the children in the canoe were. They had black hair and angular features common to our people, but their eyes were blue and they wore itheran clothing — patched trousers and a tunic for the boy, about five, and a dirty white dress for the girl, about eight. The girl had twin braids instead of the single one most Rin wore. When my mother picked up the boy, he burst into wailing sobs, squirmed loose, and curled against Yotolein.

The falcon warrior flew ahead with the news, so a crowd awaited us on the lakeshore when we returned. Fendul shooed everyone away and carried Yotolein to the healing tent. The blue-eyed girl tried to push in after them, but the healers refused to let anyone enter. My mother brought flatbread, tea, and blankets for the kids, who sniffed the food like they expected poison. They didn't speak except in whispers to each other.

Through the tent wall, I heard snatches of the healers' discussion. First they gave Yotolein a numbing tincture, then cut away the infected tissue on his leg. One woman came outside, put a knife in the fire, and went back in. I knew by the reek of seared flesh that they'd cauterized the wound. They couldn't fix everything, though. The infection had spread into Yotolein's blood. That would only heal with the blessing of our ancestral spirits, the aeldu, who weren't fond of runaways.

During all this I hung back with my temal. My father's expression shifted whenever he looked at me. Usually it was easy to read Temal — he was famous for telling stories with big gestures and bigger voices. When he cracked jokes, he laughed before they were over. Now he was silent. I squirmed, wishing he'd get my lecture over with.

Finally he asked, "Why'd you go down the river?"

I couldn't think of a good lie, so I admitted, "I was trying to attune."

Temal's face softened like melting wax. He rumpled my hair. "You were brave today, little fireweed. You saved your uncle and those kids. But you shouldn't have left the lake, and I get the feeling your friends had a hand in it. You can't see them until the equinox festival."

"That's not fair! They wanted to help me!"

"Your attuning isn't their responsibility. That's between you and the aeldu. No complaints, or you'll miss the festival, too."

I folded my arms, sulking. "Can I see Fendul?"

My parents thought Fendul was a good influence on me. As kids, we'd often played together. He'd practised for a future of bossing people around by setting strict rules for our games. After he came of age and that life became real, he had no time for make-believe. We'd drifted apart and never found anything to pull us back together.

"Fine," Temal conceded. "If you get *him* into trouble, I'll be impressed."

Cornering Fendul was easier said than done. I found him at his family's campsite, a cluster of tents painted with black-and-white kinaru. He stood deep in conversation with his parents. His father, Behadul, was the okorebai, the leader of the Rin. I couldn't just interrupt. So I stood glaring until Behadul dismissed his son with a wave, then I dragged Fendul away into the trees.

"Did you follow us?" I demanded.

Fendul glared back. He towered over me, full-grown at seventeen. "I have the whole Rin-jouyen to look after. You're not that special."

"Then how'd you know where we were?"

"My father posted scouts by the downriver branch of Kotula Iren. I *warned* you to stay away. Of course you didn't."

"Because it's absurd!" I threw my hands into the air. "We're nowhere near the coastal skirmishes—"

"Don't you wonder how Yotolein got that wound? He's a trapper like you. He knows better than to stumble into a bear clamp." Fendul sank onto a mossy log. "What I saw on the coast this summer was bad, Kateiko. People are fleeing, our kind and itherans alike. If another war breaks out, it'll spread fast."

"You say that like itheran ships might come up the river any day."

"They might. It's a major route." He raised a hand, cutting me off. "We're probably fine. But it's better to be cautious. And I'll be honest, Rokiud's the opposite of cautious. I'm uncomfortable with you hanging around him."

"Join us. Then we can all be uncomfortable."

"Can you have one conversation without sarcasm? I'm trying to look out for you—"

I groaned. When he tried to speak again, I groaned louder. A waxwing launched from a branch, chittering in annoyance.

Fendul got up and brushed moss off his breeches. "No wonder you haven't attuned. You're still a child."

Temal kept me busy with chores at our campsite — gathering kindling, patching our tent with tree resin, gutting trout for dinner, drying bogmoss to pack on Yotolein's wound. People kept coming to talk with my family or sneak a glimpse of Yotolein and the kids, who were asleep in a borrowed tent. Nili, Rokiud, and Onarem didn't come. They'd gotten in trouble, too.

Tema took a sacrificial trout to an elder for "spiritual guidance." That's how I knew my mother was really upset about her brother. Sure, she believed in the aeldu — they gifted her the swan body — but she never asked them for help or gave fish in offering. *Waste of food*, she said. She often argued about it with her elder sister, who'd sacrifice a whale if one turned up in the rainforest.

Temal didn't bother much with spirits, either. In his youth, he'd learned to carve makiri, sacred guardian figurines typically made of rioden, fir, or hemlock. People gave them as gifts, putting a fragment of their spirit into the figurine, thereby protecting the recipient. Temal wanted no part in anyone breaking bits off their spirit, so he never finished his apprenticeship. He was happier carving things fully in his control. Bowls and axe handles didn't talk back.

Years ago, when my parents got a new canoe as a wedding gift, Temal decided to carve the kinaru prow himself. The carvers said he wasn't qualified to use sacred designs. Temal said that was bearshit. It wasn't like he planned to stick a spirit in the prow. Rokiud's father started shouting. Tema got in the canoe and said, *Whoever has the right to carve this boat, get in*. Temal jumped in and sprawled out so no one else fit. The eldest carver laughed so hard she let Temal carve the prow.

I'd proudly repeated the story many times, but sometimes a prickly ball of resentment swelled inside me as I wondered if it was my parents' fault I hadn't attuned. Maybe they'd made a spiritually defective child. Or the aeldu were punishing me for my parents' disrespect. Or my parents had failed to teach me something important, had been too focused on water-calling and fur trapping. Practical stuff. *Kianta kolo* was Temal's favourite saying, *the sap will flow*. It meant that no matter how tough winter was, spring always came. He was the only Rin who put more faith in trees than in our sacred dead.

As we lay in our tent, Temal sleeping with his arm around Tema, I wondered how devout Yotolein was. The little I knew about my uncle could be rattled off faster than an *I told you so* from Fendul. Mentioning Yotolein usually started a fight among my extended family, so my parents only ever did it in private, and privacy was hard to find. Even now I could hear my cousin snoring two tents over.

The next morning I woke groggily to Temal's voice. "Rise and shine, little fireweed," he called.

Confused, I stumbled outside into misty rain. For as long as I remembered, dawn had meant water-calling lessons with Tema. She and I came from a long line of antayul — I'd earn the title after passing my test — who believed in gruelling training. Waking early, meditating in sleet and snow, never missing a day. Temal didn't have a speck of water-calling skill, but today he was the one drinking herbal tea by our campfire.

"What's going on?" I asked.

"We decided to change things up." Temal drained his mug and wrung rain from his long brown braid. "Bring your practice weapons."

Combat training. Less boring than meditation, more painful. I dug through my wicker carryframe. Other than my fishing and hunting knives, I owned an iron flail with a spiked head, a gift from my parents on my ninth birthday. Well-forged metal was valuable, so I also had a practice version, a weighted wooden ball stuck with rusty nails.

As we walked down the beach to the training grounds, I said, "Fendul thinks Yotolein got in a fight with itherans."

Temal glanced down at me. "Could be. Could not be."

"So I'm doing extra combat lessons for no reason?"

"If you're running off to be heroic, you'd better be prepared. Yesterday could've gone much worse."

I shut up, remembering his threat to extend my punishment. The equinox festival was my best chance of getting Rokiud alone.

Temal wasn't the only one worried. The training grounds, a stretch of rocky beach fenced by rope, were busy this morning. Bare-chested men and women in sleeveless shirts wrestled on canvas tarps. Archers fired at wooden targets. The site was temporary, easy to dismantle when we headed to our permanent settlement. Autumn rain would flood the beach soon after.

We warmed up with a run, our breath fogging, then I did swings with my practice flail against a driftwood log. Temal fixed my stance and guided my aim until the poor log was a mess of kindling. Next he held moss-stuffed pads and I tried to punch them. In the past, after I'd grown tall enough to reach his face, I'd accidentally given him several bloody lips.

Today my fists kept striking air. Off balance, I toppled and scraped my hands. When Fendul showed up and started practising sword thrusts, it was all over. I kept remembering our fight and wanting to hit him instead.

"All right." Temal folded his arms and looked around. "Who's distracting you? A boy or girl?"

"Temal!" I rinsed dirt off my palms. "It's not that. Just . . . maybe I should go to the elders for spiritual guidance, too."

"Ah." He scratched his neck, then tossed the moss pads aside and said, "Get your hunting knife. If you can draw blood from me, I'll tell you what I really think about your attuning. If not, you spar with Fendul."

My jaw dropped. Not only did Fendul have three years of training on me and a good deal more muscle, he'd never go easy. Once his father passed away and Fendul took his place as Okorebai-Rin, he would command our warriors. He wouldn't risk losing to me in front of anyone.

I drew my knife, did a few practice thrusts, then lunged. Temal swatted me away. I whirled, swung, got knocked aside. I ducked under Temal's arm and swiped at his ribs. He hit my hand. The knife flew from my grip and clattered onto the rocks.

"Again," I said, panting.

We circled each other. I was a small target, but that didn't help on offence. My arms weren't long enough to reach Temal's core. Then again, I wasn't trying for a fatal blow. I lashed at his forearm. He caught my wrist, twisted, and got me into a headlock. I struck at his thigh. He flipped me over and dumped me on the beach.

We lined up again. I feinted right. When he turned to block me, I grabbed his braid and yanked. He stumbled. I swung at his bare shoulder. Temal threw his weight against me. I hit the ground, wheezing.

When he bent over to pull me up, a drop of blood fell onto the rocks. Temal smiled. "Well done."

I got up with a wince. "I couldn't do that in a real fight. Itheran men don't have braids."

"Nei, but if you're thinking about that, you've made progress." Temal tossed me a waterskin and crossed to a log bench. When we were settled, he said, "Maybe you haven't attuned because you don't need it yet."

I blinked.

"You're a brave, resourceful young woman. Only when people get under your skin about seeming immature do you lose sight of yourself. The irony of life. But whatever your friends think about it doesn't matter."

"What about you and Tema? I hear you at night. You want me to attune soon."

"Of course. We hate seeing you miserable, and . . ." He chuckled. "It's hard to accept that spirits control part of our daughter's life. I'm angry at the aeldu for keeping it from you, yet I wonder if they know something I don't. In peaceful times, our second bodies guide us to our true selves. In war, they're a means of survival. What with Yotolein and the coastal skirmishes . . . I worry something worse is coming."

"Then shouldn't I attune now so I can practise fighting in my second body?"

"Wish I could answer that, little fireweed." Temal laced his fingers behind his head. "If you want to ask the elders, go ahead. It's not my place to stop you. But no matter what, I'll be here, ready to help you survive."

Yotolein kept up a fever. Healers changed his bandages and fed him broth during the brief periods he stirred awake. The blue-eyed kids wouldn't leave his side, so Tema and my aunt Isu took turns looking after them while the rest of us went out to fish or harvest duck potatoes. One evening I tried to show them a dice game, but they either didn't understand or didn't want to play.

On the fourth day, a neighbour interrupted combat training to say Yotolein was up. Temal and I hurried to our campsite and found an argument. Yotolein, sitting on a bark mat with the boy in his lap and the girl hugging his arm, faced off against Isu, matriarch of our family. Tema waved black smoke from potatoes forgotten in the fire. My cousin Emehein soothed his crying toddler while his wife nursed their fretting baby.

"You have a lot to explain," Isu said in the low voice she used for misbehaving children.

Isu was much older than Yotolein and Tema — she was actually their half-sister — but I usually forgot that. I'd never seen her speak to Tema this way. Yotolein's knuckles whitened, and for a moment I saw my own resentment in the face of this uncle I'd never met. But after a moment, he slumped with defeat.

"There's not much to tell," he said. "I left home, wandered the coast, and trapped furs to earn my keep. A few years later . . . I fell in love with an itheran woman. We got married."

Isu drew a sharp breath. No one from our family had ever married an itheran. Yotolein didn't have a wedding tattoo, which meant by our laws he wasn't married. He didn't even have the long hair that married Rin men grew.

"The kids are ours." He kissed their heads. "I brought them here for safety. We can't live on the coast anymore."

I shared an astonished look with Emehein. We had more cousins. *Half-itheran* cousins. The girl studied us with her dark eyebrows drawn. Her younger brother just stuck his thumb in his mouth and snuggled closer to their father.

Tema flung a charred potato back into the fire. "Yotolein, how dare you act like nothing happened. You were gone for seventeen years. You missed our parents' burials, your niece Kateiko's birth. She rescued you and didn't recognize you!"

I cringed, wishing I could fade into the forest. If only I attuned to a tree.

"Hold on," Temal said, touching Tema's arm soothingly. "Yotolein, where's your wife?"

Yotolein covered his kids' ears. "Her blood met the ground in a skirmish a week ago. I got wounded trying to save her."

Tema's lips worked soundlessly like a fish pulled from water, but Isu kept stone-faced and asked, "Why should we take in itheran children?"

Yotolein bristled. "They're half-Rin—"

"Are they? You abandoned the Rin-jouyen, married the itheran way, raised your children among itherans. Do they know our customs? Language? They haven't said a word to us—"

"Because they're terrified! Their mother's dead!"

I watched in a daze. I'd seen my family argue before and didn't think it could get worse. Clearly my imagination wasn't good enough.

"Come on, Kateiko," Emehein murmured. "Let them work it out."

He beckoned to his wife and they scooped up their kids. We escaped down the beach to a sandy spot where their toddler could play. Emehein and I sat in the shallows with ripples lapping at our boots. The autumn-toned cottonwoods looked like flecks of yellow paint among the shoreline evergreens.

This lake, Kotula Huin, was Emehein's favourite meditation spot. *Kotula*, the name it shared with the river feeding in and out of it, meant *flowing gateway*. Legend said our first matriarch was a kinaru who laid a giant egg on this shore, and our jouyen hatched from it. When the first Rin died, the kinaru opened a gate to the spirit world so her living and dead children would never be apart. Half our newfound cousins' ancestors were here.

"Yotolein and his kids won't get sent away, right?" I asked.

Emehein rubbed a hand over his face. "Probably not. Everyone just needs time to cool down . . . although no one holds a grudge like my tema."

I knew what he meant. Five years ago, his brother, Dunehein, married into another jouyen and moved to their settlement on the south coast. Isu had called it betrayal and refused to attend her own son's wedding. She must've felt as if she were being abandoned by Yotolein again.

Emehein, on the other hand, was the perfect son. He'd attuned young, passed his antayul test with ease, and married a woman from our plank house. He taught my water-calling lessons when Tema got fed up with my wandering attention. *Look*, he'd repeat, while I sat blindfolded and searching for the nearest creek.

With a jolt I realized something. Yotolein had an antayul tattoo, a fan-shaped mark under his collarbones. Had he taught his children to call water? I'd never met an itheran who knew how. And worse yet . . .

"Emehein," I said. "Can half-itherans attune?"

He furrowed his brows. "I'm not sure. I've heard they can if they grow up in one of our settlements, close to the aeldu, but otherwise . . ."

I shivered. Maybe it was too late for Yotolein's kids. He might've ripped away the most sacred part of their identity by raising them among itherans. Suddenly I understood why Isu was so mad.

*

Over the next few days, the remaining Rin arrived from their summer travels, meaning we could hold the dawn ceremony that roused the aeldu and told of everyone's safe return. I watched Yotolein's kids during it, wondering if they'd ever seen whirling shawl dancers or heard the echo of drums off mountains. I would've given anything for a sign from the aeldu, but my spiritual sight was as dim as the fog that filled the valley.

I glanced down the beach toward our sacred rioden. *Look*, Emehein always said. I willed the fog to shift and reveal the rioden's sprawling green branches. But when the misty curtains parted, the tree was black and bare. I blinked. The foliage reappeared.

I stood still, baffled. The land of the dead, Aeldu-yan, was said to be a lush, peaceful forest. I had no idea how or why the aeldu would show me something different.

No one else seemed to have noticed. My family was watching dancers and drummers sway around the ceremonial bonfire. But after the ceremony, Isu brusquely announced that Yotolein's kids could come to our permanent settlement. I didn't dare question it. Maybe the vision hadn't been for me.

We stowed the canoes, packed up camp into carryframes, and hiked toward the settlement. The cool damp air deep in the rainforest tasted of moss. Yotolein limped with a cane and Temal carried the little boy on his shoulders. The girl walked, clutching her skirt so it didn't snag on nettles. The kids stared at bouquets of mushrooms, salamanders scurrying along logs, curtains of witch's hair hanging from branches — but still they didn't speak. Yotolein wouldn't even tell us their names.

Hours later, we climbed the narrow wooden steps that wound up Aeti Ginu, the mountain where we lived most of the year. I stopped by a cliff to catch my breath and peer down at the zigzag of people. Through a gap in the trees, I glimpsed Rokiud chucking hemlock cones at his brothers. We hadn't gotten close enough since canoeing Kotula Iren to share more than a wave.

"Keep up, little fireweed," Temal said, and I hurried on.

Atop the mountain, flagstone paths spiderwebbed between clusters of moss-roofed buildings. Rows of bushes hung red and heavy with huckleberries. Early arrivers were dismantling the lattice fences that kept birds from eating our berries while we were away. A few young men cut waist-high grass with scythes, clearing it back from the paths.

All summer I'd looked forward to returning to our plank house — sleeping in a huge room surrounded by the familiar murmurs of seven other families, cooking in our hearth where wooden makiri of our ancestors watched in protection, doing chores by the glow of my vellum lantern painted with my fireweed crest. Now I saw it with new eyes. Yotolein's former bed had been given away. He moved across the house instead, setting up a grass-stuffed mattress on a spare dirt platform.

When my chores were done, I ran my hand over carvings on the doorframe that told the history of its inhabitants. My birth was recorded with my parents' family crests. Eventually my attuning, marriage, and death would be, too. Yotolein's history ended at his departure. I wasn't sure how his kids would be added. His daughter would inherit his crest, but his itheran wife didn't have one to pass to their son.

Like I wasn't embarrassed enough about not attuning, I wasn't allowed to work my trapline alone in case I snuck off to see my friends. At least I didn't have to go with my parents. The next morning, Tema started sewing clothes for Yotolein's kids and Temal started repairing a workshop roof, so Emehein offered to supervise me instead. Going with a cousin felt less like getting nannied.

After breakfast we traipsed into the rainforest. I'd had my own trapline for a year and knew every hillock and cave. The route started two hours' hike from Aeti Ginu and curved alongside a chattering brook where hares, martens, and other small game often came to drink. I tried to lose myself in the familiar motions of chopping overgrowth to clear the path, but my mind kept straying back to our plank house.

"Kateiko," Emehein said, and I realized I'd hacked through a fallen log into a carpet of rotting leaves. "Something you want to talk about?"

I wiped leaf muck from my axe. There were many things, but I started with the simplest. "Why'd Yotolein leave?"

"I don't remember the details. I was a child."

"You remember more than me. I wasn't born yet."

Emehein sighed, shouldering his axe. "It was during what itherans call the Third Elken War. We'd lost so many people during the first two that the Okorebai-Rin of the time commanded us to keep out of it, but Yotolein disobeyed orders and went to fight."

"Do you think he'll stay here now?"

"Maybe. Raising a family changes a man."

I frowned up at him. After marriage he'd grown out his hair into a braid, and with a toddler and a baby he was permanently tired, but otherwise he seemed the same. He was still my annoyingly calm almost-brother, as rooted in his ways as a stump in the earth. In his whole life he'd missed dawn meditation three times — after his wedding night, and when his two kids were born.

Before I could pry, Emehein pushed back a cluster of branches and said, "Ai, come look."

I peered around him. Narrow clawed prints interrupted a patch of mud, heading toward the brook. Foxes were common around here, but the prints strangely turned back with running-length strides. "Looks like something scared it."

"Maybe." Emehein stepped away. "You know what to do."

I tied yellow ribbon around a branch. I'd keep an eye on this spot. If wildlife passed through it regularly, I'd set snares here. We hoisted our axes and went back to chopping.

"I noticed something," Emehein said between swings. "When people mention itherans or the coast, Yotolein's children pay attention. I think they understand our language."

"Really? When I talk to them, they just stare."

"They've been through a lot. Have patience."

Patience. That's what my parents said about attuning and seeing my friends. Biting back sarcasm, I raised my axe to trim a sapling — and froze.

Across the brook, something slunk through the trees. Too upright for a deer, too thin for a bear.

"Eme," I whispered. "Someone's over there."

Emehein pushed down hard on my shoulder. I dropped into the mud, heart racing.

"Turn around," he murmured. "Crawl until you're out of sight, then run. Head for that pine ridge and follow it home. I'll be right behind you."

3.

FESTIVAL

Back at Aeti Ginu, we found Behadul and told him what happened. Scouts left immediately, but by the time they reached my trapline, the figure was gone. Probably it was a refugee lost on the way to sanctuary villages up north. Still, Behadul posted guards around our settlement. Lost, hungry itherans tended to get violent.

Cut off from my trapline and my friends, I had nothing to do except help Temal repair the workshop. As I whittled bark into shingles, I daydreamed about the equinox. It'd be the first day of the season we were allowed into the shrine grounds. In the morning we'd light lanterns to summon the aeldu here, then initiate newly attuned people into adulthood, which I *definitely* wasn't bitter about watching from the sidelines for yet *another* year. In the evening we'd have the feast and festival.

That gave me an idea. It was tradition to bring gifts back from summer travels. I'd brought things for my many cousins on Temal's side, who traded on different routes from us, but I had nothing for Yotolein's kids. Tema paused her sewing and showed me how to twist arrowhead leaves into a doll like I'd had as a kid. I painted it to match Yotolein's daughter — black hair, blue eyes, a white dress. Temal gave me an auburn chunk of rioden wood that I whittled into a toy canoe and painted with a kinaru prow.

On the night of the equinox, while everyone in our plank house shared platters of autumn's bounty — roast goose with chestnut stuffing and quivering cranberry jelly, flaky smoked trout, herbed mushrooms and root vegetables, crabapple preserves, flatbread smothered in huckleberry jam — I edged close to Yotolein. "I have a surprise for your little ones," I said.

He murmured to his children, who wiped jam-sticky fingers on handkerchiefs. The girl seized the doll and hugged it close. The boy's face lit up like a lantern at the toy canoe. I brought a water pail and filled it with a wave of my hand. He dropped the canoe in and splashed it around, laughing.

The girl whispered to Yotolein, who nodded. She said with a slight accent, "Thank you."

My eyes widened. "You *do* know our language."

Yotolein patted the girl's head. "I made sure they were ready in case we ever came home to the Rin-jouyen."

I crouched down to eye level with the girl. "Are you going to name your doll?"

She chewed her lip, then said, "Hymelai, Lady of the Sky. She's the goddess of archery and ravens and moonlight, and has white clouds for her dress and storm clouds for hair—"

"That'll do," Yotolein cut in. "Remember, we don't talk about Mamma's religion here."

I wanted to invite the kids to the festival but didn't know how to spend it with half-itherans. Plans had been made for me, anyway.

I'd hardly finished washing the dinner dishes when Temal's sister's middle child swooped into the plank house. Malana was eighteen and lived for nights like this, wearing soot smudged around her eyes and red feather earrings. She came holding hands with Nili's older sister, Aoreli.

"Nisali told us everything," Malana said, sprawling across my bed and shedding glittery mica powder on my blankets. "We'll make sure you dance with Rokiud tonight."

Aoreli handed me a pile of folded cottonspun. "Nili finished your new clothes. She didn't have time to embroider them, but we brought jewellery for your equinox gifts."

"How did she sew these?" I demanded. "I haven't seen her in days."

"She measured another of your cousins. You're about the same size." Aoreli kissed Malana goodbye and headed for the door, her tail of hair swinging. "See you two at the shrine."

The cottonspun was dyed dark with blackberries. I laced the shirt tight so it hugged my chest. The leggings had to be cuffed, but my knee-high boots hid that. Malana, knowing I preferred my hair loose, brushed it smooth and tucked a comb with a glass lily behind my ear. A black beaded necklace and bracelet finished my outfit. She dabbed lilac perfume on my neck, making me sneeze, then stepped back to scrutinize me.

"Gorgeous," she said with a clap of her hands. "Come on."

"Behave yourselves," Tema called. "And if you sneak off with someone, don't go behind the dyeing sheds. Itchbine grows there."

"How does she know that?" Malana whispered, and I mock-gagged.

We walked arm in arm, beads jingling. Flickering torches guided us between buildings. People waved and called cheerful greetings as we joined a line climbing to Aeti Ginu's highest point, then passed under a massive carved gateway into the shrine grounds. Atop a cliff, the three-storey shrine made a tiered silhouette in the twilight, studded with glowing windows. Rattling strings of evergreen cones swayed from the eaves.

Together we pushed open the heavy double doors and stepped into sweltering heat and noise. In the shrine centre, drummers whirled across a raised platform, pounding hide drums strapped around their hips. The ground level included everyone from toddlers learning to walk to elders who hardly could. We climbed creaking stairs to the second level where kids our age danced or leaned over railings around an open square in the floor, watching the performance below.

On an outdoor balcony, Nili had her arms around Onarem. Malana scanned the crowd for Aoreli. She had as much luck as I did finding Rokiud. Maybe he'd decided to drink brånnvin in the woods with our more troublemaking friends. Or maybe he'd gotten punished again and was stuck in his plank house.

Malana nudged me. "Should we check the top floor?"

I shook my head so hard my glass lily slipped. That's where couples went to pretend they had privacy. Instead, I danced with Malana until Aoreli showed up and they disappeared together. Left alone, I went outside to a quiet balcony and gazed across the dark expanse of mountains. Soft rain pattered on the railing. I was ready to dig a grave for my hopes when someone said, "Ai, Kateiko."

I whirled. The sight of Rokiud so close, his shaved black hair and bare chest shimmering with rain, made my insides twist up like frayed rope. "Hi," I tried to say. Instead I choked and made an awful hacking noise. I grabbed an abandoned mug and took a swig. *"Agch!"*

Rokiud sniffed the mug. "I think that's brånnvin." He dumped it over the railing and handed it back.

I called water into it and drank until I could speak. "I didn't think you were coming."

"I wasn't gonna. I thought you'd be pissed I got you in trouble."

"Huh? It's *my* fault *you* got in trouble."

He shrugged. "I feel bad anyway. Maybe this'll make up for it." He opened his palm to reveal a pearly blue seashell on a leather cord. "I wanted to find a pale purple one but, y'know, banned from the coast. This was all I could barter from itheran refugees."

I stared at it, caught off guard. So he'd been thinking about me over summer, too. He'd even remembered that pale purple was my favourite colour. "I like blue, too," I assured him. I held my hair aside so he could undo my beaded necklace and replace it with the seashell.

"Does that mean you'll dance with me?" Rokiud asked.

I nodded. He led me inside and took my waist, carefully avoiding my hair. After a borderline heart attack as I figured out where to put my hands, we settled into a rhythm. Drumbeats pulsed up through the floor into our bodies. *Aeldu save me*, he smelled nice. Like fresh-cut wood. I got the feeling Malana had found him in the canoe workshop and threatened to knock him down if he didn't come see me.

We stayed together for hours, even when his brothers or my cousins pulled us upstairs to spy on couples or downstairs to sip cranberry wine. My parents said nothing, which was the closest they'd gotten to approving of Rokiud. His help in saving my uncle and younger cousins must've improved their opinion of him.

Later, when Rokiud's hands had moved down to my hips, Nili caught my eye across the shrine and grinned wickedly. Okay, I owed her breakfast for, like, five years. When we saw Fendul watching us, Rokiud whispered, "Wanna go pick huckleberries?"

I arched my eyebrows. The bushes had been picked clean for the feast. Smothering laughter, we slunk into the night past people stargazing and drinking at the firepits. Moonlight washed everything bluish-white. At the huckleberry patch, we stepped into a dark tunnel of bushes that muffled the thumping drums. I went first on the narrow path, treading over roots and rocks, trailing my fingers along wet leaves.

"I have a question," I said. "Promise to answer honestly."

"That's a big promise."

I flicked a branch, spinning raindrops at him. "Does it bother you that I haven't attuned?"

"A little," he admitted. "But you don't need it. You're a good warrior, you're more mature than a lot of our friends, and Fendul doesn't scare you. If you want honesty, I'm kind of awed by you."

"Then why'd you suggest going down the river? You just like breaking rules?"

"Not anymore."

I turned. His tone had shifted.

Rokiud rubbed his leaf-fuzz hair. "I was serious about owing you for the canoe paint, but . . . it's not just about that."

"What do you mean?"

"Well . . . most people do their initiations together, right? Into adulthood and their jouyen role. I should've become a carver three years ago, but I kept doing dumb shit and getting in trouble. When the elders finally said they'd evaluate me, I was crazy happy. Then someone painted those stupid symbols in my canoe, and I thought it was all over.

"I know who did it — me and another apprentice had been fighting — but that doesn't matter. If I hadn't screwed around before, I could've just said I didn't make the symbols. It's my fault the elders wouldn't have believed me. I didn't think I deserved to be a carver. I was ready to give up forever . . . until you showed up with that paint and said we were gonna fix it. You didn't give up on me."

I looked up at Rokiud, his face shadowed by the huckleberry bushes. I hadn't realized he got that close to quitting. He loved canoes so much, learning ways to make them faster or sturdier or better balanced, that I couldn't imagine him doing anything else. He only skipped lessons because his temal shouted whenever he made mistakes.

"Anyway," he said, "I know how much you wanna attune. So I tried to repay the favour. And I'm not gonna ditch you for an attuned girl, if that's what you're worried about."

It was. Exactly. Even now, I couldn't shake the thought that he'd only come to the shrine because Malana had made him.

"Oh," I said, suddenly reminded. I reached into my leggings pocket and handed him a tin of candied blackcurrants. The itheran goatherds I traded with had brought them from beyond the eastern mountains. "You like these, right?"

"You remembered." Rokiud sounded impressed. He unscrewed the tin, peeled a dark berry from the clump, and offered it to me.

Maybe it was the darkness and the lingering buzz of wine that made me brave, or maybe it was his honesty. I held the blackcurrant to his mouth. He accepted, grazing my fingers. He must've swallowed, but I was distracted by how his eyes glimmered in a thread of moonlight. How had I gotten from the shrine to here, alone with the only boy who'd ever made my breath stutter?

Rokiud tipped his face down to mine. His lips were softer than I'd ever imagined. He pulled back, giving me a chance to stop him. When I didn't, he kissed me firmer, our noses bumping. I lifted onto my toes to reach better, holding his arms to steady myself.

Finally we broke apart, smiling and stunned and lightheaded. It wasn't my first kiss if stupid bonfire games counted, but it was my first real one. I slipped my hand into his and ambled down the path with him in tow, afraid I'd pass out in the huckleberries if *that* happened again.

Then Rokiud swore. "You leave soon for the salmon run, right? We won't see each other for a month."

I stopped. Misery crept in, followed by a realization. "Your salmon camp's on the part of Kotula Iren we're banned from. Where are you going fishing?"

"Not sure yet. Every family in our plank house is joining someone else's camp."

"Come to mine." I spun, knocking into him. "Fendul will be there, ugh, but it's his job to provide for Rin in need. I'll guilt him into it."

"If it means I can keep doing this." Rokiud gripped my waist and kissed me again.

Passing out be cursed. This time I gave in, pressing my palms to the canoe paddles inked on his taut chest. He tasted like the sweet-sour of candied blackcurrant.

Then we noticed voices. We twisted, searching for the source. The settlement's centre, moving east. Rokiud pulled back branches so we could peer through. Behadul, holding a torch, led a column of armed warriors past. Emehein carried his double-edged battle axe. They stopped in the grassy clearing that led to the wooden steps down Aeti Ginu. A scout took off in bird form and soared overhead.

"What's going on?" I whispered.

"Dunno, but I don't think we should stay here." Rokiud pulled me back down the huckleberry tunnel and we emerged into the glow of abandoned firepits. The stargazers had left, gone who knows where. We scurried across the flagstones toward the plank houses.

Halfway there Fendul called out. He strode toward us, sword in hand. "Kateiko, where's your family?"

"Other than Emehein? No idea. Probably at the festival."

Fendul eyed Rokiud, seeming to realize we'd left the shrine a while ago. "Follow me. Both of you."

We zigzagged between buildings, pushing through grass that hadn't been cut yet. Fendul shoved open the door to our house. Yotolein snapped his head up.

"Itheran ships rowed up Kotula Iren," Fendul told him. "They got stuck at rapids, but fifty soldiers continued on foot. They're at the base of the mountain awaiting orders. Their captain's hiking up now to meet my father. We know you've kept secrets from us, but if you come with me, you'll live to see sunrise."

Yotolein swung toward his sleeping children and stumbled. He'd hardly gotten enough strength back to move with a cane. Fendul lifted the girl out of bed and Rokiud scooped up the boy.

"Bring your weapons and whatever supplies you can carry," Fendul instructed me. To everyone else in the plank house, he said, "Stay here. Act normal. You never saw us."

I buckled my flail and knife sheaths onto my belt, threw on my cloak, and pulled the blankets from Yotolein's bed. Someone passed me a canvas bag of leftover food from the feast. I scooped up Hymelai the doll and the toy canoe and tossed them in the bag.

Outside, Fendul unlatched a wooden case and took out his irumoi, a rod covered with glowing blue mushrooms. We navigated by its watery light onto a dirt path that did hairpin turns down the mountain. Pebbles slid from under our feet and rattled away into blackness. Yotolein shushed his daughter's drowsy mumbling. Fendul turned left at a stone cairn, then right at a marshy pond.

I knew where we were going. We splashed into an icy creek and straight through a waterfall into a rocky cave. Shivering and sputtering, I dried everyone's clothes. Fendul and Rokiud set down the kids and covered them with blankets. We didn't dare risk a fire. Smoke in such a cramped space would drive us out long before anyone found us.

"Keep watch," Fendul told Rokiud and me. "I'll bring help as soon as possible."

I'd been awake since my dawn combat lesson, so Rokiud offered to take first watch. Later I woke to find my head on his shoulder. He'd let my hair drape across his skin, connecting our spirits. It was an unexpected comfort. I stayed next to him with my cloak draped over us while he nodded off.

Yotolein sat propped against the cave wall, rubbing his bad leg. I didn't know if we were guarding him as a refugee or a prisoner. While we were close enough to share each other's breath, the distance between my uncle and me still felt infinite. I knew nothing about his children fretting in their sleep. He knew nothing about the canoe carver dozing against me.

The night lightened to grey, then to sunshine piercing the waterfall and casting rainbows inside the cave. The five of us were sharing cold goose and flatbread when Fendul returned with my parents. Temal bearhugged me and assured Rokiud that his family was safe. Tema kissed my hair before rounding on Yotolein.

"I hate to repeat our dear sister," she said, "but you have a *lot* to explain."

"You first," Yotolein retorted. "What's happening?"

"Nothing," Fendul said. "It's a stalemate. The itherans are from Eremur, a province our jouyen has no treaties with. They're demanding to search our homes. My father won't let them. We could wipe out their force long before they make it up the mountain, but that's a declaration of war."

"What are they looking for?"

"Anyone connected to the Rúonbattai."

Yotolein's shoulders sagged. In an instant he looked smaller. Frail.

I looked between them. "What's the . . . Roo-on . . ."

Yotolein nudged his kids, who went further into the cave with their toys. Once they were distracted, he said, "Two itheran races hold power in this region. Sverbians were the first settlers to arrive. You'd have met them, our trading partners and allies in the Elken Wars. The people we fought against are the Ferish, who you've probably heard of by less polite names."

"Brown pigeons," Rokiud said. "I met some once on a trip south. They threw rocks at my brothers and me."

Yotolein laughed harshly. "Sounds right. Well, the Elken Wars were all centred in the province of Eremur. After the second war, Sverba and Ferland agreed to share control of Eremur through an elected council. Ferish immigrants could buy land there and vote for the councillors. That didn't sit well with Sverbians who'd just lost their families and livelihoods in war, so a few formed a secret militia called the Rúonbattai and vowed to drive the Ferish from these lands forever. They haven't succeeded yet. For every Ferish person they killed or scared away, more moved to Eremur.

"After the latest war, the one I left to fight in, a Sverbian hired me as a courier. Paid well for discretion. He never mentioned the Rúonbattai, but I figured it out. Normal people don't hire warriors to carry mail. Through him, I met my wife. She worked for him as a seamstress, sewing hidden pockets, repairing uniforms from fallen soldiers, and the like. But we realized the Rúonbattai were doing terrible things, and we wanted to start a family in safety, so we quit our jobs and moved to a remote village of other mixed-blood families.

"Some years back, the Rúonbattai went silent. I figured they'd finally been beaten. We were glad if it meant we'd escaped our past. But a couple weeks ago, an Eremur ship landed in our harbour. Soldiers stormed our village searching for Rúonbattai, looting and razing on the way. Two men tried to . . . take . . . my wife." Yotolein's voice cracked. "I killed one. The other put a spear in my wife's chest, so I grabbed our children and ran."

Stunned, I glanced at the kids, who were making up some game. How much had they seen? Their mother's dead body? Their village in flames?

"You led Eremur's navy here," Tema said, mouth twisting like she'd eaten soap. "You've endangered us all."

"It might not be Yotolein's fault," Fendul interrupted.

Everyone looked at him. He flushed red. Even though he was the okoreni, he was still speaking to elders.

"The Rúonbattai never went totally silent," he said. "Rumour is they're on the north coast rebuilding strength, and we're the most powerful jouyen up north. It's not farfetched to suspect we're aiding them. That said . . . Yotolein, if Eremur soldiers *are* after you, we can't help. Harbouring an ex-Rúonbattai could get us massacred, and you lost our goodwill by keeping dangerous secrets."

"I've been careful," Yotolein insisted. "My employer's the only Rúonbattai I dealt with, and his blood met the ground years ago. I don't tell people I'm Rin. I keep my kinaru tattoo hidden."

"What about your wife? Can anyone connect you to her?"

"The Sverbian stavehall doesn't have a record of our wedding. We didn't get marriage tattoos, either. It killed me to abandon a sacred Rin tradition, but with our past, we couldn't risk being linked."

"You have half-Sverbian children," Tema said. "*That'll* raise questions."

Yotolein ran a grimy hand over his face. "Where else can we go?"

No one answered. Aeti Ginu was the beating heart of our jouyen. If soldiers were bold enough to come here, they wouldn't hesitate to go after unprotected sanctuaries out in no man's land.

Then Fendul said, "There's a secret island down south where another confederacy once took refuge during a lungkiller epidemic. The Dona-jouyen sailed there this summer to start rebuilding it. They only accept child refugees because it's hard to get enough supplies, but—"

"I won't separate my family," Yotolein said. "We've already lost everything else."

"You're a danger to each other," Tema snapped. "Grow up and make the tough choice—"

"I'm not still your kid brother!" Yotolein smacked the cave floor, which echoed. "Those are my *children*. I won't send them off alone!"

"Easy there," Temal said. "What if Kateiko went with them?"

My jaw fell. Yotolein scrutinized me. Rokiud took my hand in his warm one, but he kept quiet.

"We taught her well," Temal went on. "She's a good water-caller, trapper, warrior, everything needed to survive. Your kids would be with family. Once we clear your name or find another refuge, you'll be reunited."

Anger flashed through me so hot I saw spots. What about *my* life here? Rokiud and I were finally together, planning for the salmon run, and instead I'd get sent away for months? *Years?* But as quick as my anger came, it gave way to searing guilt. My cousins had suffered so much. I had to protect them so they could grow up and have the life I was upset about losing.

Tema leaned back out of the glittering rainbows from the waterfall, drumming her fingers the way she did after losing an argument.

It took me a second to realize who'd embarrassed her — Yotolein, because now Tema had to face sending her child away, too.

She looked at me. "If we ask you to do an adult's job, we have to respect your decision as an adult. Leaving is your choice. And" — she raised a hand to stop me from interrupting — "think it through. You'll likely attune while you're away. Are you ready to do that without your temal and me?"

I already knew the answer. Temal believed the aeldu kept me from attuning because they had some greater plan for me, and now I believed it, too. Being unattuned is why I'd gone down Kotula Iren and found my cousins, why I could go with them now. My frustration with the aeldu was wiped away. Whenever and however I attuned, I trusted them to do it right.

"Yes," I said. "I'm ready."

4.

THROUGH THE FRAY

Together we worked out a route. My parents, Yotolein's kids, and I would travel by canoe northwest to an ocean inlet, then by ferry to Nordmur, a region claimed by Sverbian settlers, and finally by ship to the island refuge. My parents would make sure the place was safe, then come back home. The ships were crewed by Dona, our confederacy's only nomadic jouyen, of whom a few had married itheran sailors and learned the trade.

Once the plan was settled, Fendul and Rokiud went back up the mountain to get supplies and report to Behadul. We stayed hidden to practise our story. Yotolein's kids would be safer if we pretended they were my siblings and we'd grown up in the wilderness, unconnected to the Rúonbattai. That meant we had to learn about the kids fast — starting with their names, Annijka and Samúnd.

"Isu will be furious I gave my children Sverbian names," Yotolein said, redoing his daughter's twin braids as a single one in the Rin style.

Tema sighed. "It doesn't matter, since they can't go by that anymore." She deliberated, then said, "We'll call them Hanaiko and Samulein. Solid Rin names. Aeldu willing, they'll get used to it before we run into anyone."

Yotolein also admitted he'd told his children not to speak to anyone else so they wouldn't reveal the attack on their village. It was easier to be mute than to lie. We decided the kids should keep that up around other people. They were naturally shy, and Hanaiko had gotten in the habit of shushing Samulein.

Fendul and Rokiud returned at midday. Nili came with them to help carry a tent, trail food, gloves, shawls, and other gear. I folded a handkerchief around my beaded jewellery and glass lily in case I needed to barter them away. I wished I could say goodbye to Emehein, Malana, and my other cousins, but we couldn't risk Eremur soldiers seeing our faces.

Yotolein pulled his kids into his lap, an arm around each. "Be good for Mamma. Her spirit's watching from Thaerijmur. And Hanaiko, I expect you to help look after your brother."

She nodded, clutching her arrowhead-leaf doll. "I'll be brave like Hymelai."

"Temal, I wanna go home," Samulein whined.

"We can't, Samu. But you're going off on a big adventure, and you'll see lots of new animals—"

"No!" Samulein squirmed, tears welling in his blue eyes. "I don't want another 'venture! I wanna go home!"

Yotolein's mouth twisted like he, too, was trying to hold back tears. He held his sobbing son against his chest until Tema cleared her throat, then he gently peeled Samulein away.

"Your aunt's family will look after you," he told his kids. "I love you both more than life."

Leaving Yotolein hidden in the cave, we crept down the mountain, watching for soldiers. Rokiud guided us to a pair of canoes stashed by a creek. He'd made them during his apprenticeship before he was allowed to carve kinaru prows, so they were still blank and wouldn't attract attention. While my family loaded our supplies, Rokiud and I slipped away into the forest to say goodbye.

"I'll miss you," he said, cupping my jaw.

I looked up into his brown eyes. "You understand why I'm going, right?"

"Yeah. Family comes first." He kissed me, pressing his hand to the seashell nestled between my collarbones. "Wish we were going to the salmon run together, though."

Back at the creek, Nili flung her arms around me. "I can't believe you're leaving without me," she wailed. "Remember we used to talk about sailing the coast together? Trading in port markets and eating weird itheran food?"

I tried to smile. "I'll bring you back something pretty."

"You better." She stood on her toes to kiss my hair. "See you, Kako."

Fendul and I made awkward farewells. I should've admitted he had been right about itherans invading, and he should've apologized for insulting me about attuning. Instead I hugged him. He went rigid and patted my arm. "Good luck," he said.

Temal got into one canoe with Hanaiko and Samulein perched in the bow. Tema and I took the other. We pushed off down the creek, waving to Rokiud, Nili, and Fendul as they faded away into the misty rainforest.

The creek carried us several hours west onto Kotula Iren. Temal made it a game for the kids that whoever spotted an Eremur scout won.

Another hour along, the Kotula's clear blue water merged with the dark green of a smaller river, swirling together into cloudy teal. We turned upstream onto the green one and paddled north into the densest part of Anwen Bel, our name for this rainforest that had once been all ours.

At night, we hid the canoes among huge ferns and camped out of sight from the river. Samulein kept crying for his parents. Tema kept reaching out to stroke his hair the way she did when I was little, but she never quite made contact. Hanaiko sniffled in the darkness. I lay awake a long time, drawing patterns of water on the tent wall and wondering what I'd gotten myself into.

All the second day, a deluge followed us up the green river. The kids used curved bark to bail out Temal's canoe while Tema and I called water out of ours. The heavy rain muffled our voices from anyone else in the area, and my parents relaxed enough to sing Rin canoe shanties. The kids knew the words to a few and eventually joined in, slipping on the trickier pronunciations.

"Get all your noise out now," Tema told them. "You must have plenty built up."

Hanaiko sure did. It rolled in like the tide, starting with chatter about the landscape, swelling into messy wandering stories about their village. Whenever she mentioned her mamma, she choked up and plunged onto some new topic. Samulein was more like a fawn, big-eyed and silent for long stretches, whooping with laughter anytime a fish jumped or a diving bird struck the surface.

A cairn of rocks stacked on the riverbank marked the start of a portage. We split our gear into packs, then my parents flipped our canoes upside down and carried them on their heads through the forest. This had been Temal's trapline until he married Tema and could use her family's land closer to home. He led us along a muddy track to a stream, then we paddled to another cairn, lifted the dripping canoes, and walked again.

Hiking was tough for the kids, who tired quickly and got blistered feet. Their boots were only ankle-high and not waterproofed as well as ours. Slowly we wound into the northwest reaches of Anwen Bel. I'd never travelled this far into the region. Game ran freely, but we had no time to set traps. I wouldn't have left camp anyway. The closer we got to the coast, the more likely we were to run into people.

During a sleepy rainfall on the seventh day, our canoes glided through floating weeds onto open water. I scooped up a handful and tasted salt. We'd reached the inlet dividing Anwen Bel from Nordmur. I'd always imagined my first time on the ocean would be a glorious sight of leaping dolphins and endless sparkling water, but with the rain all I saw was grey waves.

Tema shifted into her swan body and flew ahead to scout. We were beachcombing when she returned. Our navigation had been right and the ferry house was a few leagues away. It was a new structure, part of the route Sverbian refugees were taking between Nordmur's largest city, Caladsten, and the sanctuary villages. Our canoes weren't built to handle ocean swells, so we stowed them in the forest and hiked down the coast among towering salt spruce and twisted shore pine, arriving just after dusk.

The ferry dock extended on stilts into a sheltered cove. Onshore, chimney smoke puffed from a cabin with a sod roof and carved doorframe, resembling a miniature plank house. Rain poured off its gutters into barrels. Temal passed dozing Samulein to Tema and picked up Hanaiko. "Like we practised," he murmured, and she closed her eyes and fell limp in pretend sleep.

As we approached, an elkhound barked and rattled a chain that held it to a woodshed. Moments later the cabin door swung open, spilling light onto the porch. A heavyset man with a yellow beard and ruddy cheeks beamed at us. "Here for the ferry?" he called in Coast Trader, the language we used with itherans. "It should return tomorrow."

Temal stopped at the porch steps. "Are you the caretaker?"

"That I am. Call me Mads. I keep the place warm for ferry passengers and direct 'em to the sanctuary villages. Come in, dry off. It be nice and toasty by the fire."

"I didn't expect a Sverbian," Temal said. "This side of the inlet is Rin land. Only members of the Aikoto Confederacy are allowed to live here."

"Ah yes. Bad luck, that." Mads scratched his beard. "The viirelei who lived here before took ill and left a couple weeks ago. I volunteered to stay until someone new arrives. But let's not stand talking in the cold. Come, come. I'll make tea."

Temal glanced at Tema, who nodded. We filed inside and laid the kids by the hearth. A canvas curtain separated the cabin in two. The front room had bark-edged tables and benches, shelves of supplies, and walls hung with fishing nets, oars, and dock bumpers. Mads put a kettle over the fire and watched curiously as Tema and I dried everyone's clothes, dissipating the rain into mist.

"Were you headed inland to the sanctuaries?" Temal asked, swinging his long legs over a bench and settling down.

"Aye indeed. Never been a fighter." Mads patted the ale belly hanging over his belt. "What brings you here? Not many folks come toward the fray."

"Family wedding in Caladsten. You know how it is. Miss one and you'll never hear the end of it."

As my parents distracted him with polite conversation, mostly lies, I wandered near the curtain to feign looking at a shelf of colourful glass bottles, then peeked into the back room. Embroidered blankets, vellum lanterns, and chests painted with seagulls, the Dona-jouyen crest. The former caretakers must've left without their things. I also saw several dirty bowls. Either Mads was terribly messy, or he wasn't alone.

Outside, the elkhound whined. Something clicked in my mind. "Mads," I interrupted, "are you taking that dog to the sanctuaries?"

He chuckled. "Sure am. Eats twice her share, but I couldn't bear to leave her behind."

I nodded. While he carried on telling some joke to Temal, I whispered to Tema in our language, Aikoto. "Rokiud said the sanctuaries had a rabies outbreak, so they banned anyone from bringing dogs. Wouldn't the caretakers have told their replacement?"

Tema's cool smile slipped. She rose. "Mads, sorry to turn down your hospitality, but I should put my children to bed."

He heaved himself up from the table. "Of course. Apologies, missus. I'll clear room on the floor. There be clean blankets, pillows—"

"Thank you, but it's not appropriate for my daughters to share a cabin with a grown man. We'll camp outside."

"In the rain? Nonsense." Mads glanced at the door, oddly fast.

Then we noticed a carved seagull on a shelf above the door. Dona caretakers wouldn't leave a sacred makiri to protect an itheran. Not by choice. Temal pressed his ear to the door, then stepped back, hand hidden under his cloak by his knives. Mads backed away, no longer smiling.

"Stay with your cousins," Tema whispered to me and took an oar from its pegs.

The door crashed open. An itheran burst in wielding a short sword. Temal grabbed him from behind and slit his throat, spraying blood across the tables.

Mads grabbed a cleaver. Tema slammed the oar into his skull, his gut, his shins. He stumbled and dropped the cleaver. She yanked a fishing net from the wall and wrapped it around his neck. They crashed into tables, Mads scrabbling at the ropes.

Samulein woke wailing. Hanaiko watched open-mouthed and frozen. I threw my cloak over them. "Don't look," I hissed, holding my flail ready.

Temal strode outside, paused on the porch, and flung his throwing dagger into the darkness. Someone screamed. He drew his sword and disappeared into the rain.

Among broken dishes and splintered wood, Tema dropped Mads's limp form. His face was blue. She stood panting, tense as wire, then seized the fallen cleaver and flung open a window shutter. She swung the blade. Something heavy collapsed into the mud. When she turned back, red speckled her face.

Tema made sure the kids and I were okay, then hogtied and gagged Mads. He groaned. She kicked his head, making his eyes roll back. "Never a fighter indeed," she muttered.

I sank to my knees. My parents were trained warriors like every Rin, but I'd never seen them in real combat. Violence had always been for other people. Not for my temal who thanked the animals he trapped for their sacrifice, or my tema who once prevented a fist-fight by sitting in their canoe to claim Temal's right to carve it.

"How'd you know someone was outside the window?" I asked.

"I felt motion in the rain," Tema said. "Now get the kettle, will you?"

It whistled, making me jump. I wrapped a rag around my hand and removed the kettle from the fire. Tema rummaged through shelves, sacks, boxes. In the kindling box she found a clinking canvas purse and dumped it out. Gold and silver sovereigns spilled onto a table, along with necklaces, rings, and brooches glinting with a rainbow of tiny jewels.

"Brigands," Tema spat. "Preying on refugees who come with all they own. Filthy *takuran*."

I flinched. She would've shown me the back of her tongue for calling anyone that — someone so awful, the earth rejected their blood and they had to be buried in shit.

Temal returned, sword in hand, dripping rain and blood. "One fled. Aeldu willing, he was the last of them."

Hanaiko peeked out from under a table where she'd been comforting Samulein. Clutching her doll Hymelai, she said, "Uncle Mikiod? Auntie Sohiko?"

"Yes, love?" Tema's voice was instantly gentle.

"I know they're bad men, but . . ." Hanaiko glanced at the dead man by the door and covered her eyes. "We're supposed to burn the bodies. That way their spirits can go to Thaerijmur."

My parents exchanged looks. None of us had ever expected to perform Sverbian death rites.

"A pyre will just smolder in this weather, and the woodshed is too small," Temal said. "We'll have to raze the cabin. First, I have something to show Kateiko."

He lit a torch and led me into the wet forest. The elkhound yowled behind us. Temal stopped by a shallow pit, illuminating six bodies submerged in muddy rainwater. Flies buzzed up into my face. I clamped a hand to my mouth so I didn't throw up.

"The Dona caretakers, I assume," Temal said, "and the itherans are likely refugees who resisted. This is what you must be ready for. Protect your cousins with your life and be careful who you trust. Itherans who murder their own kind won't hesitate to harm ours."

Swallowing, I asked, "If we burn the itherans, what should we do with the Dona?"

"I'll perform the battlefield rites here in the woods. They exist for situations like this where it's dangerous to stay long. You go help your tema."

"Wait," I said. "Back there . . . it didn't seem like the first time you and Tema . . . killed people."

Temal rubbed his neck. "During the last war, Ferish soldiers found our fishing camp. They were lost, starving, angry, and didn't speak Coast Trader. Things went wrong. It's happened a couple times since."

Memories surfaced — a winter trapping trip when Temal left during the night with his sword, a summer trading trip when Tema told me to stay in our tent no matter what I heard. I shuddered.

Back at the cabin, I coaxed Samulein out from under the table. We searched the Dona's belongings for food and clothing so my parents could change out of their bloody garments. Tema found leggings and a shirt with lacing up the sides. She stowed the gold, jewels, and seagull makiri in the purse buckled to her belt. When Temal finished piling bodies on the floor, he changed into a tunic and breeches that were too short, leaving a gap between them and his knee-high boots.

Together my parents lifted Mads, struggling under his bulk, and carried him outside to the dock. They tied the dazed man to a mooring post and left bread and water in reach. "We'll send someone to get him," Temal said. "Until then, let him be a warning to anyone who lands here."

Lastly, we drenched the cabin's interior in fish oil and spread out kindling, pillow down, anything flammable. Tema was about to toss a blazing torch inside when Samulein cried, "The dog!"

We'd forgotten it, hunkered behind the woodshed. Freeing a guard dog with fresh blood in the air was risky, but the cabin might burn down the shed with it. Temal tossed the elkhound a strip of jerky as distraction, then unhooked the chain. The dog whined, looked between us and Mads, and ran into the woods.

Tema threw the torch and stepped back. Hot oil popped and burst. We were gone before the scent of burning flesh could reach us.

We hiked long into the night, tripping in the dark, until we gave into exhaustion and collapsed in the rain. I woke to grey sky, low voices, and my parents pointing at the ocean. Four long war canoes floated east, going the way we'd come. Tema climbed down a bluff, hid among clumps of dune grass, and fired a pulse of motion into the water. Itherans wouldn't notice, but other antayul would.

I sagged with relief when the boats turned. As they drew closer, their high seafaring prows became clear, carved with the shark crest of the Tamu-jouyen. The Tamu lived to the west on two peninsulas of Anwen Bel. When the canoes landed, a woman with tattooed knuckles and a necklace of crab claws explained that they'd been patrolling the inlet, saw the fire, and came to investigate.

"I had no idea brigands had taken the dock," she said, chewing a blade of dune grass. "Good thing you were armed. I'll track down the ferryman in case he's involved, too."

"It's appreciated. In the meantime, we need to get to Caladsten." Tema rummaged in her purse and held out a sovereign. "Can you take us?"

The woman looked us over — filthy and tired, my parents in borrowed clothes, me nursing a twisted ankle from our overnight hike, Hanaiko and Samulein silent as they'd been taught. She lingered on their blue eyes. "Throw in another sov and we won't ask questions."

She sent one canoe to find the ferry, one to get Mads, and another across the inlet to warn ports in Nordmur. My family piled into the remaining canoe. We followed the coast, passing cod trawlers and herring drifters crewed by itherans, taking refuge each night in salmon camps bustling with Tamu. Boys and girls my age teased each other as they gutted fish, like Rokiud and I should've been doing back home.

Near the Tamu-jouyen's settlement at Tamun Dael, we turned north to cross the inlet. As we entered Nordmur, mist gave way to reveal mountains golden with rye and flax fields. The Tamu woman pointed. High on a rocky cape, a stone-walled keep rose straight up from blunt cliffs. Rows of timber buildings layered the surrounding slopes. Anchored ships rocked in a harbour below.

"Caladsten," the woman told me. "Know what the name means?"

Hanaiko squirmed. She loved showing off what she knew but kept quiet.

My brows crinkled. "Oceanstone, right? *Kalad* is *ocean* in Aikoto. *Sten* is Sverbian for *stone*."

"Very good. That keep used to be a Ferish trading post. The brown pigeons kept murdering our trappers, so the northernmost Aikoto jouyen — we the Tamu, the Rin, Beru, and Haka — allied with a Sverbian militia and took it over. The alliance lives on in the name." She glanced at Hanaiko and Samulein. "And in other ways."

"Is Caladsten the capital here?" I asked, mostly to distract the woman.

"Nordmur doesn't have a capital. It's not an official province. No government, no military, just people who want to farm and fish in peace. So naturally, Eremur thinks everyone here are backwater rebels supporting the Rúonbattai."

We landed just outside the city at a set of low docks. Canoes bumped against lichen padding at their moorings, some prows carved with Tamu sharks, some with Dona seagulls. We climbed a steep cobblestone street to the Aikoto gathering place, a plank building surrounded by cranberry bushes with vibrant red foliage. Kids played tag in a field. I seemed to be the oldest, but not by much, to my relief. A boy about thirteen sat on an upturned canoe, watching the game.

The boy introduced himself as Akohin Dona and said we were in time to catch the last sailing before winter. Any later, the weather would be too rough for travelling open ocean. His uncle Batohin was captain of the ship we'd be on. Batohin himself arrived that evening, a windburned man with a southern name and a northern accent. He went pale when Tema gave him the seagull makiri from the ferry house.

"I knew the caretakers," he said. "Thank you for avenging them."

He explained that he was waiting on several families from the Beru-jouyen further north. If they didn't arrive by the first frost, we'd leave without them. If they did arrive . . . the news hit me like a paddle to the gut. There'd only be enough room on his ship for children and new mothers. My parents and I would separate here.

"There's really no other sailings?" I pleaded.

"Sorry, *akesida*." Batohin truly looked apologetic. "These voyages are tough to pull off. It's a two-week trip, and the fewer itherans who know where we're going, the better."

So we waited. I memorized everything Hanaiko and Samulein said about their village that I could spin into our story. In turn, I told them about my life, careful to feed them only memories that fit our tale of growing up in the wild. The last thing we needed was a slip of the tongue.

With prodding, we discovered Yotolein had started teaching Hanaiko water-calling. She couldn't yet move a droplet, though, so Tema decided we'd do lessons together. I did practice exercises familiar enough to perform in my sleep. Samulein splashed happily in a bucket, the way we got young kids used to handling water. Only

Hanaiko protested. Some mornings she stomped off, others she sulked with her arms folded.

"She's used to being the big sister," Tema reminded me in private, "better than Samulein at everything. Be patient and encouraging. You might learn something from them, too."

Nothing useful, I thought sullenly. But over lunch I asked Hanaiko, "What'd you study in your village?"

"Book things," she said with a mouthful of flatbread. "History, 'rithmetic, spelling. Our mamma read us folk tales every night before bed. She said reading's important."

That afternoon, Temal went into Caladsten and returned with a book bound in blue leather. Hanaiko lit up as she flipped through pages of tiny Sverbian symbols and ink drawings. At night she haltingly read a story to Samulein. After he fell asleep, Hanaiko tried translating it for me, something about a craftsman who kept making silly trades with travellers.

On a misty morning carrying a chill, we gathered in the field and watched canoes with whale prows land at the docks. The Beru families had arrived.

We hiked up a muddy road into Caladsten, passing log cabins and goat pastures. In the docklands, burly men lifted crates off a barge and stacked them on wagons. Fishermen shouted from the market, "Fresh caught, fresh caught." Gulls and bluejays flocked in search of scraps.

Batohin's ship was a sleek three-masted schooner with black sails in front and white sails behind, matching the feathered crest of its namesake, the *Ridge Duck*. It was the prettiest ship in the harbour, though that didn't make me feel better about getting on it without my parents. While Tema triple-checked the satchels with Hanaiko's and Samulein's belongings, Temal pulled me aside.

"Always keep your weapons at hand," he said, "even when you're asleep. When you reach the refuge, find a sparring partner. You need to keep in practice."

I nodded but couldn't speak. The dread that had been building since we left home threatened to boil over. I buried my face in Temal's chest.

"*Wala, wala*, little fireweed," he soothed and pressed a tiny figurine into my hand.

I gasped. Carved from pale hemlock, a prowling mountain cat stood with one paw raised, backed by a swan spreading enormous wings. My parents' attuned forms. "But you're not allowed to carve makiri," I said. "You didn't finish your apprenticeship—"

"I didn't perform the blessing to turn it into a makiri. Our spirits haven't gone into it, just our love." Temal folded my fingers over the figurine. "That's heartwood from Aeti Ginu. No matter where you are, you'll always have a piece of home. And remember—"

"Kianta kolo," I said. "Winter ends, spring comes, the sap flows."

He chuckled. "See? You don't need me anymore."

Next, Tema drew me into a hug and kissed my hair. "Kateiko," she murmured. "You're growing up before my eyes. When we meet again, you could be an attuned adult. I'm so sorry I might not be around to help you through it, but no matter what, you'll manage. That's how we raised you. I'm so proud of you, my daughter. Be brave, protect your cousins, and remember your temal and I love you more than anything. We'll come get you as soon as possible. I promise."

5.

VOYAGE

Akohin showed us below deck to the passenger quarters, lit by glass prisms in the ceiling that diffused the daylight. Everything smelled like seaweed, but the floor was scrubbed and the hammocks seemed clean. I helped my cousins unpack into cubbies nailed to the wall, then handed out our dinner ration of flatbread and elk jerky, along with shards of amber-coloured sapsweet Temal had bought in Caladsten. We ate at a hanging table that rocked with the waves.

Just before we set sail, a pale young woman with a baby swaddled to her chest climbed down the ladder, stumbling in a white skirt. Ash-blonde hair escaped her brimless bonnet. Finding the hammocks full, she spoke to a Beru mother, who turned away. The pale woman soothed her squealing baby, looking for somewhere to settle.

Hanaiko tugged on my sleeve. "Samu and I can share," she whispered. "He's little."

I sighed. After the ferry house, I didn't want Sverbians near us, but in this cramped space she'd be close no matter what. I called out to her and moved Samulein's blanket from his hammock. The woman blinked, not moving until I beckoned.

"Thank you," she said in accented Coast Trader, setting down a satchel. Her baby shared her green eyes, though its wisps of black hair probably meant the father was Aikoto.

When the ship's horn blew, I lifted Samulein and Hanaiko to a porthole in turns to watch the dock shrinking into the distance. They'd been on a herring drifter before but never a ship this big. Their excited chatter pried a smile from me. Siblings and sailing were two things I'd dreamed of. Maybe this trip wouldn't be so bad.

My hope lasted until night when Hanaiko shook me awake. "Samu won't stop crying," she whined.

I rubbed crustiness from my eyes and mumbled, "Samulein, c'mere."

He crawled into my hammock, putting a knee in my stomach. I held him and sang a Rin lullaby like Tema had on the way here, but he kept snuffling and wiping his nose on my shirt.

"What's wrong?" I asked. "Another nightmare?"

Samulein nodded.

"He dreams about fire," Hanaiko said, wrapped in her blanket with Hymelai clasped to her chest. "Ever since soldiers came and . . ."

A knot twisted in my stomach. So they *had* seen their village in flames. Yet Hanaiko had still asked us to burn the ferry house brigands' bodies, because it was the kind thing to do in their mamma's religion. Maybe Tema had been right about me learning from my cousins.

Samulein stared up at a glass lantern swaying from the rafters. Its light cast odd shadows on everything. "Eko," he whispered, a nickname that'd come from him mispronouncing Kateiko. "Can you put the lantern out?"

I glanced at a night-watch sailor supervising the rows of sleeping kids. "Sorry. The crew needs to see."

"But what if it falls and breaks?"

"Then I'll put the flames out. I can call water, remember."

"What if you're asleep?"

I groaned, too tired for this. "It's a magic lantern. It can't break. Now hush."

His sniffling eventually faded, but I couldn't fall back asleep. Someone kept coughing. No one in the gathering place had been sick, so I guessed it was a Beru. Like it wasn't bad enough they'd taken my parents' place on the ship. I clutched a fistful of blanket, knowing I was being unfair.

In the morning, sailors took kids above deck to get fresh air, an hour per group. The Sverbian tied a wool cap on her baby and came with us. My cousins ran to the forecastle to look ahead. We were sailing south through Tamu-jouyen territory, following a channel between the mainland and a string of huge islands. Misty mountains passed on either side. Alders and cottonwoods had shed their yellow autumn robes, leaving only evergreens to shelter the land.

Tamu kids pointed out landmarks, a waterfall here, smokehouse there. They said close ahead was a hilly island in the shape of a shark. The other kids looked skeptical, but Rokiud had seen it on trading trips — one of the Tamu-jouyen's sacred sites, a real version of their crest. I peered at the horizon, eager to share what I could with Rokiud.

Then the watchman shouted down from the crow's nest. I missed the words in the wind, but sailors began shepherding kids below deck.

"What's happening?" I asked.

"Spotted an Eremur ship," a sailor said. "It's best they don't see you."

Hanaiko wilted. We'd hardly gotten half our time outside. She took Samulein's hand, but he grabbed the railing and held fast.

"Come on, Samu," I said. "Let's go read a story."

"Nei!" He planted his feet like a tiny wrestler. "I wanna see the shark island!"

Hanaiko pulled hard on Samulein, who wailed. She swung to me desperately. In her wide blue eyes I glimpsed the burden she'd been carrying since their mamma's death — an eight-year-old playing mother to her younger brother. Samulein got scared at night, but Hanaiko was scared all the time.

I prised Samulein's fingers from the railing and carried him to the ladder. "You can be upset inside. Now climb down like a big boy or I'll carry you. Do you want everyone to see that?"

He scowled but quit flailing. I set him on the deck. He stomped down the ladder, stomped to our hammocks, and threw himself on the floor. I got the folk tale book for Hanaiko, who started reading Samulein's favourite story about an invisible trickster spirit. He pretended not to listen, but by the time the trickster stopped a horse in its tracks and confused the rider, Samulein was laughing.

"Your sister reads well for her age," the Sverbian told me. "Who taught her?"

"Our parents," I lied.

"Yet they didn't teach you?"

I shrugged.

"Never mind. Gods know we all have secrets." The woman smiled dryly and shifted her baby. "My name's Kirbana, by the way, and my son is Kel. You'll meet my husband at the island refuge. He's a Dona carpenter, so he travelled ahead to help rebuild it."

My shoulders eased. It couldn't hurt to be polite to people we'd be living with, especially another mixed-blood family. "Call me

Eko," I said, offering her a piece of sapsweet. "How about you read the next story?"

I looked out a porthole and saw only water. We'd left the channel and entered open ocean, heading southwest. Frost flowers decorated the glass. Wind struck hard, rocking the *Ridge Duck* and twisting our stomachs. Kirbana repaid the sapsweet with candied ginger, which I'd never seen, but my cousins said was safe. It burned my tongue but eased the nausea enough to sleep. Our daily hour outside was the only time I felt okay, soothed by cold air and the billowing black and white sails.

The fourth night sailing, I woke suddenly. The portholes were dark — no, they'd been shut. Waves pounded the hull. A Tamu mother with an antayul tattoo under her collarbones met my eyes across the dim room. Akohin stirred, too. We'd all sensed the water grow frenzied.

"Storm," said Batohin, halfway down the ladder. "Wake the others and fasten everything down. It's gonna get rough."

The Tamu antayul swaddled her baby to her chest and joined me and Akohin in rousing everyone. We rolled up the hammocks, threw laundry into sacks, and packed away tables and dishes, leaving our quarters strangely empty. We'd just finished when the rain came. I felt a curtain swing toward the ship, followed by a splattering collision. Drops struck the ladder. Someone above slammed the trapdoor shut, muffling the storm and sealing us into a timber box.

"Maybe the real Hymelai is out there," Hanaiko said, whisking her doll through the air. "Mamma said storm clouds are Hymelai's hair blowing across the sky."

"Did your temal teach you about saidu?" I asked. "The spirits that control the weather?"

"Yeah!" Hanaiko sat straighter. "Temal taught us a rhyme. 'Tel-saidu make the wind blow, edim-saidu make the trees grow. Anta-saidu make the creeks flow—'" She cut off, looking wide-eyed at Samulein. He apparently didn't remember the last line, but I did. *Jinra-saidu make the fires glow.*

"Temal says saidu change the seasons and keep everything balanced," Hanaiko went on. "But they've been asleep for hundreds of years, so people don't see them anymore."

I nodded. "Saidu are so good at handling the weather, they can do it in their sleep. Sometimes, though, they bicker and cause storms. A grumpy tel-saidu meets a grumpy anta-saidu, and *crash*! Wind and water everywhere."

"How do they fight in their sleep?" Samulein asked.

"They're having bad dreams," Kirbana said. "So once they get nice dreams, the storm will calm."

I cast her a grateful smile. That conversation had been about to go opposite how I wanted.

A Beru mother sang as a distraction. We comforted crying kids, passed out blankets, and fetched buckets for battles lost to seasickness. Kirbana offered up her whole supply of candied ginger. Anyone walking around had to cling to ropes for balance. A sailor on his way to pump the bilge stumbled and cracked his head but wiped away the blood and kept going.

Eventually, even sitting upright was tough. I braced myself against a crate and put Hanaiko between my legs, Samulein between hers, and Hymelai between his. Hanaiko's braid pressed into me, but I ignored it. We were blood relatives, after all.

On and on the ship plunged, groaning in protest. Water leaked through the trapdoor. A chill sank into my skin. Rain turned to hail, rattling against the porthole covers. I grabbed another sailor heading to the bilge. "I can help," I said. "I'm nearly an initiated antayul."

"Then you're nearly allowed below," he said, yanking away.

Akohin gave me a resigned shrug. He was an antayul-in-training, too, and often worked with the crew, but he wasn't allowed below, either. There was nothing to do but wait. I was nodding off when light flooded the room, followed by sky-shattering thunder.

Samulein shrieked. Hanaiko flung her arms around him, their little bodies trembling against mine. Lightning meant a jinra-saidu was out there, too. I cursed my antayul training that let me sense leagues of icy roiling water below, our burial place if the ship sank. I grasped Temal's figurine of the swan and mountain cat, seeking the strength he'd lovingly carved into it.

A fireball exploded through the room.

Lightning crackled out in blue fingers, leaping to the iron porthole covers. The air sizzled. I felt Hanaiko's chest swell with a scream but heard nothing over thunder ripping the world apart.

It was gone in seconds, leaving black smoke and the reek of rotten eggs. Sunspots dotted my vision. I scoured my cousins for wounds. Neither seemed hurt, but something prickled my mind, rhythmic as a heartbeat.

I leapt up. The wood around the portholes had been burned open. Whenever waves struck the ship, water poured inside. I slammed my hands over a hole and tried to push the water back out, but I couldn't fight the raging ocean. "Help!" I cried.

Kirbana thrust baby Kel at Hanaiko and stuffed his swaddling cloth into the hole. She leaned her shoulder against it, straining and panting, until Akohin nailed a board over the gap. He and I hurried through the room, helping the mothers plug scorched portholes with whatever we could find.

When the hull was secure, Kirbana took Kel back and cooed until his wailing stopped. The other antayul and I evaporated seawater flowing back and forth with the pitching ship. Finally, I slumped onto the floor and held my cousins, exhausted. The storm had calmed enough that I could hear Beru kids coughing.

"Rest," Kirbana told me. "I'll rouse you if you're needed."

Not until I woke at midday did I find out how much damage the storm had wreaked. A lightning bolt had struck the mainmast, splintering it down the middle. Two sailors had been wounded by flying shards of wood. Another got his hair burned off and his feet blistered. The lightning had gone out through the portholes, sidestepping sailors pumping bilge water below.

I poked my head up from the ladder to watch the repairs. Crewmen mended the shivered mainmast with boards and ropes. Others cut up scorched sails, keeping whatever cloth could be salvaged. Half the rigging had burned away, leaving charred ropes swaying through the air. Yet when I returned below deck, I realized, laughing, that the "magic" lantern still hung intact.

Batohin decided it was too risky to sail to the island refuge in a damaged ship. Instead we'd travel to our confederacy's nearest major port, the Iyo-jouyen settlement of Toel Ginu, and repair the *Ridge Duck*. I couldn't help being excited. Emehein's younger brother, Dunehein, had married into the Iyo and moved to Toel Ginu. Visiting him would be like going home. Plank houses, solid beds, dry clothes, and real food instead of jerky and stale bread.

More ships appeared on the horizon as we sailed east. We watched from the portholes, making up stories about where they were going. One day, sailing through a busy channel between massive islands, a schooner passed so close we could see its billowing flag — white with two rearing red elk over an anchor.

"That's the navy sigil of Eremur," Kirbana said. "We're entering the province now."

I pulled back from the glass. "*This* is Eremur? But it's Iyo territory."

"Depends who you ask. Wars have been fought over the question. But right now, it's safer than Nordmur, which is probably where that ship's heading." She peered at it. "See the smaller blue flag with a white raven? That's the flag of Sverba, which means it's an all-Sverbian crew. It's easier to segregate crews since Ferish ones rig sails differently."

"How do you know all this?"

"Oh, my uncle used to be in Eremur's navy. Then he retired and bought a farm, so I lived here for a few years to help fix it up." She smiled ruefully. "Now I'm back south with a half-viirelei baby and no husband. The gossip would run rampant."

When we made anchor, Batohin went ahead on a rowboat to ask the Iyo's permission to bring refugees ashore. My cousins and I were allowed on deck to see Toel Ginu. On high coastal cliffs stood neat lines of plank houses and workshops, their timbers faded by salt wind. We marvelled over rock pillars rising from the ocean and a natural stone bridge leading to an island that housed the Iyo shrine.

Our joy soon vanished. A navy cutter appeared on the misty horizon, sailing right at us. The watchman reported it was a Ferish crew. Batohin had instructed his first mate to leave without him if needed, but with our anchor down, there wasn't time. I hustled Hanaiko and Samulein below deck like we'd been taught.

"It's probably a routine check," Kirbana reassured me. "We've done nothing wrong."

Nothing except transporting the children of ex-Rúonbattai. A shadow fell over our portholes as the cutter drew alongside us.

Strange gliding accents called out overhead, followed by gangplanks striking the deck. The wait stretched on — until blades clashed above.

"Hide," I whispered. Hanaiko and Samulein climbed into their hammock and pulled blankets over their heads. I stood in front of them, my hunting knife drawn.

Kirbana raised her eyebrows. "That's not a fight you can win."

"I won't let anything happen to them," I said.

"We'll be fine. Keep your weapons hidden and don't give anyone reason to think you're a threat. That's not a battle up there, it's a show of force. Listen. No one's screaming in pain."

She was right. I slipped my small fish knife into my boot, then stowed my hunting knife, flail, and sheaths under my blanket.

Moments later, itherans in red uniforms climbed down the ladder, their curved sword sheaths knocking against their knees. The captain announced in broken Coast Trader that they'd seized the *Ridge Duck*. Batohin's crew was under arrest and would be taken to Eremur's capital, Caladheå, to face justice. We'd be taken with them.

6.

CUSTOMS HOUSE

We reached Caladheå in the dead of night and moored among ships with furled sails and empty decks. Fog and darkness hid the city. Soldiers prodded us across a lantern-lit pier and onto icy ground, which seemed to pitch after so many days at sea. Half the soldiers took Batohin's crew away in chains, leaving Akohin with us refugees. The other soldiers shoved us into a huge sandstone building, down winding halls, and into a cavernous room.

"I know where we are," Kirbana told me. "The Customs House is the only sandstone building in Caladheå's docklands. Everything that comes through the harbour gets processed here."

In flickering torchlight, soldiers began searching us for weapons. Akohin grimaced as he handed over a dagger. Kirbana beckoned me into the shadows behind stacked crates and whispered, "Give me your blade."

I pulled the fish knife from my boot. She tucked it into the folds of Kel's swaddling cloth. We took turns holding him as a bored-looking soldier patted us down and checked our purses and pockets.

We slept on dirty flagstone, or tried anyway. I kept shivering myself awake. Samulein stared at torches on the walls, his little fists balled against his mouth. Several kids had lung sickness now, racked by coughing that echoed off the stone. Kel kept fussing. I called water into my cupped palms and let him suck up what he could.

"Don't let the guards see," Kirbana whispered. "People here aren't used to water-calling. They think it's dangerous magic."

"A bucket's dangerous if you try hard enough," I said.

When dawn light came through the windows, I could see the room properly. The far wall had a pair of wide doors, barred shut and creaking from the wind. Muddy wheel tracks and all the crates meant this was probably a warehouse. Our guards had been replaced by soldiers in grey uniforms. Kirbana explained they were Caladheå's city guard, usually just called Elkhounds.

From outside came the clatter of horses and the distant *clang*, *clang* of a bell every hour. After it rang ten o'clock, a knock sounded on the wide doors. A guard heaved up the crossbars and pushed open the doors. I drank in fresh air and a view of ships backed by deep blue ocean. Two itheran women in heavy coats and dresses climbed down from a horse-drawn wagon. They both wore wide-brimmed bonnets over tightly curled hair.

"More Ferish," a Dona mother muttered.

The wagon driver, a man with a black moustache, unloaded water pails and baskets covered by burlap. One woman broke the ice on a pail and started filling cups. The other walked through the room handing out stale bread. If someone didn't take a loaf immediately, she dropped it in their lap and moved on. As she drew near, Hanaiko and Samulein hunched over, hiding their blue eyes.

"*Sienti dereto*," snapped the woman, glaring down at them. She straightened her back and twirled a hand for emphasis. Switching into heavily accented Coast Trader, she said, "Sit proper or not eat!" She grabbed Hanaiko's braid and yanked.

Hanaiko squealed. I shoved the woman away. She stumbled, tripping on her dress hem. A loaf slid from her basket and hit the ground. She lifted a hand with a glittering gold ring and slapped me.

"Gods' sakes," Kirbana cried. "They're children!"

The woman scowled, adjusting her skirts, then kicked the fallen loaf at me. I pulled Hanaiko close and kissed her braid, trying to cleanse the stain left on her spirit by a stranger's touch. She snuffled into my shirt. Samulein wiggled between us into a three-way hug.

"You're bleeding." Kirbana fished a handkerchief from her purse and held it near my cheek. When I didn't protest, she dabbed at me.

I tried to smile. She'd learned our people's taboos, unlike the Ferish woman. When no one was looking, I called a stream of water to rinse dirt off the bread's tough crust, then tore it in quarters for us and Kirbana.

That afternoon, shouting came from behind the small inner door. "Need I remind you I am Officer of the Viirelei?" a man demanded. "These refugees are my responsibility. Why was I not fetched last night?"

The door burst open and a wiry man strode in. He was clearly Aikoto, tall with tanned skin and sharp cheekbones, but wore a tailored coat and breeches like the wagon driver from earlier. His dark hair was combed sideways and looked oddly waxy. He ignored the Elkhounds and spoke to us, switching into rapid Aikoto.

"My name is Falwen. I am our confederacy's liaison to the itheran government here, the Caladheå Council. Batohin's crew has been arrested for transporting illegal immigrants into the province of Eremur."

"That's ridiculous," a mother said. "We were in Iyo waters!"

"The border treaties are in dispute. With the suspected return of the Rúonbattai, the military has ramped up security. It is more accurate to call you prisoners of war than of the law. However, I am here to aid you. First I must register everyone in Eremur's birth records. Form a line, please."

Falwen snapped his fingers. Elkhounds brought a table, stool, quill, inkwell, and other writing tools. Falwen jotted notes as he questioned the mothers, who also answered for children of their jouyen travelling alone.

"What does he mean by birth records?" I whispered.

"That's how the government identifies your people," Kirbana said. "Registered viirelei are meant to have free passage through the province. I should warn you, though, Falwen has to answer to the Caladheå Council. Don't tell him anything you don't want him to repeat."

I pressed my fingers to my lip. In the wilderness I could protect my cousins, but here I had no idea how things worked. "What if our family . . . has a reputation?"

She smiled wryly. "Tell you what. At twenty-two, I'm far too young to be your mother, but I could pass as your stepmother. The Dona don't have permanent homes to carve their family history on, so it'll be tough to disprove. That'll give us a better chance of staying together."

"So we pretend your husband is our temal? What if Falwen asks the Dona about him?"

"Narun spent years at sea working as a ship's carpenter. We can claim he had a secret family in Nordmur. Just say as little as possible for now so we have time to work out the details."

We listened to Falwen's interrogations as we got closer, memorizing his questions and practising our answers. Eko already sounded like a Dona name, short and easy to say, and I made up new ones for my cousins. When we reached the front of the line, Falwen's gaze darted to my cut cheek.

"Who did that?" he asked.

"Um — a Ferish woman who brought food," I stammered. "She grabbed my sister's braid, so I pushed her."

Falwen's mouth twisted. "Someone else will bring your food." He wrote something with swooping strokes, then said, "Names and jouyen?"

"Kirbana Elynehl," Kirbana said. "My baby, Kel Narunind, is registered at the main Sverbian stavehall in Caladsten. I just need to register my stepchildren — Eko, Aniya, and Sohin of the Dona." She tapped our shoulders in turn.

Falwen studied us. "Who are their birth parents?"

"Their father is my husband, Narun Dona. He's overseas right now. Their mother's blood is in the ground."

"Interracial custody cases go to the provincial court. Do not hold your breath." He made more notes. "Birthdates?"

"Winter of fourteen years, summer of eight years, spring of five years. Eko is still unattuned."

"That simplifies the paperwork." More notes. "They need second names. For children in the absence of a blood relative, I must assign names. Mèrus is given to all viirelei who come via ship."

"What's it mean?" I asked.

"*Of the sea* in Ferish." Falwen filled out three stiff cards, stamped them with sigils of rearing red elk, and handed one to me. "Done. Good luck, Eko Mèrus."

*

The wagon driver returned the next morning with a dark-haired Aikoto boy in his late teens. The boy wore a hooded wool jerkin and patched breeches. Tall and brawny, he unloaded crates as easily as if they held goose down. "The Iyo-jouyen put together a collection," he said.

We opened the crates to find blankets, lye soap, bandages and gauze bags of bogmoss, clean wraps for the babies, and honey and medicinal herbs for the sick kids. There was food, too — salted jerky, berries, mushrooms, fresh flatbread made from brassroot flour. In the last crate was smoked salmon, oily and rich with the scent of alder.

As the boy passed out supplies, he whispered something to one of the mothers. She repeated it to us later. The military had offered to release us if Batohin came from Toel Ginu and turned himself in. He'd agreed and gone to prison, but there was no sign of us being allowed to leave. Akohin went pale at the news and refused to eat.

The Iyo boy came back every morning with supplies. Frost grew on the windows with each passing day. Soon everyone had caught the sickness, filling the warehouse with constant coughing. One mother asked about bringing an Iyo healer but was told only a Ferish medic would be allowed in.

"Not a chance," she muttered to us. "I've heard about those pigeons' idea of medicine — cutting, burning, poisoning. They'd kill us faster."

Hanaiko and Samulein went through violent coughing bouts followed by odd whoops of breath. My throat felt like I'd swallowed sand. Kel kept making little wheezes and sputters. I dipped my fingertip in honey and let him suckle while Kirbana read aloud from our folk tale book, propping it open for my cousins to see the illustrations. I couldn't imagine getting through this without her.

So when I woke to see an Elkhound shaking her awake, I told myself it was a nightmare. But the glint of the man's armour was too bright, the mix of sweat and spice too pungent. He said something with a thick accent, handed Kel to me, and pulled Kirbana to her feet.

"Don't worry," she assured me as she was led away. "I'm sure it's nothing."

Like we'd done nothing to have our ship seized. I rocked Kel, fretting whether his forehead was warm or if my hand was just cold. Questions swarmed my head. What if Kirbana didn't come back? If I had to care for Kel? My sick cousins were enough to handle — bored, scared, and bickering.

"Aniya, give that back," I snapped.

"Sohin started it," she complained, holding his toy canoe out of his reach.

"I don't care. You're being childish."

"I *am* a child."

There was nothing to say to that. We should've been on our way to the island refuge where my cousins could run and play in fields and forests, safe and healthy like normal kids. No one was trying to kill us here, but this was no life. I buried my face in my hand, not moving when the doors opened for our daily delivery.

As my cousins devoured their bread, a husky voice asked, "Where's that itheran woman?"

I looked up. The dark-haired Iyo boy stood over me, pulled tight like a drawstring, shoulders hunched and hands in his pockets. My answer stuck in my throat. He took Kel, changed his wrap, mushed some berries and fed him, and handed him back to me. Then he sat cross-legged and started tying knots in a length of frayed cord.

"What's your name?" I asked.

"Jonalin Tanarem," he said.

"Don't you have things to do?"

"Nei. I'm a dockhand. There's no work until a ship comes or goes."

My cousins stopped squabbling when they noticed Jonalin's knots. He showed them different kinds that locked or came loose easily, and explained their names and uses in sailing — bowlines, reef knots, rolling hitches. Then he pulled out a spool of string and asked their favourite flowers. Hanaiko said daisies. Samulein said he liked dogs, not flowers.

Jonalin bit off a length of string and began knotting it. I watched his calloused fingers in awe. A tiny daisy emerged, followed by a shaggy dog that was mostly loose string. Samulein wriggled with excitement.

"It's called macramé," Jonalin said. "Sailors use it to cover bottles and stuff, and they make pretty things to sell in ports."

"Can you teach us?" Hanaiko asked.

"Sure." He bit off more string and showed my cousins a knot to practise. Once they were busy, he glanced at me. "What about you? Dogs or flowers?"

"Um . . . cranberry blossoms, I guess. They look like swans in flight."

Jonalin worked deftly, creating a flower with petals curled back from the stamens. He strung it on a cord and dangled it over Kel, who burbled and waved his hands. I managed a smile.

"You can keep it." Jonalin squinted one eye shut. "I mean . . . if you want to."

"Could you make it a bracelet?" I shifted Kel in my arms and held out a hand.

He tied the cord around my wrist, his rough fingertips brushing my skin. Malana and Nili would've teased me relentlessly about a brawny older boy making me jewellery. Eventually a ship's horn blew and Jonalin left, but I found myself thinking about him as the distant bell tolled the passing time, wondering about his life outside these sandstone walls.

Hours later, Kirbana returned. She smothered Kel in kisses. I waited as long as my patience could hold, then burst out, "What happened? Where'd they take you?"

"An interrogation room," she said. "They wanted to know if I have any connection to the Rúonbattai. I don't, and our home stave-hall confirmed Kel is half-Sverbian, so he and I are free to go."

"*Really?* Why?"

"We're legal immigrants. This is a province of Sverba, though you couldn't tell from living here. Nearly everyone in this city is Ferish." She nodded at the Elkhounds.

"So if I said we're half-Sverbian, we'd go free, too?"

"Well . . . only with a guardian, so it still depends on a custody trial. Until then, you're wards of the province. But don't worry." Kirbana took my hand. "I'm not leaving without you."

On a blustery day, a dozen grey-clad Elkhounds filed in. One with a red band around his sleeve introduced himself as their captain. He read names aloud from a scroll, mangling the pronunciations. Children went up one by one and the captain waved them into a group. Only the mothers and babies, my cousins, and I weren't called. The captain spoke to the Elkhounds in Ferish. One lifted the crossbar from the doors, letting sleet whirl inside.

"Wait," said a Beru woman holding her baby. "Where are you taking them?"

"The orphanage," the captain said. "They'll be taken care of there."

A clamour rose across the room. Kirbana and I exchanged startled glances. A few kids started to cry.

"But that's my son!" The Beru woman grabbed a young boy's hand. "Ask Falwen, ask the Okorebai-Beru—"

"Restrain her," the captain said, raising his voice.

One Elkhound pulled the boy away. Another wrested the woman's wailing baby from her arms. She shrieked, clawing at the soldiers. A third slammed his spear into her head, knocking her over.

I watched in horror. All my warrior training told me to grab the fish knife from my boot and defend the woman. Before I could, Samulein grabbed my leg, staring at the fight. Hanaiko pressed close to my other side.

"Stay back," Kirbana whispered. "If you get involved, they'll separate us, too."

Elkhounds tied the Beru woman's wrists and held her at spearpoint. Others began shepherding kids toward the doors. More fights broke out as mothers tried to grab their kids, nephews, nieces. I heard a crack as a Tamu woman's arm snapped. She screeched in pain, barely holding onto her baby.

Akohin stood his ground, facing down the captain. "You promised to let us go," he said through gritted teeth. "My uncle went to prison on your word. He never should've trusted a brown pigeon."

"Batohin Dona was wanted for a lifetime of smuggling," the captain said. "Now move, or you'll join him."

Scowling, Akohin joined the group of kids filing out the doors. Most of the Elkhounds went with them, leaving just our usual guards, who shut and barred the door. The ocean wind faded. The Beru mother kept screaming, but the others slumped to the floor, the fight beaten out of them.

For once Kirbana didn't tell me it was nothing. Instead, sounding stricken, she murmured, "At least my claim on you held up."

⁂

Jonalin must've heard the news. Our next delivery was small enough that he came alone pulling a hand cart. He flinched at the sight of the injured women. We'd bound the Tamu woman's broken arm with a swaddling cloth, but she was delirious with pain and sickness.

More than ever, I was glad Kirbana's deception had kept us together, but it soon became clear she couldn't stay. Kel struggled to eat and his once-chubby limbs had wasted away. Damp hair stuck to his feverish forehead, yet no amount of blankets kept him from shivering. One night I woke and found Kirbana white-faced, Kel in her arms.

"He wasn't breathing," she whispered.

My insides wrenched. "Kirbana . . . you have to go. Take him to a healer."

"I don't have the money. Our ship passage cost everything I had."

I held out a gold sov from the ferry house. "Brigands stole this from Sverbian refugees. It's only fair it goes to you."

She hesitated before accepting the coin. "I'll stay in the city. I'll keep fighting for custody of you three. For now, take this." She handed me a rusty tin coin. On one side was a crown, on the other was a leafless tree with nine branches and nine roots. "If you get out of here and need help, look for that tree."

"What's it mean?"

"It's the sacred Sverbian oak at the centre of the universe, our symbol for eternity. Every stavehall has it carved outside. The clerics there will help you."

I ran my fingers over the etched branches. "My people have a sacred tree, too. Ours is a rioden. It's supposed to be evergreen, but on the equinox I . . . had a vision. It looked like this, black and barren."

Kirbana smiled softly. "Gods and spirits speak in strange ways."

She lifted a hand to my face, asking permission. I dipped my head. Gently, she stroked my tangled hair. I'd never imagined letting an itheran touch it, but she wasn't just an itheran anymore. She was family.

The day of the first snow, the Elkhound captain announced the rest of us would be deported to Tamun Dael, on the coast of the war-torn region we'd fled. My cousins and I got up, but he waved us back down. "Not you," he said.

I moved aside as the mothers swaddled their babies and filed outdoors, casting pained looks back at us. With Elkhounds pointing spears at them, there was nothing they could do. We pressed our faces to an icy window and watched them head toward the harbour.

Samulein tugged my sleeve. "Eko, when can we go home?"

"I don't know, Sohin. Sorry."

"I miss Kirbana," Hanaiko said quietly. "And Temal and Mamma. And Auntie Sohiko and Uncle Mikiod."

My throat tightened at my parents' names. "Me, too. But we'll be okay as long as we're together."

Torrential rain hit overnight, rattling the windows and dripping through the ceiling. I thought Jonalin might skip his next delivery, but he turned up soaked, looking unsurprised to find us alone. Water streamed through the wicker basket he carried. An

Elkhound guard said something wryly, and Jonalin replied with words I didn't understand.

"You speak their language?" I asked as he passed us soggy flatbread.

"Some," he said. "I work with a lot of Ferish dockhands."

I frowned, comparing his dark hair and tanned skin to our guards. "Are you really Iyo?"

Jonalin unbuckled his hooded jerkin and peeled off his tunic. Inked on his muscular arm was the Iyo dolphin wreathed by sorrel leaves, his family crest. I realized I was staring and looked away, my cheeks warm.

"I grew up in Toel Ginu and moved here for work," Jonalin said. "Me and a friend share a flat on the Iyo street nearby."

"Is that why you're doing this? You're getting paid?"

"Nei. I volunteered." He wrung out his clothes. "If my niece and nephew were locked up alone in a strange city, I hope someone would take care of 'em."

From then on, Jonalin stayed with us every day until he was called away to work. He brought another toy canoe so he and Samulein could fight battles in a water bucket, and a macramé doll to go with Hymelai. This one had white yarn hair and a teal dress.

"She's Hafai, Lady of the Ocean," Hanaiko proclaimed. "Hafai swims everywhere with two huge whales. When ships get too close, the whales open their mouths and — *snap*!" She clapped her arms together.

"You mean like . . ." Jonalin crawled across the flagstone. He spread his arms wide and scooped up Samulein, who squealed with laughter.

Hanaiko giggled and threw water at them. Jonalin grabbed her and the three collapsed in a squirmy mess. As he untangled himself, our eyes met. He grinned, showing a dimple. It felt like looking up from the deep ocean gloom at a sparkle of sunlight.

Jonalin brought news, too. Kirbana had gone to a stavehall and told the clerics that we were half-Sverbian, which is why we hadn't been deported with the others. The clerics were demanding Kirbana get custody of us.

"Why won't the military hand us over?" I asked. "We don't matter to them."

"It's not about you," Jonalin said. "The Rúonbattai were crazy religious, so if they're on the rise again, the military doesn't wanna give in to Sverbian clerics. They'd look weak. My jouyen's trying to get custody of you, too, but once itherans take our kids, we don't often get them back."

"You mean we could be stuck here *forever*?"

"Dunno." He ran a hand through his short hair, making it stick out in every direction. "Look . . . Falwen knows you're not Kirbana's stepkids. He said if you tell him the truth, he'll have a better chance of getting you out."

I twisted the macramé flower on my bracelet, thinking. I wasn't ready to tell Jonalin everything, but we couldn't spend a winter in this leaky, freezing warehouse. Maybe Falwen could send a message to Toel Ginu asking Dunehein for help.

"Aniya and Sohin aren't my siblings," I admitted. "We're cousins. Those aren't their names, either. If Elkhounds find out who they are, they'll get taken away. Or worse."

Jonalin's brows crinkled. "Well, if you want, I'll ask Falwen to come tomorrow. The Okorebai-Iyo, Tokoda, trusts him."

I took a deep breath, uttering a silent plea to my aeldu that I was making the right choice. "All right. Ask him."

⁂

The next day, Jonalin left work early and came to wait with us. He entertained my cousins, teaching them to make string figures by weaving cord around their fingers. I paced the room, going over what I'd say, yet daylight faded with no sign of Falwen.

Without me needing to ask, Jonalin slept on the floor with us. I woke to him nudging me in the faint grey light of dawn. Murmurs came from behind the inner door. I sat up blearily, my cloak crackling where my breath had frozen onto it.

The Elkhound captain entered along with an elderly man. They glanced at us and went on talking. The old man looked like an owl with rimmed spectacles, a bald head, and draping sleeves. Embroidered on his deep blue robes was a symbol like a three-blossom flower.

"A Ferish priest," Jonalin whispered. "Probably from Nen Divinus, the sancte up the street. That's where the bell is that rings every hour."

"Can you understand them?" I whispered back.

He cocked his head, listening. "I think . . . the priest says you're too old for the orphanage. Fourteen's the cut-off."

The priest spread his hands as if to say there was nothing he could do. The captain folded his arms, arguing, then sighed and beckoned to our guards.

I rounded on Jonalin. "Did you bring the priest? Was meeting Falwen all a lie?"

He paled. "Nei, I swear—"

The men came toward us. I scrambled up and stood in front of my cousins, who had woken wide-eyed. Jonalin moved next to me, towering over us all.

"What's happening?" I asked. "Are we going somewhere?"

"*You're* not," the captain said. "Now move aside."

I didn't. He pushed me, so I pushed back. He struck me in the head and I stumbled.

"Nei," I said dazedly. "They're my family. You can't take them!"

"Watch us." The captain glared up at Jonalin. "Move or I'll arrest you, boy."

"Try," Jonalin said.

An Elkhound swung his fist. Jonalin dodged, grabbed the man's arm, and flipped him. The other soldiers went after Jonalin together, dragging him down.

The captain scooped up Hanaiko. She bit his hand and kicked until he dropped her. Her squeal of pain ignited something in me. I pulled my fish knife from my boot and lunged. Catching the captain by surprise, I sliced his thigh. He staggered. I sank my blade into his gut.

"Eko!" Samulein cried.

I spun. An Elkhound had his spear to Jonalin's chest. The captain knocked my knife away and pinned my arms behind me. I struggled, too sick and weak to escape his grip.

"Take them," he grunted, his warm blood seeping into the back of my clothes.

Elkhounds picked up my shrieking, writhing cousins. The priest turned in a swirl of blue robes and held the door open.

"Nei!" I shouted. "Give them back! You can't have them! *Give my family back!*"

Hanaiko stretched out her little arms over her captor's shoulder. "Let us go!" she wailed. "Eko! *Eko!*"

I screamed myself hoarse as my cousins were carried away. The priest glanced back, his face creased with apology, and shut the door after them. My cousins' crying faded into silence.

The captain released me. I crumpled, staring at Hanaiko's dolls crushed on the dirty flagstone. Hymelai's arrowhead-leaf skirt was torn.

"Eko," Jonalin said.

I looked up. *Go*, he mouthed. *Now*.

He grabbed the spear pointing at his chest. The Elkhound holding it toppled. I seized my bloody knife from the floor, smashed its handle into a window, vaulted off a crate through the opening, landed in a snowbank, and ran.

7.

GOLDEN OAK

The carriage holding my cousins rolled away from the Customs House, rattling up a slushy cobblestone street. I tore after it. My sick lungs screamed in protest. I wove around crates, ducked under oars carried by a startled dockhand, and shoved through a group of people waiting to board a ship.

"Watch it, fleabait," a man snapped.

A crowd filled the street ahead. They parted to let the carriage pass, then closed again, swallowing it from view. By the time I reached the crowd, footprints in the slush had erased the wheel tracks. Side streets went off everywhere. I swore, coughing so hard I retched. Someone wearing grey knocked into me and I flinched, but it was just a woman carrying her shopping.

The sancte bell tolled, clear as water now that I was outside. I followed the peals. Between the shore and a vast courtyard framed by red-brick shops, the spired bell tower of Nen Divinus interrupted the sky. Out front, the carriage waited at a hitching post, but the sancte's wide stone steps and portico were empty.

Deep blue robes caught my eye. Along the side wall, the old priest unlocked an iron-banded door. Guards carried my kicking cousins inside. A strangled cry burst from my lungs. Once again, the door closed, sealing them away from me.

I sank to my knees in the filthy snow. Nen Divinus was a fortress. Each stone slab in the walls was the length of my arm, and the multi-coloured windows were too high to sneak through. Going straight in the front doors would be like running into a bee nest.

Looking across the courtyard, which was filled with rows of wooden stalls, I realized it must be the city square. Jonalin had mentioned visiting his aunt Segowa's embroidery shop here. Maybe she could contact Dunehein in Toel Ginu. She at least deserved to know Jonalin might've been arrested. I swallowed my guilt. No time for feelings. *I'd* get arrested if I wasn't careful. My cloak sported a bloodstain from the captain and rips from the broken window.

I spotted a beggar woman and said, "Ai. I'll pay you ten pann to trade cloaks with me."

She took the deal wordlessly. Her cloak was thin, patched, and too short, but the hood concealed my hair. From behind I could pass as Sverbian. In an alley, I washed the blood from my fish knife, then tucked it back into my boot.

I elbowed through a mat of people filling a laneway between stalls. The range of goods was dizzying — jars of preserves, lace and ribbon and silk in every colour, bins of striped candy, scented soap, metal tools, jewellery in glass cases. A few laneways in, I found an Iyo dolphin crest embroidered on a square of leather nailed to a wall. I glanced inside and froze. An Elkhound spoke to a middle-aged Aikoto woman with a long braid.

"I swear I haven't seen her," the woman said. "I'd notice a child covered in blood."

"Harbouring a violent criminal is a serious offence," the Elkhound said. "You don't want more trouble, do you?"

"Of course not. If anyone from the Iyo-jouyen sees the girl, we'll turn her in. But if you'll excuse me, right now I need to find my nephew. Has he been taken to the prison yet?"

Heart thudding, I shoved out of the laneway, sliding on ice and turning corners at random. I collapsed in a park. A month of being sick and locked up had wrecked my body.

Yesterday I wouldn't have believed the Iyo would hand me over, but it was too much of a coincidence that I'd admitted to lying about our identities, then a priest turned up instead of Falwen. If they also blamed me for Jonalin's arrest . . . Either way, Elkhounds would search the Iyo street. It was near the docklands, so I stumbled inland instead, keeping the weight of the ocean at my back.

Endless red-brick buildings lined the hilly roads. Carriages jolted past, splattering up slush. Whatever district I'd reached, everyone seemed to be Ferish and wealthy. Chattering women with lambskin mittens and gold earrings held their skirts above the snow. Men in thick fur hats passed me with hardly a glance. "Street rats everywhere these days," one grumbled to his friend.

The scent of cooking food made my stomach growl. I followed it down stone steps into an enclosed courtyard decorated with fir boughs and hanging glass snowflakes. Food stalls filled the place with heat. An itheran woman spooned steaming beans into hollow buns as fast as she could take people's money. I held out coins like everyone else, but she ignored me.

Confused, I tried again with a man slicing meat off a roast, but two women talking loudly pushed me out of the way. At the next stall I broke into a coughing fit and the shopkeeper shooed me off with a disgusted look. A baker couldn't understand me and kept gesturing at his bread rolls. I was wondering if I should just take one and drop money on his counter when a girl in a dirty green dress poked me. She looked about twelve, skinny as a fencepost with tangled black hair.

"He ask, meat or fruit?" she said with a gliding accent. "What you want?"

I didn't want to risk eating animal heart, a sacred organ, so I said, "Fruit."

"*Pérossetto*," she told the baker. He answered, and she told me, "Two pann."

I paid and bit into my roll apprehensively. It was soft and filled with berry jam.

"Why you here?" the girl asked. "Viirelei not come to this place."

"Lost," I said, my mouth full of bread.

"Where you go?"

I chewed and thought. Kirbana had given me a rusty coin and told me to look for the sacred oak symbol on a stavehall. The clerics were my last hope. I wouldn't tell this girl what I was looking for, but if I got to a Sverbian district, I'd find a stavehall eventually. "A Sverbian market," I said. "Do you know where one is?"

She nodded. "Old quarter. I take you?" She pointed at the baker's rolls, then her mouth. "For . . . ?"

It was a fair price, so I bought her a meat-filled roll. She grinned and beckoned.

"I'm Lucreza," she said as we climbed the stone steps back to the street. "What you want at market? I help?"

"Nei, thanks," I said. "I just need to find one."

Lucreza shrugged and led me north. Blackened timber buildings with sagging roofs appeared, scattered among the brick like hunched old men. I knew the history of Caladheå. My family had once lived here and saved a stavehall from a fire that destroyed half the city. That was over sixty years ago, though, in the Second Elken War. I wasn't sure if the building still stood, or if this was even the same area.

"Shortcut," Lucreza said, turning down an alley.

I stopped at its entrance. Every window was boarded over. The alley was empty. I backed up — and a cudgel smashed into my head.

Hands grabbed me. Blind with dizziness, I rammed my elbow sideways and heard a *crunch*. My purse straps tore as someone ripped it from my belt.

I reeled backward, yanked my fish knife from my boot, and brandished it at a scrawny boy holding my purse. "Give it back or I'll gut you."

An older boy wrested the knife from my grip. He dragged me down the alley and shoved me against a wall, holding the blade to my throat. Behind him, Lucreza wiped a bloody nose with her sleeve. The three of them all had black hair and pinched faces. Siblings, probably. I swore.

The eldest spoke in gliding Ferish and plucked my leggings. Lucreza snorted and said something that made the younger boy laugh. She took my purse from him and rummaged through it, unfolding the handkerchief with my glass lily and the beaded jewellery I'd worn at the autumn equinox. She pocketed them along with my money. Next she pulled out Temal's carved figurine of the swan and mountain cat.

"Nei!" I slammed my fists into the wall. "Don't touch that!"

The older boy pressed the knife closer, cutting my neck. "*Afrettari*," he snapped at the others.

Lucreza dropped my purse in the slush. As she turned to leave, the younger boy squeaked. An ice spike hovered in mid-air, pressed to his chest.

"If I die, he dies," I said.

"Mage," the older boy spat. He backed up, grabbed the figurine from Lucreza, and threw it at my feet. "Take it. But you hurt my brother, I find you. Skin you in sleep."

I scooped the figurine up and edged away. At the end of the alley, I let my spike melt and splatter onto the ground, then ran. My head throbbed. I threw up on a bush and kept running, spitting to clear my mouth.

In an icy lot, I slipped and went sprawling. I groaned and rolled over. Nearby hung a sign carved with a tree, but my vision shifted too much to count the branches. I peered at the long building behind it. Steep shingle roof, white window frames, timber posts for walls. It sure looked like a hall built of staves, but no way could I have found one just like that . . . unless the aeldu were guiding me.

I heaved myself up and careened through the nearest door. Straw crunched under my feet. An odd musty scent filled my nose. I stumbled into a stall, toppled onto a straw pile, and passed out.

"Ah! *Bøkkai*!"

I jerked awake. A man stared at me, startled, holding the reins of a silver horse. A sword hung at his side. I flattened myself against the wall, gripping an ice spike.

"Amja, amja." The man raised his free hand in peace. With a thick accent he said, "Why are you sleeping in the stavehall?"

"I need help," I said breathlessly. "Are you a cleric?"

He looked confused, then cracked a smile. "Ah. I said the *stable*," he repeated. "For an inn, the Golden Oak. Its pub has spirits of the other sort."

I sagged with disbelief. A pub of drunk itherans was the last place I wanted to be. I tried to get up, only to double over coughing. Pain shot across my throat. I clamped my hand to it and found blood where my wound had reopened.

"Gods' sakes." The man's voice was suddenly gentle. He untied a waterskin from the saddle. "Here. Drink."

I sniffed it and sank my mind inside. The contents felt like plain water, not poisoned or laced with alcohol. I sipped it warily.

He hitched his horse and crouched next to me, brushing a lock of brown hair out of his eyes. Most of his hair was tied back loosely. Scars crossed his forehead and the bridge of his nose. "Would you like to come inside?" he asked. "Warm up and have something to eat?"

I shook my head. I was done following people into traps.

"Should I take you to a real stavehall?"

I shook my head again.

The man's brow furrowed. "How about I bring you some food?"

I shrugged. Whatever made him leave. He headed down the aisle, and I crept to the stall gate, listening to his footsteps move deeper into the stable. I was about to go the other way when a door creaked.

"Ah, it *is* you, Tiernan," said a new voice. "I saw you from the pub window."

"I will join you later," the horseman, Tiernan, said. "I just found a viirelei girl sleeping in a stall. She looks like she has been through a gristmill."

"Really?" the new voice said. "There was an incident in the docklands this morning. A viirelei girl stabbed an Elkhound captain and fled."

Tiernan scoffed. "Not much of a captain to lose against a child."

"A child warrior. Violence runs in those people's blood—"

"Mind yourself, Nerio," Tiernan said sharply. "Even if this is the same girl, she is half-dead and terrified. She needs help."

Their voices dropped low. I peeked around the corner. The second person was a dark-haired teenage boy with a longbow strapped to his back. Embroidered on his black uniform were two rearing elk.

"Kaid," I muttered. I aimed at the ceiling rafters behind them, formed a ball of ice, and let it drop. It shattered. They whirled. I bolted for the outer door.

Orange sunset glinted off the icy lot. Yet again, I staggered through the streets, panicking. If Tiernan told that soldier I needed a cleric, the stavehalls wouldn't be safe for me. I had nowhere left in Caladheå. I needed to get out while I could, then figure out how to get Hanaiko and Samulein out, too.

By accident, I came across farmers packing up a market. While a woman adjusted her horse's harness, I climbed into her wagon and burrowed into a pile of dusty sacks. We drove across rattling cobblestones, then a bridge over rushing water, and stopped while the woman spoke to what sounded like Elkhounds. I bit a sack and forced myself not to cough.

Finally, we jerked back into motion. The Elkhounds' voices faded. I lifted a sack and saw snowy fields all around. I was free — as long as I could survive.

8.

WHITE WOLF

Somewhere on a muddy road, I slid off the wagon. It rolled ahead into the growing dark. Farmhouses with firelit windows dotted a rolling plain around me. I headed for the nearest one and slunk through the shadows until I found the cellar door. It was locked. I tried the barn and found a basket of bruised apples and carrots near the horse stalls. I felt bad for stealing until I remembered the farm was on land stolen from the Iyo-jouyen. A historic agreement between the Iyo and Rin said I had a right to take whatever I needed from their land to survive.

Savouring an apple, I looked at the stars to get my bearings. I knew that this plain, the Roannveldt, separated the rainforest Iyun Bel into halves. Toel Ginu was in the south forest, but I couldn't go there to find Dunehein. Segowa had said the Iyo would hand me over to the military. Being alone was safer. I marked an arrow north in the snow, then went to sleep in the barn.

A rooster crowed at sunrise. I filled my pockets with food, kicked snow over my arrow, and left before the farmers stirred. I hoped to forage something on the way, but all I found was shaggy white goats and snowy fields. My legs ached by the time I glimpsed a long dark smudge of forest across the horizon. When I reached the first tree, I collapsed under its leafless branches.

Something prickly jabbed me. I pawed through the snow and uncovered a mat of deep red plants still holding berries. I laughed and stuffed a handful into my mouth, leaves and all. I'd never seen bearberries grow so far from the high mountains.

Deeper in North Iyun Bel, the forest canopy blocked the snowfall, so only a dusting of flakes had reached the ground. I found a patch of frozen mushrooms, but just in time noticed a black and orange newt hibernating under them. Coal newts were so toxic the whole patch would be contaminated. Near dusk I reached a wide creek with ice on its banks, as good a place as any to camp. I bent branches into a shelter, gathered armloads of conifer needles for a bed, and dried moss and wood for a fire. My flint had been in my purse when Lucreza stole it, so I rubbed sticks together to make sparks.

In the morning, I stripped naked and stepped shivering into the creek. I hadn't seen my body since leaving home two months ago. My bones stuck out everywhere. I bathed, scrubbed and dried my clothes, and dressed by the fire. Teeth chattering so hard they ached, I examined what little I had — Temal's carving, my seashell necklace from Rokiud, and my macramé bracelet from Jonalin. No tools, weapons, or money.

"I can do this," I told myself. "Tema always says the rainforest provides."

I started by making a fishing pole — a branch for a rod, my unravelled bracelet for a line, a thorn for a hook, berries for bait. After several tries I snagged a trout, which I gutted messily with a sharp rock.

Fish wouldn't keep me alive long, though. I needed bones for tools and furs for warmth. No matter how much I wanted to huddle by my fire, staying here meant dying. I compromised with a torch. I snapped a disc-shaped fungus off a rioden trunk, hollowed it out, filled it with flammable resin, and stuck in a forked branch for a handle.

Figuring the creek flowed back toward the ocean, I followed it east instead, searching for animal tracks or droppings. I was shocked at how few I found. Jonalin had mentioned Iyun Bel was heavily over-trapped by itherans, but I hadn't understood how bad it was. My years of trapping experience weren't for nothing, though. I dug a pit, disguised it with branches and leaves, and got safely back to my campsite by nightfall.

A day later, I sat cross-legged skinning a hare with my makeshift rock knife. It kept snagging and I couldn't work it properly with my hands so stiff from cold. I nicked my thumb and had to soak up the blood with bogmoss I'd foraged from a damp clearing. The hare's pelt was mangled by the time I finished. I was putting the meat to roast when a whine split the silence. My head snapped up. A pure white wolf cowered in the bushes.

"You're far from home," I breathed. Traders had brought white wolf pelts from the northern tundra, but I'd never seen one alive.

The wolf crept closer, limping. I thrust my torch forward. It stopped and whined again. We stared at each other. Its thick coat made it look big, but its ribs showed through a bald patch caked with dry blood. It was too weak to hunt.

I raced through options. Fight and maybe lose. Run and lose my food. Desperate, I threw the hare's heart. The wolf snatched it up and slunk off. I slumped with relief. I'd dreaded eating a sacred organ anyway.

Next morning, I spotted the wolf gnawing something. I eyed the wolf, flipping my rock knife. Its pelt would make a good mantle, and I might get a little meat off its bones, but it'd be wasteful to kill it without a proper skinning knife. I shuffled closer to my fire and daydreamed about burying my face in that cloud of fur.

Then it hit me. *Bones*. I sidled toward the wolf and realized it was gnawing a huge rib. I followed its tracks, heading west along the creek for the first time. Near the bank, mossy antlers stuck up from the foliage. I tore up dead ferns and found an elk skeleton, spread across the ground and hidden under snow and rotten leaves. *Buried treasure*, I thought with a grin.

I broke a shard from the lower leg bone, then ground it to an edge. The bone dust sent me into coughing fits. I gathered frozen ropeweed from the creek shallows, knotted its fibres into cord, and wrapped it around the knife handle for grip. My hands were chafed by the end, but it felt good to have a real knife again. So good that when the white wolf slunk up to watch me clean fish, I threw it the guts.

"You live another day," I said. "Tomorrow I'll work on trapping you."

That evening, howling sounded through the forest. I paused to listen. Voices drifted up the creek. I doused my fire, tore apart my branch shelter, and swept out my arm, pulling snow from the trees and draping it in a sheet over the ashes, bloodstains, and tracks of my campsite. I dropped onto my stomach in the bushes just as a long narrow boat appeared on the water.

Six men in red naval uniforms rowed it, talking in what sounded like Ferish. A seventh man holding a crossbow sat in the stern. He laughed, deep and throaty. None of them noticed smoke lingering from my fire. The boat glided past, steering around patches of ice on the banks. Soon it was gone.

I rolled over and exhaled, forming a misty cloud. The howling faded. Moments later, the wolf limped up and looked at me, seeming to expect something for sounding the alarm. I grudgingly threw it a trout I'd saved for breakfast. "Guess I can't kill you now," I muttered.

It was too late to rebuild my shelter, and I didn't dare relight the fire in case the soldiers saw the glow. I raked up the coals instead and huddled by their feeble warmth, hands tucked under my arms, trying to forget the white fur mantle I'd never have.

I woke wet and shivering. Sleet fell on my face. Darkness choked the forest, the sky so blank I hardly knew which way was up. I scrabbled around for my coals, finding only snow. I swore and tried to dry my clothes, but my mind moved slow as mud and my hands shook wildly.

"Come on," I said through chattering teeth. "Come on!"

Droplets shot out of my cloak and hit me in the face. Nothing else happened. Where was the wolf? I would let it gnaw my leg off in exchange for curling against its warm body. I pushed myself up and stumbled forward, branches jabbing into me. Sleet turned everything into a swirling mess. Then with a *crack*, the ground gave out.

I plunged into iciness. Shrieking, I swallowed water and choked. My flailing hand struck something hard. I grabbed it and clawed my way up, first onto solid ice and then sharp rocks. I collapsed spluttering and panting.

Images flashed through my mind. Fendul, nine and scrawny, falling through lake ice. His mother screaming. Tema melting the ice, Emehein diving in and grabbing his limp body. *Cold water kills faster than weapons*, Tema had said.

A hard little nut of terror formed in my stomach. I was going to freeze to death. Someone would find my skeleton like I found the elk, and no one would even know who I was. My blood would never rest in the soil of Anwen Bel. My spirit would be lost here in a rainforest that wasn't home.

The nut turned into a fiery coal, searing my insides. Heat flooded into my arms and legs. Suddenly burning up, I peeled off my soaked clothes and flung myself into the snow. Falling sleet kissed my skin.

A soft wet nose nudged me. I reached out and touched fur. "Wolf," I mumbled. "Feed on me. Grow strong. Take us back north."

And everything faded.

Smoke. Fish. Rot. The smells prickled my nose. A sparrow chirped, clear over the lazy swoosh of water. I tried to rub my face and scratched myself. I yelped. At the same second, something barked very close by.

My eyes snapped open. In front of me were two white paws. I couldn't work out how the wolf and I were tangled together. Nothing felt right. Around us, glittering snow lay on trees and bushes that seemed oddly grey. I lifted my hand and a paw moved instead.

I screamed. It came out as a strangled howl.

Nei, I thought frantically. *That's not me!* I bit the white-furred leg. Pain shot through my arm. I bit again and again, tearing off skin in search of my real body. Nothing came except blood, just as weirdly grey, but with a metallic scent so hot and fresh it was like breathing molten iron.

I thrashed, spattering blood. I backed up and the paws came with me. Branches snagged my shoulder. I yanked away and felt fur rip from my skin. A whine scratched out of my throat. I staggered and collapsed, blind with pain, sides heaving.

Slowly, a blue dot came into focus among all the white and grey. Confused, I limped close. A pearly seashell on a broken cord lay in the snow. How did a seashell wind up deep in the rainforest?

Rokiud. Memories trickled in — his hands fastening the cord around my neck, his body against mine as we danced in the shrine, his lips on mine among the huckleberry bushes. *I know how much you wanna attune*, he'd said. This was it. I finally attuned. Alone, on the run, to an animal not from my homeland. And I had no idea how to shift back.

I pictured shifting into my human form. Nothing happened. I flexed my muscles, pushing outward, trying to break free of wolf flesh and sinew and fur. Sharp cramps forced me to give up. I tried to stand on two legs and toppled into the snow. *Help me*, I begged the aeldu. *Change me back!*

Maybe I needed to focus on something specific. I thought of the times I'd been most aware of my body. Laughing and spinning as Nili taught me a shawl dance. Singing from a mountaintop with Malana. Kissing Rokiud. Sparring with Temal, dodging and striking. Meditating with Tema and feeling rain on my skin. The thought of never doing those things again stung more than my bitten leg.

Not that it mattered now. None of my training had kept Hanaiko and Samulein safe. Nothing I wanted from coming of age — my initiation tattoos, Rokiud's attention, Fendul's respect — mattered unless I got my cousins back. I imagined tearing through Nen Divinus as a wolf, biting and snarling and clawing anyone who got in my way, then rising into human form and hugging my cousins.

Tears burned my eyes. I froze. Wolves didn't cry.

Everything prickled like an itch spreading all the way to my toes. I clung to that thought of holding my cousins, saying their names, stroking their hair. Imaginary-them wove their little fingers into mine. *Eko*, they'd shout, wriggling with joy. *You came back for us*.

My bones juddered. A tail pulled back into my spine. Fur faded into skin. I sat up, trembling. Bloody bites covered my left arm. Trampled snow stung my bare legs. I was stark naked.

"Kaid," I swore. Temal had told me stories of people lost in the wilderness. On the brink of freezing to death, they got hot flashes and tore off their clothes in confusion. I kicked through the snow, found my frozen clothes, thawed them, and dressed clumsily. At least there was one good thing — if I'd attuned with my clothes on, I'd have torn them beyond use. Learning to shift anything other than the body took practice.

Soon I was back at my campsite, warming by a fire and holding bogmoss on my bloody arm. Only then did I realize how precious a gift the aeldu had given me. In my wolf body, I could sleep outside all winter and never freeze. I could live here in Iyun Bel as long as it took to rescue my cousins.

Hiking back north to Anwen Bel to get help was out of the question. I was weak and sick, only had a rough idea of the way home, and travelling through mountains alone in winter was suicide. All it'd take was a broken leg to wind up like the white wolf that couldn't hunt. Here, I could build up strength and work on a better plan than barging into Nen Divinus.

Everything would require money. Bribing Elkhounds and priests, paying ship fare, buying a proper weapon to defend us, aeldu knew what else. I'd need to buy supplies I couldn't make. It was another blessing that trapping season had just begun. By Iyo law, I could only trap on their land for survival, not profit, but technically I'd be selling furs for my cousins' survival.

I held Temal's carving of the swan and mountain cat, running my thumb over the sanded edges. *Kianta kolo*, he always said. *The sap will flow*. One season of hard work, then when the trees woke and flowers bloomed, I'd take my earnings and go get my cousins.

9.

CHILD OF THE FOREST

Attuning became easier over time. After a few nights, I could shift back with my clothes and knife intact. Not only did I avoid getting cold while undressing, but I didn't need to look at my bare arm where my kinaru crest should've been tattooed. I wouldn't feel like a real adult until I got initiated.

As my cough faded and my strength grew, I ventured further along the creek. To the west, I found a Sverbian-style log cabin and a frosty glass building that held some kind of greenery. To the east, I discovered a cluster of plank buildings in a valley that had been logged flat, leaving stumps jagged with saw marks. A lone figure shovelled snow. The valley was too open for me to sneak up, so I shifted into my wolf body to listen. The figure was singing in Aikoto.

It turned out to be an old Dona man. He explained that this was a lumber camp that stopped work every winter. Itherans paid him to live here and watch for poachers. Most years it wasn't a problem, but recently a ship hauling animals from the northern tundra — caribou, muskoxen, and white wolves and foxes for some rich lord's collection — had wrecked on the nearby coast. My new body had a bounty on its head.

So I destroyed my traps and went east. The white wolf followed. We skirted Crieknaast, a border town of Sverbian immigrants, and camped in the foothills of high mountains. The wolf stuck around about a month, showing up less as its limp faded. When I left out a cloud weasel heart and found it frozen the next morning, I knew the wolf had gone for good.

Every day I wondered if staying out here was the right choice. Dunehein would help me, but I couldn't think of a safe way to return to the coast. If I got arrested or killed, no one would know our cousins were in the orphanage. So I stayed put, indecision keeping me as frozen as the foothills.

Midwinter hit hard. Wind carried huge gusts of snow from the mountains. I made fur mittens and a mantle, stitched scraps of deerskin into a sturdy shirt and leggings, and packed my nice cottonspun clothes in a waterproof box to protect them. I wove my seashell necklace into a thin braid of hair so I wouldn't lose it again. Out of boredom during a snowstorm, I carved beads from trout vertebrae and braided those in, too.

Familiar people moved through my dreams. Nili twirled in a kinaru shawl, Emehein floated in the lake under our sacred rioden, Malana flew among the stars as a goldeneye duck. Rokiud led me through never-ending huckleberry tunnels. Sometimes Jonalin took his place, calloused fingers twined into mine.

The winter solstice passed, followed by my fifteenth birthday. On a clear morning, I loaded pelts onto a sled and hiked down to Crieknaast. A townsperson directed me to a furrier, where I pretended not to speak Coast Trader so the woman behind the counter wouldn't ask questions. I looked like a child of the forest anyway. I left with sovereigns clinking in my purse, outweighed by the ache of wishing I had someone, anyone, to talk with.

It might be enough money to get Hanaiko and Samulein back, I thought. I got halfway through dismantling my tanning racks before the familiar nut of fear formed in my stomach. I'd only get one chance to make a bribe. If it went wrong, I'd get thrown in prison along with Jonalin. He'd sacrificed his freedom to give me this chance. Being reckless and getting arrested would be a shitty way to thank him.

Kianta kolo, I reminded myself. A better time would come.

The day I saw the first flower of spring, I also heard the voice.

"What is happening?" a man said with a heavy accent. "Jorum. Jorum!"

I stopped halfway through loosing a dead squirrel from a snare. The voice rose higher, sharper. I crept through the forest. The snow that still lay thick in the shadows gave way to a muddy clearing. Near a stream, a man in leather armour spasmed on the ground. A brown-haired man crouched over him. Four horses lay wheezing on the grass. A teenage boy in a black military uniform watched, looking dazed.

"Run to Crieknaast and fetch a medic," the brown-haired man said. "Hurry."

"I . . ." The boy touched his face. A longbow slipped from his hand. "Tiernan, I . . ."

"No." Tiernan caught the boy as he slumped. "Not you, too, Nerio!"

Heart juddering, I backed away. A twig snapped under my foot. Tiernan looked straight at me. *Help*, his eyes pleaded. Like a kick to the gut, I recognized him — his face, his name, his silver horse. He'd found me sleeping in the Golden Oak's stable. Been kind to me.

I edged as close to the spasming man as I dared. Spit and vomit foamed onto his straw-coloured beard. His rope-like braid lay across the grass. The sides of his head were shaved, exposing a bloody gash where his skull kept striking the sword strapped to his back. An iron shield lay a few paces away.

"Did they eat or drink recently?" I asked, my voice hoarse from disuse. "Touch any strange plants?"

"We watered the horses half a league downstream," Tiernan said. "My comrades refilled their waterskins. Then Jorumgard said his face felt numb, and . . ."

I crossed to the stream. Clear water burbled past, sending up a cool mist. Black newts with vivid orange bellies wriggled in the shallows like four-legged burning coals. "Yan kaid."

"What?" Tiernan demanded.

I whirled. "Get that man sitting up. Open his mouth."

Nerio, grey-faced and sprawled on the grass, said, "Why should we trust—"

"Gods' sakes, boy, be quiet," Tiernan said.

Together we hauled Jorumgard upright. He was heavy, his spasming arms kept striking us, and I didn't dare touch his hair. Tiernan held his shoulders and forced his jaw open. I emptied my waterskin into his mouth and waved my hand back and forth, pushing the water around to rinse every crevice. I pulled it back out in an orb and flung it on the ground.

"You next," I told Nerio. I refilled my waterskin with clean water from the air and tossed it at him. "Wash your hands, stick a finger down your throat until you throw up, then rinse your mouth. Don't swallow."

“Will that cure them?” Tiernan asked, easing Jorumgard back down.

“Maybe. I’m not a healer.”

“I thought you knew what you were doing,” he snapped.

“*I* thought you’d recognize poisoning. Now help me with those horses.”

He held each one’s head, talking to them soothingly, while I rinsed their mouths and tried to ignore how close their enormous teeth were to my hands. The smallest horse, a pack pony, had crushed its bundles when it fell. As Tiernan checked on his comrades, something toppled off a tree. I searched the undergrowth and found a dead kingfisher with wide eyes and limp grey wings. I took it to the others.

“Watch,” I said.

Nerio propped himself up on one elbow. Moments later he said faintly, “*Sacro dios*.”

A newt crawled out of the kingfisher’s open bill. I picked the slimy critter up and said, “Coal newts ooze poison. Safe to touch, lethal to swallow. These ones just came out of hibernation to breed. The water is liquid death now.” I carried the newt to the stream and tossed it back in.

Tiernan bowed his head. “I apologize for snapping at you earlier. Is it asking too much for you to stay the night?”

I looked them over and sighed. Jorumgard had passed out, still twitching. Nerio’s chest rose in shallow gasps as he stared at the kingfisher.

“Let me get supplies from my camp,” I said.

I returned in late afternoon, dragging my sled. The two sick men slept under a canvas shelter, clammy and shivering. I spread warm pelts over them and gave Tiernan a bogmoss packet to bandage Jorumgard's head wound. He'd just finished when Jorumgard turned red and sweaty. I pulled off the pelts and laid a damp cloth on his forehead.

Their travel gear included a dented cooking pot, so for dinner I stewed meat scraps and mushrooms. Tiernan salvaged bits of hard dried flatbread from the crushed bundles and sprinkled them into the stew. Their waterskins were contaminated beyond saving, so I started stitching new ones of thin leather lined with elk bladder. On my instructions, Tiernan burned their old skins and sprinkled salt around the campsite to keep newts from crawling in.

"I suppose we never introduced ourselves," he said, settling by the campfire. He took out a folding knife and began whittling a stick. "I am Tiernan Heilind. That other man is Jorumgard Tømasind. The boy, Nerio Parr, serves with the 5th Royal Eremur Mounted Archers."

"What are you doing out here by the border?" I asked between pulling stitches tight with my teeth.

"Travelling. What about you?"

"Surviving."

Tiernan half-smiled. "May I ask your name?"

"Lucreza," I said, the first one that came to mind.

He didn't question me having a Ferish name. Instead he said, "We owe you, Lucreza. Jorum and I are mercenaries, so we take debts seriously. How can I repay you?"

I paused with sinew thread in my mouth. I'd have to face the military eventually to get Hanaiko and Samulein back, and asking a favour from this man seemed safer than bribing or fighting soldiers. He didn't seem to recognize me as the girl who stabbed an Elkhound captain.

"Name your request," he said. "It can be our secret, I swear to the gods."

"The Caladheå guards . . . stole something from me. I just want to get it and go. I don't want trouble."

Tiernan's dark brows knit together. "Am I right to guess that retrieving this thing is dangerous, illegal, or immoral?"

I shrugged.

"None of those are dealbreakers, but . . . there may at least be a safe way. Let me think on it."

We worked to the sound of crackling flames and whispering wind. Every so often I snuck glances at him. He had soft grey eyes, and alone here in the dusk his voice was gentle, but everything else — his harsh tone earlier, his scarred face, the sword at his side — made me feel like a deer with an arrow trained on me.

Tiernan cleared his throat. He'd whittled a newt that clung to the stick with delicate toes. It beamed at us with big innocent eyes.

I burst out laughing. "You made it cute!"

"We need some joy today." He held it upside down in the fire. The figurine's back started turning dark while its belly of fresh-cut alder remained pale orange. "I always carve the wildlife of places I go. It helps me understand new lands. Remember them."

"Where are you from?"

"Sverba. I moved here, ah, must be nine years ago. Clearly I have more to learn about this province."

I brimmed with questions. What was Sverba like, why he came here, how the newt figurine didn't catch fire. But the more I said, the more I risked spilling my secrets, and I was too tired to speak carefully. I covered a yawn with my elbow.

"Get some rest," Tiernan said and blew soot off his carving. "You have done more than enough."

I curled up facing away from him. I didn't think I could actually sleep. Since attuning, I'd spent every night in my wolf body. Grass against my cheek and hard ground pressing into my hip felt strange now. Yet as dark fell, my eyes slid closed.

Sizzling sounds woke me. Tiernan had laid strips of meat on hot coals in the fire. He noticed me rise and said, "I checked on Jorum and Nerio. The worst seems to have passed."

"Good." I sat across from him, warming my hands over the flames.

He passed me a square of flatbread and a strip of steaming meat. "Military rations. Hardtack and salt pork."

"What's a pork?"

Tiernan chuckled, not realizing I was serious. "Pour some water on that bread to soften it. You'll break a tooth otherwise."

Skeptical, I did as told. It was like eating mushy woodchips.

"I thought about your request," Tiernan said. "I have three options for you."

"I'm listening."

"My comrades and I are doing reconnaissance. If all goes well, we shall return to Caladheå within a month and retrieve your item then. Option one — we steal it back. Jorum will help, but Nerio will not. He swore an oath to uphold the law. Option two — we ask Nerio's father, a respected cavalry captain, to have your item returned in gratitude for saving his son's life. That would normally be the best way.

"However, I sense that something else keeps you out here alone." He gave me a searching look. "Thus, option three — come on this mission. You have skills and knowledge we do not. At the least you will be paid, and the more help you provide, the more you can ask in return. A pardon, for example. You would not be the first outlaw I have met on the road."

I stared at Tiernan. Entering Eremur illegally, attacking an Elkhound captain, fleeing my captors . . . all my supposed crimes could be gone. "What's your mission?"

He glanced at the shelter. No one stirred inside. "Are you familiar with the Sverbian Rúonbattai?"

"I've heard of them."

"We recently learned of a place called Brånnheå, the Burning Stronghold. It was the Rúonbattai's base until five years ago when they abruptly disappeared. We are going to find Brånnheå. It may reveal why they went quiet and if they are truly back. Some in the military suspect that new people have stolen the name for the fear it inspires. Either way, anything you help us discover is an excellent bargaining chip. Nerio's father has a vendetta against the Rúonbattai."

I chewed my hardtack slowly, thinking. "A burning stronghold sounds dangerous."

"Not to me." Tiernan scooped up a handful of flames. They simmered above his palm, turning blue, then white. He didn't flinch.

My eyes widened. I'd never seen anyone call fire.

He scattered the flames like sowing seeds, and they vanished. "These new Rúonbattai are only rumoured to be active up north. We do not expect to meet any in Brånnheå. If we do, we will protect you."

I brooded while finishing breakfast. If Tiernan and I got caught breaking into an orphanage, at best we'd go to prison. Earning a pardon and bargaining for my cousins was safer. But if my secrets died with me on this mission, my family might never learn where Hanaiko and Samulein wound up.

"Okay," I said. "I'll come. But I have to tell you something."

Tiernan waited.

I drew a deep breath. "My name's not Lucreza. I'm registered as Eko Mèrus, but *that's* not my name, either. It's Kateiko Rin. If something happens to me, I need you to visit a stavehall. Ask the clerics to find Kirbana Elynehl. Tell her my registered and real names, and tell her the kids I was with are in the orphanage. She'll figure out the rest."

"Kateiko," Tiernan repeated. He scratched his stubbled jaw, looking thoughtful. "Names have power. You deserve to use yours. Perhaps . . . might I call you Katja? That is how it would be shortened in Sverbian for a young girl."

Kat-ya, he pronounced it, like a knife tip flowing into a curve. Not the bluntness of Eko or the strangeness of Lucreza. It felt . . . whole. A name I could own, and a name that could protect me.

10.

TURQUOISE MOUNTAINS

Nerio emerged from the shelter with limp black hair hanging around his face. Wet leaves stuck to his muddy uniform. I pointed him toward a pond to bathe in. He slumped off silently and returned clean, his damp hair tied back with a ribbon. His face still looked grey and drawn. I handed him a newly sewn waterskin.

He eyed it, then my leather clothes and fur mantle. "Do you have a permit for trapping here?"

"Do you have one for being an ungrateful ass?"

A laugh boomed nearby. I swung around. Jorumgard was up, rocking unsteadily.

I hadn't seen him standing until now. He was huge for an itheran, a looming wall of muscle. His flaxen hair was coming loose from its braid. Combined with his pale skin and the bloody bandage on his head, he looked like a ghostly Aikoto warrior.

"Who's the girl?" he asked, thumping down by the fire. He bit through a slice of hardtack without bothering to soften it.

"Katja is the reason you and Nerio are alive," Tiernan said. "Those newts in the stream are poisonous."

"Aye indeed?" Jorumgard glanced at me. "Well, *I'm* grateful. I've seen soldiers go down like that and never knew why. We could use you around."

"My thought exactly," Tiernan said. "Which is why Katja is coming to Brånnheå."

Nerio choked on his water. "That is not your decision—"

"I am aware you command this mission, Nerio. That means if it fails, *you* will tell your superiors you refused the help of a skilled viirelei. Take her wages out of mine if you must."

"She is a child. This is the military, not a nursery—"

"I'm fifteen," I said, annoyed.

Tiernan spread his hands. "There you are, Nerio. Same age you enlisted."

"S'nothing new, anyway," Jorumgard said through a mouthful of hardtack. "The Iyo nation used t'have their own regiment in Eremur's military. Best scouts in the land. But I'm sure Nerio knows that, coming from a military family."

Nerio's cheeks went red. "Fine," he muttered. "She comes."

Jorumgard slapped his thighs. "Then let's see if we're fit for service yet. Spar with me, boy."

"Sit still and rest," Nerio replied. "You were near death yesterday."

"I'll spar," I said. "I'm out of practice."

Jorumgard scrutinized me. "Sure, that's a fair fight. You're pint-sized and I'm poisoned." He heaved himself up and held a strip of salt pork in the air, grinning. "All yours if you can reach it."

For a moment, I was annoyed at him, too. Then an idea struck me. Months ago in combat training I'd said to Temal that itheran men didn't wear braids, yet here was one who did. I pulled my gloves on and beckoned to the open clearing.

Jorumgard followed, grinning wider. He was too solid to knock down, but his balance was off. We circled each other. I lunged a few times and he dodged easily. I feinted right. He whirled the other way. I grabbed his swinging braid and kicked at his foot. He toppled like a tree. I stepped over him and plucked the salt pork from his grip.

He roared with laughter. "Tiernan, you didn't hire a scout. You hired a little warrior!" He stretched out a calloused hand for me to help him up.

I took it. Instantly I went flipping through the air. I hit the ground, stunned. Once my vision cleared, I cracked up laughing, too.

Tiernan shook his head, chuckling. I looked at Nerio, sure I'd proven I wasn't totally helpless. But he looked . . . angry. With a wrench in my gut like I'd been flipped again, I remembered what he'd said in the Golden Oak. *Violence runs in those people's blood.*

I went off alone to dismantle my trapline and campsite. I finished tanning the pelts I'd left on racks, then packed them into waterproof boxes along with my tools. Tiernan had told me to only bring whatever food and healing supplies I had on hand.

Over dinner he said, "Katja tells me she cannot ride. She had better go with you, Nerio. You two are the lightest."

Nerio looked as horrified as I felt. I'd expected to walk.

"Katja rides with me," Jorumgard said. "My horse can handle another person. And it's more appropriate, if you follow my drift."

"I don't," I said, bemused.

"Well, a girl your age riding with a man wouldn't be right. But I go for menfolk myself, so you needn't worry."

"Oh!" Suddenly I understood. "Yeah, okay."

Tiernan and Nerio exchanged a look, but I didn't mind this way at all. Jorumgard reminded me of Dunehein, another big warrior with a bigger laugh and a fondness for teasing people.

In the morning, Jorumgard put his sword and shield with the pack pony so I wouldn't get tangled in them, then padded the back of his saddle with a blanket. His horse, Skarp, was a massive white stallion with feathery hooves. Jorumgard slung his braid over his shoulder and pulled me up behind him.

"You know about our hair taboo?" I asked, taking hold of his waist.

"I had a fling with a Dona man in my younger days. Seemed strange that he let me kiss him but not touch his hair. I got used to it, though."

We headed east, climbing steep muddy tracks into what the men called the Turquoise Mountains. I had all sorts of questions for Jorumgard. He said he'd been born in Sverba's capital, Kånheå, a walled city on the shore of a mighty river. At six, he started training for the queensguard, the Kånehlbattai. At eighteen, he joined them, living in a stone fortress and standing guard in a throne room hung with the shields of fallen enemies.

"Nei," I said in disbelief. "You protected a *queen*?"

Jorumgard shifted the reins and pulled up his sleeve. Tattooed on his inner wrist was an ornate crown matching the gold sovs in my purse.

"There is a reason Nerio refuses to spar with him," Tiernan said behind us, riding his silver gelding, Gwmniwyr. "Not even I can beat Jorum when he is healthy."

"It's meant to be a life position," Jorumgard said. "We're raised with ancient warrior ways, growing our hair long and offering animal sacrifices to the gods. I'd only served a year when I pissed off the wrong warlord and had to flee. Eremur needed soldiers something bad, so I came here and took a contract to protect a wealthy Ferish lord. A few had already been assassinated by Rúonbattai."

"Doesn't that mean you were fighting your own people?" I asked.

"The Rúonbattai aren't my people. Sure, they're Sverbian, but they're war criminals, too. They razed villages, sunk immigrant ships, whatever they could do to take Eremur back to the days before any Ferish showed up. That's where their name comes from. Sverba used to call this region Rúonmur, the Rain Land. It's still rainy, but everything else has changed and there's no going back."

"What happened to the lord you were protecting?"

"Oh, he died of pox." Jorumgard shrugged. "Good timing for me. Nerio's father, Antoch Parr, had just been promoted to captain, and he hired me and Tiernan to help hunt down the Rúonbattai. Ol' Parr wet himself with joy at getting both a mage and an ex-Kånehlbattai."

"You should speak more respectfully of my father," Nerio said from the front of our convoy. His horse was a chestnut mare called Saetta. "Not many people would hire a royal deserter."

"I kid, I kid. Captain Parr's a good man. Kept us on after the Rúonbattai went silent. Then again, he's in the camp that believes they never truly disappeared. He told me he'd like to run for the Caladheå Council, but can't bear to retire from military service if 'those damned rebels are still out there.'"

"They are," I said.

Nerio twisted to look at me.

I hunkered down behind Jorumgard's armoured bulk. "That's what I heard in Anwen Bel, anyway. They've been rebuilding strength."

Nerio said nothing, but for once he didn't seem annoyed. He turned forward again and kept going, leading us higher into the mountains.

We made slow progress. The horses were weary from poison, and my legs grew sore from straddling Skarp's broad jolting back. I had blisters everywhere. We camped on a slope overlooking a long stretch of water, the northern arm of an ocean inlet that came unusually far inland. Nerio went off alone and brought back a goose with an arrow in its chest. Jorumgard buried its heart for me, another Aikoto practice he'd learned from his Dona lover.

Tiernan showed me our route on a map. We were near Dúnravn Pass, a major route through the mountains to the eastern plains, but instead of taking the pass, we would enter a vast tunnel network. Through the tunnels, we'd travel past southern Eremur, which overlapped Kae- and Yula-jouyen territory, into the Kowichelk Confederacy's land. Brånnheå was somewhere there underground.

"I've never heard of these tunnels," I said skeptically.

"The southern ones were natural. Earth mages from Ingdanrad" — Tiernan's finger slid to a city deep in the mountains — "improved and expanded them. Other than sailing up the inlet, they are the only way to reach Ingdanrad, one of the few places mages can live free from persecution, so they are kept secret. We can travel unnoticed and safe from blizzards or avalanches. The tunnels are even beautiful in their own way."

I definitely didn't believe that. Open air was beautiful to me. Aeti

Ginu's shrine was built on a high cliff so our aeldu could live close to the sky. When we reached a yawning gash in the mountainside, the ground stained with bat droppings, only the promise of getting my cousins back kept me from sliding off Skarp and turning around.

The tunnel was wide enough for us to ride side by side. Tiernan conjured a fire orb that floated ahead, lighting the way. A short distance in, the horses' steps grew muffled and we stopped. The fire flickered out. I clung to Jorumgard until my eyes adjusted, then I gasped. Glowing bluish-green grass carpeted the tunnel. Mica glittered in the smooth rock walls. Altogether, it felt like standing on the bottom of a motionless river.

Tiernan smiled at my shock. "Most people think the Turquoise Mountains are named for their glacial lakes. To anyone who has lived in Ingdanrad, as I did my first year in this land, they are named for these tunnels."

"How does grass grow down here?" I asked.

"Mages bred it with bioluminescent mushrooms. It lives on mineral water that seeps through the rock. Its light is helpful, but more importantly, it is food for the horses. We can travel for days without surfacing."

Within hours, I'd lost all sense of direction. The tunnel rose and fell, twisted and turned. Occasionally it forked into other tunnels. Tiernan navigated with his map, a compass, and signs engraved on the walls. Nerio tracked the time with a pocket watch and told us when to stop each evening. Jorumgard filled the silence by telling stories, real ones from military campaigns and imaginary ones from Sverbian folklore.

I didn't learn much about Tiernan except that he and Captain Parr had become friends while fighting the Rúonbattai. He dodged my questions, saying Jorumgard was a better storyteller. Instead he asked me about all sorts of things — my water-calling, the Aikoto Confederacy, the southern lands where we were headed. I didn't know much about them. I'd only ever met a few Kae and Yula traders, and most Kowichelk had gotten wiped out by foreign diseases.

Slowly I pieced together Nerio's story. He was Ferish and born in Caladheå, enlisted after the Rúonbattai disappeared, and got assigned to the same regiment as Tiernan. They'd served together for two years until Tiernan got reassigned. Nerio was nineteen now and had been given command of this mission in place of Captain Parr, who'd recently been wounded in combat up north.

"None of the other captains are keen to travel with a mage who can burn them alive," Tiernan added dryly. "I cannot imagine why."

During rests, Jorumgard and I sparred for real. The few of my blows that landed hurt me more than him. He knew his strength, barely hitting back hard enough to bruise. He taught me how to defend against itheran soldiers — aim at gaps in their armour, take out a rider's horse, and avoid the shield, which doubled as a weapon. Tiernan also offered to teach me riding. In the evenings, he put his saddle on the pack pony and led me up and down the tunnels, explaining how to sit and hold the reins. After each lesson he made me groom the pony and wipe down its gear, saying that the best riders looked after their horses.

Every night I collapsed sore and exhausted. Now that the shock of the tunnels had worn off, I was tired of looking at them, tired of hardtack and horse sweat and man sweat. I hadn't made any progress proving myself to Nerio. I didn't have a way to help at all. Natural springs provided clean water and there was nothing to trap down here, only rats and spiders and weird albino lizards. All I could do was wait until we reached Brånnheå.

11.

BRÅNNHEÅ

Twelve days into our journey, golden light appeared ahead. The tunnel broadened into a rocky cavern where shafts of sunshine fell through a crevice. Bats hung from the ceiling. I glanced up, squinting, and saw immense stone walls rising to a thread of blue sky.

"That is the marker," Tiernan said. "The entrance to Brånnheå is here, probably concealed by magic. The Rúonbattai had several mages in their ranks."

"Then how are we supposed to find it?" I asked.

He smiled slightly. "You and I are not without power."

I slid off Skarp, glad to stretch my legs. The men dismounted as well and began exploring. There were no passageways or signs, no obvious features at all besides the sunlit crevice. Even the turquoise grass didn't grow here. The bare rock floor was slick with bat droppings.

Something wet landed on my head. I flinched before realizing it was just water. Droplets slid down the crevice and landed in tiny puddles. I chewed my lip, thinking. Snow would be melting on the surface at this time of year, but this place wasn't flooded. I pulled water to me and let a stream fall from my hand. It flowed across the uneven ground, hit the wall, and disappeared.

Tiernan came over. Looking closer, we saw a crack between the floor and wall. "Good thinking," he said and slid his hand along the rock. He stopped on a patch of red lichen and pressed it. A horrible grating sound erupted forth. Dust showered onto us as a jagged stone panel slid aside, revealing another tunnel.

"Strange," he said, examining faint marks on the panel. "The magic in these runes is inactive. I think the opening trigger is mechanical. It is like the Rúonbattai shut the door but did not lock it."

"You seem to know more magic than just calling fire," I said.

Tiernan smiled again. With paper, charcoal, and a writing board taken from his saddlebags, he copied the runes, sketched the door and cavern, and drew the start of a new map. Finished, he tucked the papers into a leather satchel that he slung over one shoulder, and we mounted again.

The tunnel sloped down, growing hot and damp. Jorumgard kept shifting the reins to wipe his palms on his trousers. My hair was sticking to my neck when we reached a set of tall open wooden doors. Beyond sprawled an enormous misty cavern of black rock. Velveted with patches of glowing red, orange, and yellow lichen, it looked like hot coals under smoke.

Jorumgard chortled. "That's the Burning Stronghold? We won't need Tiernan's firepower after all."

"Do not be so sure," Tiernan said. "That rock is basalt, and unless I miss my guess, these tunnels were originally lava tubes."

We rode through the remains of farmland, now just gently sloping earth surrounded by crumbling stone fences. Murky water trickled through irrigation trenches and down into a glassy lake. Across the lake, a stone bridge led to an island with a single tree. Its white bark gently pulsed with light. One gnarled branch hung thick with red leaves, but the others were barren. A ring of glowing shrubs surrounded the tree.

Closer on the lakeshore stood a garrison of basalt bricks. Its open gates revealed a courtyard littered with bones. Our horses snorted and refused to enter, so we went in on foot. Lichen-speckled skulls grinned next to femurs, ribs, and rusty weapons as if they'd been tossed like dice. Arrows stuck in rotting doors.

"*Någvakt bøkkhem*," Tiernan swore. "No wonder the Rúonbattai went silent."

Jorumgard kicked a pale blue shield emblazoned with a white raven and crossed swords. "That's their sigil, all right. A bastardized Sverbian flag."

"Who attacked them?" I asked.

"No idea," Nerio said, examining a curved sword. "This is Ferish, but there is no record of Ferland or Eremur sending troops here."

I used my boot to sift through a jumble of shattered bones. "Looks like carrion eaters tore apart their corpses. I don't know of any cave animals big enough to do this, though."

The buildings were all basalt except one made of timber posts. I'd never seen a stavehall, but I recognized the leafless nine-branched oak carved on a gable. Jorumgard shouldered open the door and traipsed in. Nerio muttered something about unholy ground and left to keep exploring. I stayed back, taught not to enter other cultures' shrines, but Tiernan beckoned me in.

The hall was large, dim, and reeked of mildew. Tiernan knelt by a rectangular pit of charred wood. It burst into flames, illuminating the room. He sat cross-legged and began to sketch. The skeletons here were intact, crumpled against pillars or sprawled across the floor. Jorumgard and I walked along a wall looking at smoke-stained murals of battles and blasted earth.

"That's Bøkkhem," Jorumgard said, pointing at a blackened plain where ghostly figures twisted in torment. "Sverbian tradition is to burn our dead. The flames guide their spirits over an ocean to Thaerijmur. Otherwise, the god Bøkkai steals lost spirits and keeps 'em in his kingdom forever. Rumour goes the last Rúonbattai leader, Liet, always kept a cleric around so he could be sure of his body being burned. Wise considering how many people wanted him dead."

"Is Liet his first name? It doesn't sound like a Sverbian second name."

"It's probably not his real name at all. Someone with that many bounties on his head would need to hide his identity."

At the hall's far end we found an altar of solid basalt, stained with dry blood and dusted with bone powder. A steel knife with a carved obsidian handle lay on it. Above, an elk skull with massive antlers hung from the vaulted ceiling.

"Ritual sacrifices." Jorumgard spun the knife, testing its balance. He handed it to me. "There you go, little pint. You'll want something stronger than your bone knife if we run into those carrion eaters."

I tucked it into my belt, slightly afraid spirits would swoop down and kill me for stealing. It felt like the nearest skeleton was watching me through hollow eye sockets.

High shelves lined the wall behind the altar. A few had been smashed, but the rest held objects in decay — tallow candles, rotting bowls, curling goat horns, flasks with peeling labels. Encased in a cube of yellow resin was a carved wooden kinaru, its long neck extended and wings spread. With a jolt of horror, I wondered if it was a makiri. When Jorumgard wasn't looking, I pocketed the cube. Kinaru didn't belong here.

Tiernan was packing up his papers when a knock echoed from the doorway. Nerio called, "There is something you all should see."

We went out the garrison's back gates, which lay in splinters. In the cavern wall ahead, a pair of wooden doors had also caved in. Nerio led us around the lake, past the bridge and island, to a steamy tunnel entrance surrounded by broken boulders. So much heat poured from it that I felt faint. The steam clouds puffing out dispersed into the mist that drifted across the cavern.

The wall nearby had a mural with mouldering paint. One panel showed people entering a steamy tunnel. The second showed them running back out with terrified expressions. The third panel had flaked away. The fourth showed mangled bodies, and the fifth showed people stacking boulders in the tunnel entrance to seal it.

Jorumgard bent down to peer below the mural. "There's a date. Sixty years ago, probably when the Rúonbattai first settled here. Seems like they found something bad, blocked off the tunnel, and painted a warning. Just our luck to find it open again."

"Katja, any idea what they might have discovered?" Tiernan asked.

I hesitated. "It'll sound crazy."

"Go on," he said gently.

"Well . . . this tunnel is probably a volcanic steam vent. My people have stories about sacred animals called oosoo, like enormous salamanders that live in steam vents. Legend says that jinra-saidu and anta-saidu — fire and water spirits, I mean — mated and birthed an oosoo, which then birthed the Kowichelk Confederacy. I've never believed it, though. *My* confederacy's mother animal isn't real."

"The mural could be symbolic," Jorumgard said. "You know, *here be giant lizards*, like sea monsters on maps. Whatever keeps people from falling into a volcano."

"Maybe." Tiernan scratched his jaw, which had grown a dark beard during our journey. "I cannot make sense of this place. It is steeped in strange magic."

"Take Katja to the lake island," Nerio said. "I know you want a look at that glowing tree. Jorumgard and I will keep exploring the garrison."

Tiernan and I looped back to the bridge, crossed it, and halted at the island. The tree sprawled high overhead, pulsing steadily with light. Its red-leafed branch was healthy, but its barren ones wept pitch from open sores. Bits of shed bark littered the rocky ground. The surrounding ring of shrubs held clusters of pale purple flowers that gave off an overwhelmingly sweet scent. A strange sensation came over me, like I'd been here before and would be again.

"Nine branches," Tiernan murmured. "Nine roots, too, I imagine."

"Is it dying?" I asked.

"The sacred oak is eternal, always dying and always living. It is not supposed to be this unbalanced, though. This tree has been corrupted. Can you feel it?"

I nodded. The fine hair on my neck prickled like I was being watched. I remembered the dawn ceremony last autumn, looking through fog at the sacred rioden on the shore of Kotula Huin, seeing it turn black and bare. Curious, I lifted my hand and pulled tendrils of mist away from the oak.

The glow died. The red leaves and the flowers faded into nothingness, leaving the oak and shrubs barren. I blinked. Everything snapped back into place.

"Did you see that?" Tiernan breathed.

"Yeah," I said, equally stunned.

"Wait here." He stepped onto the shore and approached the shrubs. They glowed brighter. The tree's pulse quickened. He touched a shrub, waited, then drew a dagger and cut off a cluster of flowers.

Nothing happened. He tucked the flowers into his satchel and smiled at me.

Then Jorumgard shouted from far away, "Tiernan!"

We whirled. Figures charged across the misty ruined farmland, one on horseback and several on foot. Their shields glinted pale blue. A soldier went down with an arrow in his chest, and I realized Nerio was firing from the garrison.

"Stay behind me," Tiernan said.

We dashed back up the bridge and along the lakeshore. The foot soldiers streamed into the garrison. The horse and rider veered around it, galloping along shore toward us.

Tiernan threw a fireball. It fizzled, choked by the mist. He threw a stronger one that grazed the rider's arm. He wasn't aiming for the horse like Jorumgard taught me to. The rider closed the distance and swung a spear. Tiernan parried with his sword, cloak whirling, but the next swing nicked his arm. He'd lose unless he could get on level ground.

I pulled a whip of water from the lake and lashed out. My whip coiled around the rider, yanking him off. He hit the ground hard. The horse reared, hooves flying. Tiernan struck at the man, who blocked with his raven-sigil shield. I watched, terrified to interfere and risk hurting Tiernan.

Something moved in my peripheral vision. I ducked. A sword whistled over my head. I kicked out, tripping my attacker. He fell on top of me. We rolled, grappling, fire-coloured lichen spinning around us. I got hold of my new knife and stabbed. The man grunted and loosed his grip on me. I scrambled away —

— and Tiernan plunged his sword into my attacker's heart. The man's eyes went wide. He writhed, coughing blood. Tiernan helped me up. The other man he'd been fighting was already dead.

"I could've taken him," I said, panting.

"I know." Tiernan caught the horse's reins. He soothed it with Sverbian words, then swung into the saddle and pulled me up behind him.

We raced into the garrison, jumping the collapsed gate. A battle raged outside the stavehall. Jorumgard fought three soldiers at once, roaring and swinging his sword like it weighed nothing. He smashed his shield into a man, knocking him back, and beheaded him with a single strike. Whirling, he drove his sword through another and pulled it out with a spray of blood.

"*Fyndestjolv*," the last man spat.

"*I'm* the traitor?" Jorumgard bellowed. "The queen would skin you bastards!" He slammed his shield into the man's skull.

The man dropped, neck broken, his head hanging at a horrid angle. Jorumgard lowered his sword and shield. Blood trickled down his cheek. All I heard was his heaving breath — then a bow cracked. Down an alley, a soldier toppled with an arrow in his eye.

Nerio stepped into view. "Time to go. There may be more coming."

It took some searching to find our horses. They'd fled the front gate and scattered through a maze of basalt columns. Skarp had left a trail of broken rock. Riding double would slow us down, so Tiernan kept the attacker's horse and told me to take Gwmniwyr, the calmest one. I mounted apprehensively. Just as we left the basalt maze, the horses backed up, braying loudly.

Colossal rust-red lizards slunk across the cavern. Their bodies were as long as canoes, and their tails doubled their length, dragging through lichen and sending up clouds of orange dust. Slime glistened on their pebbly skin. A few found the dead men by the lakeshore, opened huge jaws, and began tearing the corpses apart.

"Yan taku," I said.

Other oosoo crawled toward the garrison, turning their heads back and forth, snapping out sharp tongues. They smelled blood. Already they were between us and the caved-in doors, wherever those went. Across the lake, oosoo swarmed the ruined farmland in search of the soldier Nerio had downed. We were cut off from the tunnel we'd entered by, too.

"Katja," Jorumgard said, sounding strangled, "do they eat living things?"

"I think they eat whatever they want," I said faintly.

He and Tiernan drew their swords. Nerio nocked an arrow.

"Don't attack them!" I cried. "There's a story about someone who killed an oosoo. Jinra-saidu woke up in a rage and erupted a volcano."

"How else do we get past them?" Nerio demanded.

"I don't know, let me think! They live in caves — they're used to darkness, something bright would stun them—"

Tiernan conjured a fire orb. It guttered in the mist. "It is no good. I need fuel to make a decent fire in this humidity."

Oosoo in the farmland, disappointed at the slim pickings, crawled toward us. Thick ropes of saliva hung in their open mouths. Our horses tossed their heads, wide-eyed and neighing.

Nerio's bow cracked. An oosoo squealed horribly, flailing. Arrow feathers stuck out of its eye.

I swung to Nerio in horror. "I said not to hurt it!"

"Would you rather get eaten?" he snapped, taking aim again.

I lashed out with a water whip, knocking the arrow from his hands. The wounded oosoo thrashed. Its tail smashed into a fence, sending stones flying. With a final whine, the creature hit the ground and went still.

The earth rumbled. Jorumgard swore.

Tiernan paled, looking across the cavern toward the steam vent. "Run!"

We all took off. Tiernan led, weaving among the oosoo. I clung to Gwmniwyr's mane, barely hanging on, trusting him to follow his owner. He leapt an oosoo's tail, landed hard, and kept running.

The ground shook again. Rocks rained down on our heads. Tiernan made a fire orb as his horse leapt the rubble of the caved-in doors. Gwmniwyr streaked after them, following the light up a tunnel. It curved left, right, left, going on forever.

Sunlight appeared ahead. We burst onto a grassy hillside, squinting in the brightness. Clean air flooded my lungs. Nerio and Saetta emerged behind us, then the pack pony driven on by Jorumgard and Skarp. We rounded hill after hill until the horses collapsed, foaming with sweat.

I slid from the saddle. Behind us stretched an immense, snow-capped mountain range. Smoke wafted from a nearby peak. Ripples ran through its slopes, sending waves of snow and earth cascading down. The ground shook again —

Fire erupted from the peak. Thick grey plumes billowed into the sky. Molten lava spilled down the mountain in glowing rivers.

"Take cover!" Tiernan called.

I stood transfixed, watching a wall of smoke roll toward us. Jorumgard yanked me down and covered me with his bulk. The last thing I saw before the smoke hit was Tiernan glowing orange, crouching with one hand to the sky.

12.

PLAINS OF NYHEMUR

The flood of smoke felt endless. Jorumgard and I huddled together with our sleeves to our faces, coughing so hard we retched. The searing heat felt like being in a furnace, yet it was dark as night. I couldn't see the other men or the horses.

Gradually, the world brightened and their figures appeared in the gloom. We all had burns and blisters, but Tiernan looked worst, like he'd taken the brunt of it for us. Soot covered his face and clothes.

I pushed myself up and rounded on Nerio. "Takuran idiot. You nearly got us killed!"

"*You* said oosoo were not real," he snapped. "Why should I believe anything you say?"

"Tiernan hired me to tell you things! That's literally why you're paying me!"

Jorumgard pulled us apart. "Enough. Arguing won't fix anything."

Fucking brown pigeons, I thought, scowling. Akohin had been right. It was a mistake to trust anyone Ferish.

"We may as well camp here until we can see," Tiernan said. "Unless Katja can call a rainstorm to clear away the smoke?"

"Only if you want acid rain," I said. "I can filter enough water to drink and wash our wounds, but that's about it."

Tiernan rubbed his watering eyes. "All right, then. We stay here."

Insisting his burns could wait for treatment, he led Nerio away to care for the horses. Jorumgard stripped off his leather armour and sweaty, filthy tunic. He had a circle of runes tattooed on his chest. A deep cut on his arm needed stitches, but my painkillers would make him hallucinate or bleed faster, so he just bit his scabbard strap while I sewed him up.

Once I'd moved on to bandaging the wound, he said, "Give Nerio time. He'll come around."

"It's a little late." I switched subjects before I lost my temper again. "What did that soldier say about being a traitor?"

Jorumgard scoffed. "*Fyndestjolv* means *enemy shield*. It's an insult for people who switch sides and take a different shield sigil, or in the case of a mercenary like me, no sigil. The Rúonbattai claim that because they fight for all Sverbians, all Sverbians should support 'em, even though they want to tear apart treaties our monarchy made with Ferland. Bloody lunatics. I won't lose any sleep over leaving their corpses in a volcano."

I kept working in silence. It didn't feel like anyone deserved to be buried in lava, but I didn't know what to think about the Rúonbattai. There'd been too much strangeness in Brånnheå, from the glowing oak to the kinaru figurine trapped in resin.

Nerio came up while I was scrubbing blood from my hands. His mouth twisted like he was searching for words. Finally he said, "I should have listened to you. I am sorry, Katja."

I blinked. An apology from him was like watching rain fall up.

"I . . ." He fiddled with a strap on his archery wristguard. "Spirits like that do not exist in my religion. The military has no precedent for that kind of battle. Nevertheless, I would rather be guilty of heresy than causing my comrades' deaths."

I flicked water off my hands. The sight of him still made me want to hit him.

"What do you think will happen?" he asked.

"Well, you murdered a sacred animal. So you're cursed now."

Nerio blanched. I felt a prickle of guilt.

"Honestly, I don't know," I said. "This is the first time I've heard of a saidu waking in centuries. I would tell the Kowichelk Confederacy, but they'll want your head on a stake. My advice is to ask Falwen, Officer of the Viirelei, to contact the Yula. They're the closest Aikoto jouyen to here."

He nodded, still looking unnerved. "Very well."

Tiernan had first watch, which he started by marking invisible runes in the air that would flare with light if anything approached us, then another set of lava-resistant runes. When he returned to the campfire, he noticed me still awake and beckoned me over. I reluctantly sat across from him, wrapping my cloak tight against the cool evening air.

"Did Nerio apologize?" he asked.

"Yeah. That doesn't mean I forgive him."

"He is not the first soldier to be blinded by religion. The best we can do is learn from and own our mistakes."

I looked down at the glow of firelight on my hands. "You didn't trust me, either."

"How so?"

"You killed that soldier for me, but you let Jorumgard take on three at once."

Tiernan sighed, pinching the bridge of his scarred nose. "Have you killed anyone before?"

"Nei, but—"

"Nor should you have to. Taking a life marks a person. Guilt, regret, questioning your life path — as if part of your spirit dies as well. Can you genuinely say you had no qualms about killing that man?"

I picked at my fingernails, which were still flecked with Jorumgard's blood. Tiernan had a point.

"It was not a criticism of your combat skills. Protecting you means more than keeping you from physical harm." He smiled ruefully. "As it turns out, I needed your help, too. You downed the rider and gave me a fighting chance."

"I realized you weren't going after the horse."

"Jorum says I love horses more than I love people. He exaggerates, but it may be my downfall one day. Sentiment is a weakness."

"It's not," I said quietly.

Tiernan glanced up from putting kindling on the fire.

I took a deep breath. "Our first meeting wasn't in the mountains. Last autumn, you found me sleeping in the Golden Oak's stable. I'd just gotten mugged and had no food or money. You gave me water and offered to take me to a stavehall."

His brows furrowed. "I did not realize that was you."

"I look different now. I mean, not bone-thin, bleeding, and wrecked from lung sickness. But I remembered you because you were kind."

"Then perhaps it is a weakness more people should have." He smiled again, though it seemed dimmer. "Get some sleep. Jorum will wake you for your watch."

Strong wing blew in the next day, clearing some of the smoke. Tiernan and I climbed a hill to see our surroundings. We'd surfaced in the eastern foothills of the Turquoise Mountains. Ahead lay waves of green plains marbled with rivers and patches of woodland, the south reaches of the province of Nyhemur. Thick haze lingered over it all.

We rested in the first village we found, a cluster of timber buildings surrounded by goat pastures and freshly plowed fields. In exchange for a donation to the stavehall, the lone cleric agreed to let us sleep in an abandoned log cabin. The grocer brought us food. He paled at the sight of Nerio and me, stuttering something I didn't understand.

Jorumgard stood up, head scraping the rafters, sword strapped to his back. "Is there a problem?" he asked, and the grocer scuttled out.

The food was my least favourite Sverbian dishes — whitefish and fermented cabbage, with rye sourbread for the morning — but anything was better than hardtack. With a fire in the hearth and the chirp of crickets floating through a window, it was surprisingly pleasant. Nerio and Jorumgard fell into debate over the battle that had destroyed Brånnheå.

"The Rúonbattai might not have fought other humans at all," Nerio said. "Perhaps oosoo broke into the garrison—"

"Oosoo didn't get into the stavehall. Those skeletons were intact. So unless they committed mass suicide . . ."

I still wasn't talking to Nerio, so I switched my attention to Tiernan's work. He spread papers across a rough wooden table and started making charcoal sketches of Brånnheå. It was like looking at a dream. The parts he'd paid attention to were detailed, while everything around them was hazy.

"I wish we'd had more time to explore," Tiernan said. "I have no idea how those soldiers knew we were there."

I pulled his drawing of the nine-branched oak toward me. "Do you believe in omens?"

"Why?"

"It's just . . ." I rested my chin in my hands. "The Rin-jouyen has a sacred rioden. Last autumn I saw it turn black and barren, and a few days later, soldiers invaded my homeland. Yesterday we saw a dead version of the oak, then soldiers showed up again."

He set down his charcoal. "I have never put much stock in omens. However . . ."

"What?" I pressed.

"The sacred oak is said to be the centre of the universe from which every world grows." Tiernan scooped up a handful of woodchips from the kindling box. He began placing them on the sketch, overlapping the branches and roots. "Traditional Sverbian scholars say the worlds include this one, Thaerijmur, Bøkkai, and so on. Interreligious scholars say they include every culture's living and dead lands."

I frowned. "You think we saw another world?"

"Maybe. Were you looking for one?"

"I was last autumn. I wanted to see my people's land of the dead to get answers from my ancestral spirits, the aeldu. But our sacred rioden wouldn't be dead in Aeldu-yan. It's a living forest, a resting place."

Tiernan shrugged, brushing sawdust from his palms. "There could be thousands of worlds. If the physical manifestations of sacred trees are a conduit between them all, we could theoretically see any of them."

"Even if I wasn't looking yesterday?"

"You may have looked subconsciously. Once you have seen through the veil, it becomes easier to do again, and that oak's magic may have amplified your sight."

"I guess it's better than seeing death omens." I studied his sketch, then pointed at the flowers below the oak. "What do these symbolize?"

"I have no idea. They are not in any other depiction I have seen."

"Do you still have the cutting?"

Tiernan handed me the cluster of pale purple flowers, slightly wilted and crushed now. Their glow had faded. The petals' sweet scent brought forward memories of kissing Rokiud among the huckleberries.

"I think they're lilacs," I said. "I've never seen any, but I used my cousin Malana's lilac perfume last year."

He made a note in angular symbols. "A strange choice by the Rúonbattai. Lilacs have no meaning in Sverbian religion."

I looked back at his sketch. The charcoal shrubs were small, no more than a few strokes each. I twirled the lilacs, imagining how they'd look in a life-sized sketch.

"Can I use your drawing tools?" I asked abruptly.

Tiernan slid blank paper and a charcoal stick across the table. First I drew a kinaru wreathed by two fireweed stems, aching to realize how vague my memory of the design was. Next I drew a nine-branched, nine-rooted oak wreathed by two lilac clusters.

"This is my family crest," I said of the first sketch. "The bird's for the Rin-jouyen and the fireweed's for my father. Every Aikoto person has a crest with the same structure, passed from father to daughter and mother to son. If I designed one for a Sverbian, I'd use the raven from your flag instead of the oak, but itherans wouldn't know it has to be an animal."

He straightened up. "Katja," he murmured. "Forgive me for not mentioning this before, but . . . your nation is suspected of connections to the Rúonbattai."

"I know. The navy wanted to search our settlement because they thought we were harbouring Rúonbattai. We weren't, though." I swallowed hard, hoping he didn't notice my white lie. Yotolein hadn't been Rúonbattai at the time. "Besides, our crests aren't secret. Beru adults get them tattooed on their necks. The Rúonbattai could've seen them anywhere."

"Still, this could implicate your people. Are you willing to include it in our report?"

I sat on my hands, thinking. The more I helped the military learn about the Rúonbattai, the better my chances of getting a pardon and my cousins back, but it wasn't worth casting suspicion on our whole confederacy. "Can we leave it out for now?" I asked. "I want to talk to my own people first."

"Very well." Tiernan dropped my sketches on the fire, where they curled and burned. "It stays between us."

Sleeping in villages whenever possible, we rode north up the plains. It all seemed the same to me. Endless grass blowing in the wind, pollen floating through the air and turning ponds yellow, a smell of damp soil whenever we passed farmers plowing fields. All that changed was the sky, shifting from watery blue to star-studded, steel grey, or flat black.

A crooked signpost at a dirt crossroads marked the turn west into Dúnravn Pass. Creeks in the pass ran high and fast, fed by snow melting on the mountain peaks. On the far side among the lower slopes, budding catkins hung thick on cottonwood trees. Nearly a month after leaving my old campsite near Crieknaast, I returned. Our supplies were so low that I had no trouble bundling my stored pelts and tools onto the pack pony.

Torrents of rain were falling when we reached the outskirts of Caladheå. Elkhounds in a guardhouse saw Nerio's uniform and waved us past. Jorumgard led us through the old Sverbian quarter to the Golden Oak, declaring we'd earned a hot meal. I paused by the sign hanging out front. The carved tree had nine branches thick with leaves. Little birds rested on its twigs and a dog snoozed underneath it. Anywhere else it would've felt welcoming, but in the stable I shrank into myself like a turtle, remembering the last time I'd been here.

"Come inside," Tiernan said. "The stablehand can tend the horses tonight."

We passed into a crowded, smoky room. I'd barely taken in the long candlelit tables when a voice called, "My boys return!"

"With a pint-sized warrior!" Jorumgard boomed, slapping my back so hard I stumbled.

A man sporting a bushy yellow beard came forward, grinning and tucking a rag into his stained apron. "Only a few days later than expected. Dinner tonight be a roast, but get cleaned up first, or the reek of you will scare away my patrons. I'll have the maid draw some baths."

I soon learned that Tiernan and Jorumgard lived here when not on campaign. We each paid six pann for a night's room and board, half-price for military service. A mousy girl showed me to a chamber with a wash basin and a merry hearth fire. Seeing her struggle to haul in a heavy bucket of water, I ushered her away, saying I could handle it. Once she was gone, I called steaming water into the basin, stripped off my leather clothes, and sank into the bath.

Even the rough lye soap and frayed washcloth felt luxurious. I scrubbed off dirt and sweat, turning the water murky brown, then unbraided my fishbone beads and seashell and combed the tangles from my hair. The bite marks from my first attuning had healed into ugly scars on my left forearm. After drying off, I dressed in the blackberry-dyed clothes Nili had sewn two seasons ago. The leggings were too short and the cottonspun clung tight to my hips and chest. Uncomfortably aware I'd soon be around drunken, leering itherans, I wrapped my cloak around me like armour.

Back in the pub, I edged through the crowd. A group of Sverbians laughed uproariously at some joke. A mother and father kept telling five squirmy blonde girls to sit still. Beyond the warm pools of candlelight, a man with a hood over his eyes smoked a pipe. I thought one chair held a tall pile of rags until the pile snored and faceplanted on the table.

My companions cleaned up well. Tiernan had shaved off his beard and looked younger, more like when we'd first met. Jorumgard, still bearded and towering over everyone, attracted looks from women who clearly didn't know he wasn't interested. Nerio's freshly starched uniform earned him a few suspicious glares.

The four of us settled on benches with bark on their edges. The innkeeper, Nhys, brought plates loaded with roast goat, herbed vegetables, and rye flatbread to soak up the gravy. I couldn't remember food ever smelling so wonderful. He set down brånnvin for Tiernan and Jorumgard and ale for Nerio and me.

"Military tradition," Jorumgard told me. "One drink if you come back alive, a whole lot more if you don't."

I sipped the ale and spluttered. The men laughed good-naturedly. When they weren't looking, I called water into my mug to dilute it.

The evening passed full of food, chatter, and song from a few rowdy patrons. Rain lashed the windows and everyone who traipsed in looked like they'd been swimming. There was so much to look at and listen to that I nearly forgot what lay ahead, but when our plates were clear of third helpings, Tiernan got up.

"Let us go somewhere quiet," he said. "We have much to discuss."

He led us upstairs. As another patron came out of a room, I glimpsed a bed inside, but we went instead to a sitting room with bookshelves and a thick woven rug. Pipe smoke lingered in the air. Tiernan stoked the fire and we settled on padded chairs. The maid brought tea and spiced cake, curtsied, and left.

"The day you two got poisoned," Tiernan began, "Katja and I made a deal. As thanks for saving your lives, I agreed to retrieve an item the Elkhounds stole from her. In addition, if she helped with our mission, I would arrange . . . other things she may need."

Nerio tapped the arm of his chair, frowning. "You did not see fit to mention this before?"

"I know you do not approve when Captain Parr makes deals like this—"

"Yet you did it anyway, behind my back—"

"What did the Elkhounds steal, little pint?" Jorumgard interrupted loudly.

I bit my lip, wishing I'd drank more ale for courage. "My cousins."

Nerio stilled. Tiernan looked floored. Jorumgard swore and got up, running a hand over his hair.

"We'd been held in the Customs House for a month as illegal refugees." A lump grew in my throat. "Everyone had lung sickness and started getting sent away. Then a priest came and said something about the orphanage, but I was too old. The Elkhounds took my cousins. I stabbed their captain trying to fend him off, but . . . I lost the fight. So I ran."

"Gods' sakes," Tiernan said softly. "I had no idea."

"I thought you'd arrest me if you knew. I wanted to earn a pardon before asking for it."

"No one's gonna arrest you," Jorumgard said. "I should've been hanged for royal desertion. If I can walk free in Eremur, so can you."

I scoffed. "Itherans look at you and see a blank shield, someone they can use. The Elkhounds never gave me that chance."

Nerio sat back, lacing his fingers together. He was silent awhile, then said, "I will bring it up with my father after we make our report tomorrow. That is all I have authority to promise."

13.

RAINY DAY

I was poking at my breakfast of rye porridge when a skinny boy came by, stacking dirty dishes on a tray. He looked familiar. As he got closer, it hit me — the nephew of Batohin, captain of the *Ridge Duck*. His dark eyes were sunken and his skin was tight over his cheekbones. He wore faded, mended trousers and a tunic that hung so loose his body didn't seem to exist.

"Akohin?" I said.

He dropped a mug. It rolled across the table, leaving a thin trail of tea. He grabbed it and said, "I'm working."

"Can't we talk?"

"Not here."

"Use the kitchen," said Tiernan. "Nhys will not mind."

Frowning, Akohin beckoned me through swinging half-doors. The kitchen was steamy from a vat of porridge hanging in a massive hearth. No one else was there. Akohin set the tray down by a basin of soapy water, pushed up his sleeves, and started washing dishes.

"How in Aeldu-yan did you get here?" I asked, pulling up a stool. "I thought you were in the orphanage."

"I was," he said, so flatly it sounded like his voice had gone under a rolling pin. "One of the few Aikoto kids there who's actually an orphan. Then I turned fourteen and the priests said I had to go. I overheard them planning to send me to work in a silver mine, so I ran away."

"How'd you escape?"

After a long pause, Akohin said, "I attuned. A raven landed on the windowsill, and . . . well, you can guess. My bunkmate broke the window so I could fly out."

I tilted my head. "And you stayed in Caladheå? Wouldn't you rather live with our people?"

He shook his head, sending limp black hair over his eyes. "I'm Dona, remember. My great-great-grandparents abandoned the Rin to form a new jouyen. That's *why* we're nomadic. No one wants us back."

"But—" I stopped as the mousy maid came in. Switching into Aikoto so she wouldn't understand, I said, "You might get caught. You'd be safer with the Iyo."

Akohin snorted. "Who do you think convinced my uncle to turn himself in? Now he's rotting in prison for nothing. Oh, but it's fine because the Iyo-jouyen don't need to harbour a Dona outlaw anymore." He dried his hands on a rag and grabbed a bucket. "I need more water."

Baffled, I followed him to the back alley. Pouring rain gathered in muddy puddles. "You were training to be an antayul. Why come outside?"

"Itherans don't like magic," he said, filling the bucket from an overflowing rain barrel.

"Do you mean the maid? She'd probably appreciate not hauling water all over the inn. I could go talk to her—"

"Nei!" He grabbed my wrist.

Instantly I had a knife at his throat. Akohin dropped the bucket, dousing us in icy rainwater. He looked as stricken as I felt. I sheathed the blade, muttering apologies.

"Guess we both got messed up," he said bitterly.

"What do you mean?"

He refilled the bucket, not meeting my gaze. "I . . . can't call water anymore. Not since the orphanage. I didn't think I'd attune, either."

My jaw fell. I'd never heard of someone losing their antayul skills — and my cousins had been there longer. I wasn't sure I could handle seeing them like this, flattened and broken with the light gone from their eyes. All I knew was I had to get them out.

I stayed silent, mired in my thoughts, as I rode through Caladheå on the back of Jorumgard's horse. I hardly noticed the passing city until we climbed a steep hill. At the top, two stone elk reared above a set of huge iron gates that looked like they stayed permanently open. Mud and leaves had built up around them. Guards in soaked blue coats stood perfectly still even as rain dripped off their faces.

"The Colonnium," Tiernan told me, pointing through the gates at the biggest building I'd ever seen. It was built of cream-coloured stone with arched windows. Birds swooped around a domed tower in the centre. "Eremur's government and military both have headquarters here."

We crossed a sodden lawn to the north wing, stabled the horses, and entered a grand hall. Rain drummed on a grid of skylights. Elk-sigil banners hung on each wall — black for the army, red for the navy, grey for Elkhounds, and blue for Colonnium guards. Men in uniforms of the same colours watched me curiously. A harried-looking woman mopped mud from the tile floor.

Nerio led us down an echoing corridor. Guards bowed to him and opened a door. Inside, several men sat talking around a large painted table. Their uniforms all had red silk bands around their sleeves, marking them as captains.

A tall, broad-shouldered man rose to his feet. His long black hair was pulled back with a ribbon. He looked plenty strong enough to wield the curved sword at his hip, though one arm currently hung in a sling. He cracked into a grin. "Nerio, my son. Heilind, Tømasind, what a relief." He used his good arm to embrace Nerio, who pulled away, looking embarrassed. He and Tiernan embraced, too, thumping each other's backs, then he and Jorumgard. Lastly he turned to me.

"Father, meet Katja," Nerio said. "We are back safely because of her."

Surprise flickered across Captain Parr's face. He gave me a deep bow. "Then I am honoured to meet you, Katja. That must be quite a tale. Please, sit."

"I must object," said a naval captain who was so windburnt he resembled an old hazelnut. "First we bring a mage into our war council, now a viirelei?"

"Katja helped us fight Rúonbattai inside Brånnheå," Nerio said. "She knows more about their current status than you, Captain Ilus."

Ilus's mouth moved wordlessly. Parr's lips twitched with a smile as he pulled out a chair for me.

Only when seated did I notice the table was a map of Eremur and its surrounding lands. Stone figurines dotted the terrain. Parr moved a horse from the southern mountains to the dot marking Caladheå, and I realized it symbolized us. Carved ships with colourful flags speckled the ocean, which was painted in a deep glassy blue.

Nerio did most of the talking, detailing our trip. Tiernan spread his drawings of Brånnheå on a clear patch of table, showing different parts of the cavern and garrison. He'd dried and pressed the lilacs on paper. The captains had plenty of questions, but at the part about an oosoo's death triggering a volcanic eruption, they fell silent.

"Nonsense," Ilus said finally. "Is this a joke?"

"I bid you not question my son's integrity," Parr said. "The war council has discussed stranger things."

"But no one has ever mentioned these creatures, or these fire spirits—"

"The Kowichelk Confederacy has," I said.

Ilus sniffed. "I meant no one of *repute*."

"Go to Brånnheå and see for yourself," Tiernan said waspishly. "The oosoo will be happy for another meal."

Jorumgard snorted and tried to turn it into a cough.

"This feels disturbingly like fighting the Rúonbattai last time," Tiernan went on. "Liet always knew where we would be and what we would do. My guess is he survived the Brånnheå massacre and is attempting to rebuild their former strength."

Parr twisted an ornate ring on his finger, looking weary. "You have given us much to consider. May I suggest we adjourn for lunch? A break should improve everyone's manners."

The other captains pushed back their chairs and filed out, murmuring to one another. Once the door closed, Nerio said, "We have something else to discuss, Father."

"Go on," Parr said.

"Katja and her younger cousins came here as refugees. The city guard separated them and took her cousins to the orphanage. Katja tried to fight off the guards — you may have heard about a captain getting stabbed in the Customs House. I believe she deserves a pardon and the return of her relatives. There is nothing moral about tearing apart a family in crisis."

Parr studied Nerio with an odd look. "How far you have come. I thought you might forever take an overly rigid view of the law." He turned to me. "I do not blame you for trying to protect your cousins, Katja. Love for one's family is not a crime. May I ask how old you are?"

"Fifteen," I said, my mouth dry.

"Good. At sixteen, you would be tried as an adult, but our laws are forgiving of children. Moreover, your help investigating the Rúonbattai has been invaluable. I can offer more than a pardon. I will make you a legal resident of Eremur so you can take refuge here as long as you like."

"What of her cousins?" Tiernan asked.

"They will be released and granted residency, too. The priests cannot object. The orphanage will be overcrowded soon if we are indeed facing another war."

It was so quick, so simple, I could hardly believe it. I felt warm and light, as if I could float away.

Parr got up and crossed to a side table with writing supplies. "Who are your cousins, Katja?"

"They're registered as Aniya and Sohin Mèrus. They're listed as my siblings, though. Oh, and I'm registered as Eko Mèrus," I added, flustered.

He wrote with bold strokes. "It will take time to arrange. However, I am instructing the priests to let you visit your cousins today." He stamped the letter with a red elk sigil. "Tømasind, would you mind taking Katja to the orphanage? I am sure the war council has more questions for Nerio and Heilind."

Jorumgard rose, grinning. "I'd be happy to."

Nen Divinus was as I remembered, grey and gloomy with spired towers that cut the sky. Behind the sancte was the orphanage, made of the same grey stone and surrounded by an iron fence. It was plain and boxy with four storeys of small windows. One window was boarded up, probably where Akohin had escaped.

The orphanage lobby had a faint odour of bleach. A young itheran boy stood on a ladder washing the windows. He stared at us, then started scrubbing twice as hard. Behind a desk sat a woman covered in billows of deep blue cloth. All I could see was her face. She scowled at our muddy footprints and set down her knitting. I held out Parr's letter with shaking hands.

The woman yanked it from me, read it, and tossed it on the desk. "Padro Filip!" she hollered.

A young priest came down a corridor, hands folded under his draping blue sleeves. The three-blossom symbol embroidered on his robes had been burned into my memory. Before he could speak, the woman thrust the letter at him. He read it twice, then looked up.

"We have no children by these names," he said.

It felt like he'd stuck a hook in me and ripped out my guts. "They're here," I protested. "I saw a priest take them into the sancte last autumn."

The man's brow creased. "I only took this position recently. Let me ask the senior *padro*. Wait here, please."

"Don't worry, little pint," Jorumgard whispered. "We'll find 'em."

Filip returned with a balding man who wore identical blue robes. The older priest lifted spectacles on a gold chain around his neck. He read the letter, frowning.

"Yes, I think I recall these names," he said. "However, if Padro Filip says they are not here now, they are not."

"Where'd they go?" Jorumgard asked.

"Good sir, do you think I keep the registry in my head? Thousands of children have passed through these doors. Come back in a few days—"

"It seems I wasn't clear." Jorumgard stepped forward, bearing over the priest with all his height. "Find out where they went. *Now.*"

The old priest puffed out his chest. "This is a holy place. Heathens have no authority—"

"Fuck authority," Jorumgard growled. "I have no fear of small gods and smaller men."

The old priest spluttered. Filip pulled him away, whispering in rapid Ferish.

"I will check the registry," Filip announced. "Sit, please."

The woman pointed at a bench. Jorumgard thumped down, drew his sword, and ran his nails along its edge. I sat next to him, allowing the tiny part of my mind that wasn't drowning in panic to be grateful for his help.

The young boy mopped away our muddy footprints, finished scrubbing the windows, and scampered off. The ceiling creaked, followed by faint voices overhead. At least an hour had passed when Filip returned. Jorumgard rose and I followed.

"Aniya and Sohin Mèrus left here three months ago," Filip said. "They were given up for adoption."

"*Adoption?*" Jorumgard repeated. "To who?"

"Unfortunately, I am not allowed to tell you. They are no longer wards of the province, therefore no longer in the military's jurisdiction."

My knees gave out. Jorumgard caught me. I distantly noticed

his hand on my hair, him bellowing, Filip cringing. None of it mattered. Nothing else would ever matter again.

At the Golden Oak, I immediately went to the kitchen. I couldn't pretend any longer that I could do this without my own people. Nhys's live-in employees got afternoons off, so he directed me to Akohin's room. I knocked several times before the door opened.

"Ai, it's you," Akohin said sullenly.

The room had two beds and chests of drawers. One bed was neatly made with knitted blankets. The other was rumpled and surrounded by bits of straw. Tacked to the wall around the rumpled one were torn pictures of women posing on haystacks.

"Those belong to the stablehand," Akohin said, rolling his eyes.

"Right," I said, too distracted to care. "Listen, will you take a message to Toel Ginu? I'll pay."

"Why?"

"I — I was just at the orphanage. Hanaiko and Samulein got adopted."

"Oh." His voice cracked. "I didn't know. It must've happened after I left."

"Can you find my cousin Dunehein and ask him to come here? I know you don't like the Iyo, but Jonalin's family won't be happy to see me."

Akohin glanced at the rain-streaked window. "I think I can fly to Toel and back before nightfall. You better not wait here, though. If the stablehand finds a girl in our room, I'll never hear the end of it."

He left me in the kitchen. Nhys offered me food, but I couldn't eat. I didn't realize hours had passed until Akohin returned with wet hair plastered to his forehead. He said Dunehein was on his way, canoeing up the coast with his Iyo wife, Rikuja. That didn't sink in either until Dunehein appeared, soaked and windswept, filling the doorway with his bearlike frame.

"Kako," he said throatily. He bent down and hugged me so hard my ribs ached. "Oh, little cousin, it's good to see you safe."

The bravado that carried me through the winter crumbled. Suddenly I was crying into his shirt, too choked up to speak, clutching his long tangled hair to touch the spirits of my family again.

Rikuja hugged me from the other side. "*Wala*, *wala*," she soothed. "It's okay."

"Best take her upstairs," Nhys said gently. "Her room be the fourth door on the left. I'll send dinner up."

Dunehein guided me there. It was an old but clean room with faded curtains and scratched pine furniture. I collapsed onto the bed and pulled the patchwork quilt around my shoulders. Dunehein sat next to me, making the bedstead groan. Rikuja took a chair at the small table. The maid brought a tray of soup and rye buns, gave me a handkerchief, and left with a sympathetic smile.

"We have more cousins," I got out. "Yotolein—"

"I heard," Dunehein said. "Emehein flew here right after you left Aeti Ginu. He said you and the kids were going to a Dona refuge. Aeldu save us, if we knew you wound up in Caladheå instead—"

"No one knew. We registered with different names. But listen, Dune. Hanaiko and Samulein are gone. I should've come back sooner—"

"Gone? Where?"

"Adopted. The orphanage gave them away."

Dunehein slammed his palm against the wall. Someone on the other side hollered for us to be quiet. "Takuran pigeons," he said through gritted teeth. "All right. Tell us everything."

I started with when we left home. Dunehein kept interrupting with questions. At the ferry house part he crushed a rye bun, and during the Customs House part he bent a spoon in half. Rikuja stayed quiet, but when I mentioned finding Jonalin's aunt with an Elkhound, she spoke.

"Oh, love," she said. "Segowa had to say she'd turn you in. Jonalin got charged with assaulting Elkhounds and helping a violent captive escape. He could've been locked up for decades if his family didn't pretend to cooperate. Did you really believe after all the Iyo-jouyen's efforts to get custody of the refugee kids, we'd just hand you over?"

"I wasn't sure," I said in a tiny voice. "Back home, everyone was mad at Yotolein for lying about the Rúonbattai and leading the military to us. The Iyo knew *I* lied, and then I got Jonalin arrested."

"No one blames you for that. Jonalin protected you willingly, and he says he'd do it again."

"That's a discussion for another time, though," Dunehein said. "Let's hear the rest of Kako's story."

I explained how I spent the winter trapping, then travelled to Brånnheå. By the time I finished, the rain had stopped, leaving us in silence except for the dying fire. Dunehein paced the small room, grinding one fist into the other. I hadn't seen him this mad since his mother refused to attend his wedding. Rikuja sipped a mug of tea, letting him work out his anger.

"You're right, you shoulda come to us sooner," he said. "I'm surprised you didn't sneak into Toel. You've never been scared of anything."

"I wasn't scared," I said indignantly. "But everyone always tells me to be cautious. I'm the only one who knew our cousins had gone to the orphanage. I had to find a way to tell you without getting caught."

Dunehein's shoulders eased. He dropped onto the bed and slung a hefty arm around me. "Here's a secret about being an adult — nothing's simple. If I knew our cousins were in the orphanage, maybe I coulda got them out months ago. Still, adoption's better than prison or death. Being cautious was better advice than anyone knew."

"Why?"

"Tokoda, the Okorebai-Iyo, has been . . . strange about the Rúonbattai. She won't talk about 'em. You were right not to tell anyone about Yotolein. The fewer people who know he used to be Rúonbattai, the better our chances of getting his kids back."

14.

FAMILY NEAR AND FAR

"I'm going to the Iyo gathering place to hire a messenger," Rikuja said next morning. "Someone older than Akohin, preferably. We need to contact your family and ask them to come south."

"Tell 'em to be careful," Dunehein said. "They might get hauled in as illegal refugees, too, and aeldu help us if someone recognizes Yotolein."

"Someone like *them*," I said quietly.

Tiernan and Jorumgard were winding through the pub toward us. They didn't seem surprised to see me with other Aikoto. Dunehein just looked them up and down, then said, "It's clear who you are."

"Jorum told me what happened," Tiernan said. "We wondered if we can help."

Dunehein glanced at me. I nodded. I didn't fully trust them yet, but I wouldn't be here without them.

"Falwen, the Officer of the Viirelei, might have the adoption records," Dunehein said. "I don't know my way around the Colonnium, though. Can one of you show me to his office?"

"I will," Tiernan said. "I am going there anyway to meet with the war council."

"We'd better find Kirbana Elynehl, too, since she's listed as the kids' stepmother," Dunehein went on. "Kako says Sverbian clerics might know where she is."

"There are two major stavehalls in Caladheå," Jorumgard said. "One here in Førstown, the old quarter, and one in Shawnaast. I'll check both."

"I'll come," I began, but Tiernan cut me off.

"Stay here until your pardon has been finalized," he said.

Once they left, I wished I'd insisted on going. Akohin wasn't much for conversation. I curled up in the sitting room and paged through books I couldn't read, looking at illustrations of plants and animals. One had diagrams of a caterpillar turning into a butterfly. I felt like I was stuck in the cocoon phase, waiting, waiting, waiting.

Rikuja came back first. Jonalin's cousin had agreed to fly to Aeti Ginu, although I half-expected him to come thrash me for getting Jonalin arrested. Dunehein returned next and said Falwen wasn't allowed to give out the records but had "let slip" that our cousins were now registered with the surname Sartere. Around dusk, Jorumgard knocked on the doorframe.

Kirbana entered carrying her son, Kel. Her bonnet hung by its strings behind her neck, revealing a messy ash-blonde bun. She was flushed and out of breath. "It's really you," she said faintly upon seeing me. "Thank the gods."

Kel was a toddler now, dark-haired and squirming. Kirbana released him on the rug. I hugged her, too relieved to speak. I'd grown taller than her. She had to stand on her toes to kiss my hair.

As we separated, I caught Dunehein's look of surprise. Jorumgard grinned and slipped out of the room.

"Kel survived the lung sickness thanks to you," Kirbana told me, tears sparkling in her green eyes. "Your money paid for a good medic. I'm so sorry I couldn't help your family in return."

Over dinner, she explained that a month after I fled Caladheå, she'd gotten a custody hearing in the provincial court. "It didn't work, though," she said, coaxing Kel to eat a spoonful of mashed turnip. "Apparently the navy found an ex-Rúonbattai in my home village. They didn't have grounds to arrest me, but they didn't trust me enough to release the kids to me or my husband."

"Is your husband here?" Rikuja asked.

Kirbana shook her head. "I haven't been able to contact him." Her words came out thickly like she, too, had a mouthful of turnip. "He's supposed to be helping run the island refuge, but only a few Dona captains know where it is, and none have come here since Batohin's arrest. I can't tromp up and down the coast looking for them with a toddler to care for."

It struck me how young she was. I'd thought of her like a softer version of Tema, wise and mature with a husband and child, but she was only eight years older than me. The whole time in the Customs House she must've been terrified and lonely, too, but never showed it, always telling us we'd be okay. I felt a warm rush of gratitude.

"Have you been living in Caladheå alone?" Dunehein asked her.

"Not quite," Kirbana said. "I'm working as a wet nurse for a Sverbian family. The wife passed away after giving birth. I don't like living in someone else's home, to say nothing of breastfeeding a dead woman's baby, but it's a stable place for Kel. Better than where you spent the winter, Eko."

"Oh," I said, startled. "That's not my name. It's Kateiko."

Kirbana laughed. "I wondered why that big man who fetched me kept calling you Katja. I was afraid he had the wrong person. Anyway, we live here in Førstown, so I'm nearby if you need anything."

"So are we. I mean, if *you* need anything."

She squeezed my hand. We felt more equal than we used to. Less like mother and daughter, more like sisters.

After Kirbana left, I went to the pub in search of Jorumgard. I found him bellowing a song, one arm swaying in the air with an ale mug, the other arm around a reedy Sverbian man who looked both unnerved and captivated. I went back upstairs and knocked on Tiernan's door instead.

"Yes?" came his muffled voice.

I poked my head in. His room matched mine with a similar patchwork quilt and faded curtains. Tiernan sat hunched, his hair loose and rumpled like he'd been running his hands through it. His drawings of Brånnheå had spilled from the table onto the floor like a waterfall. The dried, pressed lilacs were tacked to the wall. He waved me in with a tired smile. I perched on the bed and explained about the Sartere name.

He tapped his quill on an inkpot, thinking. "I believe it is Ferish for *tailor*. Many Ferish tradesmen take the name of their profession and pass it down through generations. Might it apply to your family?"

"Nei," I began, then stopped. Yotolein's wife had been a seamstress for the Rúonbattai. "Maybe. I mean, we're trappers, so we learn to sew leather and pelts. It's not our main work, though."

"In that case, the Sarteres are probably a family who adopted your cousins. I will ask Nerio if the name sounds familiar." Tiernan jotted a note.

"I have another favour to ask," I said hesitantly. "But it's big, and I don't have anything left to bargain with."

He turned in his chair to face me. "You have nothing to lose by asking."

"Captain Parr said I wouldn't have been tried as an adult for the Customs House fight, but . . . someone else *was*. An eighteen-year-old dockhand named Jonalin Tanarem had been looking after us. He held the Elkhounds off so I could escape, and he got arrested instead. He's in prison now. Can we do anything for him?"

Tiernan rubbed his jaw, leaving a small smear of ink. "We may be able to shorten his sentence. Parr would need to pull some strings, though, and while he is compassionate, he is also opportunistic. He may ask you to return the favour. Are you prepared for that?"

I bit my lip. "What might he ask for?"

"Nothing terrible, and I will make it clear that it is not a binding agreement."

"Then I'm prepared. I owe Jonalin that."

Tiernan made another note. "I will see if we can hurry it through the courts."

"Could I see him in the meantime?"

"I am afraid not. Only family can visit prisoners."

I thanked him and left. His papers had reminded me of something else from Brånnheå. I dug through my belongings, found the kinaru figurine trapped in a resin cube, and went to Dunehein and Rikuja's room. Their muffled voices cut off at my knock. Dunehein answered.

"Aeldu save us," he said, taking the cube. The yellow resin glowed in the candlelight. "That looks like a makiri inside. Where'd you get this?"

I described the basalt altar. Looking disturbed, he passed it to Rikuja. She was a skilled woodworker, one of the few people entrusted with carving the Iyo-jouyen's history on their shrine walls. She turned it this way and that, studying it from every angle.

"The kinaru is flawlessly carved," she said. "It sure looks like a makiri, but encasing it in resin blocks spirits from getting in — or worse, getting *out*. No Rin carver would do that."

"You think someone else put it in resin?" Dunehein asked.

"Probably. My guess is the Rúonbattai wanted to protect it from rotting in those damp caves, and had no idea what the side effects could be. But we should ask your temal when he arrives, Kako. He'll know better than me."

News came two nights later. I was in my room listening to rain spatter the window when someone knocked. Rikuja entered with her braid half-undone, the bark cord that marked her as a shrine carver hanging loose among the strands. She was barefoot and had clearly been getting ready for bed.

"The messenger's back," she said.

A teenage boy followed her in. He was built like a sapling, tall and skinny. Raindrops sparkled on his shaved head. Nili would've called him lush, though his nose was crooked, probably from an old break, and his nervous grin revealed a chipped tooth. "*Hanekei*," he said, raising a hand.

I was so caught off guard by our traditional greeting that I stammered through returning it. I really had been away a long time.

"I'm Airedain Kiyorem," he said. "Jona's cousin. I visit him in prison every month and he's been worried about you, so when

Rikuja asked for someone to fly to Aeti Ginu and talk to your family, I volunteered."

"Did you find them?" I asked breathlessly.

"Some of 'em." He tried to jam his hands in his pockets, but his breeches were so wet the pockets stuck. "Not your parents or Yotolein, though. Your aunt Isu claimed they went trading, but your cousin Emehein told me in secret that no one knows where they are. Your temal's whole family is missing, too."

"*Missing?*"

"Yeah. It was creepy. A bunch of plank houses were boarded up, half the firepits were abandoned, and everyone was pissed off. They kicked me out of Aeti Ginu before I could ask anything else."

I sank onto my bed like I'd been punctured. Nothing made sense. It couldn't be about Yotolein's ties to the Rúonbattai if Temal's relatives were gone, too. Something had gone horribly wrong.

Dunehein looked as stunned as I felt. "Is anyone coming? Emehein?"

"Nei," Airedain said, sounding truly sorry. "No one at all."

I moved through the next few days in a fog. I needed identification to get my pardon and military wages, but I'd lost mine when Lucreza and her brothers mugged me. Dunehein took me to Falwen's office and re-registered me as Kateiko Leniere. The surname meant *carpenter*, the closest the Ferish language got to Temal's role as a woodcarver. Nerio gave me paperwork I couldn't read and a clinking bag of coins.

It all felt pointless. I was a carpenter's daughter without a father. I had legal residency in a province I'd never called home. I had wages for a mission I'd only taken to get my cousins back, and they were still out of reach.

One evening, another knock came at my door. I opened it to find Akohin with a dish rag over his shoulder.

"Some brown pigeon wants to see you in the sitting room," he said.

"What? Who?"

"I dunno. A soldier." He stalked off.

I headed down the hall into the candlelit room. Captain Parr stood by a window, looking out at the stable lanterns glowing in the darkness. His arm was still in a sling. At the sound of my footsteps, he turned and bowed.

"Miss Leniere," he said with a sad smile. "Nerio told me about your cousins. I am so sorry. I looked into it, but—"

"They're not in the military's jurisdiction," I said dully.

"Yes. However, I have some good news." Parr gestured to the padded chairs.

I perched on the edge of one. He settled into another, shifting the sword at his hip.

"Firstly, my son took your advice and contacted the Yula nation. They visited Brånnheå and found the entire cavern destroyed by lava, yet the oosoo colony is alive and well. Heilind also informed members of the Kae nation who live in Ingdanrad and study saidu. Together they will monitor the volcano."

I nodded. "Good."

"Secondly, Heilind and I appealed Jonalin Tanarem's case. We argued that since Falwen placed your family in Tanarem's care, Tanarem was morally obliged to protect you, even if that meant assaulting the guards trying to separate you. Since it was his first offence and his behaviour has been excellent, we got his sentence reduced to one year in prison, plus one year in a parole house."

"What's that?"

"A guarded boarding house for convicts. Tanarem can live and work freely during the day, as long as he remains within Caladheå and returns to the parole house by curfew."

I bit my lip, thinking. Jonalin wouldn't be able to visit his plank house or the Iyo shrine in Toel Ginu, but at least he had family here. "Tiernan said you . . . might want a favour in return?"

"Do not worry about that now." Parr leaned forward. "Think of this as a good faith arrangement and focus on finding your cousins."

I managed a wavering smile. "Thank you, sir."

The news about Jonalin pulled me partway out of the fog. Nerio brought me the rest of the way. He'd visited a tailor's shop in the Shawnaast district on the pretense of needing his uniform mended. The owners were a middle-aged Ferish couple who, according to gossip, had never borne children, but Nerio had seen schoolbooks on a counter.

"How do we approach them?" Rikuja asked.

"Carefully," Nerio said. "The Sarteres seem very traditional. Well mannered. Try to appear . . ."

"Civilized," she finished, her lip curling with derision.

He flushed and looked away. "In essence, yes. Ferish attire would be ideal, though Sverbian would do."

The next afternoon, Kirbana helped me into her best outfit, a white dress and moss-green bodice that laced up the back. The stiff boning forced me to stand straight. She pinned up my hair and tied on a brimless bonnet. Rikuja coiled her braid on her head and changed into a dress borrowed from the maid. Her tattoos showed through the threadbare sleeves, so she draped a shawl over her shoulders.

"Not those," Kirbana said as I reached for my knives. "You're going to negotiate, not terrify them."

"My temal told me to always have weapons—"

"Kirbana's right," Rikuja said. "Trust me, itherans are scared enough of Dunehein."

We met him in the corridor. His hair was tied back with a ribbon, and he wore a leather jerkin, tunic, and trousers borrowed from Jorumgard. The seams strained around his shoulders and he kept pulling at the sleeves. "Thank the aeldu you befriended the biggest Sverbian in the land," he joked.

He, Rikuja, and I crossed a wooden footbridge over the Stengar river into Shawnaast. Old timber buildings sagged among rows of identical red-brick shops. Carriages clattered over pollen-coated flagstones. This had been a separate Sverbian town once, until Ferish immigration became legal and people flooded into Caladheå and across the Stengar. That was around when the Rúonbattai formed.

Shawnaast had grown fast and wild since. Even with Nerio's directions, we kept getting lost. Most roads were unmarked and some signs had been painted over or scratched out. Finally, we found a brick shop with blank-faced mannequins in the window. I gaped at a ruffled silk dress with enormous lace cuffs and a skirt puffed out by frilly petticoats. Wearing that dress would be an accident waiting to happen.

Inside, the shop was a riot of texture. Fabric of every kind lined the walls — soft velvet, ribbed corduroy, gauzy muslin, silk and wool and cottonspun patterned in paisley and gingham and damask. Most of the cloth was dyed dark, but a few bolts of scarlet and amber and turquoise stood out like jewels. Nili would've spent hours admiring everything.

A man leaned over a table, cutting a bolt of bleached linen. His short black hair was grey at the temples and a few wrinkles lined his eyes. He set down his shears and bowed stiffly, restricted by his brocade waistcoat. His high-collared shirt seemed to choke his voice as he said, "How may I help you?"

Dunehein bowed back. With forced calm he said, "It seems you've adopted our cousins. Last we heard, they were registered by the names Aniya and Sohin."

Mister Sartere went as white as his linen. "I — we—" he stammered.

"We just want to talk," Rikuja said. "Is your wife available?"

"She . . . she . . . oh, goodness. We better go upstairs." He called out in Ferish, flipped over a sign in the window, and beckoned us to a spiral staircase.

Missus Sartere met us at the top. She reminded me of a wren, wide-eyed and fluttery. Her skirt folds draped like wings. "Guests!" she chirped. "Come into the sitting room. Forgive me for not having tea ready—"

She went on twittering as she ushered us into a bright, airy room with flowery wallpaper. At her instruction we sat on a horsehair couch, which was so smooth I had to plant my feet to keep from sliding off. The room smelled thickly floral even though the vases held only silk daisies. Every surface was covered with lace tablecloths or doilies.

"Well," Mister Sartere said, settling onto a padded armchair. "Let's have some introductions. I'm Viènzo Sartere and this is my wife, Giana. Who might you be?"

"Dunehein Iyo and my wife, Rikuja," Dunehein said. "This here is my cousin Kateiko Leniere."

"Are Aniya and Sohin here?" Rikuja asked, looking around.

"Oh, no, they're at school," Viènzo said. "But goodness, the priests told us the children had no living relatives."

"We ain't—" Dunehein cleared his throat. "We aren't sure what happened. Kateiko and the kids came to Eremur as refugees, but the younger two got taken to the orphanage."

"That's where we found them," Giana said, beaming. "We planned to adopt Ferish children until we spotted Aniya and Sohin. Such beautiful orphans. Big blue eyes, exotic names, and ever so well behaved. Who wouldn't fall in love with them?"

Rikuja looked taken aback. "They're not orphans, though. Their father must be terribly worried, so we'd like to bring them home with us—"

"Home?" The smile froze on Giana's face. "This is their home."

We stared at her.

Viènzo spread his hands. "You must understand. Giana and I always dreamed of passing the shop onto our children, but we've never been blessed with any. Aniya and Sohin will be our legacy. We're a proper family at last."

"But they're *our* family," I said, bewildered.

"Well, you say their father is alive, but there's no trace of him. There's no proof you even know them—"

"Proof?" The word burst out of me. "Like knowing Sohin has nightmares about fire because his home burned down? Or Aniya named her dolls after Sverbian goddesses, then lost them when soldiers tore us apart? I bet *you* don't know that, though. They stop talking when they're scared."

The Sarteres exchanged a look. "See here," Viènzo said uncomfortably. "You can't turn up unannounced and expect us to give up our children—"

"They ain't yours," Dunehein growled. "How many times we gotta say it?"

"Calm yourself, sir," Viènzo snapped. "You are upsetting my wife."

Giana had gone pale. She clutched her chair and fanned herself.

"The kids have suffered a lot," Rikuja said, hands clenched in her lap. "It's best for them to go back to a life they know—"

"But what kind of life is that?" Giana cried. "Living in the sticks and eating raw meat? Worshipping heathen gods? We'll give them an education, a livelihood, a safe and peaceful home. We can civilize them—"

Dunehein jerked to his feet, knocking over a vase. It hit the floor and shattered. Giana shrieked.

Viènzo leapt up. "Sir! I demand you leave at once, or I'll call the city guard to remove you!"

Dunehein leaned over the man. He reminded me of Jorumgard bearing over the old priest. But he didn't swear, didn't draw a weapon, didn't utter a threat. He just made a disgusted sound and strode out.

15.

APOTHECARY

I seethed all the way back through Shawnaast. I'd never hated anyone as much as the Sarteres. I hated their fake manners and fake flowers and fake love for my cousins. I hated that they could steal someone's family, then threaten us with arrest just for wanting them back.

In the Golden Oak, I went straight to my room. I didn't want to hear Rikuja's calm voice and remember I hadn't controlled mine, to see Dunehein's blazing temper and know I couldn't have stood so close to Viènzo without hitting him. Nerio's words rang in my head. *Violence runs in those people's blood.* He was wrong about my family, but the nagging thought he was right about me just made me angrier.

I hated these stupid clothes, too. I tore off the bonnet and yanked at the bodice laces. They tangled in a knot. The more I tugged, the worse it got, and I couldn't see behind me to fix it. I pulled my boots off and threw them at the wall. I'd forgotten Jorumgard's room was on the other side until his muffled voice said, "You okay, little pint?"

I flung open my door, ready to yell at him for calling me that. Instead I gaped. He'd undone his braid and his straw-coloured hair fell loose past his elbows. The sight felt weirdly private, which let me shelve my pride and admit through gritted teeth, "I'm stuck."

Jorumgard couldn't hide a smile. "Can't say I've ever helped a lady undress before." He untangled the knot, then said, "Come down to the stable yard. You look like someone who needs to throw a few punches."

Next morning, sore and bruised from sparring, I went downstairs and found Dunehein and Rikuja sitting with Tiernan and Jorumgard in the pub. Rikuja pushed a plate of toast at me, smiling distractedly. Tiernan was reading aloud from a newspaper, something about monthly rates.

"We're looking at places for rent," Dunehein explained. "We'll get a home, steady jobs, whatever it takes to seem 'civilized' to the Sarteres. Then we'll ask permission to visit our cousins, and eventually get 'em back for good."

"You're going to rent somewhere in Caladheå?" I asked.

"Nei, in the ocean. The fishing's better."

I rolled my eyes, though secretly I was glad to hear him crack a joke. He was starting to sound more like himself again.

"We'll live in Shawnaast if we can afford it," Dunehein continued. "If not, the Iyo street in the Ashtown district. Depends on the work we can get."

"Try the lumberyard," Jorumgard said. "You've got the strength for it. As for Rikuja, households are always hiring domestic help. Shawnaast is the district for families with lots of money and lots of kids."

"Where can I work?" I asked.

"Nowhere," Dunehein said. "You're going to live with Rija's family in Toel Ginu."

"I am not," I said indignantly. "Hanaiko and Samulein have never met you. Besides, they got adopted because I stayed away too long. I'm not leaving again."

Looking exasperated, he swung to Rikuja. She smiled into her tea as if to say *I told you so*.

"Fine," Dunehein said, flinging out an arm and knocking over a mug. "You ain't working just anywhere, though. There's no way in Aeldu-yan I'll leave you with people like the Sarteres."

"May I make a suggestion?" Tiernan said. "A friend of ours, Marijka Riekkanehl, supplies herbs to an apothecary in that part of Shawnaast. She says the shop owner is always overworked."

"What's an apo . . . athopo . . ." I gave up.

"Someone who sells medicine and does basic healing. I have been meaning to visit Marijka anyway and ask her about those lilacs from Brånnheå, so I can ask if the shop owner is . . . accepting of viirelei."

Dunehein folded his arms. "I guess it can't hurt to ask."

One week later, Dunehein and I left our new flat and headed to the apothecary. The smells of spice and musk guided us to the right building. It was two storeys of red brick like the Sarteres', but the windowsills held pots of real flowers basking in spring sunshine. A bell tinkled as I opened the door. Inside, dusty shelves held containers organized by size, from heavy-looking ceramic jars to crystal vials, all with faded and peeling labels.

A short round woman stood behind a stone counter weighing herbs. A few stray curls of grey hair hung past her high collar. "You're Kateiko?" she barked.

"Yes," I stammered, curtsying awkwardly.

"None of that. One bad curtsy and it's a whole batch of tincture shattered on the floor." She added weights to the scale as she talked. "I'm Missus Agata Solus, but call me Agata, understand? I got no time for fanciness. Now, Tiernan Heilind said he'd write you a reference."

I held out the letter. Agata skimmed it so fast her green eyes were like darting beetles.

"Level-headed while men are dying, recognition of poison, field surgery — good, good. This place isn't for the weak of stomach." She pocketed the letter. "I need help with chores. I'll pay eight pann a day, three days a week. That work for you?"

I nodded.

Agata thrust a frayed apron at me. "Put that on. I'll feed you lunch, and you'll finish around four o'clock."

"You okay with this?" Dunehein whispered as I tied the apron on.

"Well, she's nothing like the Sarteres," I whispered back.

"If it goes bad—"

"I know where to find you and Rija. You at the lumberyard, her at the river washing rich itherans' laundry."

He ruffled my hair and left. I turned back to Agata, waiting for instructions.

"Nica!" she hollered.

A girl leaned out from a doorway. She looked like a younger, slimmer Agata with the same green eyes and small mouth. Her auburn curls were damp and her face was flushed. A fluffy white cat wound around her skirts, twitching its stub nose.

"This is Nicoletta, my granddaughter and apprentice," Agata said. "She's sixteen, but don't be fooled. She knows the work like a piper knows his pipes. Nica, this is our new chore girl, Kateiko. I'm putting her in your charge."

Nicoletta eyed me. "Hm," she said.

First Nicoletta showed me the back rooms. The steamy kitchen was dominated by a huge oak table. Bowls of herbs, roots, minerals, and slimy animal bits covered the table's scratched surface. Pots bubbled in a brick hearth. The surgery room had a cot and a rack of steel tools for lancing boils, cauterizing wounds, and other minor treatments. Staircases went down to the cellar and up to their home. The back door opened onto an alley with gutters full of slime.

"Stay out of the shop front," Nicoletta instructed. "We don't need customers asking you for medical advice. Don't go upstairs unless told, and *never* go into the surgery when we're treating a patient."

She put me to work in the kitchen. No matter what, she found some way to scold me. I used too much water mopping the floor, not enough water washing dishes, and the wrong soap for scrubbing bloody linens. Seeing her struggle to reach a jar, I took it down, only for her to snap that I wasn't to touch anything without permission.

In what felt like no time, we moved onto making lunch. Nicoletta handed me a compressed brick of dried black leaves, then scoffed when I asked what to do. She showed me how to scrape bits off with a knife and brew them into a bitter tea. Lunch was wheat buns and *spianèzi te papriconne*, a blindingly spicy soup. I ate in silence. Agata and Nicoletta talked in gliding Ferish, ignoring me until Agata turned and examined my borrowed dress and bodice.

"Those won't do," she said. "I don't need anyone thinking

you trained under Sverbians when our soldiers are out hunting Rúonbattai. Nica, you'd better lend Kateiko a dress."

Nicoletta dropped her spoon. "But Grandmera, I've only got my good muslin and—"

"Your old gingham. You can spare that."

"But — what if she ruins it? It's supposed to go to my sister!"

"I'll buy a new dress," I cut in. "I've got money saved."

That was the wrong thing to say. Nicoletta shoved aside her bowl and got up. "When you're done," she told me airily, "there's dead mice in the cellar that my cat, Luna, killed. Get rid of them."

I left the apothecary wondering where to find a Ferish dressmaker. I sure wasn't going back to the Sarteres. Distracted, I walked straight into someone. Halfway through apologizing, I realized it was Tiernan.

"Did Dunehein send you to check on me?" I demanded.

He chuckled. "No. I went to the lumberyard and asked him what time you finished. I have news, although it is not a conversation for the sidewalk."

Still suspicious, I said, "Come over then. I'll make dinner. Dune and Rija won't be done work for a while."

I took a few wrong turns trying to remember the way to our new home on Shawnaast's northern edge. We'd rented a flat in a string of red-brick rowhouses, which had identical small scrubby yards and rusty iron staircases leading to the second storey flats. Our neighbours were mostly Ferish men — bricklayers and mill workers, judging from the their torn dirty clothes. I climbed our stairs, fumbled with the lock, and beckoned Tiernan in.

Our flat was a single room. We'd been sleeping on the floor with furs left over from my winter trapping. The Iyo had lent us cookware and scraped together a food donation. Rikuja had promised to build a shelf over the iron stove, the closest we could get to Rin and Iyo tradition of placing makiri over a hearth, but for now Temal's figurine of the swan and mountain cat lived on the windowsill alongside the kinaru in a resin cube.

Tiernan looked around uncertainly. He'd never been in my room at the Golden Oak. I didn't know etiquette for inviting a Sverbian man into an Aikoto home on a Ferish street, and I was too tired of propriety to care. It didn't suit us.

"Leave your sword there," I said, pointing at our pile of hunting knives. "Then can you build a fire?"

He obliged. I took a trout fillet from our cold-storage box, which I'd packed with ice chunks, and put the fillet to bake in the stove's roasting slot. Then I sat cross-legged on a bark mat and began mixing brassroot flour and water into dough. It was nice to be around someone who didn't care if I called water.

"What's your news?" I asked.

Tiernan settled on another mat. "The military has established a regiment of special forces to investigate the Rúonbattai. Captain Parr has been given command of it due to his zealousness about destroying them, and he has appointed Nerio as one of his lieutenants. They are bringing Jorum and me to the front."

The blood drained from my face. "To Nordmur, you mean."

"Yes. We leave the day after tomorrow."

Sudden anger pulsed through me. "Jorumgard says the Rúonbattai are war criminals, but all I've seen is soldiers tearing apart my homeland to find them. Now you'll be doing it, too."

Tiernan rubbed the scar on his nose. "War is never straightforward. Let me try to explain. A year ago, were you afraid of Ferish people?"

"Nei. I mean, we fought them in the past, but I'd never met any."

"What about now?"

"I'm scared of Ferish soldiers," I admitted. "And priests. And I'm scared the Sarteres will have my cousins forever."

"How far would you go to get them back?"

I frowned at him, accidentally kneading my dough into shreds.

"The Rúonbattai thrive on fear," Tiernan said. "Without it, they are fleas nipping at a powerful beast. With it, they can poison and kill the beast. Fear is the greatest weapon in the world."

"That's my point. It's not *them* I'm afraid of—"

He raised a hand until I fell silent. "A year ago, the military heard rumours the Rúonbattai had surfaced in Nordmur. The reaction was swift. People like Captain Parr wanted to root them out before they began repeating the crimes for which they are infamous. We found signs of the Rúonbattai, yet no evidence they committed a single violent act since their return other than attacking us in Brånnheå.

"Instead, the military has been violent, a military largely made of Ferish soldiers. People like you learned to fear them. Here in Eremur, Ferish civilians are terrified about the Rúonbattai's return. They distrust your people and mine, suspecting us of supporting the Rúonbattai. Fear has poisoned the land. It brings out the worst in people and breeds hatred and cruelty, which breeds more fear.

"I have to wonder, who started rumours of the Rúonbattai's return? Did someone know that simply suggesting it would provoke chaos and turn our races against each other? Does someone *want* people like you to hate the Ferish so much that you would hurt them? Kill them? Do whatever it takes to drive them out of your homeland? Who craves that more than anything?"

I looked up from laying dough in a frying pan. "You think the Rúonbattai meant for all this to happen?"

"It is certainly in line with their goals. Given how many of them died in Brånnheå, it is also not surprising they would need to weaponize others."

"But that means they baited the military into going after innocent Sverbians. After people they claim they're protecting."

"Yes. And yet they call Jorum and me traitors." Tiernan ran his hand over his face. "Believe me, I do not condone the military's reaction, but I cannot stand by and let the Rúonbattai wreak carnage. Gods know how much further they will go. What I can do is stay at Captain Parr's side and steer him toward a less brutal approach. I understand if my involvement is . . . unforgivable to you."

His voice caught. He could've just told Dunehein he was leaving, but he'd tracked me down to tell me directly. He seemed to care how I felt about it.

"I don't know," I said. "I can't forgive something that hasn't happened yet."

Tiernan nodded. "If we ever meet again, we can discuss it then."

That's when it sunk in. He might not come back alive. Even if he did, I hoped to be long gone with my cousins by then. At least our last meal together was better than our first meal of scrap stew. I served the baked trout and warm flatbread with fresh raspberries and herbal tea, a typical spring dinner for my people. We talked about nothing important, but we knew our time together was ending.

Once we'd cleaned up, Tiernan said, "I apologize for failing you, Katja. I promised to retrieve your cousins."

"You helped me get a pardon, a job, and this flat so I can be near them. There's nothing else you could do — except kidnap them."

"Do you want me to?"

I sighed. "Fleeing from soldiers got us into this situation. Dunehein says we should try to get our cousins back legally."

He shrugged. "If you change your mind, come find Jorum and me at the Golden Oak before we go."

"I won't. But can you ask Jorumgard to come here tomorrow? I'd like to say goodbye."

"Of course." Tiernan buckled his sword back on, then hesitated. "If I may . . . I would like to give you something to remember us by." He reached into his jerkin pocket and drew out the coal newt he'd whittled. The alder wood had faded to palest orange.

I took it gingerly. He wasn't a makiri carver, so it wouldn't carry part of his spirit, but it felt powerful all the same.

16.
CATERPILLARS

On a day off from work, I lurked outside the Sarteres'. Giana emerged hand in hand with two kids who trudged along with their heads down. The sight made me crumple. I hardly recognized my cousins. They wore identical blue coats, crisply ironed and trimmed in white, with matching breeches for Samulein and a skirt for Hanaiko. Her straight black hair now hung in tight curls under a wide-brimmed bonnet. Giana had not only touched her hair but *changed* it.

I followed them to a huge grassy yard surrounded by a wrought-iron fence. They went through the gates, up a gravel path bordered by colourful flags, and to a large four-storey building of red brick. My cousins went in alone and Giana left. Soon after, a bell clanged nine o'clock. I waited in a nearby alley. At noon, hundreds of kids in blue uniforms spilled into the yard, ate and played games, then filed back indoors. At half past three, Giana came to get my cousins. There wasn't a moment I could talk to them alone.

Another morning, I followed Giana, Viènzo, and my cousins to a spired stone building, one of the minor sanctes in Shawnaast. A blue-robed priest on the steps greeted them. Everyone chatting in the garden wore elaborate prints with lace and gold jewellery. I had no hope of blending in with my new plain grey dress. I hadn't even bought a bonnet, since I hated the look of them.

"Better stop following 'em," Dunehein said that night. "We don't wanna spook the Sarteres. Just do your work and stay out of trouble."

I obeyed reluctantly. Seeing my cousins again had lit a fire under my skin. I daydreamed about finding Yotolein and bringing him to the Sarteres. He'd sweep into the shop, a storm of hatred and rage, and sweep back out with a child in each arm. It felt hopeless, though. Even if I could find him, he'd probably leave the Sarteres' shop in handcuffs.

Kianta kolo, I told myself. *The sap will flow*. But the promise felt hollow when spring was already here and I kept losing as many people as I got back.

The flowers outside the apothecary shed their blossoms. Cottonwood catkins burst open and covered the ground in white fluff. As the last of it washed away in rain, a swarm of caterpillars flooded Shawnaast. It looked like a wriggling shroud had fallen over the district. The streets turned green with smushed caterpillars. On my afternoons off, I went to the Golden Oak to see Akohin, who said in all his travels along the coast, he'd never seen an influx this bad.

Nicoletta didn't handle it well. I was scrubbing the surgery floor, cursing my stiff corset, when I heard a screech. I hurried to the back alley. Nicoletta whacked a crate with a broom, knocking off caterpillars. With every whack she shrieked in incoherent Ferish.

"Is that a delivery?" I asked.

"Yes — the idiot — just left it—"

I pushed her inside. After checking she wasn't looking through the window, I called water from the rain barrels and blasted the crate clean. I tossed away the last few caterpillars and dragged the crate into the kitchen. Nicoletta was pouring tea into her favourite cup, blue porcelain with painted roses.

"Why is it wet?" she demanded.

"Tea is always wet."

"The *crate*, you ninny." Nicoletta pried its lid off, releasing an aroma of herbs and soil. The canvas bags inside were dry. All she said was "Hm."

Agata bustled into the kitchen, her face flushed. "I'm off to help the midwife," she said, tossing bleached linens into a basket of vials and jars. "The grocer's daughter went into labour early. I might not be home until tomorrow." She grabbed her shawl and hurried out.

"So I have to go through all this myself?" Nicoletta grumbled, kicking the crate.

"What is it?" I asked.

"Useless, probably. One of our suppliers broke his leg, so his son's doing the foraging instead, but the doorstop of a boy doesn't know what anything is. He keeps bringing weeds and acting like they're made of gold." She picked a bag at random and upended it, dumping muddy round roots into a bowl. "Are these supposed to be onions?"

"They look like brassroot. It's hard to tell without the flowers." I cut one open and licked the inside. My tongue burned. I made a face and spat into the fire. "Never mind. It's chokeroot. There's enough poison here to kill a mountain goat."

Nicoletta slammed her cup down, splashing tea over the table. "You think you're so clever, don't you? So tough and talented?"

"What?" I said, taken aback.

"I read your reference letter. You washed out a soldier's mouth, like that makes you some great healer. *I've* spent my whole life learning this—"

"You have to be right about everything, don't you?" I snapped. "If you'd rather watch your customers die frothing at the mouth—"

A yowl interrupted me. We both whirled. Shrieks and hisses came from the back alley.

"Luna!" Nicoletta cried. "She keeps fighting with the baker's cat. Oh, no!" She grabbed the broom and ran out.

I gripped the table and drew long, slow breaths. The memory of Jorumgard spasming on the grass had rattled me. I'd hardly gotten back to scrubbing the surgery when the bell over the front door tinkled. A boy called out in Ferish. I scrambled up, swearing and twisting my petticoats back into place.

I found the boy in the kitchen, sitting on the table and eating a wheat bun. He looked younger than me, skinny with a mess of curly auburn hair. His shirt collar was unbuttoned and his rolled-up sleeves revealed scabby elbows. On the floor lay a blue-and-white coat and a scuffed leather satchel.

"Who are you?" I asked.

"Matéo Solus," he said with a mouthful of bread. "Agata's grandson. Who are *you*?"

"Kateiko Leniere. The new chore girl."

"Kateiko sounds like a boy's name."

"In my language, Matéo sounds like a girl's name," I replied, still grumpy.

We stared each other down. Suddenly he grinned.

"Fair enough," he said, hopping off the table. He was a palm-width shorter than me. "Where's Grandmera? My mother sent me to get some stuff."

"Uh — Agata's helping the midwife. And Nicoletta's out chasing her cat."

"Again? Whatever, I'll get it myself." Matéo stuffed the rest of the bun in his mouth, grabbed his satchel, and headed into the front room.

I followed him. If he really was Agata's grandson, I couldn't tell him to get out, but I didn't want to let some random kid steal medicine. He pulled a crumpled paper from his pocket and began browsing the shelves, sliding jars and vials into his satchel.

"You seem pissed off," Matéo said. "Was my sister giving you a hard time?"

"Nei," I said, determined not to complain.

"Liar. Want me to put caterpillars in her tea?"

"Huh? Why?"

"'Cause she's Nica," he said like that explained everything. He stopped at a shelf that was empty except for dust. "Where's the laudanum?"

My cheeks flushed. "I don't know what that is."

"Really? It's poppy essence and grain alcohol. People use it for pain, coughs, sleep, pretty much everything."

"Ai, wait — I do recognize that. The military bought most of it, so Agata put the rest in the surgery for patients. She—"

Once more, an ear-splitting shriek interrupted me. I thought it was a cat again until Nicoletta screeched, "MATÉO!"

He grinned. "Guess Nica found her tea."

My jaw dropped. Nicoletta swooped into the doorway, clutching her hissing cat. She looked ready to explode, red-faced and puffed up. I clapped a hand over my mouth to hide a laugh.

"You horrid little . . ." Nicoletta released her cat, who streaked away. She stormed across the room and whacked Matéo with the broom. "Get whatever Mera needs and go home. And don't think I won't tell her about this!"

Matéo raised his hands in mock apology. On his way to the surgery, he winked at me. "Good luck, chore girl."

Later, I realized Matéo's coat had looked familiar. Agata confirmed he attended the same school I'd followed Hanaiko and Samulein to. I wasn't sure if I should ask him about them, though. He didn't seem trustworthy, unlike Nicoletta, who I trusted to consistently be in a sour mood. After our spat, she started giving me tasks like dissecting frogs and stewing pig heads, declaring that I should be used to it as a trapper.

Akohin tolerated me venting my annoyance. He found the stablehand as difficult as I found Nicoletta. When the caterpillar flood settled down, we packed a lunch and went to Bjørn Park, the largest park in Shawnaast. A Sverbian wedding was happening under a long timber shelter decorated with flowers. Fiddle music drifted toward us. I sprawled out in the shade of an alder while Akohin examined its branches tented in gauzy sheets of cocoons.

"I wonder what caused all these caterpillars," he said. "Odd weather, maybe. This spring seems warmer than usual."

"Maybe that jinra-saidu down south is getting revenge," I said, only half-listening.

"That's not the only saidu who's awake, you know." Akohin pulled a few cocoon strands loose and watched them sway in a breeze. "Remember the story of a tel-saidu who learned our language? The Iyo call him Ainu-Seru and itherans call him Suriel.

Anyway, he never went dormant. My great-great-grandfather Imarein Rin lived with him."

I frowned. "I'm Rin and I've never heard of Imarein."

"That's not surprising. He got really messed up — sleeping with a knife, screaming in the night, thinking he was still in battle — so at sixteen he ran away to find Ainu-Seru."

"When did he have your great-grandparent then?"

"Oh, he knocked up a Dona girl before running away. I don't think he ever found out."

I winced. Akohin said nothing else. My mind wandered, slotting us into the roles of troubled Dona and Rin teenagers hooking up. I stifled a laugh. Kissing Akohin was about as appealing as kissing the cocoon-laden alder, and he'd never shown interest in anyone at all.

My daydreams didn't work with anyone else, either. Jonalin was in prison. I had no idea where Rokiud was. Somehow in a city of a hundred thousand people, I felt totally alone. I tore up a handful of grass, wondering if the blades would look like caterpillars in Nicoletta's tea.

The next time Matéo turned up, he dropped his leather satchel on the kitchen floor and rummaged through a cupboard before noticing me. He waved, his mouth full of biscuit, and held out a tin. I inspected a biscuit before eating it. It was dry, peppery, and completely normal. Maybe I'd judged him too quickly.

"Ai, do you know Aniya and Sohin Sartere?" I asked. "They go to your school."

"How old are they?"

I had to think about that. "Sohin's six. Aniya's ninth birthday is any day now."

"Then I don't know 'em," Matéo said in between bites of his third biscuit. "Every year is in a different grade. I'm with the fourteen-year-olds."

"Really?" I raised my eyebrows. "Keep eating. You need to grow."

He stuck out his tongue. "Who are the kids?"

"My cousins. They got adopted by a Ferish couple who won't let me see them. The couple doesn't believe we're related."

Matéo looked at me, chewing another biscuit. Something stirred deep in his eyes, which were so green they looked like mossy pools. "I'll ask around. Some of my friends have siblings that age."

Hope buoyed me through my next shifts. I kept glancing at the doors and peering through the windows for any sign of Matéo. Nicoletta scolded me for not paying attention to my work. After a week, I started to think Matéo had forgotten. My family wouldn't matter to him.

Then suddenly he was there, dropping his satchel and grinning. "Found 'em!"

My paring knife slipped and cut my thumb. I swore and sucked away the blood.

"I was looking in the wrong place," Matéo said. "Your cousins got put in remedial classes 'cause they don't understand Ferish."

"Are they okay?" I asked, fumbling through shelves of bandages. "What'd they say?"

"Nothing." He nabbed a handful of salted beans from a bowl. "They looked scared of me. You better talk to 'em yourself."

"I can't—"

"Sure you can." Matéo glanced around, making sure we were alone in the kitchen. "I'll go upstairs and get Nica's old uniform. You put it on, come to school at lunchtime, and pretend you're a student. I'll take you to 'em. My brother's friend's sister says they always eat in the same part of the yard."

I took the uniform home and tried it on. The coat sleeves and skirt were far too short, but Matéo had pointed out it was the end of the school year and everyone had outgrown their uniforms. I wasn't desperate enough to do it without permission, though. I asked after dinner, when Dunehein was contented by a full stomach and Rikuja had finished putting salve on her hands, which were cracked from hours of scrubbing laundry.

Neither of them liked the idea. Instead, to my mixed relief and dread, Dunehein decided it was time to visit the Sarteres again. Over the next few days we got letters from our landlord and employers, confirming we had a home and steady work, and we all arranged time off for the first day of the weekend, when the kids wouldn't be in school or at the sancte.

We barely got into the Sarteres' shop. The moment Viènzo recognized us, he threw us out. Dunehein stood his ground on the sidewalk, huge hands balled at his sides, asking somewhere between a beg and a bellow if we could please just *talk* to our cousins. People leaned out of neighbouring shops to stare. Not until Viènzo started shouting at them to call the Elkhounds did Dunehein turn away, shaking so hard I thought he might shift into his grizzly bear form.

"Hope you kept that uniform," he told me in a low voice.

Matéo met me at the schoolyard gates, mischief sparkling in his smile. He took two squished buns from his satchel and gave me one. "Eat that and act normal."

I followed him across the yard. Students of all ages filled the lawn, basking in brilliant sunshine and swatting at clouds of moths that kept landing in their lunch pails. Boys played catch and girls jumped rope. A harassed-looking Ferish woman hurried among the kids, breaking up scuffles and separating couples holding hands.

Several older boys had sprawled across a group of stone benches. "Hey, Solus!" one called. "Who's your girl?"

"*His* girl?" another boy jeered. "He's half her size. Looks like he belongs to *her*."

A third boy, built like a cart with a broad chest and no neck, got up and stood in our way. "She's pretty," he said, tossing a small leather ball from hand to hand. "How'd you snag her, Solus? Your grandmera start selling love potions?"

"Why, you need one?" Matéo said. "That's the only way *you'd* get near a girl, Covonnus."

"Don't get smart with me," Covonnus snarled.

"I won't. It's wasted on you." Matéo tried to move around him.

Covonnus moved with him. "Where you two sneaking off to?"

"We caught a snake, so we're gonna release it out the back gate. Wanna see?" Matéo opened his satchel.

Covonnus blanched, stumbling backward and dropping his ball. The other boys laughed. Matéo smirked and pulled me away from them.

"What was that about?" I asked.

"That boy kept pestering Nica when she went here, so I put a garter snake in his lunch pail. Turns out he's scared shitless of 'em. He blacked my eye for it, but I kept slipping him snakes until he left Nica alone."

I didn't know what was more baffling — being scared of harmless little snakes, Matéo defending Nicoletta, or anyone mistaking him and me for lovers. I pushed all those thoughts aside. I thrummed with nervousness at finally talking to Hanaiko and Samulein, rehearsing what I'd say, wondering how to explain we didn't know where their father was.

Matéo led me behind the school to a birch copse. He stopped, looked around, went into the copse, and came back pulling empty cocoons off his uniform. "This is where I found 'em last week," he said.

My hopes plummeted. "Maybe they're scared you'll talk to them again."

He chewed a ragged fingernail. "They're probably still inside, then. Their classrooms are on the top floor."

I looked up at the four storeys of red brick and gabled windows. "Am I allowed up there?"

"Sure. The teachers will be on the ground floor, anyway. That's where the office is."

I was so close that giving up would be unbearable. We slipped into the back lobby, which smelled strongly of paint from a half-finished mural of the ocean. Another wall had cork boards covered in papers. Moths fluttered around the ceiling rafters. Matéo, not bothering to wipe his shoes on the doormat, bounded up a staircase. Three girls coming down jostled out of his way.

On the fourth floor, we emerged at the corner of two dim corridors. Daisy chains decorated the walls. Matéo moved along the left corridor, trying doors. They were all locked except one. Over his shoulder, I glimpsed wooden desks and benches — then he slammed the door shut.

"*Merdo*," he swore, grabbing my hand. He dragged me down the hall. "A teacher's inside."

"So? You said we're allowed up here—"

"*You* are. C'mon, hurry."

Matéo pulled me into a shadowy alcove full of shelves, brooms, mops, and crates. Coal dust covered the floor and cobwebs hung from the ceiling. It was all I could do not to sneeze.

"I'm kinda . . . banned from this floor," Matéo whispered. "Don't ask why."

"What happens if you get caught?"

"Never mind that. I'll distract the teacher while you look for your cousins—"

"Nei!" I seized his wrist. "Someone took the fall for me once before. He's in prison now. I'm not letting that happen again."

Matéo blinked. "Well, it's not that bad. But I'll get expelled."

A floorboard creaked, followed by approaching footsteps. We flattened ourselves against a wall — and together we noticed our tracks in the coal dust. It was too late to sweep them away. Struck by an idea, I grabbed Matéo's face and kissed him.

"*Sacra flore*!" a woman cried.

Matéo looked too shocked to speak. I whirled and drew up to my full height, blocking him from view.

"It's my fault," I said. "I brought him here."

The teacher squinted at me. Her misty eyes, curly white hair, and woolen shawls reminded me of a sheep. "What's your name, girl?"

"Lucreza," I said wildly. "Lucreza Leniere."

"A Ferish name, yet you speak Coast Trader to a teacher?"

"I—" My mind blanked. "Well—"

I glanced behind me. Matéo had his head down, fumbling with his satchel. As the teacher yanked me into the corridor, Matéo dropped something.

Glass shattered across the floor. Huge hairy wolf spiders skittered out of the wreckage. The teacher shrieked and stumbled away, holding up her skirts. Matéo leapt over the spiders and said, "Run!"

We barrelled back the way we'd come. A group of students was blocking the staircase. We turned down the other corridor instead. As we passed an alcove, I glimpsed two small startled faces. I hit the wall to slow my momentum and spun back around. Hanaiko and Samulein sat on a wooden bench, staring open-mouthed at me.

"You're here," I gasped. "You're really here."

Hanaiko got up. Trembling, she moved in front of Samulein like she was guarding him.

"It's me," I said, stunned. "Eko, your cousin. Don't you recognize me?"

She nodded.

"I've been trying to see you, but the Sarteres wouldn't let me. We have another cousin here — Emehein's brother, Dunehein. Remember those names? Kirbana and Kel are in town, too. We all miss you."

Hanaiko's blue eyes glittered with tears. Her lips moved, but no sound came out.

I dropped to my knees in front of her. "What?" I breathed. "What'd you say?"

"You left us," she whispered. "In the orphanage."

"I'm so sorry. I would've gotten arrested if I came for you. I spent all winter trying to find a way. Please forgive me—"

But Hanaiko was shaking her head. Behind her, Samulein curled into a ball, hiding his face.

A bell clanged, making us jump. Matéo appeared at my side and said, "We gotta go. Classes are about to start."

"Come with me," I begged my cousins. "I'll take you home to our family. You never have to see the Sarteres again."

I reached toward Hanaiko. She flinched. At that single motion, that terrified flinch, my heart cracked in half. Nothing I said or did in this corridor could mend what was broken.

17.

REUNION

Worn out and defeated, I dragged myself to my next shift at the apothecary. Matéo showed up after school. We sat on crates in the alley, shelling beans into a bucket, an excuse to talk alone. Now that the shock of my cousins' rejection had faded, another question had floated into my mind.

"Why'd you do it?" I asked. "Why take me somewhere you're banned?"

"I like a challenge." Matéo flicked a bean pod at me.

"I'm serious. Helping someone you barely know can't be worth getting expelled."

His grin faded. "Has Nica told you anything about our family?"

"Nei. She mostly just lectures me."

He glanced at the windows and door, although they were shut to keep out moths. "We all got really sick a couple years ago. Our baby sister died. One brother went blind, and another — well, his muscles are all jerky and he can't talk right anymore. Now they go to a special boarding school in southern Eremur. With Nica living here at the shop, there's only three of us kids left at home. I know what it's like to miss your family."

I gaped at him, tossing beans at the bucket and missing. "Is that why Nicoletta's always in a bad mood?"

Matéo rolled his eyes. "Don't ask me to explain Nica. She came out of our mother's womb screaming about the mess."

I snorted. "Well, thanks anyway. Not many people would've done that for me."

"Not many people would've used a kiss as a distraction." His ears went red under his messy curls. "The priests say people aren't supposed to kiss until they're engaged."

"Really?" I clapped a hand to my mouth. "Kaid. I'm sorry."

He shrugged, back to grinning. "I didn't mind. What's life without breaking some rules?"

Matéo seemed to have meant what he said, since he started coming by the apothecary more often. I found myself looking forward to his visits. I should've been figuring out ways to earn back my cousins' trust, but thinking of them was like picking an open sore. Instead I kept drifting into daydreams of kissing Matéo. I formed a bad knack for dropping things whenever he was around, as if I needed another way to annoy Nicoletta.

Her scolding got so bad that I decided to invite Matéo somewhere else. I didn't have much time left. Their brothers at boarding school would come home soon for summer holidays, so he'd be busy with them. At work, I twitched every time I heard the bell at the front door, prompting Agata to offer me a dose of hellseed tincture to calm the nerves.

In midafternoon, the bell was followed by Nicoletta's shriek. I bolted into the front room. A line of people was filing in — Dunehein, Rikuja, Kirbana with Kel in her arms, and four muddy, windswept figures. I stared at the leather and braided hair and weapons crowding the room. The three muddy men were barechested and the woman wore a sleeveless shirt, showing their tattoos. Nicoletta clutched her cat, Luna, struck silent.

"God above us all," Agata said behind me.

"You—" I held the counter, my knees weak. "Where — how did you—"

Temal scooped me off the ground in a bear hug. A moment later, Tema was kissing my pinned-up hair. I couldn't stop grinning. Yotolein gave me a tight nod. Kirbana introduced the fourth muddy person as her husband, Narun Dona. He smiled warmly and went back to cooing over his son. Kirbana was so wide-eyed with love and awe she looked ready to make another baby.

"Oh, little fireweed," Temal said, hugging me again and beaming. "You've grown."

Agata sent me off, saying to take as much time away from work as I wanted. My family had heard a short version of what happened to my cousins, which explained why Yotolein was only glaring at me, not throttling me. Once we'd crammed all nine people into our flat, Kel scooting around on bark mats, Temal began to tell their tale. He spoke low and serious, not in his normal storytelling way with big voices and gestures.

"Something happened in the Rin-jouyen about two months ago, an argument of sorts. I'll get to that in a bit. Afterward, we left to get Kateiko, Hanaiko, and Samulein from the island refuge. It took weeks to find a Dona captain who could take us there. Nordmur is in shambles. Eremur's navy took over Caladsten and a few other major towns. They're checking every ship in the ports, trying to find Rúonbattai.

"At the refuge, we learned the kids never arrived. We met Narun there, who said his wife and child hadn't made it, either. He thought they'd missed the last sailing before winter, but I remembered seeing a Sverbian woman with a baby board the *Ridge Duck*, so Narun came back to the mainland with us to look for you all. By luck, we met a Dona woman who'd sailed with you and got deported back north. She said Kirbana had been awaiting a custody hearing. We didn't have high hopes you'd still be in Caladheå, but we came south and snuck into town. An Iyo boy named Airedain told us you're living here."

"We sent him to Aeti Ginu two months ago," Dunehein said. "He must've gotten there just days after you left."

Tema smiled wryly. "I imagine he got quite the reception. Isu has disowned us."

"What in Aeldu-yan happened?" I asked, pouring tea. We didn't have enough mugs, so I had to serve some in bowls.

"Things have been strange for a while," Temal said. "You saw it yourself, Behadul banning us from the coast and being evasive about why. When Eremur's navy showed up at Aeti, some of us got suspicious. We spent the winter following Behadul and his family to secret meetings with Sverbians. Over time, we realized they were working with the Rúonbattai."

"But—" I stammered. "Fendul made it sound like the navy were wrong to suspect the Rin. It's *true*?"

"Yes," Yotolein said with disgust. "Behadul threw me under the cart, claiming the navy followed me to Aeti Ginu. He let me send my children away to protect them from my supposed crimes instead of admitting *his* family are the traitors."

Images from Brånnheå flashed through my mind — the oak and lilacs planted like an Aikoto crest, the kinaru in a resin cube. I felt sick. Kirbana's expression dawned with understanding, probably as she pieced together why I was afraid for anyone to learn about Yotolein.

"We didn't reveal our discovery right away," Temal went on. "With Ferish soldiers storming Nordmur, it's hard to argue against the Rúonbattai. But then we learned something we couldn't ignore. The Rúonbattai leader, Liet, is trying to wake the saidu and use them as a weapon against the Ferish."

"Yan kaid." I set down the teapot. "I've seen what an angry jinra-saidu can do."

Tema squeezed my hand. Her pained smile said enough.

"Nothing's worth messing with nature that way," Rikuja said, at the stove reheating stew. "Saidu are ancient spirits, not dogs that can be trained to do someone's bidding."

"Exactly," Temal said. "So we told the rest of the Rin, and one of our people challenged Behadul as okorebai. Behadul kept his position by claiming he doesn't support that particular plan, but I don't trust a proven liar. We left Aeti the next day along with my family, Nisali's, Rokiud's, and about two hundred other people. There hasn't been a schism like this since the Dona-jouyen formed."

Dunehein folded his hands over his face. "And my mother and brother are on the opposite side?"

Tema scoffed. "You know what Isu and Emehein are like. Loyal to the Rin even if it kills them."

"Both sides agreed to keep the reason for the schism quiet, though," Temal said. "Other jouyen will be less tolerant of the Rúonbattai alliance."

"What happens next?" Rikuja opened the dish cupboard, realized the bowls were being used for tea, and started ladling stew into flowerpots she'd recently built. "Are you leaving the Rin for good?"

"Maybe. We haven't decided yet."

"The Dona-jouyen will accept deserters without too many questions," Narun said with his arm around Kirbana. "I don't know where my okorebai is these days, though. Our priority was finding our families."

"Which has been harder than expected," Yotolein added with a scowl my way.

"Don't blame Kateiko," Kirbana cut in. Pink patches appeared on her cheeks. "She fought as soldiers tore your children from her arms, and you wouldn't believe the lengths she's gone to get them back."

"We know where they are, at least," Dunehein said. "And the Sarteres can't claim the kids are orphans now that you're here, Yotolein. Problem is, they threaten to call the Elkhounds whenever we go near them. If you get caught being in Eremur illegally, you'll get locked up faster than you can say knife. The military started cracking down on immigration when the Rúonbattai returned."

"Then what am I supposed to do?" Yotolein demanded. "Let brown pigeons keep my children?"

"Be here legally." The words left my mouth before the idea had fully formed. "I earned residency and a pardon by helping the military. You could, too."

His mouth twisted. "I'm not turning mercenary for soldiers who murdered my wife."

"You might not have to. Just sell secrets about the Rúonbattai. The captain who pardoned me, Antoch Parr, leads the regiment investigating them."

"It's a thought," Rikuja said slowly. "But it'd be hard to give anything away with outing the Rin."

I pressed my fingers to my lips, thinking. "We could go through Tiernan. I already found something linking us to the Rúonbattai — sort of a magical garden in their old base, designed like our crests — and he promised not to tell anyone. He can pass some info to Parr and use the rest to guide the military away from us."

"Do you trust him?" Tema asked.

It took a second to realize she was asking me, not Dunehein or Rikuja. Like my opinion mattered. I looked at the coal newt on our makiri shelf, remembering my last conversation with Tiernan. He'd been right that the Rúonbattai were dangerous. And above all else, he'd always been kind.

Kirbana was the only one of us who could write, so I dictated a letter and she took it to the military headquarters to be sent to Tiernan. Narun wanted to barter for residency, too. They were thinking of staying in Caladheå. For now, Narun got enough carpentry work to rent a flat in Førstown, letting Kirbana quit her wet nurse job and move out of her employer's house.

Twice a day I checked our postal box, which had rusted shut from disuse. The passing time felt like having constant vertigo — cooking with my parents again, spending my days with them instead of at work, rolling over in my sleep and bumping into someone where before there had been space.

Spring turned into summer. The markets stopped selling raspberries and started selling huckleberries. Iyo sold us chokecherries, salmonberries, and brassroot at good prices because itherans didn't buy them. On a hot evening, with our windows open to let in the breeze, we heard footsteps on the iron stairs outside. I stuck my head out a window. Tiernan and Jorumgard were climbing up, their sword hilts glinting orange in the twilight.

"Hello, Katja," Tiernan said with a smile.

I flung open the door. "I didn't think you'd come in person."

"We told Captain Parr it would be worth the information we brought back. I hope that is true."

Jorumgard thumped my shoulder, grinning. "Good to see you, little pint."

I beckoned them in and made the introductions. My parents raised their hands and said our traditional greeting, but Yotolein kept his arms folded. Being stuck here while his kids were so close had done nothing for his mood. Dunehein laid out two more bark mats. I passed out iced tea, a luxury of being able to freeze water in any weather.

"Your letter was rather sparse," Tiernan told me. "I take it these are the people who need residency?"

"Yeah, plus Kirbana's husband. They're staying in Førstown. And . . . my uncle Yotolein might need a pardon."

"What for?"

Yotolein answered like the words were being dragged from him. "I spent eight years as a courier for the Rúonbattai. My late wife, Tove Karinehl, worked for them as a seamstress. That's all, I swear. We never fought for them, never knew their plans."

Tiernan frowned. "Your work undoubtedly got people killed. You must have known that."

"I took the job right after the Third Elken War, after seeing Ferish soldiers slaughter my people and yours. I thought anyone hurt by the Rúonbattai deserved it. When I couldn't lie to myself any longer, I quit. I've had nothing to do with them for over a decade."

"I can sympathize." Jorumgard pulled up his tunic sleeve to reveal the crown tattoo on his wrist. "I used to be a Kånehlbattai in Sverba. I'd bet my sword I did more harm in one year than you did in eight, telling myself I was protecting my people. Like you, I wised up and deserted, leaving queen and country behind."

I choked on my tea. "You told me you fled because you pissed off a warlord."

He chuckled dryly. "A warlord who wears the crown of Sverba."

Yotolein was looking at Jorumgard strangely. His brows were furrowed, but the set of his shoulders had eased.

"There is good news," Tiernan said. "In all our time investigating the Rúonbattai, I have never heard the names Yotolein Rin or Tove Karinehl. As far as the military knows, there is no crime to pardon. I suggest keeping it that way. The bad news is I doubt your knowledge of the Rúonbattai is relevant anymore. Most of their force was killed and Brånnheå was destroyed."

"Oh, it's relevant," Temal said. "We've been following their allies for months."

Tiernan and Jorumgard exchanged a look.

"Let's be clear, though," Tema said. "Our daughter trusts you to only use our information against Sverbians. Our people are our responsibility. If the military attacks the Aikoto Confederacy, we'll declare open war."

Tiernan sighed, tapping his mug. "Jorum and I can only promise so much. We will be judicious with your information, and we have some influence over Captain Parr, but we are foreign mercenaries. We cannot stop the military from acting."

Temal nodded. "That's about what we expected."

Fading sunlight dyed the room red as he, Tema, and Yotolein described how the Rin had helped the Rúonbattai — providing food and canoes, allowing passage through Anwen Bel, spying and passing information. My family knew meeting spots, supply routes, even the names of a few Rúonbattai. Tiernan took notes on it all. What really caught his attention was Liet's plan to wake the saidu.

"Gods help us all," he murmured, and Jorumgard's expression echoed his words. "How does Liet intend to wake them? Murdering more sacred animals?"

"I doubt it," Tema said. "The Rúonbattai know about that jinra-saidu destroying Brånnheå, and killing kinaru to wake tel-saidu would end the Rin alliance. They'll hold out for a better way."

"There *is* one tel-saidu who stayed awake," Rikuja said. "Ainu-Seru, the mountain owl. Liet won't be able to use him, though. He just wants to be left alone."

The mention of kinaru reminded me. "Tiernan, Jorumgard, there's something about Brånnheå I didn't tell you," I admitted. I took the resin cube from our makiri shelf. "I found this in the stavehall, behind the altar. We think the kinaru inside is a Rin makiri."

Tiernan raised the cube, examining it. Lamplight shone through its clear depths. "What is a makiri?"

"A sacred guardian figurine," Jorumgard said.

My family looked at him in surprise.

"I had a Dona lover once," he explained. "He taught me some things."

Yotolein gave him another odd look, but I didn't have time to ponder it. Temal was already speaking.

"Jorumgard has the gist of it. If a carving receives the right blessings, it becomes a potential vessel for the human spirit. A person then gifts it to someone — usually a relative, lover, or friend — transferring a fragment of the gifter's spirit into the makiri in the process. It's mostly symbolic while the gifter is alive, but after they die, the fragment 'lives on' in a sense, offering protection.

"Aeldu knows why the Rúonbattai had this one, or if there's a spirit fragment inside. I trained as a makiri carver, but I can't sense anything through the resin, and the usual ways of removing it — sanding, solvents, and so on — might damage the spirit. I've never heard of anyone sealing up a makiri before. It's barbaric."

Tiernan's brow crinkled with thought. "I could melt the resin, if you trust me to."

"I don't know if itheran magic is precise enough for this. No offence."

"Tiernan can do it. I watched him make this." I picked up the carved coal newt, perfectly burnt to match a real newt's colouring.

Temal looked grudgingly impressed. "Go ahead, then. I can't in good conscience leave a spirit trapped."

Tiernan held the cube in his palm and closed his eyes. Heat radiated from him. The resin glowed orange and melted like hot wax. He held it over a bowl to catch the drippings, then rinsed the figurine in our water pail, sending up billows of steam. Quickly he handed it to Temal.

We watched with bated breath. Temal closed his fist around the kinaru, then ever so slowly unfurled his fingers. His eyes fixed on the wood as if in deep conversation. The temperature had dropped back to normal by the time he looked up from his reverie, blinking.

"Waredul Rin," he said.

Tema gasped. "Behadul's grandfather? An Okorebai-Rin is in there?"

"Yes, and has been for a long time. He died twenty-five years ago. I remember because it's the year I attuned. While I'd rather believe the Rúonbattai stole this, it seems Behadul's family might've allied with them much earlier than we thought."

"Yan taku," Dunehein said. "That means they were allied through the Third Elken War, and the Rúonbattai's most violent years after it."

Rikuja got up and paced in the small gap between us and our beds. "It could be much earlier than *that*. Not just the Rin, either.

I think some Iyo supported the Rúonbattai. Kako told us about glowing lilacs in Brånnheå. There are lilac bushes around Toel Ginu's shrine, but they're not native to this region. The seeds were a gift from Sverbians fifty years ago."

I sucked in a breath. "That's right. I recognized the scent because Malana had lilac perfume, but I forgot that your family brought it on a trading trip."

"Well, it doesn't seem like that alliance held," Tema said, tilting the bowl of melted resin. It had cooled and hardened into a clump. "We didn't see any trace of Iyo involvement. Better keep an eye on Tokoda, though."

"As for this" — Temal held up the makiri — "now that I've unsealed it, Waredul can hear us, which I'm not comfortable with. I'll take it to the river and release his spirit into the water. Hopefully he finds his way back home."

"I suppose that ends tonight's conversation, then." Tiernan got up and stretched. "It has certainly been informative. Thank you. I will write to Captain Parr and arrange your residency."

18.
LADY OF THE WOODS

One steamy, sticky afternoon, I came back from the downtown fish market and found Temal on the staircase outside, whittling a bowl. Curls of wood fell through the stair gaps to the ground. Tema's voice came through the shuttered window, cut off by Yotolein's shouting.

"What's going on?" I asked.

Temal patted the space next to him for me to sit down. "A courier brought our papers. Yotolein insisted on going to the Sarteres' right away. We told him to bring you, Dunehein, or Rikuja, someone the Sarteres know, but he was too impatient."

My stomach dropped like it'd fallen through the stairs, too. "How badly did it go?"

"Well, the Sarteres believe he's the kids' father. But they asked why he sent Hanaiko and Samulein away, where he's been, all that. They refused to let him see them unless he answered. Yotolein lost his temper, so the Sarteres called him a savage who's not fit to raise children, and . . . you can imagine. Viènzo's got a broken nose now. We had to drag Yotolein out."

I put my head down into my folded arms. "Oh, kaid."

Temal sighed. "Sometimes I think he hasn't grown up. Then again, maybe I'd be acting the same way if they had you."

I didn't dare go inside until Yotolein calmed down, so I left. But as I crossed a footbridge over the Stengar, I realized there wasn't anyone I wanted to see in Førstown. Tiernan and Jorumgard had left on military business, using the info we'd given them. I couldn't handle Akohin's sullen silences. I couldn't face Kirbana kissing Narun and cooing over Kel — a happy, intact family.

With nowhere to go, I leaned on the wooden bridge railing and watched people on the muddy bank. Women scrubbed laundry and men fished. Barefoot children played in the water, splashing around to cool off. It took me a few minutes to realize who five kids with curly auburn hair must be.

I walked down toward them. Matéo was pulling a small rusted trap out of a weedy patch. A girl held the hands of a boy about Samulein's age, helping him walk through the water. His steps were jerky, but his face glowed with a smile. Two more boys shrieked and giggled as they splashed each other. One kept turning his head, and I guessed he was Matéo's blind brother, listening for the other boy.

"What are you catching?" I asked Matéo.

He looked up and grinned. "Leeches. Grandmera needs 'em."

"How come?"

"Leeching," he said like it was obvious. He pulled a slimy black lump from the trap and tossed it into a bucket of water. "You know, to suck out bad blood. Haven't you seen the leech tank at the apothecary?"

I blanched. "Agata uses those on people?"

Matéo snickered. "So you *are* scared of something."

"I am not. It's just that blood's sacred to my people. I'd never bleed someone as medicine."

"Then you'll never work in the surgery." He put a minnow head in the trap and dropped it back in the river. "And now I know how to freak you out if we ever get in a fight."

I shoved him. But secretly, I liked the thought of seeing him often enough to fight. It was the closest to a happy thought I had.

Stormy was the nicest way to describe Yotolein's mood. I went back to work as an excuse to avoid my family's endless arguments about what to do next. Like in my daydreams, Yotolein wanted to barge into the Sarteres' and take his kids, but I'd never bothered to imagine *where* he'd take them. My parents refused to return to Aeti Ginu, and nowhere else in Anwen Bel was safe anymore.

I felt bad about avoiding Akohin, since his only family here was an uncle in prison. But on my way to visit him one day, I got sidetracked. Tiernan and Jorumgard were in the pub eating lunch and poring over papers. They waved me over.

"When did you get back to Caladheå?" I asked, lifting my skirt to swing my legs over the log bench.

"Last night," Jorumgard said. "But never mind about us, little pint. You look gloomy enough to sink a ship."

I heaved a sigh. "The Sarteres won't give my cousins back. They called Yotolein savage, heathen, a whole bunch of horrible things."

"No," he said, thunderstruck. "They're keeping his own children from him?"

"My offer to kidnap them still stands," Tiernan said.

"Believe me, we're thinking about it. My friend Matéo offered to set snakes loose in the sancte as a distraction."

Tiernan's brow creased. "Snakes in the sancte," he murmured, pushing a chunk of whitefish around his plate. "That might work."

"What? I didn't mean it seriously—"

"Neither did I, but your friend is onto something. In Ferish religion, snakes represent evil. Remember I said fear is the greatest weapon in the world? We need a metaphorical snake, some way to intimidate a god-fearing couple without letting them use Elkhounds as a shield."

"I know that look," Jorumgard said. "You've got an idea."

Tiernan nodded. "Thanks to the Rúonbattai, nothing scares Ferish people more these days than Sverbians. I think we ought to arrange a visit with the children's mother."

"But her blood's in the ground," I said.

"The Sarteres have no proof of that." A smile pulled at Tiernan's mouth. "Nor that she is mortal."

"Remind me who I'm supposed to be?" I asked as Kirbana painted white dots on my face.

"Thymarai, Lady of the Woods," she said. "Goddess of fertility, love, beauty, and, for some reason, juniper trees."

"What a leap from a child of the forest," I muttered.

Half my disguise was from my winter attire. This being a summer night, I sweltered in my shirt and leggings made of scrap leather. Kirbana had glued a pair of deer antlers to my scalp and draped feathery lichen from them. My hair fell in thin braids decorated with my trout-vertebrae beads.

Kirbana had offered to be Thymarai, since she looked more like a Sverbian goddess with her pale skin and hair, but I refused to put her in danger when she had a baby at home. It had to be me, anyway.

Reuniting Yotolein and my cousins felt like the only way to earn their forgiveness.

Jorumgard and Dunehein would act as *bjørnbattai*, legendary bear shapeshifters and my guards in myth and reality. They each wore their hair in a high rope-like braid that swung when they moved. Both men were shirtless. Dunehein had painted black bands over his Rin and Iyo tattoos, but Jorumgard left exposed the circle of runes inked on his muscular chest. Yotolein kept eyeing Jorumgard as if wondering what kind of man he was letting near his kids.

"Nearly done." Kirbana wiped paint from her fingers, then tied a band around my head. A deerskin fringe hung from it, hiding my eyes. "There."

"Not bad," Tema said. "I wouldn't recognize my own daughter."

I turned my head, testing my vision through the fringe. Balancing the antlers forced me to stand perfectly straight. I felt different. Powerful. I sheathed my weapons — bone hunting knife on one hip, the obsidian-handled knife from Brånnheå on the other.

Dunehein and Jorumgard hid their eyes with leather fringes, too, then buckled fur mantles around their shoulders. Tiernan, Yotolein, Tema, Temal, and Rikuja donned black cloaks and pulled hoods low over their faces, disguised as my spectral attendants. Kirbana leaned out the door, checking the street.

"All clear," she said. "Good luck."

I descended our stairs into the night. It was cooler outside and deathly silent. The windows in the nearby rowhouses were dark. Tiernan extinguished the street lamps with a flick of his hand, leaving us bathed in moonlight. I strode down the middle of the road, flanked by Dunehein and Jorumgard. Five hooded figures glided behind us. A few blocks on, a man staggered out of a pub, gaped at us, and bolted away.

We filed into the alley behind the Sarteres'. Matéo, proud that his snake idea sparked something real, had gotten the Sarteres to hire him as a window-washer, then spied through their second-storey windows to see the layout. He'd left the ladder. Temal propped it against the wall next to Hanaiko and Samulein's bedroom window.

Tiernan pressed his hand to the back door. The lock sizzled and melted, scorching the wood around it. He pushed the door open and went in, carrying a fire orb to light the way. The rest of us followed, all except Temal and Rikuja, who stayed in the alley as lookouts.

We'd entered a kitchen. Steel pots shone in the firelight. Tiernan led the way into the shadowy tailor shop, up the spiral staircase, and into a corridor. Yotolein opened his kids' bedroom door. Hanaiko was asleep in a wrought-iron bed, her dark hair splayed across the pillow. Samulein rolled over in a matching bed, whimpering. Yotolein slipped in and shut the door. He wanted to reassure them before the Sarteres began screaming.

I opened the Sarteres' door and scanned the room. A four-poster bed with closed velvet hangings, ornate wooden cabinets, dressing gowns hung on hooks. My heart seized when I saw a person, but it was my reflection in a mirror. Snoring came from the bed. I breathed deep, inhaling the sickly floral scent I hated so much.

You're not Kateiko Rin tonight, I reminded myself. *You're Thymarai, Lady of the Woods.*

I moved to the foot of the bed. The fire orb drifted between my antlers, warming my head. Dunehein and Jorumgard flanked me, huge and hulking with their fur mantles. Tiernan guarded the door while Tema went to the window and pulled moisture from the damp night. Mist surrounded us. I signalled. Together, Dunehein and Jorumgard wrenched down the velvet hangings.

Giana stirred first, squinting in the firelight. She saw us and screeched. Vienzo bolted upright, his nightcap falling off. His broken nose had healed crooked.

Jorumgard spoke in a low rasp, playing up his Sverbian accent. "You have stolen from the gods. The Lady of the Woods demands her children back."

"We — what?" Vienzo spluttered. "Who are you? What madness is this?"

"You have stolen from the gods. The Lady of the Woods demands her children back."

"Get out, demons!" Vienzo flapped his hands at us. "Shoo!"

Dunehein growled, a low rumble with a trace of his grizzly form. He grabbed Vienzo's collar and hauled him out of bed. Jorumgard pulled Giana out. A whimper escaped her. The Sarteres wore nothing but thin nightshirts, Giana's fluttering as she trembled, Vienzo's revealing his bare, knobby knees.

"Take us to the children," Jorumgard said.

Vienzo made a jerky gesture at the door. Dunehein dragged him toward it. Vienzo blanched, noticing Tiernan's hooded form in the darkness. I paced after them, the fire orb floating along with me. At my cousins' bedroom, I touched the door and snapped a water whip on the other side, warning Yotolein.

Dunehein kicked the door open. We filed inside. Yotolein stood hand in hand with his kids, his hood off, face exposed.

"You," Vienzo snarled, lunging forward.

Hanaiko and Samulein flinched. Dunehein hauled Vienzo back. Yotolein just smiled.

"The Lady of the Woods demands an oath," Jorumgard rasped. "You will never come for her children. You will never come for their father. If you do, we know where to find you."

"*Her* children?" Giana shrilled, glowering at me. "We've been raising them for months! What kind of mother abandons her children?"

I drew my knives and twirled them. The fire orb between my antlers crackled.

"Fine," Vienzo said in a choked voice. "Take them, just leave my wife and me alone—"

"No!" Giana whirled on him. She'd gone deathly white. "How can you let them go? After all this time—"

"Silence, woman!" he snapped back.

Giana crumpled onto the floorboards. Tears slid down her cheeks. "My darlings," she croaked, reaching toward the kids. "Is this what you want? A heathen father and this — this demon woman?"

Hanaiko, holding a rag doll, pressed closer to Yotolein. Samulein clutched a plush bear and stared above my head. We'd warned Tiernan about Samulein's fear of fire. I raised a knife to the orb and gave a gentle flick. The fire drifted away to a corner of the room. I sheathed my knives and knelt in front of my cousins, my back to the Sarteres, then lifted my deerskin fringe just enough for Hanaiko and Samulein to recognize me. Slowly, they nodded.

A wail erupted from Giana. She crawled toward us, but instead of going for my cousins, she seized my arm. Jorumgard and Dunehein swept forward. I lifted a hand to stop them. Giana didn't look angry, and somehow I felt bad for her. Maybe she really did care for the children.

"Tell me," she pleaded. "Will they be safe? Will they be loved?"

I dipped my antlers in a nod.

Giana gave a strangled sob. "Then . . . we swear. We won't come for them or their father."

Tema glided toward the window and pushed it open. A thick cloud of mist swirled in. Yotolein scooped up Samulein and held him out through the window. I sensed Temal hidden in the mist, standing atop the ladder and taking Samulein safe in his arms. To the Sarteres, it looked like a wide-eyed little boy vanished into another world.

19.

TAKING ROOT

At dawn, I slipped out of our crowded flat and sat on the dewy stairs. The morning was cool and crisp. I expected everyone to sleep late, so I was surprised when Yotolein came out with two steaming mugs of tea. He gave me one and settled down next to me.

"I owe you my thanks," he said. "And an apology for how I've been treating you. You've done far more for my kids than I had any right to expect."

I managed a weak smile. "I love them, too, you know."

"That much is clear." Yotolein gazed across the street, hands wrapped around his mug. "Your parents raised you well. I hope I can do the same with Hanaiko and Samulein."

"Have you decided where to take them?"

"Well . . . I'm thinking of staying here in Shawnaast."

"Really?" I said, astonished.

"They've already been uprooted twice, fleeing our village and then Aeti Ginu. Their school has a Sverbian track they can transfer to. Tove wanted them to have an itheran education." He smiled bitterly. "I hate to admit my wife had anything in common with the Sarteres."

"But . . ." I bit my lip, afraid of provoking his temper. "Our ways are important, too. Emehein said half-itherans can only attune if they grow up close to the aeldu."

Yotolein sighed. "I've known a lot of mixed-blood families. I think what matters is whether people grow up *believing* they can attune. Hearing the legends, seeing their family do it, understanding why we're given our second forms."

"So if Hanaiko and Samulein had stayed with the Sarteres . . ."

"They'd probably lose that belief." He sipped his tea. "We won't only be around itherans, anyway. The Iyo street is close enough to visit, and Narun and Kirbana are staying in Caladheå. It's safer than going back north. They agreed to re-register my kids as Hanaiko Kirbanehl and Samulein Narunind, keeping them listed as Narun's in case something happens to me."

I didn't reply. Protecting my cousins had driven me for so long, but now I had to face my own uncertain future. If I didn't go home to the Rin, I'd never be initiated as an adult or an antayul. Never get my kinaru and fireweed crest tattooed on my arm. I'd pretended to be so many things since leaving home — a big sister, a trapper who didn't speak Coast Trader, a schoolgirl, the Lady of the Woods — that I didn't know who I was anymore.

By Rin tradition, Hanaiko should've received her first weapon on her ninth birthday. We were two months late. Yotolein wanted to give her a Sverbian weapon in honour of her mother, so Jorumgard took us to a blacksmith. Hanaiko picked out a simple steel dagger that was small enough for her to train with. Jorumgard, grinning, said he expected to find another pint-sized warrior whenever he returned. He and Tiernan were going back to Nordmur to serve alongside Captain Parr.

My parents started talking about going north, too — not home to Aeti Ginu but to find the other Rin who'd left it. The deserters had been thinking of constructing a new settlement in Anwen Bel, which would take a lot of work. Building homes and workshops, setting traplines, planting berry patches, carving new canoes, building weirs and smokehouses before the autumn salmon run began.

A different idea had taken root in my head. I kept weighing what I wanted to do and should do. When Yotolein asked me to help enrol his kids in Sverbian classes and replace the uniforms and supplies they left with the Sarteres, I realized my *want* and *should* were the same thing.

I held off until my cousins were asleep, but my patience didn't last much further than that. Halfway through the adults' conversation, I burst out, "I want to stay here."

Tema turned to me, astonished. "Why?"

"To look after Hanaiko and Samulein. I can help teach them Rin culture, combat skills, water-calling—"

"No," Yotolein cut me off. "I already made you leave home to protect them. I won't let you give up more of your life."

"That's just it," I persisted. "The life I had is over. I've lost my home and trapline, Isu and Emehein have disowned us, I can never trust Fendul again, and I'm sure Rokiud's moved on. But I have a life in Caladheå now. I have friends here, family, a job."

Tema scoffed. "You're too skilled to be a chore girl for itherans."

"I know. I'll ask Agata to take me on as an apprentice."

Yotolein's face twisted. "You'd train under a brown pigeon? Their idea of medicine is barbaric."

"I don't like all of it," I admitted, vowing to never mention the leech tank. "But Agata can cure things our healers can't, and I can teach her things I know."

Temal was studying me. "I hadn't marked you as a healer, little fireweed."

"Me neither, but . . ." I swallowed hard. "In the Customs House, Kel nearly died of lung sickness and all I could do was give Kirbana money for a healer. When I found Jorumgard and Nerio dying of poison, it was a fluke I knew how to treat them. All my warrior training can't save people from nature. I don't want to leave things to chance again."

Tema's expression softened. She hugged me. "Oh, my child. When we parted, I knew you were growing up. Here you are with a wiser head on your shoulders than most people in this land."

"Does that mean I can stay?"

"You're an attuned adult. We can't tell you where to go. Whether you can live with Yotolein and his kids is up to him."

Yotolein folded his arms, drumming his fingers. I could guess what he was thinking. He wanted help, but living together these past two months had been awkward enough.

"Rija and I had a feeling this might happen," Dunehein said. "We're happy to stay in this flat with Kako. The tenant downstairs is leaving soon, so Yotolein and his kids can move in there. We'll be close without tripping over each other."

"You're sure?" Tema asked skeptically.

"I'll look for a better job than scrubbing laundry," Rikuja said, showing her dry cracked hands. "But otherwise, we don't mind. Dune left the Rin-jouyen to marry me. Caring for his cousins is the least I can do."

"Let's not make anything permanent," Temal said. "Sohiko and I will return to Anwen Bel. If the other Rin deserters are building a settlement, we'll help out. They'll need us over winter to trap furs. Then in spring . . ."

"Kianta kolo," I said.

He ruffled my hair. "When the sap flows, we'll come visit you. If you're still happy here, stay. If not, you can come live with us in the settlement. You'll always have a home with us."

"Two of my grandsons are leaving town, too, back to boarding school," Agata said as she ground beetles into powder. "Guess we're getting back to normal."

"Well . . ." I made sure Nicoletta wasn't in the kitchen, knowing her opinion would scupper my chances. "I actually have something to ask you."

"Ask, then. Time's a-ticking."

"Will you take me as an apprentice?" I said in a rush.

Agata's small mouth pursed. "I admit you're overqualified for chores, but this is a delicate business. People's health is at stake. The wrong ingredient or dose can be disastrous. I need to know you'll be responsible and take the work seriously."

"I will, I promise—"

"Don't promise. Convince me. I'll get you doing some basic tasks, and if you do well for a few months, I'll take you as my apprentice. Sound fair?"

As I nodded, I caught sight of a row of labelled vials. "Um — will it matter that I can't read?"

Agata spat in a bowl and held it out. "If I say that's wine, will you drink it?"

I blinked. "Nei."

"Words can lie. The substance can't. I'll teach you to recognize what's in the container, not on the label. But unless you've got a flawless memory for recipes, you'd best start learning to read."

I nodded again. "I'll find a way."

"Good." She handed me the bowl. "Wash that, then get cleaning the surgery. Those stains aren't wine, either."

The first month of autumn flew by. In some ways it did feel normal — living with just Dunehein and Rikuja again, enduring Nicoletta's scoldings, seeing Matéo in his school uniform — but instead of three full shifts a week, I worked four shorter ones so I could walk my cousins to and from school. They were slowly opening up, starting to talk again and sometimes even smile. Hanaiko tried a few hairstyles, first pinning hers up like mine, then a single braid, before settling on the twin braids she'd worn so long ago.

She shyly asked me to make a Thymarai outfit for her rag doll, which Giana had put in a lace-trimmed bonnet and skirt. I made a deerskin dress and a headband with twigs for antlers. Samulein decided his plush bear was a *bjørnbattai*. We carried them all over Bjørn Park, making up adventures and playing hide-and-seek in the bushes.

On my weekdays off, I walked to Førstown and helped Kirbana with chores in exchange for reading lessons. She suggested I start with Coast Trader, which used an adapted version of Ferish writing. I could get used to the letters while learning spoken Ferish at work, and eventually combine them into reading Agata's medical textbooks.

Kirbana wrote curving symbols with a slate and chalk, telling me what sounds went with them. I was instantly confused. *J* was a hard sound in Aikoto names like Jonalin, but a soft *y* sound in Sverbian names like Jorumgard. It wasn't used at all in Ferish, where the hard sound was written with a *g*, like Giana. Kirbana said Trader was like a crow, stealing bits from multiple languages and patching them together.

Samulein had different problems. His new teacher said he didn't interact with other kids and was always distracted. Matéo suggested enrolling him in the school's athletic league with his ten-year-old brother Rico, running laps and playing ball games on their lunch break. It helped a little. Samulein burned through enough energy to sit still during afternoon lessons, and Rico told off kids who called Samulein a mutt.

Hanaiko occasionally came home crying because kids had teased her, but she loved the schoolwork. For an assignment to write about someone who'd helped her, she wrote about the two strangers who helped reunite her family. Since she couldn't hand that in to her teacher and reveal our ruse about the Lady of the Woods, we mailed it to Tiernan and Jorumgard. A response came in Tiernan's graceful handwriting, saying he'd never seen Jorumgard cry until reading Hanaiko's letter.

Yotolein was determined to balance his kids' Sverbian and Aikoto education. One weekend, we took them to the Iyo gathering place in Ashtown to meet kids their age. The next, we paddled down the coast to a river delta where Rikuja's three brothers, their wives and kids, and several other Iyo families were camped for the salmon run. Yula traders visited the campsite and we taught my cousins to barter smoked salmon and whitefish for woven jackets and blankets.

On the autumn equinox, we visited Toel Ginu. Normally non-Iyo weren't allowed into the shrine, but Tokoda let us, understanding how important it was for Hanaiko, Samulein, and Kel to grow up familiar with our ways. Thousands of carvings on the walls detailed the Iyo-jouyen's history. Rikuja explained the meanings to the kids — births, deaths, attunings, marriages, battles, new okorebai and okoreni. Hanaiko was fascinated. Samulein was happier running up and down the stairs and counting dolphin carvings.

During the ceremonial dance to summon the Iyo's aeldu to the shrine, Rikuja pointed out Jonalin's family. His mother, Makinu, and his three sisters whirled and swayed with the other dancers. They wore blue cottonspun shawls with white beading so it looked like sparkling waves flowed around them. His father, Ranelin, stood with his cousin Airedain in the line of drummers, pounding huge drums painted with the Iyo dolphin crest.

I met his parents that night at the festival. Jonalin was built like his father, tall and broad-shouldered, but the similarity stopped there. Ranelin's laugh boomed like his drum and within minutes he was teaching Samulein a loud clapping game. Makinu, her words as graceful as her dancing, said it was a blessing my family could attend even if her son couldn't.

In a wavering voice, Hanaiko asked where he was. Makinu knelt to eye level and said Jonalin cared about us so much, he'd broken itheran law to protect us, and sometimes the law was wrong and not fair to people like us. Hanaiko asked if we could write a letter thanking Jonalin. Makinu said it was a wonderful idea and Airedain, who'd attended Sverbian school in Ashtown, would read the letter aloud next time he visited Jonalin in prison.

I wondered what Jonalin would be doing if he was here — playing with his niece and nephew, dancing and drinking with friends, or tangling with a lover in a dark corner. I remembered from him stripping off his rain-soaked tunic that he didn't have tattoos for drumming or shawl dancing, so he hadn't taken either of his parents' jouyen roles. Standing here in his shrine, it felt like I didn't know him at all.

⁂

Back in Caladheå, Matéo and I started hanging out in the evenings. I invited him to come fishing in the Stengar, where I grossed him out by pulling a salmon's guts out through its mouth. He invited me to explore the old town hall, which was abandoned, crumbling, and taken over by roosting pigeons. School was cancelled for Shawnaast's harvest festival, so we took Rico, their twelve-year-old sister Inesa, and my cousins for a day of food and music and games.

Nicoletta was the only thorn in my side. At the apothecary, she told me to stir a pot of simmering roots and *absolutely not* let it boil, but the fire was too strong and she refused to let me move the pot. When her back was turned, I waved my hand over the water and called out some heat. A moment later she peered at the gently simmering contents. "Hm" was all she said.

Another time, an amber-coloured infusion I'd just finished making got mysteriously paler. A quick water-calling check told me someone had diluted it. I pulled out the excess water, bottled the infusion, and went on with my work. Out of the corner of my eye, I saw Nicoletta frown, then knock one of my bottles off the shelf.

My hand shot out on instinct. The bottle shattered on the floor, but the liquid stayed in midair, a floating amber streak.

"God above us all," Agata breathed.

Nicoletta stared at me with a mix of fear and triumph. "Mage," she hissed. "I knew it."

Horror-struck, I threw the infusion into an empty bowl. Voices flashed through my memory. Kirbana warning me that itherans feared water-calling, Lucreza's street-rat brother spitting *mage* like a curse, Tiernan explaining that some military captains refused to travel with a fire-caller.

Agata picked up the bowl. She tipped it back and forth, sniffed the infusion, took a spoonful, and tasted it. "What else can you do, girl?"

"Just control water," I managed to say. "Heat it, freeze it, fill a bucket, or dry things out."

She clicked her tongue. "Yet you've been hauling well water for months? Imagine what you could've done with that time. And having ice all year? We can numb wounds, preserve ingredients — I hardly know where to begin!"

Nicoletta looked like I'd just kicked her cat. "But Grandmera—"

"Don't 'but Grandmera' me. I saw you knock that bottle over. If the infusion had been wasted, it'd come out of *your* pay. Now clean up that glass."

Sulking, Nicoletta got the broom. I made an excuse of needing something from the cellar. Alone down there, I broke into a grin. Nicoletta could sabotage me however she liked. Agata wouldn't fire me now.

20.

LAUDANUM

Eager to tell Akohin the latest about Nicoletta, I skipped my next reading lesson to visit him. Trees hung with brilliant red, orange, and yellow foliage. Fallen leaves crunched under my boots. Everyone said it was an unusually warm and dry autumn, but today felt like it was beautiful just for me. I hummed as I went into the Golden Oak and knocked on Akohin's door.

The stablehand answered, reeking of horseshit. Hay stuck out of his hair. He frowned and said, "Didn't you know? Akohin left."

"What?"

"He quit a few days ago. Said he was leaving town."

"What?"

I pushed past him. Akohin's knitted blanket lay folded on his bed. His drawers were open and empty. After so much of my family went missing, he wouldn't just leave without telling me anything.

He must've left something to explain it. I looked under his bed, then lifted the straw-filled mattress. A cleaver lay on the bedstead.

"Did you put this here?" I asked.

The stablehand shook his head, looking unnerved. I triple-checked everywhere, testing for loose floorboards and false drawer bottoms. Nothing else seemed out of place. I brought the cleaver to the kitchen, where Nhys took it with a chuckle.

"I lost that months ago," he said. "Where'd you find it?"

"Under Akohin's mattress," I said hollowly.

Nhys's face fell. "Ah. It went missing not long after I hired him. I wondered if he was a thief, but an old cleaver be a strange thing to steal."

"Do you have any idea where he went?"

"Afraid not. All he said was he doesn't want anyone to go searching for him."

My insides knotted. I told myself there could be a good reason, like maybe his uncle Batohin escaped prison and they had to flee. I dropped by Kirbana's flat, but she and Narun hadn't heard news of Batohin or any other Dona.

On my way home, crossing through Bjørn Park, Akohin's words hit me. This was where he'd told me about his great-great-grandfather Imarein Rin. *He got really messed up — sleeping with a knife, screaming in the night.* Akohin had been trying to tell me about himself, and I'd been too distracted with my own problems.

It wasn't just that one day, either. I'd avoided him because his misery made *me* miserable. I could've invited him to the equinox festival at Toel Ginu, convinced him the Iyo didn't hate him, made him feel safer. I swore and slammed my hand against an alder trunk. My palm came away scratched and bloody.

I could *search for him*, I thought wildly, but already knew it was pointless. His attuned form was a raven. He could be halfway across the ocean by now, and maybe he really didn't want me to follow. Maybe he left because I'd already failed him.

It proved difficult to tell Batohin that his nephew was missing. Only family could visit him in prison, and even if he could read, I didn't want the guards to intercept a letter about a runaway from the orphanage. In the end, Falwen visited the prison. He returned with news that Batohin didn't know where Akohin might've gone, either.

The autumn rain came all at once, like some dormant anta-saidu had been hoarding it and lost control. Shawnaast's streets turned into rivers and Yotolein's ground-level flat kept flooding. I dictated a letter to Hanaiko, asking Tiernan and Jorumgard to let me know if they saw Akohin up north. A damp envelope arrived in our postal box, addressed in smudged ink to *Pint-Sized Warriors*, with a reply promising they'd keep an eye out.

Good and bad news came from my cousins' school. They were far behind, having missed half a year and then been put in Ferish classes for another half. Hanaiko was catching up. Samulein wasn't. Rain cancelled lunchtime athletics so often that he had too much energy and couldn't focus. Yotolein and I weren't sure how to help. Our education had been outdoors, trapping and calling water and training in combat.

Temal's younger brother, Geniod, arrived as a rain-soaked bald eagle. He'd always been my favourite uncle on that side, kind-hearted and cheerful, and he didn't have a partner or kids to look after, so he'd volunteered to bring news of our family and the other Rin deserters. They'd settled in southeast Anwen Bel, as far from war-torn Nordmur as possible, on a forested mountain much like Aeti Ginu. People had jokingly called the new settlement

Nettle Ginu because of all the brambles they'd had to clear, and the name stuck.

To keep the reason for the schism secret, Behadul and the deserters had agreed to pretend the settlement was to guard Anwen Bel's southern border from Eremur. A few Rin-born Dona had been allowed to join Nettle Ginu on strict oaths of secrecy. For a moment I hoped Akohin might've found his way there, but Geniod said they'd seen no trace of him.

Rain turned to sleet, sleet turned to snow, and after a few false starts, winter settled in. One clear day, Agata went out to do house calls and Nicoletta took over handling customers. I listened from the kitchen, trying to learn what I could. To my surprise, a deep male voice speaking in fluent Ferish said my name with an Iyo accent. A moment later, Nicoletta swept into the kitchen, huffing.

"He's asking for you," she said.

Wary, I handed her the spoon for the pot I'd been stirring, smoothed my apron, and went up front. Agata hadn't yet agreed to take me as an apprentice, let alone given me permission to deal with customers.

A boy of about nineteen waited with his hands in his breeches pockets, shuffling his feet. His dark hair was shaved short and he had a sunken look that didn't match his considerable height. His eyes wandered and his pupils were dilated. I wouldn't have recognized him except for his hooded jerkin and familiar posture, that look as if he'd been pulled tight by a drawstring.

"Jonalin?" I said.

He blinked several times. "Kateiko. It *is* you."

I managed a smile. "You got out last week, right? Rikuja mentioned it."

"Uh . . . yeah. I've got another year in a parole house in Ashtown, though. No idea why they transferred me there. Most people bribe their way in."

I'd never decided whether to tell Jonalin about my deal with Captain Parr. It depended what Parr asked in return, and that request hadn't yet come. I fumbled for a change of topic. "Um . . . did you get our letter? Hanaiko wrote it, but we all pitched in."

"Yeah." Jonalin ducked his head. "It made prison worth it."

Wanting to melt from embarrassment, I sidled behind the counter. "Do you need medicine?"

"Ai, yeah." He pulled his left hand from his pocket. His two smallest fingers were gone, the knuckles wrapped in bloody bandages.

I gasped. "What in Aeldu-yan happened?"

"It's stupid. I got a job at the brick-making kilns, then dropped a load of bricks. My fingers got crushed too bad to save. I can manage without 'em, but I can't find a good painkiller. Willowcloak makes it bleed more, I'm allergic to Sverbian needlemint, and tulanta, well . . ."

"Hallucinations."

"Right. This room is full of bees. They sing." Jonalin smiled crookedly. "Airedain said you work at a Ferish apothecary, so I thought you might know something better."

I leaned into the kitchen. "Nicoletta, laudanum is used for amputation pain, right?"

"Yes," she said without looking up.

"And it's safe? It doesn't thin the blood, or—"

"Of course it's safe," she snapped. "We give it to babies, for god's sake. Just be careful with the dose."

I went into the surgery, sniffed a flask of bitter red-brown liquid to make sure it was right, then returned to the front. I had to say Jonalin's name to pull his attention from the imaginary bees. "This is our strongest painkiller. It'll make you throw up, but it works."

"How much is it?"

"Twenty pann. It'd be cheaper if we could grow the ingredients locally, but we have to import a special type of poppy seed."

Jonalin rubbed his neck with his good hand. "I'll think about it—"

"Just take it. I owe you." I pushed the flask across the counter, took twenty pann from my purse, and put it in the till. "Mix five drops of laudanum into a mug of water. Wait at least three hours between doses, and don't take it with other painkillers or alcohol."

He picked up the flask, looking confused. "Well . . . thanks."

I paused, pretty sure he missed what I just said. "Jonalin, is anyone taking care of you?"

"Uh . . ." His eyes flickered toward the bees. "My old flatmate left town. My parents came up from Toel when I got out, but they went home a couple days ago. They don't know about my accident. Aire's been helping me with stuff."

"Tell you what," I said. "I need to get Hanaiko and Samulein from school. Why don't you come? We can all go to the Iyo gathering place." And I'd find Airedain so I could relay the instructions to someone whose senses were bee-free.

I'd hardly gotten into the apothecary the next morning, shaking snow off my thick wool coat, when Agata snapped her fingers at me. "You. Upstairs."

Startled, I followed her to their sitting room. It was small and cozy with overstuffed brocade armchairs and a shelf of well-thumbed medical books. The smell of spices wafted up from the kitchen. I'd been here plenty of times, cleaning or fetching things, but never been ordered in like this. Agata pointed me at an armchair, stoked the fire, and hung a kettle over the flames.

Finally, she eased herself into the seat across from me. Tapping her foot, she said, "Nica says you sold laudanum to a young man yesterday."

"Yes, but—"

"Without training. Without permission to touch the medicine stores or the till."

"*Yes*, but—"

"Hush, girl. I said I'd take you as an apprentice if you acted responsibly. Does this sound like the actions of a responsible apothecary?"

"He was in pain!" I cried. "He lost two fingers! If he kept taking tulanta, he might've followed imaginary bees off a pier and drowned. I had to help him. I owe him pretty much my whole life."

Agata's beetle-green eyes narrowed. "Go on."

My words poured out. "I know laudanum's used for amputations because your son takes it. I know he lost a leg in military service, and that's why Matéo picks up laudanum so often, for his father. I checked with Nicoletta that it's safe, then I did the sale because amputations upset her. I know it was the right flask because I stocked the surgery, but I checked the contents anyway."

"What dosage did you prescribe?"

"Five drops in water, because he's underweight."

"And you expected a hallucinating person to remember?"

"Nei. I took him home and told his cousin. You always make house calls if customers can't care for themselves."

Agata's eyes became slits. "How do you know all this?"

"I listened. That's how my people learn, by listening to our elders."

Ever so slowly, her scowl turned into a smile. "Make the tea, girl."

"Huh?"

"God above us all, what happened to listening? Make the tea. I'm an old woman with arthritis."

I bustled around, scraping flakes from the tea brick, putting it to brew, laying out cups and saucers. Agata always took tea with milk, so I hurried down to the kitchen and fetched the pitcher. Not until I'd handed her a finished cup did she speak again.

"In this business, compassion matters as much as discipline, and it takes effort. You have to listen hard to what people do and don't say. You have to handle patients at their worst, whether they're confused, scared, bloody, smelly, infected, or shitting like a horse."

I spat tea over myself. Flustered, I called the droplets out of my skirt and dumped them on my saucer.

"Nica's still learning compassion," Agata went on like nothing happened. "But you seem to have gotten that lesson somewhere, so we'll move on. I expect you here bright and early tomorrow."

"I've got tomorrow off—"

"Not anymore. My apprentices work five days a week. You'll have weekends off for your cousins." She sipped her tea, then added, "And for my grandson. Don't think I haven't listened, too."

"Let me get this straight," Matéo said, rolling a knee-high ball of snow along the ground. "You broke almost every rule Grandmera has. Nica ratted you out. Then *she* got criticized and *you're* an apprentice now?"

"That about covers it," I said, idly pulling a trail of snowflakes through the air.

We were in Bjørn Park, watching Rico and Inesa have a snowball war with my cousins. Their shrieks of laughter shattered the air. Couples strolled past on shovelled paths, hand in hand and oblivious to the world. A young woman with an auburn bun and a blue Colonnium uniform sat on a bench reading a newspaper. We were nowhere near the Colonnium, so it puzzled me why she was here.

"What are you making?" I asked skeptically.

"A snowman." Matéo plunked another large snowball on the first.

"That looks nothing like a man."

"Duh. It doesn't have a head yet. What are *you* making?"

"I haven't decided. Maybe . . ." With a few moments of water-calling, I shaped snow into a giant snake, coiled around his snowman and ready to strike.

"Show-off." Matéo threw his snowman's head at me.

I yelped. Before long, we were tearing across the park in our own snowball war. I tripped on my thick woolen petticoats and went sprawling. Matéo flopped down next to me, red-cheeked and panting. Snow glittered in his messy auburn curls.

"There's one bad part," I said. "I have to move my reading lessons with Kirbana. So . . . I can't see you as much."

He looked over at me. "What if I teach you instead?"

"Really?"

"Sure. You wanna learn to read Ferish, right? We can use my old school primers."

My heart turned upside down at the thought of reading together, snuggled up by a fireplace. I ached with wanting to kiss him. It felt like ropes pulled me toward him, urging me on. It wasn't proper for him, though. I didn't know how anyone could live like this until they were engaged.

Then before I knew what was happening, Matéo leaned toward me. His lips brushed mine.

Grinning, he said, "Race you back to the others."

21.
BREAK

The next time I took my cousins to school, Matéo was waiting at the gates. He didn't smile. He didn't even meet my eyes. Instead, he led me away from the gates and the curious looks of other students.

"My parents don't want me to see you anymore," he said.

It felt like the snowy sidewalk had given way beneath me. "Why not?"

"Well . . ." Matéo fidgeted with his satchel strap. "They think you're . . . a bad influence."

"Because of what, our kiss? How could they know?"

"Nica was in the park." He sounded disgusted. "She also told our parents you're friends with a viirelei who just got out of prison. And she knew someone wore her school uniform, because when she got it out of storage for Inesa, she found a ripped seam. So she asked her old classmates, and some of them saw us there. She told our parents *that*, too."

"Kaid." I leaned against the tall wrought-iron fence and covered my face with my hands. "Did they tell the school? Are you expelled?"

"No, but . . ." Matéo dug his boot into the snow. "My parents threatened to send me to boarding school. Then I won't see *any* of my family."

An invisible knife twisted in my stomach. I knew how it felt to be separated from family, and it was the one thing Matéo feared most. There was no fighting against it.

The warning bell clanged. In the yard, kids began heading toward the school. Matéo bit his lip, still not looking at me.

"I'd better go," he said. "Sorry, Kateiko."

I stood alone on the sidewalk until my limbs were stiff with cold, finally realizing I was late for work. I pulled my shawls tight and headed for the apothecary, my rage building with every step. Snowflakes swirled around me. I went through the alley, flung open the back door, and stormed into the kitchen.

Nicoletta was dicing roots. She dropped her knife as I drew close. I shoved her, sending mops and brooms clattering.

"How dare you?" I demanded. "Sabotaging me is one thing, but how *dare* you drag Matéo into it! Using your own brother against me? That's low!"

"Who says it's about you?" she sneered. "Maybe I'm just protecting him from getting seduced by a shameless whore."

I slapped her.

Nicoletta reeled, her mouth open in shock.

"That's for Matéo," I said, breathing hard. "You don't know the first thing about protecting family. Do you have any idea what he's done for you? He put a snake in Covonnus's lunch pail to make that bludgehead leave you alone. Covonnus gave him a black eye for it, and Matéo kept doing it anyway!

"You know why he snuck me into the school? So I could talk to my cousins who got stolen from me. Matéo had just met me, and he did it anyway, because he understood. He cares about family more than anything. Yet *you're* such a selfish bitch that you threw your own brother under the cart!"

Nicoletta's lip trembled. Her eyes welled with tears.

"What in bloody hell is going on here?" said a low voice.

We whirled. Agata stood in the doorway.

"She . . ." Nicoletta touched her red cheek. "Kateiko *hit* me."

Agata's lips pressed so thin they nearly vanished. "Nica, go upstairs. As for you, girl" — she pointed a gnarled finger at me — "I don't tolerate violence against my family. Get out and don't come back."

That evening, Dunehein found me curled in bed, shivering under a pile of furs and blankets. I'd cried myself dry long ago. The fire had burned down to embers, filling the room with a dull red glow. My hairpins lay scattered across the floor where I'd thrown them.

"Looks like you've had quite the day, little cousin." Dunehein stoked the fire and sat next to me, brushing sawdust from the lumberyard off his clothes. "Let's hear it."

I let the story unravel, from kissing Matéo in the park and being happier than I could remember since leaving Aeti Ginu, to getting broken up with and fired in under an hour. By the end, I was sniffling again.

"It's stupid to cry," I muttered. "I've been through worse."

Dunehein pulled me into a warm hug. "I don't think it's stupid. You've suffered a lot, and you finally got to feel good. Of course it hurts to lose that."

"I wish I could go home," I said in a tiny voice.

"Me, too, sometimes." He stroked my tangled hair. "No one would judge you for leaving."

"But I don't know where home *is* anymore. If I go to Nettle Ginu, I'll have to start my life all over. If I go to Aeti Ginu, it feels like betraying all my family who left."

Dunehein chuckled. "Ain't that always the problem. You can change jobs and lovers, but you can't change your family." He was silent awhile, and I wondered if he was thinking of Isu and Emehein. Finally he said, "You don't need to decide anything now. Take some time to recover. If you want, Rija and I will take tomorrow off work. We can do whatever you like."

More than anything, I wanted to be with our own kind, people who'd never say the awful things that Nicoletta and the Sarteres and so many other Ferish had. That brought up a terrible thought. If Jonalin went back to the apothecary, he'd find Nicoletta and Agata instead of me.

"Can we go to Ashtown tomorrow?" I asked. "There's someone I need to check on."

The upside of getting fired was I had time to look after Hanaiko and Samulein during their school's winter break. They'd fallen behind on antayul lessons, so every morning, we traipsed into the snowy woods outside Shawnaast where we could practise without itherans seeing. In afternoons, we went to Ashtown so my cousins could play with Iyo kids. It distracted them from asking why we didn't see Rico and Inesa anymore.

Jonalin couldn't work until his hand healed, so he spent a lot of time with us in the Iyo gathering place, an open building with red-brick pillars supporting the high roof. He barely spoke, which balanced out since now that Hanaiko had started talking again, she never stopped. Jonalin's patience was unending. He didn't complain even when Samulein climbed all over him and jostled his injured hand.

Whenever my cousins ran off to play, Jonalin and I were left in awkward silence. He kept trying to tie sailor's knots in a frayed cord, seemingly a nervous habit, then giving up in pain and hiding his injured hand in his pocket. Hoping to cheer him up, I teased him about a pretty Iyo girl who kept smiling at him, but he scowled and told me to cut it out.

I drew back, surprised. "Sorry. I was trying to be nice."

"By using my messed-up love life to forget about yours?" He gave me a hard look and then stalked off.

I stared after him. Apparently, I'd found the limit of his patience.

The next day — pale, clammy, and speaking like he was in a dream — Jonalin apologized and opened up. He told me that for a year he'd been seeing a Ferish baker's daughter named Téresa. Then he got arrested, and she didn't want anything to do with a man convicted of assault. Because they weren't married, she couldn't visit him in prison to break up with him, so Airedain had to do it for her.

Heartbroken, Jonalin had grasped at his only way to reach Téresa — by mail. He couldn't read or write, but a Ferish priest offered lessons to inmates who attended weekly religious rites, so he buried his dislike of priests and took the deal. Every month when Airedain visited, he helped Jonalin write letters to Téresa. She never replied.

Jonalin had never mentioned her, even during our month in the Customs House when he was still seeing her. I wasn't sure she was real. His hands trembled with a telltale sign of tulanta hallucinations. He rambled about everything he'd missed while in prison. His eldest sister had given birth again. His next eldest sister had gotten married. Airedain had graduated school, the first in their family. Jealousy soaked Jonalin's voice.

"Never now," he kept muttering. I asked if he was talking about Téresa. He didn't remember telling me about her. He didn't even recognize me. Unnerved, I sent my cousins down the street to their friends' home, a nearby Iyo man to find their healer, and another man to fetch Airedain from his greengrocer job.

Moments after they left, Jonalin's eyes rolled back and he slumped over. His breathing was shallow. I could barely feel a pulse. I searched the pockets of his hooded jerkin and discovered half-empty flasks of laudanum, tulanta, and some clear smoke-scented alcohol. In horror, I realized he'd overdosed.

I held his face and called his name. He started vomiting. I rolled him onto his side so he didn't choke. An Iyo woman brought charcoal powder, which I dissolved in water and coaxed Jonalin to drink. It would absorb the laudanum, but I didn't know how to treat whatever else he'd taken. Every time his eyelids fell, I got him talking about anything that came to mind. If he passed out, he might never wake again.

Only when the Iyo healer arrived did I slow down enough for things to sink in. I didn't know if Jonalin had overdosed on purpose. I didn't want to know. *This is all my fault* kept repeating in my head. Not only had I given him laudanum, but if he hadn't gotten arrested protecting me, he wouldn't have lost everything — his lover, health, dockhand job, flat and flatmate, even his freedom to go home to Toel Ginu.

Hours later, Airedain came to my flat and said Jonalin was okay for now, but they'd gotten into a blazing argument. Airedain had sent word to Toel Ginu asking Ranelin and Makinu to come look after their son, which ignited the last thing Jonalin had left — his pride. He was already pissed off about needing to borrow money from his family. Airedain also confirmed everything about Téresa was true but asked me to pretend I never heard it.

A gulf separated Jonalin and me. In my last days of being fifteen, I'd never felt so young. I had no idea how to help a nineteen-year-old who might want to die. Secretly, I just wanted to sulk about my own problems. But after abandoning Akohin, I couldn't abandon Jonalin, too. So I settled on being there as a friend. I wouldn't tease him again, pry into his secrets, or subject him to my usual sarcasm. I'd learn a new kind of friendship just for him.

The day that school started again, I saw Nicoletta at the gates, recognizable from a distance by auburn curls falling from under her bonnet. She carried a wicker basket on one arm.

"Kateiko," she called out, hurrying over. "I'm here to apologize."

"Took you long enough," I said.

Her cheeks went pink. "I wrote a letter, but Matéo reminded me that you're still learning to read. Please, can we talk?"

Grudgingly, I followed her into the schoolyard and sent my cousins to the building. A few students gave Nicoletta and me curious looks, but the yard soon emptied as everyone went inside. We settled on a frosty stone bench.

"These are for you." She lifted a handkerchief covering the basket, revealing deep brown cookies that smelled of molasses. "Grandmera says apologies should always come with food."

"Did you poison them?"

Nicoletta's mouth twisted. "No. I took your advice, if yelling and swearing at me counts as that. I took time off work and went home while Matéo, Rico, and Inesa were on winter break. We baked these together."

I bit into one. It was so gingery my eyes watered.

She folded her mittened hands in her lap. "I should explain something first. I'm supposed to inherit the apothecary, but my mother doesn't think it's proper for a woman to run a shop. If she gets the tiniest whiff I can't handle it, she'll marry me off to some ugly old man. So I try to be perfect, but whenever I mess up, I'm afraid I'll never be good enough to run the place.

"Then you swept in, and you were good at everything. You had this great reference from the military, you knew about plants I didn't, you're a *mage*. Nothing even grosses you out. Grandmera thought you were a gift from god. You probably thought I hated you, but the truth is I was jealous."

"Of me?" I said incredulously. "I don't know half the stuff you do."

Nicoletta scrunched up her face. "It wasn't just that. Grandmera told me to lend you a dress, and instead you could afford a new one. Even my petticoats are hand-me-downs from cousins. Then Matéo started spending all this time with you, and it felt like you were stealing my brother away. When I saw him kiss you . . . I had this horrible thought that if he married you, Grandmera might give the apothecary to you two."

I was speechless. I'd only thought of engagement as the gateway to kissing Matéo. I'd never imagined what marriage would mean for us.

"Anyway," she said, blushing bright red, "I know that's not an excuse. I was selfish and stupid, and I hurt you and my brother. I'm sorry."

"Sorry doesn't fix things," I muttered.

"I tried to fix them." She picked at loose yarn on her mitten. "I told our parents I lied about everything, but they believed me more when I was being mean. *Don't* comment," she cut me off.

I held up my hands in peace. "So . . . I've got no chance with Matéo?"

"Not while he's in school. You could wait a few years, but to be honest, it'll never be easy. Our parents would disown him for marrying a viirelei."

I sighed, thinking about everything Yotolein had suffered for marrying a Sverbian and raising mixed-blood kids. Maybe things between Jonalin and Téresa had been rocky before his arrest.

"But . . ." Nicoletta peeked out from under her bonnet. "I fixed one thing. I convinced Grandmera to hire you back."

"What? How?"

"I said I deserved to get slapped. Don't laugh! And I told her we'll never find a better apprentice. She's stressed about all the work piling up, and I hate going out in the cold to fetch well water. I understand if you don't want to come back, though."

I scraped a gloved finger across the frosty bench, thinking. Jonalin's overdose had scared me off wanting to give anyone medicine again, but the Iyo healer had gently told me that people in Jonalin's state would always get ahold of something. Things would always go wrong, people would always need help. The question was whether I wanted to learn how to help them. With that, I knew what I'd say when my parents visited in spring and asked if I wanted to stay in Caladheå.

"I do," I said.

Nicoletta sagged with relief. "Does that mean you forgive me?"

I eyed her dubiously. "Maybe."

"That's fair." She got up, then said, "Oh, I nearly forgot. Matéo said it's your sixteenth birthday, so we pooled our money to buy you a gift. Hang it in your window to catch the sunlight." She handed me a package from the basket.

I untied the string and unfolded the paper. Inside was a stained-glass butterfly. "Caterpillars," I said, starting to laugh.

22.

A YEAR WITHOUT STARS

Once Jonalin and I both went back to work, it became tough to see him. There wasn't much time between our shifts and sunset, which was his curfew. Our days off didn't overlap. So one weekend I brought him lunch at the brick-making kilns in Ashtown, then one weekday he brought me lunch at the apothecary, and we settled into a routine.

He said he missed seeing the stars. Back when he was a dock-hand, he'd worked such odd hours he couldn't sleep at night, so he'd wandered the shore or gone canoeing. Neither his cell in prison nor the parole house had windows. He said sometimes he woke in total darkness and felt like the sky had been wiped blank. After a year without stars, I wasn't sure he'd survive another.

I started looking at the sky before bed. Next time I saw Jonalin, I described each night to him. I told him about storm clouds, falling snow, and shimmers of green and blue light on the horizon. His eyes drifted out of focus like he was picturing it, saving it for later. Over the weeks we followed the moon cycle and the slow movement of constellations.

Jonalin told me the prison guards had shaved off his hair. He had no idea what happened to the shorn bits. Iyo tradition dictated they should be burned to return to the earth, but for all he knew they were still lying on a cold stone floor, those bits of his spirit trapped in prison forever. I wanted to reach out and stroke his head, to touch the remains of his spirit and say he'd be okay, but it felt like a hollow promise.

He asked how my reading lessons were going, and I admitted they weren't. My dashed hopes of learning from Matéo hurt too much. I scraped by at work by memorizing recipes and drawing symbols on labels. Even Samulein, who struggled to pay attention when snow or sleet cancelled lunchtime athletics, was making more progress than me. Hesitantly, Jonalin suggested he could teach me.

It felt like the Sverbian trickster spirit was playing a cruel joke. At one point, I would've been flattered that a brawny older boy wanted to help me. Now, everything was wrong. Jonalin didn't look or act or smile like he used to, we were both hung up on Ferish people we could never have, and every time I saw him, I remembered touching his neck to find a pulse.

Lessons were a good excuse to keep watch over him, though. On days he visited me, he brushed coal ash off his clothes in the alley, greeted Agata and Nicoletta politely, and gave Luna a scratch under the chin. He was a shadow stepping into my daydream of Matéo — the two of us curled up by the sitting room fireplace, reading Ferish children's stories in Nicoletta's old school primers, sharing *pérossetto* rolls and smoked salmon.

Gradually, his hair grew into its usual rumpled state. Hauling bricks put muscle back on his bones. By the time my parents visited in spring and met Jonalin, he looked like his old self. His mood seemed permanently sunk, though. He couldn't come with us to the equinox festival in Toel Ginu. He couldn't even go canoeing in case Elkhounds thought he was skipping town.

The festival reminded me how strange it was he hadn't become a drummer or shawl dancer like his parents. Ranelin told me he'd wanted to take his son as an apprentice, but Jonalin didn't like performing, while Airedain took to it like a duck to water. I knew what it was like to feel out of place in a family. I couldn't even borrow Hanaiko's and Samulein's schoolbooks because they were written in the angular symbols of Sverbian.

On days I visited Jonalin, we perched on huge piles of bricks overlooking the kiln yard, brushing a perpetual rain of coal ash off our lunch. In late spring, trying to keep my night sky descriptions interesting, I tried doing them in Ferish. Hiding a smile, Jonalin corrected my grammar, explaining that the language had different types of words for tangible and intangible things.

"Take light, for example," he said. "*Luma* means a lantern, torch, something you can hold. *Lumos* is the light that comes from them. Now take stars. Aikoto people have the story of Orebo who wanted the moon's beauty so much that he broke off a moonbeam, but it shattered and made the stars. In Ferish religion, starlight is the aura of god. It's untouchable, so their word for star is *stelos*, not *stela*."

"You sure learned a lot from the prison priest."

His smile evaporated. "Not all of it by choice."

I sighed. Somehow I always managed to upset him. He started to get up even though he hadn't finished eating.

"Wait," I said, pulling him back down. "What do stars mean to you?"

Jonalin pulled a frayed cord from his pocket and started tying knots. He'd gotten good at doing it with two missing fingers. Eventually he said, "When I was twelve, I went canoeing and got lost in a storm. I wound up on open ocean and couldn't see the stars to navigate. Then I saw an osprey circling a patch of clear sky, just enough for me to find land. A few days later I attuned to the osprey. It felt like . . . as long as I could see the stars, I'd survive anything."

My heart ached. No wonder he missed them. I'd have broken the moon myself if I could give him its light.

"Sometimes I think about flying home to Toel. I could make it back here by curfew, but if I get caught . . ." Jonalin looked sideways at me. "I don't wanna lose everything again."

He brushed ash from my cheek. The rough feel of his fingertip lingered on my skin. For a second, I wondered what it'd be like to kiss him.

I stamped that thought out. I was just confused from missing Matéo, and tipping this fragile balance could send Jonalin spiralling into another overdose. I had to be the untouchable light that kept him on course. *Lumos*, not *luma*.

Jonalin's curfew got later as the days got longer. He took me to a pub downtown, the Drunken Otter, and introduced me to his friends, Beno and Hélio, Ferish immigrants he used to work with at the docks. Their rough humour brought out a side of Jonalin I'd never seen, the conversation full of cursing and dirty jokes. Tipsy from spiced wine, I asked them for Ferish swear words to scandalize Nicoletta with. Beno taught me *bastardo*, Hélio taught me *sacro dios*, and Jonalin taught me *cingari tia mera*, which he warned would get me punched in the mouth anywhere else.

Still, the evening was weirdly depressing. Beno and Hélio kept cracking jokes about travellers they'd seen at the docks and mentioning exotic things they'd unloaded from cargo ships, then realizing Jonalin had been in prison at the time. When Beno called me Téresita, Jonalin went off at him with all the swear words I'd just learned and more. I didn't understand why until the next day when Nicoletta explained it meant Little Téresa.

It was easier hanging out with Airedain and his older sister, Lituwa, whose endless bickering gave Jonalin and me excuses to share weary, eye-rolling smiles. The first hot evening of summer, around Jonalin's twentieth birthday, the four of us went swimming at the Iyo docks. Lituwa had sewn me cropped leggings and a shirt that showed my midriff — the most skin I could show without Elkhounds arresting me for public indecency, she said.

As I pulled off my cottonspun summer dress and exposed my swimming outfit, I caught Jonalin staring. Heat spread over my body. I couldn't tell if he was looking at the ugly scars from when I first attuned and bit my forearm. He turned away as if he'd seen nothing and stripped off his tunic. Then it was my turn to stare, but not because of his sinewy arms and taut chest. Scrapes and bruises covered his skin. He claimed it was from roughhousing with Airedain, but every time I saw him shirtless over the summer, he had new bruises.

The injuries didn't stop him from kicking a leatherball around with Samulein behind the Iyo flats. He knew from Airedain's time at school that boys who did well at sports got teased less. Other evenings, we roasted hazelnuts in a campfire and Jonalin told stories he'd heard from sailors, doing his best to answer Hanaiko's questions about faraway lands. He said it was the closest he could get to seeing his niece and nephews.

In autumn, Kirbana and Narun moved into a two-room flat across the street from mine. They were expecting another baby. When it came — a girl named Sena — Jonalin brought a blanket embroidered by Lituwa. He stuck around to play with Hanaiko,

Samulein, and Kel, who'd been feeling ignored. It was strange to realize I couldn't imagine life without him anymore.

One chilly day in early winter, Jonalin left the parole house for the last time. We stayed up all night with Airedain, Lituwa, and their Iyo friends, drinking in the gathering place. It was supposed to be a celebration, but I didn't know how to feel. I was too nervous to ask what came next.

When Jonalin went outside, I followed, worried about leaving him drunk and alone. He stopped in the frosty field behind the Iyo flats, gazing upward. I stood next to him and craned my neck. Some tel-saidu must've drifted through and cleared out smoke from the kilns. Thousands of stars sparkled across the sky.

"It's beautiful," he murmured.

I glanced sideways at him, silhouetted against the glittering lights. "Yeah. It is."

Jonalin slipped his arm around my waist. I froze. *He's drunk*, I reminded myself.

With that, my medical training kicked in. I put my thumb on his wrist and counted his heartbeats. They were normal. His chest rose and fell steadily, pressed against my side.

"I never thanked you," he said.

"For what?"

"This." He waved at the sky. "Giving me the stars for a year."

My throat tightened. I had so many questions, but he deserved to enjoy tonight. *Kianta kolo*, I thought. A better time would come. I rested my head on his shoulder and sank into his warmth.

In the darkness, I sensed water slide down his cheeks. His body was free. Maybe now his spirit could find freedom, too.

23.

FOURTH ELKEN WAR

“Morning,” I called, blown into the apothecary alongside eddies of snow. I wiped my boots on the mat, straightened my black work dress, and headed into the steamy kitchen. “It’s chaos out there. People are crowded around every newspaper stand, shouting and swearing at each other. I bought a *Caladheå Herald*, but the wind nearly tore it from my hands.”

“Leave it on the table,” Agata asked, stirring a pot in the hearth. “I’ll read it in a minute.”

Nicoletta thrust a bowl of salted beans at me. “Happy birthday! Seventeen beans for seventeen years. It’s Ferish tradition, remember.”

“I’m not eating those,” I said, hanging up my coat and bonnet. “I have nothing to prove to you.”

“Fine.” She rolled her eyes and held out a tin of molasses cookies instead. “I left out the ginger since you don’t like it.”

I tried one. It was a mix of foreign spices — cinnamon, nutmeg, cloves. Nicoletta wasn't usually so thoughtful, but maybe this time of year woke her lingering guilt. These days, Matéo and I barely exchanged more than awkward smiles.

"What do you need me to do?" I asked, warming my hands over the fire.

"Make some more beeswax salve," Agata said without looking up. "People keep asking for it. God knows every winter seems to get drier."

I tied on my apron — Lituwa had embroidered my fireweed crest onto it with bright purple thread — and got to work. "Ai, Nica," I said over the heavy oak table. "Did you hear about the charity social next month? It's a fundraiser for the veterans' league. You should invite Paolo."

Nicoletta turned pink like she did at every mention of the shy young man who delivered milk each morning. "I keep telling you, it's not proper for a girl to invite a boy—"

"And I keep telling you he'd do anything you ask."

She huffed. "If it's so easy, *you* invite someone."

"Like who? Matéo's still not allowed to see me, Jonalin and I are just friends, and—"

I was cut off by shattering porcelain. Agata stood open-mouthed, the newspaper in one hand, the other still grasping at air. Tea spread across the floor among the fragments of her cup.

"God above us all," she said. "It happened, girls. The Fourth Elken War has begun."

⁂

"Read the list again," Dunehein said, running a hand through his long hair.

Kirbana, cradling Sena in one arm, pulled an oil lamp closer and read from a newspaper spread on her table. "'The Rúonbattai captured the following towns — Caladsten, Gåmelheå, Thúnveldt, Hafenaast . . .' The rest are fishing villages."

"And they're all in Nordmur?"

"Yes, all places that Eremur's military was occupying. Caladsten's the biggest concern. Twenty thousand people live there, or *lived* depending how bloody the uprising was — oh, shh, sweet child." Kirbana handed her crying baby to Narun. "Put her in the crib, though I don't expect she'll sleep tonight."

He carried Sena into their bedroom, where Hanaiko and Samulein were playing marbles and keeping Kel from swallowing them. I'd started thinking of Kirbana's kids as my nephew and niece. Their home was always messy, loud, and smelling of vinegar, and I loved it. We'd gotten so used to being there that Rikuja, Yotolein, and I were making dinner.

"What worries me is the Rúonbattai captured all these towns in one night," Yotolein said, distractedly cutting raw elk into slivers. "That takes a *lot* of manpower. They didn't have that many soldiers when I worked for them."

"You don't think the Rin-jouyen . . ." Dunehein began.

"Behadul's too cautious to enter a war, especially since a third of his warriors are staying in Nettle Ginu for good. No, I think Liet has been secretly recruiting. It wouldn't be hard to drum up support from Sverbians who've been under military invasion for three years."

"Did Tiernan and Jorumgard mention anything in their letters?" Rikuja asked me.

I shook my head. Hanaiko and I had gotten into the habit of writing letters to the men. They replied once a month or so with light-hearted campaign stories, but never mentioned their serious military work, wary of mail getting intercepted by Rúonbattai. Their last letter had been sent from Caladsten. All day, the fear they were dead gripped me so hard I couldn't breathe.

"Kako?" Rikuja said.

I looked up from washing duck potatoes. The room swam back into focus.

"What's going to happen at the apothecary?" she asked.

"Oh, um — Agata said during the last war, the military requisitioned most of her medicine. We'll need to work day and night to make enough for customers, too. Inesa will drop out of school to help with chores, but I won't have time to walk Hako and Samu there."

"We can walk ourselves," Hanaiko called from the bedroom amid the clink of marbles. "I'm ten and a half, remember. I might attune tomorrow. Then I'll be an adult and can do whatever I want."

Despite the tension that had settled in the kitchen like smoke, Yotolein chuckled. Leaning over to drop diced elk in the stew pot, he whispered to me, "Independent little brat. No one can doubt she's related to us."

Soon we were all busy. Dunehein got home late every night from the lumberyard, which was supplying wood to repair Shawnaast's old docklands. The navy needed space for new ships. Rikuja and Narun got hired as carpenters for the dock construction, the saddlery where Yotolein worked got flooded with orders from Eremur's mounted forces, and Kirbana sewed military uniforms at home.

At school, Hanaiko joined a girls' wartime club, cutting cottonspun for bandages and collecting scrap metal for weapons and armour. Matéo and Rico joined a military club doing infantry drills and learning survival skills. Samulein, upset that seven and three-quarters was too young to join, started acting up in class. Yotolein reluctantly started giving him combat lessons alongside Hanaiko even though he was more than a year away from getting his traditional first weapon.

One unusually warm day, as melting snow dripped from the apothecary eaves, someone pounded on the back door. Nicoletta and I reached it at the same time. Paolo stood in the alley holding the reins of his sweat-lathered workhorse.

"I was just at the harbour," he panted. "Three schooners with Eremur's navy flag, one mooring in the Shawnaast docklands. They're carrying wounded soldiers from Caladsten."

"I've got supplies ready," Agata called from inside. "Nica, give the inventory list to the ship medic and tell him to pay us later."

Nicoletta and I grabbed our coats. Inesa fetched the wicker baskets full of laudanum, bandages, bogmoss, and more. As we went outside, I had a thought.

"Can you ride to the brick-making kilns and find a young man named Jonalin Tanarem?" I asked Paolo. "We could use an experienced dockhand."

He mounted his horse and rode off. Nicoletta and I hurried through the streets, baskets swinging on our arms. In the harbour, the ship was moored at a newly rebuilt dock. Naval soldiers in red uniforms came down the gangplank, carrying men on stretchers. Nicoletta whimpered as they came up the dock toward us. One man was missing a leg just like her father. I squeezed her hand reassuringly, then we got to work.

Every so often, I glimpsed Jonalin carrying stretchers. The stream of them felt endless. Several soldiers had bled through bandages, gotten splints knocked loose, or developed infections, and the ship's medical supplies had run out on the journey. We fixed what we could here on the slushy shore, gave them painkillers, and loaded them into horse-drawn wagons. A clerk using a crate as a makeshift table recorded where they were sent.

"Ridiculous," came a sharp voice. "Parr Manor is my home. Surely I can send my own friend there."

I spun. Nerio was arguing with the clerk. He'd grown up, now a young man with a trimmed black beard and elk pins on his uniform. Nearby, Tiernan supported Jorumgard, whose leg was in a splint. They all bore faded cuts and greenish bruises, but they were *alive*.

"Only captains can override the rules," the clerk said, tapping his quill.

"I am a lieutenant of the 1st Royal Eremur Special Forces." Nerio thrust out his arm, circled by a yellow band. "My father, *the captain* of this regiment, sent me here to carry out orders in his absence."

"Then get a writ from your precious father," the clerk snapped. "Now move along, Lieutenant."

Nerio made a disgusted sound. Tiernan helped Jorumgard shuffle aside. I finished tying a man's bandage and hurried over to them.

Jorumgard cracked into a grin. "Little pint!" he cried. "I'd hug you if I wouldn't fall over."

"What's going on?" I asked. "I heard an argument."

Nerio spat out the answer. "My father and I volunteered our manor as a military hospital, but only enlisted soldiers can stay there, not mercenaries. We have nowhere to send Jorumgard."

"Never mind," Jorumgard said bracingly. "I'll stay at the Golden Oak. Maybe Nhys can put me up in a storage room so I don't need to climb stairs with a broken leg."

"Stay with us." I spoke on impulse but instantly knew it was right. "Yotolein's flat is ground level, and mine's right above. We'll take care of you."

"I doubt your uncle wants a stranger living with his kids—"

"You're not a stranger. We've been writing to you for a year. Besides, with all of us working so much, Yotolein will like having someone else to keep an eye on his kids."

Paolo had stuck around to help Nicoletta, so I called him over and reeled off a list of instructions — transport Jorumgard in his milk wagon, pick up supplies from the apothecary, and send Inesa to the school to get Hanaiko, who'd show Paolo where we lived. He cast a doleful glance at Nicoletta before going to fetch his wagon. Nerio raised his eyebrow at me, looking reluctantly impressed.

I was starving by the time I reached Yotolein's flat, so I was glad to find dinner still warm. Yotolein was talking to Tiernan and Jorumgard, whose leg was propped on a wooden chest padded with folded cottonspun. Tiernan was whittling a crutch. I kicked off my muddy boots, hung up my filthy apron, and plunked a brånnvin bottle on the table.

"One drink if you make it back alive, more if you don't, right?" I said.

Jorumgard thumped my back in appreciation. "We'll need the 'more' tonight."

Yotolein rounded up his kids. "All right, little monsters. Go see Dune and Rija. Time for the grown-ups to talk alone."

They scuttled outside. Yotolein handed out cups of brånnvin while I helped myself to a rye pastry filled with stew. He made *blødstavgren* different from the traditional Sverbian version, using elk's blood instead of goat's. His whole home was like that. The mattresses were on the floor, the Aikoto way, with Sverbian patchwork blankets. The shelves held books, inkpots, and quills alongside boxes made from carved rioden wood.

"So," I said, "you must have a lot to tell."

Tiernan downed his brånnvin before answering. "I think I triggered the war."

"You *what*?"

He set aside his whittling, rifled through a scuffed leather satchel, and passed a paper to me. "Look familiar?"

It was an ink sketch of a leafless tree with nine branches and nine roots, wreathed by two lilac clusters. One branch and one root were blood red. I recognized it as the way I'd drawn the glowing oak from Brånnhea, like an Aikoto crest, but this wasn't my drawing. Tiernan had burned mine when we discussed it in Nyhemur.

Tiernan rubbed his scarred nose. "That design was on a tapestry in the archives of a Caladsten stavehall. The tapestry oozed dark magic. I felt strange around it, as if I had seen it before and would again, just like in Brånnhea. A cleric told me it was a sacred object donated to them twenty years ago and they had strict orders not to touch it. Twenty years ago, Liet had just become the Rúonbattai's leader. I thought maybe one of his clerics donated it to ensure its protection. So, curious fool that I am, I stole it."

"Oh, no," I muttered.

"I had the tapestry for a day, long enough to copy the design and briefly study its magic. Out of nowhere, Rúonbattai stormed our barracks. It was the first time since Brånnheå that they'd attacked us, and they went straight for the tapestry. Jorum held them off while I torched the bloody thing. Once they saw it burn, they retreated. A few days later, they captured Nordmur." Tiernan poured more brånnvin and downed it again. "After three years of moving in the shadows, it cannot be a coincidence that they struck now."

"It might be," Jorumgard said wearily, like they'd had this argument before. "No one can capture that much land on a whim. They've been planning for ages."

"Who did they recruit?" Yotolein asked. "Local Sverbians in unrest?"

"Oh, I'm sure they got some." Jorumgard shifted his leg and winced. "That's probably who fought in the fishing villages, people liberating their homes. But Gåmelheå got hit by mercenaries from Nyhemur, and in Caladsten, we got hit by mercenaries from Sverba. I recognized their shield sigil."

Yotolein whistled. "Foreign mercenaries can't come cheap."

"Or fast. It takes the better part of a year to send recruiters to Sverba and back."

The two men fell into discussion of tactics. It seemed like they'd get along fine while Jorumgard stayed here. I turned back to Tiernan and asked, "Did you figure out anything about the tapestry?"

He hesitated. "I have . . . theories."

"Try me."

"Well . . . I once told you sacred trees may be a conduit between thousands of worlds, including living and dead lands. Most living ones are probably *shoirdrygen*."

I chewed my lip, translating from Sverbian to Coast Trader. "Shard realms?"

"*Splintered worlds* is the usual translation." Tiernan got a branch from the kindling box and settled back in his chair. "Imagine this is a world. It grows normally over time. Then some catastrophe strikes it, ripping apart time itself. Each shoirdryge develops its own timeline, a future growing apart from the other half." He pulled out a folding knife, cut through the branch end, and peeled apart the splintering halves.

"What kind of catastrophe? Like earthquakes or volcanoes?"

"Far worse. Theological scholars have suggested various options, all of which you will be happier not knowing."

"And there are thousands of worlds like that?"

"Maybe. I think we are *in* one."

I blinked. "How can you tell?"

"I suspected it when we had that vision of the dead Brånnheå oak. It would be quite the coincidence for two worlds to have an identical arrangement of oaks and lilac bushes, down to the exact layout of branches. The more likely explanation is at some point after the Rúonbattai planted the garden, the world split. In our shoirdryge, the oak survived. In the other, it died. The same may be true of your sacred rioden you saw turn black and barren.

"Likewise, the Rúonbattai donated the tapestry before the split. In this world it was well maintained, yet I saw it dusty and mouldering in the other world. Once I moved it to our barracks, I had visions where it vanished, exposing the wall behind it. I could no longer see the dusty version because their locations were no longer parallel."

"Aeldu save us," I said, rubbing my eyes.

Tiernan smiled wryly. "Complicating things further, if the split did indeed happen after the tapestry donation, then it was in the last twenty years. Jorum, Yotolein, and I were already born. You, Hanaiko, and Samulein may not have been. You may not exist there."

"That's . . . a bizarre thought."

"One that makes your family here all the more precious. I advise not dwelling on it. If the other shoirdryge exists, it seems to have no material impact on ours, and we have a war to focus on. Which leads to my other theory about the tapestries."

I scoffed. "I don't know how to ignore my non-existence, but go on."

Tiernan tapped the red branch on his drawing. "This is higher than the red-leafed one in Brånnheå. No matter how we draw them, this cannot be the same branch. I think they are different trees. And if there are two, there may be more. Nine, in fact."

"So . . . anywhere you find a magical oak surrounded by lilacs, you find a link to the Rúonbattai?"

"Right, and look here." Tiernan pointed at the white branches. His delicate ink marks showed peeling bark and weeping pitch. "The Rúonbattai *designed* this tree to be sick. The one in Brånnheå was intentionally corrupted, not dying from malice, neglect, or disease. I have no idea why someone as devout as Liet would tamper with a sacred symbol, but we found people who might know."

"Who?"

"A Ferish mercenary band called the Ombros-méleres — the Shadow Soldiers. They specialize in assassination, suspected of killing a Caladheå councillor, a high priest in the southern colonies, and a member of Ingdanrad's mage assembly. Little is known about them, but Captain Parr has contacts in unsavoury places. It seems an Ombros-mélere got talkative after too much mezcale and told his drinking companion about a disastrous campaign in Brånnheå."

"Yan taku." I sat back in my chair. "That's who massacred the Rúonbattai?"

Tiernan nodded. "Rather more brazen than their usual contracts, so whoever hired them must have paid well. Parr was trying to arrange a meeting with their commander when the war broke out. He is too busy to leave the north now, so Nerio has taken over negotiations."

I glanced at my apron hung on a peg, the embroidered fireweed stained with blood, pus, dirt, and spilled tinctures. Treating itheran soldiers didn't feel useful enough when a war was raging next to my homeland. "Take me to the meeting."

"Katja—"

"Nei, listen. The Rúonbattai want to use saidu as a weapon, right? My people grow up learning about saidu. They're our stories, our spirits, our lands. Nerio ignored me in Brånnheå and made a jinra-saidu erupt a volcano."

He gave a dry laugh. "Nerio certainly learned his lesson. Trust must go both ways, though. Are you willing to tell him that your nation is allied with the Rúonbattai?"

I looked at Yotolein and realized he'd been listening. He reached over the table and squeezed my arm.

"The Okorebai-Rin threw us under the cart," he said. "We don't owe them protection."

"I'm worried about protecting *you*," I replied.

"The Ombros-méleres commander might reveal the alliance," Jorumgard said. "It's better to tell Nerio ahead of time."

I knotted my fingers into my skirt, weighing all the times Aikoto people muttered about trusting brown pigeons against Nerio's help reuniting my family. "Okay. I'll tell him."

24.

OMBROS-MÉLERES

A week later, Jonalin and I left the gathering place at sunset. I needed a cover for being in Ashtown and he was glad for any excuse to be out at night. We pretended to wander, actually heading for a brick building with a horseshoe nailed over the door. Half a dozen horses stood under shelter, munching hay and puffing out clouds of frosty breath. The sound of ringing metal came from inside.

The Ombros-méleres used a farrier as a front for mercenary work. Their soldiers and clients came and went like normal people whose horses needed shoeing. Tiernan's silver gelding, Gwmniwyr, and Nerio's chestnut mare, Saetta, were already here. Since I didn't own a horse, I'd asked Paolo to come, giving us an excuse to stop. He'd agreed in exchange for a good word about him to Nicoletta, which he didn't need, but it had delighted her.

Paolo waved from where his workhorse was hitched. Jonalin and I stopped to talk. I glanced around to check we weren't being watched, whispered my thanks to the boys, and slipped inside. Three figures awaited me in the entryway — Tiernan, Nerio, and Captain Parr.

"Oh," I said, startled. "I wasn't expecting you, Captain."

Parr took my hand in his, glittering with rings, and kissed it. "My ship just got in. I am glad to see you well, Miss Leniere."

Nerio greeted me with a nod. I'd expected him to be furious that we'd hid the Rin-Rúonbattai alliance so long, but he'd been oddly understanding. He beckoned us into a large open room. A sweaty man worked at an anvil near a blazing hearth. Smoke and steam wafted toward the high ceiling. A middle-aged woman held a neighing stallion as a second man nailed a horseshoe to its hoof.

"Last shoe," the woman called to us. "Won't be long."

Once it was done, she came over, wiping her forehead with a rag. She walked with a slight limp, a curved sword swinging at her hip. Her dark hair was drawn into a severe bun that emphasized her strong jaw. The spaulders of her black leather armour rested on muscular shoulders.

Parr bowed gracefully. "Sofia Mazzina. How nice to meet you."

She gave a smile that didn't reach her eyes. "Commander Mazzina to you. I wondered when you'd find me, Antoch."

Nerio arched an eyebrow. "You know him?"

"By reputation. I'm ex-military myself." She looked Nerio up and down. "You must be the Parr boy."

"Lieutenant Parr to you," he replied coolly.

"As for this one . . ." Commander Mazzina studied Tiernan. "You're not tall enough to be the Kånehlbattai, so you must be the fire mage. I did my research. But I don't know the viirelei girl."

"Call me Katja," I said.

Her glance went to my waist. "No weapons. Can you fight?"

I snapped out a water whip. It curled around her rag and yanked it from her grip, sending it fluttering to the ground.

Mazzina's smile turned cat-like, showing her teeth. "I've heard about Antoch's unusual choice of associates. Come upstairs and we'll talk."

She unlocked a door and led us up narrow sooty stairs into what felt like a mockery of a sitting room. Wrought-iron benches with scattered cushions ringed a varnished table, and a dusty wine rack stood next to shelves of old books, but no one could relax here with the constant ringing of metal below. Giana Sartere would've had a heart attack at the dirt worn into the floorboards.

"I invited you here in good faith," Mazzina said, running a finger over the wine bottles. She chose one and uncorked it. "Shall we toast to mutual desires? This is a beautiful spiced red from Ferland."

At her urging, we settled on the benches. I knew what she was doing. In the Aikoto Confederacy, sharing food was a show of wealth and power. Mazzina didn't want to come off as some common mercenary asking for money. She filled five crystal goblets, passed them out, and settled on a bench, draping an arm over the back. Not until we'd each taken a drink did she speak again.

"So," she said. "Antoch, I know you lead the fight against the Rúonbattai. I assume now that you're in open war, you want to hire the Ombros-méleres."

"Perhaps," Parr said, twirling his goblet. "First we want to ask you about Brånnheå."

Mazzina went very still. "What do you know about that?"

"We have been there," Tiernan said. "We saw your comrades' skeletons torn apart by oosoo. We want to know who hired you and what happened."

Her lips pursed. "I don't spill secrets for free."

Parr tossed a small clinking bag on the table. Mazzina glanced inside it and settled back against the bench.

"It's quite the story," she said. "Many years ago, my mercenaries and I ambushed some Sverbians in Dúnravn Pass. Killed the lot of them. As we tended our wounds, the wind rose through the mountains and a voice spoke to me. I couldn't see the speaker, but he said he saw the battle. He introduced himself as Suriel."

I put my goblet down so fast wine sloshed against the edges. "Ainu-Seru. He's an air spirit. The only saidu who didn't go dormant."

Tiernan straightened up next to me.

"That's the one," Mazzina said. "Suriel's been watching the Turquoise Mountains for . . . well, who knows how long? He saw the Rúonbattai go underground sixty-odd years ago to construct Brånnheå. Twenty years ago, during the Third Elken War, he witnessed a meeting. It wouldn't normally have been held above ground, but the Rúonbattai were in chaos. Their leader had just been killed. Their chosen replacement was Liet, who decided to withdraw from the war and enact a plan he'd been devising. He wanted to wake the dormant saidu and use them against the Ferish."

Mazzina paused as if expecting a reaction. When she got none, she went on, fingering her goblet stem. "The Rúonbattai's withdrawal ended open war over Caladheå, but as you know, they grew powerful under Liet's leadership. I give him due respect as a strategist. If anyone can figure out how to wake the saidu, it's him. Suriel ignored this for years, until it became . . . a personal concern."

Parr leaned forward. "Why?"

"I don't know exactly. Suriel was never very open. He said he'd had a human companion who recently died, and it seemed like he thought other saidu would interrupt his mourning. So he spoke to me. He'd seen that my Ombros-méleres were skilled soldiers who didn't hesitate to kill Sverbians, and he hired us to destroy Liet and the Rúonbattai before they woke the saidu."

"How did he pay you?" Nerio asked with disbelief. "Surely spirits do not deal in silver and gold."

"Suriel doesn't need money, but he can find it. Imagine how many people have died in the Turquoise Mountains over hundreds of years — travellers, smugglers, soldiers, gold prospectors. Suriel knows where their plunder rests." Mazzina raised her crystal goblet and smiled.

"Looting the dead, an ancient mercenary tradition," Tiernan said dryly.

"Hold on," I said. "Why did Suriel need to hire humans? He could just crush the Rúonbattai with an avalanche."

"Above ground, yes," Mazzina said. "But Liet rarely left Brånnheå. Maybe he knew he was being watched. Either way, sending Suriel underground is like trapping a storm in a snuffbox. He's weaker, slower, disoriented. So after months of spying, learning the tunnel layout, and stealing magical keys to bypass the rune wards, I devised a plan.

"Ever seen terriers on a fox hunt? My plan was to sneak in through the west tunnel, the one marked by a sunlit crevice. We'd storm Brånnheå and drive the Rúonbattai out through the east tunnel like foxes from their den. They'd surface on the plains of Nyhemur and Suriel would hit them with a blizzard. We attacked in midwinter. It *should've* worked perfectly. Instead, we found the west tunnel already open."

I remembered that tunnel. Near the sunlit crevice, Tiernan and I had discovered a secret wall panel with inactive runes. At the tunnel bottom, the wooden doors to Brånnheå had stood open.

Mazzina paused to top up our wine goblets. "Against my better judgment, I led my soldiers in. The cavern looked abandoned. We rode through empty farmland into what seemed like an empty garrison — and we got ambushed. It was a trap. Yet my mercenaries fought hard. We were winning until the Rúonbattai unblocked a third tunnel."

"The volcanic steam vent," Nerio said.

She nodded. "Huge salivating lizards crawled out, drawn to the carnage. It turned into a bloodbath. Suriel realized something had gone wrong, so he broke through the east tunnel to give us an escape route. You probably saw the caved-in doors and the garrison's splintered gates. I assume the surviving Rúonbattai fled west, deeper underground. Many probably died of their wounds before reaching the surface."

Tiernan winced. "Did you ever see Liet?"

"Oh, yes. Hard to miss a man swinging a flaming battle axe, and he had a cleric at his side, just like everyone says."

"So he *is* a fire mage. I had heard rumours."

"Damned good soldier, too. He must've been forty or fifty and fought like a man in his prime. Could've been an ancient Sverbian warrior. Long braided beard, tattoos on his face and hands. I saw him go down in combat and figured he was dead. Without his leadership, the Rúonbattai couldn't come back from a thrashing like that, so I believed the job was done. Suriel insisted we not pursue their allies."

Mazzina's eyes lingered on me. I kept my face blank. She had no way of knowing I was Rin, and I meant to keep it that way.

She continued, "Three years ago, I learned the military was storming the north in search of the Rúonbattai. Realizing Liet might've survived, I found Suriel and offered the Ombros-méleres' services again. We searched everywhere, but the Rúonbattai weren't *doing* enough to be tracked. They were just fearmongering. Oh, we fought a few battles, but never saw Liet again."

Parr set his goblet down. "So you never noticed their war preparations?"

"We quit before those started." Mazzina leaned back against her bench, crossing her legs. "Suriel called our contract off the autumn before last. He didn't care anymore if Liet woke the dormant saidu. Maybe he finished mourning his human companion, so there was nothing left to interrupt."

"Or you are holding out on us," Parr said.

"I swear I'm not. I doubt anyone can understand what motivates an ancient spirit."

Parr shrugged, twisting a gold ring on his finger. "Earlier, you mentioned 'mutual desires.' Would you consider working for Eremur?"

"To fight the Rúonbattai again?" Mazzina laughed. "No, sorry. I want them dead, but I won't send my mercenaries back into that hell without Suriel. I'm not too proud to admit I would've died in Brånnheå without him."

Parr and Tiernan exchanged a glance. The Ombros-méleres were the mercenaries they'd wanted most, the only ones who knew what they were up against.

"One more question, then." Tiernan opened his satchel and slid his drawing of the nine-branched oak across the table. "Have you ever seen this design?"

Mazzina picked up the paper. "Yes, I think so. A wealthy merchant was funding the Rúonbattai. His estate had a rock garden like this, with white minerals for the tree, red for one branch, and pale purple for the flowers. I didn't have much chance to examine it. We went to kill the merchant and found Rúonbattai soldiers waiting for us."

"Where is the garden?"

"Ah, you already asked your last question," she said silkily.

Tiernan slid a silver half-sov across the table next to the bag from Parr.

"The estate's just outside Hafenaast," Mazzina said. "The garden was destroyed, though. Our horses kicked the rocks everywhere."

Parr rose and gave a slight bow. "Thank you. This has been . . . illuminating."

⁂

"I thought your family said Suriel keeps to himself," Tiernan said to me in Yotolein's flat.

Captain Parr had gone to military headquarters at the Colonnium while we came here. I glanced upward, triple-checking Hanaiko and Samulein were still in my flat. They were supposed to be asleep, but roars, laughter, and thumps told me they were playfighting with Dunehein, shaking dust loose from Yotolein's ceiling. Jorumgard was trying not to laugh.

"It's half true," I said. "Mazzina is right that Suriel had a human companion. After the First Elken War, an orphaned teenage boy named Imarein Rin ran away to live with him. No one had heard from them in decades, though."

Yotolein looked up from mending a rip in Samulein's school uniform. "I've heard that story. As a teenage runaway myself, I took an interest in other Rin ones. I didn't care much about Imarein, though. I wanted to be a warrior and he didn't."

"You're a man after my own heart," Jorumgard joked, earning a smile from Yotolein.

I poured herbal tea into mugs and handed them out. "I'm surprised Mazzina didn't mention the Rin. Suriel must've seen them with the Rúonbattai over the last sixty years, and when Mazzina talked about chasing their allies, she gave me this pointed look."

"I noticed," Tiernan said. "I thought she was fishing for more money."

"She, ah . . ." Nerio coughed. "When I found out my father was coming, I paid Mazzina to not mention the Rin."

Tiernan frowned. “Parr can be ruthless, but we may have to tell him. The Rúonbattai crushed us in Nordmur—”

“Which means all eyes are on my father,” interrupted Nerio. “If he attacks the Rin, every other viirelei on this coast will be suspected of treason, too. Look at Katja’s experience coming here as a refugee.”

“Parr knows that. He is a master of doing things quietly—”

“I said no!” Nerio smacked the table, making the mugs rattle. “Tiernan, I love you like a brother, but I will pull rank if needed.”

Tiernan sat back, stunned. “Fine. If you insist.”

Yotolein and I traded bemused glances. It was odd enough having a Ferish lieutenant in his home, let alone one lying to protect us.

“I think we need something stronger than tea.” Jorumgard shifted his bandaged leg, grabbed a bottle of golden whisky, and poured a shot into everyone’s mugs. “If we can’t hire the Ombrosméleres, what’s our next step?”

“Flip Liet’s plan on him,” Yotolein suggested. “Ally with a saidu first. If you convince Suriel to rejoin the fight, Mazzina might follow.”

Nerio sipped his drink and grimaced. “Setting aside the risk of dealing with an unpredictable spirit, how would we find him?”

“I can try,” I said. “Rin are children of kinaru, which are children of air and water saidu. I’m linked to Suriel.”

Tiernan shook his head. “You would have to travel the mountains in midwinter. That is hardly safe.”

“I spent a winter living out there.” I smiled grimly. “I’ve got a body built for it.”

25.

WHITE RAVEN

In the dim hour between night and dawn, I followed an icy road out of Caladheå and north onto the Roannveldt plain. All I brought was my bone hunting knife and a few tools in a purse strapped to my belt. I needed to remember how to survive in the wild. Hidden in a field of tall winter rye, I shifted into a white wolf.

Even after so long away from this body, the paws and tail and heightened senses felt natural. I loped into the depths of North Iyun Bel, its thick canopy sheltering me from the rising sun. At the frozen creek where I'd first attuned, I shifted to human long enough to catch and eat a trout, then kept running east along the water. Past my old campsite, past familiar bends in the creek, past the logging camp where the same elderly Dona man sang as he shovelled snow.

Short winter days didn't leave many hours for travel. I slept on the creek bank, warm in my thick pelt. The second day, I passed Crieknaast and reached the foothills of the Turquoise Mountains where I'd once spent a winter trapping. The third day, I headed into the rocky valley of Dúnravn Pass. Between mountains I caught glimpses of the shining ocean inlet. The air grew thinner and colder. Wind whistled through the pass, gusting sheets of snow over me.

Of any jouyen, the Iyo had the most legends about Suriel. Rikuja had told me to find the end of the inlet, then look for the tallest mountain. I spotted it on the fourth day, silhouetted against clear sky. Its peak was Suriel's domain — Se Ji Ainu, the Pillared Mountain. Misty waterfalls spilled from its heights into chasms. This was the closest I could get on foot. I shifted back to human and tucked my mittened hands under my arms.

"Suriel?" I called. "Ainu-Seru? My name's Kateiko Rin. I've come to speak with you."

An icy breeze sent my skirt swirling. It spiralled up my body, rustling my braid and making the hair on my neck stand on end. I stood petrified. My fingers were numb by the time a raven drifted through the air, black wings spread wide. It landed on a boulder and cawed.

I lifted a hand. "*Hanekei*," I said, the Aikoto greeting for the first time people meet.

The raven launched off the boulder and shifted in midair. Akohin landed on the ground, human and naked. I gasped.

"Your greeting's wrong for me," he said. "Ainu-Seru appreciates it, though."

I dropped to my knees in the snow. "I should've realized you came here. You told me Imarein was your great-great-grandfather."

Blushing, I forced myself to look, to *see* him. No longer skittish and sickly, he'd grown into a lean, windburned sixteen-year-old. His once-black hair was now white and shaved close to his head, glittering like frost. Like me, he'd never received his initiation tattoos. Where there ought to have been a seagull inked on his upper arm, there was now a kinaru.

"I was always Rin in spirit," he said, noticing my gaze. "All my Dona ancestors came from Rin bloodlines. I'm as much a child of kinaru as you are."

I managed a weak smile. "More than me. I didn't attune to a bird."

Akohin tilted his head. "Come for a walk. I want to show you something. But you need to come like me."

"What do you . . . oh." I sucked in a breath. "Won't I freeze? Aren't *you* freezing?"

"Ainu-Seru will take care of us. Have faith."

I hadn't worn my petticoats, corset, and bonnet, but I still had several layers. I stripped off my fur mantle, coat, dress, and boots, hesitating at my loose linen chemise. I'd never been fully naked in front of a boy, but Akohin and I had never been that way together. This was about baring the truth of myself — stripping away shame, deceit, all the identities and disguises I'd worn like armour. Shivering, I pulled off my chemise, then unbraided my hair.

Akohin beckoned. We began to hike through the pass. The snow stung my bare feet. As we walked, a hot breeze gusted around us, swirling my loose hair. Snow melted under us with each step, exposing damp earth.

"I'm sorry," I said. "For not paying enough attention, I mean. You were mad at me, right?"

"Yes. Although that wasn't fair of me." He sighed. "I wanted to tell you things, but I couldn't say what mattered most. It's strange, isn't it? How hard it is to say, 'I'm scared. I need help.'"

"Agata told me compassion takes effort. We have to hear what people *don't* say, too."

"She's smart. I'm glad she's in your life."

I glanced sideways at him, noticing we were the same height. "Was there anything else you wanted to tell me?"

Akohin was silent awhile. He turned and started picking his way down a steep slope dotted with scraggly pines. Icicles hung from their branches, but in front of us, the snow melted to reveal a rocky path. I followed, gripping lichen-speckled boulders and leafless shrubs for balance.

"Remember the stablehand at the Golden Oak?" he said. "The one with pictures of women on haystacks? He teased me about you. When I said you were just my friend, he asked if I liked boys instead. He didn't seem to care either way, but he couldn't understand that I'm not attracted to *anyone* that way."

My brows creased. "I wondered about that. It's okay to not have those feelings, you know."

"I know that now. But back then, everything about me felt wrong. I couldn't call water anymore, I was a Dona living in Iyo territory, an Aikoto working at a Sverbian inn. And the orphanage . . . well, I still have nightmares." Akohin jumped down to a ledge and landed nimbly, his soles curling around the rocks. Melted snow flowed off the ledge in rivulets. "The only thing that felt right was attuning. It seemed like a sign. Do you know where the name of this pass comes from?"

I dropped onto the ledge after him. "*Dúnravn* means something like *pale raven* in Sverbian. They're mythical birds who travel with Hymelai, Lady of the Sky. That's why the flag of Sverba has a white raven."

"Right. The first Sverbians here saw pale birds in the sky, felt the power of this place, and thought it was home of their sacred ravens. Our legends tell of kinaru living here, but of course a kinaru couldn't land on my windowsill at the orphanage. I wondered if Imarein's spirit gifted me a raven body as a way of asking me to follow his path. I didn't think we had enough in common, though."

"Why not?"

"Well, he was a warrior, while I just kept a knife under my mattress. And he had a lover, however briefly. But once I got here . . . Ainu-Seru told me the truth. Imarein never felt attracted to anyone, either, but after being around itherans in the war, he felt pressured and confused like me. Here, there's no pressure. No fear. No soldiers, priests, or other kids telling me what I should be."

"So you're happy here?" I paused my descent to look around. Far below us, the inlet stretched away to the southwest, sparkling in the sunlight. "You're not lonely?"

Akohin shook his head. "We're never lonely now."

I couldn't hide a shudder. His words had sounded wispy, not like his voice at all.

The melted path led us into a forest covering the lower slopes, quiet and still except for our footsteps and trees rustling in the hot breeze. All the wildlife had gone into hibernation or migrated south for winter. I'd forgotten how it felt to walk barefoot on a carpet of half-decayed pine needles, to have the wind on my skin and branches snagging my hair.

After an hour, we emerged on the inlet shore, greeted by the smell of seaweed and salt water. Frozen tide pools thawed around us. It was hard to believe I'd travelled inland for days and was this close to the ocean.

"Where air and water meet," Akohin said, echoing my thoughts. "Where children of kinaru belong."

He reached toward the inlet. A wave rolled across the shore and over our feet, depositing kelp strands on my toes. The water felt as warm as a bath. Akohin raised his hand. The wave split into ribbons and coiled around us, steaming in the breeze.

After all he'd suffered, he could call water again. This place had fixed what the orphanage had broken. I touched his bare chest where he would've had an antayul tattoo, saying what words couldn't. He released the ribbons, letting them drain back into the inlet.

"Are you ready to meet Ainu-Seru?" he asked.

"If he's willing."

The wind rippled across the ocean. Sheets of mist rose from the surface. They grew and spread into a colossal raven filling the sky, wings folded, head cocked to look at me. It glittered in the sunlight, sending out thousands of rainbows.

Awestruck, I knelt on the shore's wet pebbles. "Ainu-Seru. I'm honoured to be in your territory."

Warm air brushed my bare arm where my kinaru tattoo should've been. A hollow voice wrapped around me, making my skin tingle. *Kateiko Rin. Speak.*

Akohin gestured for me to stand again. I repeated what Commander Mazzina had told us. When I finished, Akohin tilted his head as if listening to something.

"It's true," he said. "Ainu-Seru was . . . traumatized by Imarein's death. They'd been companions for more than eighty years, and they had a bond stronger than humans can ever share. Ainu-Seru's grief was driving him to do terrible things. Things that could throw our world into chaos. Other saidu would've tried to stop him, so he hired Sofia Mazzina to destroy the Rúonbattai before they could wake the saidu."

"Did you know that when you came here?" I asked Akohin.

"No, nor that my great-great-grandfather had died only seven years prior. It's sad to think I could've met him. But Ainu-Seru and I connected right away." Akohin smiled oddly. The mist raven ruffled its immense wings, sending waves across the inlet. "My presence makes his grief easier to bear. He doesn't want to do terrible things anymore, so it doesn't matter if the dormant saidu wake or not. That's why he called off the search for the Rúonbattai."

"It matters to everyone else," I said. "The jinra-saidu in Brånnheå nearly killed my friends and me, even though I tried to save the oosoo."

That jinra-saidu is disoriented came Ainu-Seru's voice. *It does not remember itself.*

I squinted into the raven's brilliant glare. "Would every saidu be like that once they wake?"

Ainu-Seru paused. *Maybe.*

His uncertainty made me shudder. "So if Liet manages to wake them, he won't be able to control them?"

No. Nor does he wish to.

"Then what's the point?"

Akohin answered. "Liet wants to wake saidu in southern Eremur, where nearly everyone is Ferish, and let them wreak chaos. Once they see itherans damming rivers, clear-cutting forests, and ripping open the ground to mine ore, they might kill the workers to restore the balance of nature. Or they'll just destroy everything in a confused rage."

I sucked in a breath. "That's genocide. And it endangers everyone else there, Sverbians and Kae and Yula."

"Yes. Scorched-earth warfare at its finest."

"Caladheå's in northern Eremur, though. Liet can't win without—" I stopped, the links clicking into place. "The Rúonbattai use fear as a weapon. Agata's parents and thousands of others immigrated here to escape famine in Ferland. If rampaging saidu cause food shortages, Ferish people will pack up and leave again."

Akohin nodded. "Liet thinks Sverbians will dig in their heels and stay. They'll buy fish and game from our people, and Liet will bring earth mages from Ingdanrad to repair Sverbian farms and improve the harvest."

"Mass starvation for everyone else doesn't bother you?"

"It terrifies me. That's the problem. I'm Rin by blood, but I wasn't raised as a warrior like you. And Ainu-Seru doesn't want to fight anymore. It . . . disturbs him. Changes him. If we get involved, we'll make it worse. We just want to live here in peace. I hope you can forgive that."

I reached over and held his hand. "Of course. I won't pressure you."

Akohin smiled again, and this time it looked natural. "You're welcome to visit anytime. It's nice having a human friend again. For now . . . we have one more thing to show you."

The mist raven spread its wings. It launched from the ocean, drenching us with spray, and flew toward Se Ji Ainu. Akohin and I watched the sky together. After a few minutes, he pointed.

Pale shapes flew through the air, growing larger. They soared overhead, so enormous they blocked out the sun. Their undersides were white, along with mottling on their long necks, making them hard to spot against the sky. But as they wheeled and flapped their wings, I saw that their outer feathers were black.

"Kinaru," I breathed. "So our sacred animals exist, too."

Akohin whistled, high and warbling like a loon call. A few kinaru landed on the inlet, sending up torrential splashes. They peered at us with brilliant red eyes. He waded toward one and stroked its wing. It clacked its pointed bill and lowered its head to nuzzle him. He whispered to it, then climbed on its back and held out a hand to me.

"I can't make you attune to a bird," he said. "But I can show you how it feels to fly."

26.
LIKE FLYING

My whole journey home, the memory of flying with Akohin stuck in my head. We'd drifted over the inlet, our kinaru mount skimming its webbed feet through the water and sending up clouds of spray, then soared over the mountain peaks. Ainu-Seru had come with us, a warm breeze lifting us so high I saw the sprawling snow-covered plains of Nyhemur to the east. I could've spent a lifetime flying.

That wasn't the life ahead of me, though. I'd promised to help Yotolein raise his kids, caring for soldiers had felt good, and my parents had raised me to be a warrior. But in other ways, I felt as lost as Akohin once had. I could hardly be called Rin anymore. I was the only one in my family to wear Ferish clothes, to be learning their language, to cook their kinds of food.

The deepest ache was I didn't have a companion of my own — like Akohin and Ainu-Seru, Dunehein and Rikuja, or even a brother-in-arms like Tiernan and Jorumgard. Sometimes I saw Hanaiko and

Samulein studying together and wondered if I should've gone to school with them. Everywhere I went, I was outside other people's relationships.

Back in Caladheå, I headed to the Golden Oak, pausing to examine the leafy nine-branched tree carved on its sign. It was just a sign. No odd feeling, no red branch, no lilacs. I found Tiernan in his room, poring over notes, and told him about Liet's plan to have saidu destroy southern Eremur. He listened with furrowed brows, tapping his quill against the inkpot.

"That explains why Liet captured Nordmur," Tiernan said. "He must be building a safe haven for Sverbians. This is quite the discovery, Katja."

"It feels like a failed mission," I said. "I didn't recruit Suriel, which means we won't get the Ombros-méleres, either."

"Those were long shots. Now we know to stockpile food and ramp up monitoring saidu in the south." He pulled a paper across his desk and began scribbling. "I will write to my mage contacts in Ingdanrad and have Falwen warn the Kae and Yula nations. You get some rest."

This life is worth it as long as I'm useful, I told myself. But that night, as Dunehein and Rikuja whispered in their bed and I lay alone, the loneliness felt like ropes holding me to the ground. I couldn't fly like this.

Nicoletta ambushed me the moment I entered the apothecary. She was glowing. "I did it, Kateiko! Yesterday! I don't know what came over me, I just — I asked Paolo to the charity social. And he said yes!"

Behind her in the kitchen, Inesa mock-gagged. I bit back a laugh and said, "That's great, Nica."

Nicoletta twittered on about what she'd wear, who else was going, where it'd be held. Part of me was happy for her, but another part, coiled like a snake in a pit, seethed with jealousy. I distracted myself by thinking about Akohin, which made me feel guilty for repeating my mistakes by ignoring Nicoletta, which made me resent her more.

"Girl!" Agata barked.

I flinched. Nicoletta and Inesa had flinched, too, but it was me Agata stared at.

"You're about to cut your fingers off." She pointed at the cleaver I held above a pile of chopped roots. "What's gotten into you?"

"Nothing. I just—"

"Being a danger to yourself isn't nothing." She flicked a wet rag at me. "Go home. Come back when you're not going to become another patient."

Red-faced, I trudged through slushy streets back to northern Shawnaast. Kids hawked newspapers, shouting headlines in different languages. A woman approached me asking me to sign a petition against drafting soldiers. I muttered an apology, knowing Eremur needed more men. Instead I dropped a few pann in a bowl held by a scarred old man collecting for the veterans' league.

In my flat, I stripped off my dress, petticoats, and corset, then took out my hairpins and let my brown locks fall loose. I got into bed wearing just my linen chemise. Sunlight poured through my stained-glass butterfly, casting rainbows on the makiri shelf over the stove. Normally Temal's swan and mountain cat, Tiernan's coal newt, and a pair of dolphins from Rikuja's parents comforted me, but today it seemed pathetic that I was home alone with them.

I needed a distraction. I rolled out of bed and spread papers over the floor. Tiernan had given me copies of his drawings, including what he imagined the rock garden looked like before the Ombros-méleres destroyed it. Counting the tree in Brånnheå and the tapestry in Caladsten, three of these Rúonbattai oaks were gone now. I had no idea where to look for six more, if they even existed.

A knock interrupted my thoughts. I groaned, not wanting to get dressed just to answer the door.

"It's me," came Jonalin's deep voice.

I sighed with relief. He'd seen me in less clothing when we went swimming. "Come in," I called, shoving my papers aside.

Jonalin slouched in, his short dark hair tousled from the wind, and put down packages wrapped in newspaper. "I heard you were back. Thought you might want decent food after travelling."

I unwrapped the packages. Flatbread and smoked salmon from the Iyo, jam-filled *pérossetto* and cheese from Ferish merchants. He knew what I liked. I sniffed the salmon with a contented sigh and set the flatbread on the stove to warm.

He sat cross-legged. "I went to the apothecary first, but Agata said she sent you home. You okay?"

I hesitated. He'd bought my life here with two years of his, so I didn't want to upset him by admitting I was miserable. Besides, the fact that he cared enough to check on me made me feel a little better. "I'm just tired. Meeting Ainu-Seru was . . . intense."

Jonalin nodded. He took out a cord and started tying knots without looking.

"Are *you* okay?" I asked, picking bones from a chunk of salmon. "I've hardly seen you since the war started."

Jonalin ducked his head. "Actually, I want a favour. But we don't gotta talk about it now."

"It's fine. Ask away."

"Well . . ." He untied his knots and started over. "When my curfew ended a couple months ago, and I could work late again, I asked for my old dockhand job back. The port authority said no. I'm a 'threat to border security.'"

"Oh, no," I said with a mouthful of salmon. I hastily swallowed. "Then I called you to carry those wounded soldiers—"

"That's the thing. The navy let me help. So while your military friends are in town, maybe you can ask them to write me a reference?"

"Sure. I owe you that. But why go back to being a dockhand? So you can work with your friends again?"

"Nei. I mean, yeah, but that's not all of it." Jonalin squinted one eye shut. "Ever since I was a kid . . . I've dreamed of working as a sailor. I love the ocean, wind, open sky, the sound of billowing sailcloth and snapping ropes. Being on a ship feels like freedom."

"Like flying," I murmured.

A smile tugged at his lips. "Yeah. It's no surprise I attuned to an osprey. I wanna see the world, but our people never leave this coast. So at fifteen, I moved here, got a job at the docks, and made friends with Beno and Hélio. They taught me to speak Ferish and find my way around a ship."

"Oh," I said suddenly. "*That's* why you always practise sailor's knots."

Jonalin stuffed his cord into his pocket, blushing. "And why I started learning to read in prison. Well, one reason. Now I can use nautical charts and stuff. Then I got a job at the kilns to build my strength back. But not many itheran crews hire Aikoto, let alone ex-convicts. I need some way back into the trade. Some way to prove myself."

I felt kind of awed. Ever since his overdose, I'd been afraid to ask him anything personal, as if he were loose yarn that would unravel with the slightest tug. But he was so much stronger than I'd realized. Life had dealt him an incredibly shitty hand, and he made it work. Which meant the whole last year I'd been watching over him . . . maybe he'd been watching over me, too.

"Why didn't you ever tell me?" I asked.

Jonalin rubbed his jaw. "It seems selfish, abandoning the Iyo for this. You left your jouyen to protect your cousins."

"Then *you* got arrested protecting them. You're the least selfish person I know, Jonalin."

He shrugged.

I pressed my fingers to my lips, thinking. "There's got to be better jobs in the docklands. What about training as a ship's carpenter like Narun? The navy just commissioned more vessels."

"You think your friends could get me an apprenticeship?" He looked like he hardly dared to hope.

"Can't hurt to try. I'll ask Captain Parr since he's got the most influence. After the info I just gave the military, we've got a bargaining chip."

Jonalin's grin lit up his face, showing the dimple on his right cheek. I couldn't remember the last time I'd seen it.

We smelled burning flatbread at the same time. I swore and tossed it onto a cutting board. When I sat back down, I found Jonalin holding Tiernan's drawing of the oak tapestry.

"I've seen this crest before," he said.

"*What?* Where?"

"In prison, carved on the upper doorframe in the exercise yard. I think I was the only one tall enough to notice it."

"Yan taku. Kaid!" I looked around wildly. Yanking on my dress, I said, "I need to find Tiernan. Go downstairs and tell Jorumgard what you just said. Sorry — thanks for lunch!"

I ran headlong into Førstown and arrived gasping at the Golden Oak. Tiernan told me to stay there with Nhys and be on guard. He spoke with such fierceness I obeyed. I watched through a window as he rode Gwmniwyr galloping down the street, sword swinging at his side.

An hour later, Tiernan returned. He'd found the crest exactly where Jonalin said. It had the same strange magic as the tapestry and the Brånnheå oak, making him feel like he'd been there before and would again. He also had a vision of it overgrown with lichen, matching his theory of seeing damaged crests in a shoirdryge. Desperate not to repeat the tapestry incident, he'd torched the carving immediately, killing whatever dark magic it held. It was the first oak to be destroyed without a fight.

In Shawnaast, we found my family crammed into Yotolein's flat, anxious and confused. Jorumgard had sent Jonalin as a runner — or rather, a flier in his osprey body — to fetch everyone. It was too late in the day to bother going back to work and school, so they stayed, discussing things over dinner. Jorumgard entertained Hanaiko and Samulein by shaping mashed rutabaga into monsters.

None of us knew why the oak crest had been in the prison, but Tiernan had a guess how it got there. Nearly twenty years ago, the military had accused several Sverbian mages of massacring Ferish immigrants during the Third Elken War. Yotolein said the mages were definitely Rúonbattai, and probably guilty. They'd been held in prison during their trial, then gotten mysteriously murdered there. The Rúonbattai alive today might not have known the crest existed.

As we cleaned up dinner, Dunehein nudged me. I followed his gaze. Jorumgard was on the floor with his broken leg stretched out, helping Hanaiko with her history lesson about Sverba. Yotolein held a squirmy Samulein in his lap, but his attention was on Jorumgard.

"Cute, ain't they?" Dunehein whispered.

"The kids or the adults?" I whispered back.

He just grinned. "What about you? Alone with Jonalin, then running outside half-dressed?"

I whacked him. He chuckled.

But as I watched Jonalin, a feeling surfaced that I hadn't had time to puzzle out earlier. I *saw* him now. He sat straighter as he asked Narun about Dona ships, spread his burly arms to indicate hull sizes, stopped hiding his three-fingered hand to demonstrate some obscure knot. His whole body was unfurling, a sail blooming in the wind.

A toy canoe clattered to the floor and bounced under the hot stove. Kel reached for it with a chubby hand. Jonalin scooped the toddler up, saving him from a burn, then fished the toy out with the fire poker. As he brushed soot off his palms, our eyes met. He smiled. It felt like I'd tumbled off a dock into the ocean. I floundered, aware of nothing except him.

I took my time deciding what to do about Jonalin, wanting to be sure my feelings were worth acting on. Even if he felt the same way, I'd been *lumos*, the untouchable starlight, for so long that stoking the flame of *luma*, the lantern, would change everything. There had to be safer people in Caladheå to quell my loneliness with.

Nicoletta took me to the charity social where I danced with Paolo's friends. At the market, I eyed boys and girls, debating if I found them attractive. I even spent time thinking about Matéo, but he felt like a painful memory, like an old sprain. Samulein commented that I'd started smiling whenever I talked about Jonalin. Hanaiko said I was being stupid and obviously belonged with him.

Yet an old secret nagged at me. Jonalin still didn't know why his sentence got shortened, and now that I was bargaining with Captain Parr again, it'd be hard to keep hiding it. Nicoletta insisted both my confessions should come with food. She taught me how to make *glissetto*, bread rolls containing a stew of chicken offal. Jonalin had once mentioned he wanted to try it, but Ferish bakers included the heart, taboo to us.

With a wicker basket on my arm, I headed into Ashtown's grimy streets. Lituwa waved as I entered the Iyo gathering place. Smoke and the smell of melting deer fat wafted from the hearths. It was busy tonight with people preparing camp food. The smelt spawn had been coming earlier every year, and several Iyo would soon head to their fishing grounds. I knocked on the door of the overnight room. Most people who slept here were visitors, but Jonalin was living here until he found a flatmate. An Iyo woman holding a crying baby answered my knock and called over to him.

Jonalin got up from his bed and tucked a battered leather-bound book under his pillow. "Everything okay?"

"Yeah." I tried to calm my thrumming nerves. "Can we talk? Alone?"

He grabbed a tallow candle and we climbed a staircase to a loft over the main room. It was mostly used for storage — crates of spare blankets, dusty shelves of tools and chipped dishes, pegs hung with coiled rope and fishing nets. Jonalin pushed aside a stack of snowshoes that had toppled over. Away from the loft edge, we were out of sight unless someone stood on the far side of the main room and deliberately looked up.

"Homemade and heart-free," I said, handing him a *glissetto*.

Jonalin nodded his thanks, took a bite, and nodded again approvingly. He thumped onto the floor and leaned against a crate, long legs drawn to his chest. His breeches had holes in the knees. I sat with my legs folded under me, wishing I had my own cord to tie knots in.

"It's time I admitted something," I said. "I'm the reason you got out of prison early."

His eyes crinkled in confusion.

"I asked Tiernan for help. He and Captain Parr appealed your case, and in exchange, Parr could ask me for a favour. I didn't want to tell you without knowing what it was, but he's never asked. I don't think he will."

"Why'd you do that?" Jonalin suddenly sounded angry, like I'd cracked him open.

I blinked. "Because you didn't deserve to be in prison."

"But why do you care?" He tossed his *glissetto* back into my basket. "You always say you owe me. Is that the only reason you're nice to me?"

"Nei! That's not—"

"'Cause I didn't fight the Elkhounds for you. I did it so I could live with myself. I couldn't keep watching those aeldu-cursed pigeons tear families apart." His hands curled into fists, his knuckles white. "I shoulda done something sooner. Poisoned the guards or whatever. I'd give up everything again, *everything*, to stop those fucking takuran."

I flinched. Still, I forced myself to look, to see the anger in his face and the hunch of his shoulders.

Jonalin took a deep breath. "You don't owe me anything, Kateiko, especially not your pity. And I'm not gonna be like your military friends, trading debts with you. If you don't wanna be here, leave."

"I want to be." I bit my lip, knowing he deserved honesty. He was strong enough to hear the truth. "Listen, please. I've never pitied you. I've been fucked up by guilt. Last winter, I saw you nearly die here in this building from medicine I gave you. But talking with

Akohin made me realize . . . people are more than their pain. I've been blind to so much. Now it feels like I'm waking up. Opening my eyes."

"What do you see?" he asked in a husky voice.

"The rest of you. You're sweet and thoughtful, but brave and tough when needed. Passionate and determined. Good with kids. Smart enough to read in your third language. And really, really lush." My heart juddered. "I like you as more than a friend, Jonalin. But I have no idea how you feel about me."

Jonalin laughed bitterly. I waited, balancing on a knife point. A tide of voices rose and fell below us. Our candle guttered in warm air rising from the hearths. Finally he said, "Aire taught me a game where you either answer a clear question or take a clear drink. Why don't we skip the vodka and just ask questions?"

"Um . . . sure?"

"You've built this amazing life. You're a healer, you've got powerful friends, you live in fucking Shawnaast where people can tile their floors with gold. What could you want with a homeless ex-con who's got a shitty job making bricks?"

"My job involves looking at rich itherans' actual shit. Want to trade?"

His mouth pressed into a thin line. Maybe he wasn't ready for me to *completely* open up, sarcasm and all.

"Sorry," I said, abashed. "Look—both our lives shattered that day in the Customs House. Thanks to you, I got a head start on rebuilding mine. You've only been free for a couple months, and you're working hard to get back on track. I respect that. I know how tough it is."

Jonalin's eyes narrowed. "All right," he conceded. "Your turn to ask something."

I blurted it out before I lost my nerve. "*Do* you like me?"

"Yeah. For a while now."

"Oh" was all I could say. It felt like my body was filling up with warmth. Every speck of dust in the loft was so beautiful I could cry.

"You flinched earlier," he said quietly. "When I talked about fighting Elkhounds. Are you scared of me?"

I shook my head. After Téresa left him for being convicted of assault, of course he'd be sensitive about it, but I understood better than anyone why he did it.

Jonalin shuffled across the floor. Only when he was close enough to block out the candlelight did I fully realize how big he was — tall, barrel-chested, with arms that could break me. I cupped his jaw. My hand looked small against him.

He kissed me, barely skimming my lips. My breath hitched. His hooded jerkin hung open, so I slid my hand down to his chest, feeling his muscles through his worn tunic. He felt tense as a snare wire, like he was holding back.

"Does it . . ." I swallowed hard. "Does it bother you that I never got initiated as an adult?"

"Nei. You attuned and earned the right, and that's enough for me. Does it bother *you*?"

"A little," I admitted. "I'm still figuring out what I am."

Jonalin folded his intact hand over mine, holding it against his chest. "I'm not exactly traditional, either, wanting to travel the world and stuff. But I'm not gonna run off tomorrow. So we can go slow. Okay?"

I nodded. "Slow sounds good. There is . . . one thing I want to do tonight, though."

Shaking, I lifted my free hand. Jonalin lowered his head, giving me permission. I touched his messy brown hair. He inhaled softly. I curled my fingers into the strands, feeling the depths of his spirit. I couldn't promise he'd be okay, but I could promise to be here for him.

Our next kiss was longer, shy and fumbling and unsure. He smelled like smoke and burnt clay from the kilns. Up here in the loft, with the ocean wind whistling outside, it didn't feel like falling for Jonalin. It felt like flying.

27.

THIN ICE

So began the happiest weeks of my life. When Nicoletta and I could both find time, we went on double outings with Paolo and Jonalin, and when we got called to tend arriving soldiers, the boys came to help. It felt like we all fit together. Jonalin was my keystone, the piece I needed to bridge the halves of my world — Aikoto and Ferish, family and friends, home and work.

He changed his shifts to spend weekends with me. Soon after, he and Airedain moved into a flat. Supposedly Airedain was sick of living with Segowa and Lituwa because he couldn't bring girls home, but it also gave Jonalin and me somewhere more private than the gathering place or my flat where family was always coming and going. Hanaiko and Samulein, egged on by Dunehein, teased me whenever I got home late.

Marijka Riekkanehl, Tiernan's herbalist friend and one of our apothecary suppliers, had been helping at the military hospitals. In her spare time, she examined Jorumgard and declared his leg was healed. Able to climb stairs again, he left Yotolein's flat to stay at the Golden Oak. Hanaiko kept asking if he could visit to help with her history lessons. Samulein wanted him to join their combat training. Flustered, Yotolein said Jorumgard had important work to do.

The Caladheå Council, spurred on by my discovery that Liet wanted to create a famine, quietly began preparing. Paolo's milk suppliers were encouraged to breed their goats. At the docks, Beno and Hélio unloaded crates of rye, barley, and flax seeds to be shipped to farmers on the Roannveldt. My family and I put together a plan for the Iyo to catch and preserve fish to sell to Eremur. Tokoda agreed and Nerio passed it on to the Council, who signed the agreement with record speed.

Jonalin and I used the chance to take my cousins fishing in his canoe and earn a little extra money. One weekend, while we cleaned our catch at the fish market, a war protest turned violent in the nearby city square. We hurried back to Shawnaast. I opened the door to Yotolein's flat and found him in a deep kiss with Jorumgard, hands in each other's hair. I shut the door and shooed my cousins across the street to Kirbana's home.

No one else had seen, but the men had heard the door. Yotolein came to my flat later, embarrassed but smiling. We sat together in sock feet drinking warm mead from a pot on the stove. Jorumgard had brought some from the Golden Oak earlier as an excuse to come over.

"I thought you'd be surprised," Yotolein said.

"I guessed two years ago," I said. "Jorumgard took off his tunic to act as my *bjørnbattai* and you couldn't take your eyes off him. Why do you think I suggested he stay with you?"

"Brat." He ruffled my hair, knocking the pins askew. "I'd appreciate if you don't tell anyone. My kids like Jorum, but . . . it's complicated."

"How come?"

"Several reasons." Yotolein gazed into his cloudy mead, then shook off his musings. "What about you? Am I likely to find you and Jonalin doing something secret?"

I elbowed him. "It's only been a few weeks."

"Get *his* tunic off and you'll change your song. I'm old, but I'm not blind."

My jaw dropped. Yotolein laughed, and I felt a surge of joy that he'd come into my life. We had lots in common — hot tempers, trouble finding our place in the world, and attractions to big men with big hearts. So it was easier to ask him questions I would've squirmed to ask my parents.

"Am I . . . *allowed* to sleep with someone? Legally, I mean. I'm not an initiated adult."

He tapped his fingers on his mug, thinking. "The aeldu are the highest power in the Rin-jouyen, and they marked you as an adult by gifting you an attuned form. So legally you're allowed. Morally, it's up to you and your lover. You don't have to follow the customs of a jouyen you don't live with."

"Then . . ." I squirmed a bit, anyway. "How do I know if I'm ready?"

Yotolein chuckled. "The same way I knew after deserting the Rin as a teenager. If you trust your lover and you both want it."

It felt like a wall crumbled in my mind. Long ago, I'd chosen to trust the aeldu with my attuning, and they hadn't let me down. My wolf body got me to Akohin, which got me to realizing my feelings for Jonalin. My ancestors had given me this chance at happiness. And I wanted to be with Jonalin. I trusted him.

But I couldn't tell how *he* felt. Whenever I tried to go past kissing him, he clammed up. If I suggested spending the night together, he made some excuse or pretended he hadn't heard me. I couldn't shake the fear that I was still a child in his eyes. When I asked again if it bothered him, he got annoyed that I didn't believe him the first time, leaving *me* annoyed that he wouldn't tell me the problem.

And so, happy as those weeks were, it felt like we stood on thin ice over dark shapes waiting to catch us in salivating maws. Military recruits marched through the streets with starched uniforms and newly forged swords, nervous boys about to become men. Their mothers and sisters and lovers threw flowers as they passed, calling blessings and goodbyes. I watched the men board transport ships in Shawnaast's docklands and wondered which ones I'd treat when they came back wounded. Which ones wouldn't come back at all.

Hanaiko, usually brimming with chatter, sometimes went silent for hours. Before the war she claimed to have grown out of dolls, but she started taking Thymarai to bed every night, placing the twig-antler headband next to her pillow. Samulein had started fighting with Ferish boys in the school's athletic league. Rico had quit to focus on the military club, so he wasn't around anymore to tell them off for teasing Samulein.

I rarely saw Tiernan anymore. He'd been moody since returning from the north. The few times I found him at the Golden Oak, he was in his room with stacks of crumbling old books and a bottle of brånnvin. His beard had grown long. He said he was working on a theory, but refused to tell me about it, claiming I was better off not knowing.

On my way to work one day, I found the street blocked by people shouting and crying over newspapers. The Caladheå Council had announced a military draft, calling to arms every unmarried itheran man between twenty and twenty-five. Jonalin told me that evening that his friends Beno and Hélio were getting sent to a training camp down the coast. The next time I saw Paolo, who was nineteen years and nine months, he looked as pale as the milk bottles in his wagon.

*

The snow melted, and for once, Yotolein's flat didn't flood. Jonalin's father, Ranelin, brought us jugs of reeking smelt oil from their family's fishing camp. It was a welcome taste of spring to eat it drizzled over bread, but the Iyo were worried. The spawn had been too early, too small, too short. Snowfall had been light over winter and the spring rains hadn't come, making the rivers run low.

For me, another worry grew with the passing time. I checked our postal box every day and found no letter about Jonalin's apprenticeship. His mood began to sink again. I knew it was trivial to Captain Parr, who was busy leading a war, but I *had* gotten information about Ainu-Seru that no one else could.

As the spring equinox approached, we arranged time off work to visit Toel Ginu for the festival. I was excited to go inside Jonalin's plank house and dance with him in the shrine. Maybe being home would relax him a little and we could slip off to an empty workshop.

Three days before the equinox, Paolo's friend Elian came into the apothecary. We'd danced at the charity social, but all I remembered was he worked at a millinery making fancy hats and had stepped on my skirt. He leaned on the counter while I put together his order.

"You know, there's another fundraiser this weekend," he said. "A dinner at the waterfront hotel downtown. Your hem would be safe."

I glanced up from weighing herbs. "Paolo told you I'm seeing someone, right?"

"The kiln worker?" Elian waved a hand. "He couldn't afford tickets."

Someone cleared their throat. I whirled. Jonalin's broad frame filled the kitchen doorway. Elian jerked upright, stammering. I pushed Jonalin back into the kitchen and sent Nicoletta up front to deal with Elian.

"Why," Jonalin said quietly, "is some itheran talking about your skirt hem?"

"It's nothing," I said. "I danced with him at that social last month—"

"Days before saying you like me?"

I winced. "I was confused, figuring things out—"

"Wow." He tossed paper packages onto the table. "I came to make you dinner, but I see you found a rich pigeon to buy it for you."

"Right, blame this on me," I snapped. "How dare I work out my feelings instead of being an emotionally repressed jackass."

Hurt washed over Jonalin's face. "Good thing you're coming to the equinox festival. You can dance with every other Iyo man, too." He backed away.

"Oh, sure. Walk out." I rolled my eyes.

"What, I should stay so you can insult me?" Jonalin scoffed. "You're not who I thought you are."

"Nei, I'm not!" I slammed my hand on the table. "I can never be myself around you. I can't even be sarcastic because you take everything so fucking seriously. I don't know who *you* are, either. You won't say how you got those bruises last summer or why you won't spend the night with me. The most you've ever told me is while you were strung out on painkillers!"

Jonalin looked like I'd slapped him. He shoved open the back door and left, letting it slam shut.

I swore. A pot hanging in the hearth abruptly boiled over, spilling water into the fire. I'd spent so long being the untouchable light that he'd never felt how hot I could burn.

After work, I went to his flat to apologize, but found only Airedain and some Sverbian girl. Airedain said Jonalin didn't want to see me. He didn't show up the next day or the next. When I got home the night before the equinox, wondering if he'd even go to the festival, Samulein burst outside waving an envelope. It was addressed to *Kateiko Leniere* in bold strokes and sealed with plain red wax.

The letter was written in Ferish. I understood maybe half of it, but I got the gist. Captain Parr was back from Nordmur, and he'd summoned me to Parr Manor tomorrow morning.

I left Caladheå by the southeast road, heading into the Roannveldt. At the end of a dusty lane bordered by willows, I found a vine-covered brick manor, its roof tiles green with age. The military hospital had taken over. In the slushy half-moon courtyard, men unloaded crates stamped with Eremur's red elk sigil. Bandaged soldiers limped across the grounds, supported by nurses. A guard tapped two fingers to his forehead in salute as I entered.

Inside, nurses scurried across the lobby. Beyond an open door I glimpsed a room with tall windows and a crystal chandelier. Whatever furniture had been there was gone, replaced with rows of cots occupied by wounded men. Their groans echoed off pale sandstone walls. Bleach and camphor stung my nose.

Nerio appeared and grabbed my arm. Strands of his black hair had escaped their ribbon and hung around his face. With his beard growing longer, he was starting to look like Tiernan.

"Keep calm," he whispered. "Admit nothing. Promise nothing."

Fear prickled across my skin. "What's happening?"

"You will see. I am sorry, Katja. I never should have let you deal with my father."

Nerio steered me through a corridor, filled with portraits of sombre-looking itherans, into a library. The gilt lettering of leather-bound tomes sparkled on the shelves. One entire wall was covered by a map with elegant gold script. Captain Parr sat at a desk of varnished wood, sifting through papers. He was cleanshaven, wearing a red silk waistcoat over an ironed shirt.

Parr rose and kissed my hand. "Miss Leniere, thank you for coming. Make yourself comfortable."

I fumbled off my coat and bonnet with shaking hands. He hung them next to his black military coat, then gestured me toward a cluster of brocade seats gathered around a low table. I sank onto an armchair while he took a couch. Nerio perched on the desk with his arms crossed.

"How have you been?" Parr asked. "Your family is well?"

"Fine." I fought to keep my voice level. "How are things up north?"

"We are coping. When the first round of drafted soldiers deploys, I will lay siege to Caladsten and starve Liet's mercenaries. Two can play at causing famine." Parr's lip twitched with disgust. "Surely though you are more interested in why I invited you here."

He took an envelope from his breast pocket and slid it across the table. The front said *Jonalin Tanarem* in curling script. The back had a red wax seal with Eremur's navy sigil, two rearing elk over an anchor.

"A shipbuilding apprenticeship as requested," Parr said. "I trust you will pass it on."

If I can find Jonalin, I thought. "Thank you, sir."

"Speaking of Tanarem . . ." Parr spread his arms across the couch back. "Do you recall offering to do me a favour in exchange for appealing his sentence?"

A cold feeling settled in my stomach. "I didn't promise anything."

"Of course." He smiled reassuringly. "I hope you will see this as mutually beneficial, though. Do you know the name Gúnnar Halvarind?"

"Nei."

Nerio finally spoke. "Halvarind is a Caladheå councillor. He comes from old gold in Sverba. We have long suspected he is funding the Rúonbattai, but cannot prove it. He is smart, careful, and has public support. If we raid his home or office, and he is innocent, we will anger thousands of Sverbians. We could trigger a coup."

I frowned. "So you want *me* to prove it?"

"You are a resourceful young lady," Parr said. "I am sure you can investigate without arousing suspicion."

"That's—" I glanced at Nerio, who shook his head. "We're swamped at the apothecary."

Parr followed my gaze. "Ah," he said coolly. "My son got to you first."

Nerio glared back at him. "It is too dangerous. I begged you to reconsider, Father, but if you will not, go ahead. Show Katja how you negotiate."

Parr's smile evaporated. He rose, fetched another envelope from his desk, and placed it on the table. This one was addressed in the angular symbols of Sverbian. "Would you like to know what this is, Miss Leniere?"

I waited.

He moved closer, bringing a scent of spiced cologne. "By all appearances, this letter was sent to Kirbana Elynehl by Torsten Njalind, an ex-Rúonbattai from her home village. If the Caladheå guard finds it, they will arrest Elynehl and her husband. They will then investigate why Hanaiko Kirbanehl and Samulein Narunind of the Dona nation live with Yotolein Rin, a man of no relation. Your cousins, Kel, and Sena will be taken to the orphanage."

I clapped a hand to my mouth. I felt like throwing up. This whole life I'd built was a glass house. Parr had seen inside it, and he could shatter it.

He leaned over me, his black hair spilling over his shoulder. "How sad it will be when guards discover stolen jewellery in the home of Jonalin Tanarem, an impoverished labourer desperate to impress his lady friend. Four months off parole and already a repeat criminal. How tragic when your pardon is revoked and you are not here to save him from another overdose—"

"Enough," Nerio snapped. "There is no need to rub salt in the wound."

Parr straightened up. "It is your decision, Miss Leniere. Investigate Halvarind or watch your loved ones crumble."

I jerked upright. I was nearly tall enough to look him in the eye. "*If* I go after Halvarind," I said, breathing hard, "it's to take down the Rúonbattai. Not because I'm afraid of you."

His smile returned, growing like a feeding leech. "See? Mutually beneficial. I expect your answer before I sail north in two days." He slipped the second letter into his pocket, bowed, and left.

The moment the door shut, I rounded on Nerio. "You knew this would happen?"

"Something like it." Nerio collapsed into another armchair. "When Tiernán revealed his plan to negotiate with my father on your behalf, I feared it would be the start of something terrible. But how was I to deny the return of your cousins? To keep Jonalin in prison unjustly? To let the threat of deportation stop Yotolein from reclaiming his children?"

"You—" I dug my nails into my palms. "*Sacro dios*. Fuck! You should've warned me!"

He ran a hand down his face. "I thought I could manage my father. I was wrong."

The wind whistled through a gutter outside, bringing Akohin's words to me. *I wanted to tell you things, but I couldn't say what mattered most. It's strange, isn't it? How hard it is to say, "I'm scared. I need help."*

Taking a deep breath, I studied Nerio. He looked beyond exhausted. Dark rings circled his eyes. At twenty-one, he was a lieutenant for one of the most powerful men in the military. I imagined the fear of betraying Parr, the guilt of exposing the last relative he had, the blow to his pride in admitting his mistakes.

"I sent for Tiernan, Jorumgard, and Jonalin as soon as I learned about this meeting," he said. "You do not have to make this decision alone."

I swallowed hard. "Jona and I had a fight. He's avoiding me."

Nerio smiled bleakly. "I was clear about the gravity of the situation. If he cares about you, he will come."

28.
OAKS & LILACS

The ticking of a grandfather clock marked our wait. I slumped on a window seat, cheek pressed to the pane, gazing at a sprawling lawn and thinking. I could gather my family and flee to Nettle Ginu, taking refuge with my parents. Our safety wouldn't last, though. It never did.

Something soared past outside. I leapt up and flung open the window. An osprey flew in and perched atop a bookshelf, swivelling its head. Seeing just Nerio and me, it took off and shifted in midair.

Jonalin hit the ground and kissed me hard, pressing his hands to my hair. "I'm so sorry," he breathed. "Aire told me I was being stupid, that I should talk to you—"

I choked out something between a laugh and a sob. "*I'm* sorry. I was horrible to you."

Nerio was still collecting himself from the shock of an osprey shapeshifting in his library. Before he could speak, hooves thudded on the lawn. I looked out the window. Tiernan dismounted from

Gwmniwyr, Jorumgard from Skarp, his golden braid swinging. A moment later, I heard footsteps in the hall, then the two men entered, sweaty and windswept.

"What on earth is going on?" Tiernan asked.

Nerio shut the window and sighed. "What was a long time coming. My father just asked Katja to investigate Councillor Halvarind. If she does not, he will go after her loved ones."

"Parr has it all planned," I said. "He'll frame Jonalin and my family, arrest them, and send the kids to the orphanage."

"*Cingari sia mera*," Jonalin muttered. "I'll kill that bastard."

"Antoch wouldn't do that," Jorumgard said with disbelief. "He's always been good to us."

"Yes," Nerio said. "No other captain would hire a former Kånehlbattai and a foreign mage. My father builds relationships on false kindness so he can continue using people — the powerful as allies, the rest as sacrificial lambs." He looked disgusted.

Tiernan shook his head. "Antoch knows Katja is our friend—"

"It does not matter. His hatred of the Rúonbattai trumps everything. If he knew the Rin are aiding them, he would have slit Katja's throat in this room."

A horrified cry escaped me. Jonalin reeled like he'd been hit. He pulled me into his arms and kissed my hair.

Tiernan folded his hands in front of his face. "Gods help us. Nerio, all this time I thought you were overreacting."

Nerio laughed harshly. "My whole life has been an underreaction. I am half-tempted to resign from the military in protest, but I would get drafted back in. Speaking of which . . ." He handed Jonalin the naval envelope.

Jonalin broke the seal and read the contents. He tore the paper in half and tossed the pieces on the table. "I'm not taking anything from that man."

Jorumgard paced the room, his boots sinking into a thick rug. "So what now?"

"I have to go after Halvarind," I said. "If he's really funding the Rúonbattai, he's as dangerous as Parr."

"We'll help—" Jorumgard began.

"No," Tiernan interrupted. He pressed his fingers to his temples. "Wait. Just . . . let me think. Say nothing."

He sounded so intense we obeyed. The voices, footsteps, clanks, and rustles of the hospital went on. Finally Tiernan looked up again. There was a strange clarity in his face.

"This is an opportunity," he said. "It could confirm my theory."

"*Någvakt bøkkhem*," Jorumgard swore. "I was afraid you'd say that."

"Katja, Jonalin, you have the choice to leave now," Tiernan said. "If you stay, what I will explain may change you forever, but it could give us the key to defeating the Rúonbattai."

Still in Jonalin's arms, I looked up at him. He didn't speak, but he didn't leave.

"Get comfortable," Nerio said, heading for the door. "I will bring something from the kitchen."

Jonalin and I moved to the brocade couch. I felt ill at the thought that Parr had recently sat here. Jorumgard settled on my other side, the padding bowing under his weight. Tiernan tossed his jerkin over an armchair and rolled up his tunic sleeves. He was quiet awhile, apparently deciding where to begin.

"Whenever we plan a move against the Rúonbattai, they know," he said. "That has been the hallmark of Liet's leadership. I have been trying to figure out how he learns our plans. Spies are the obvious explanation, but it would mean they have also infiltrated the Ombrosméleres, the most secretive mercenary band on this coast. My theory is both simple and unfathomably complex. Liet knows what will happen because he literally sees it happen."

I sucked in a breath. "You mean . . . seeing the future?"

"Exactly. A tiny number of mages can see through time, both past and future. Ancient Sverbians claimed the ability was a gift from the gods, so it has remained acceptable even though other forms of magic are distrusted. A few temporal mages throughout history documented their observations, which now circulate as religious texts. That is what I have been researching."

"How does it work?" I asked. "I've seen fortune tellers in the market, and it seems like bearshit."

"Temporal magic is not about tea leaves and omens. It is more like . . ." Tiernan glanced at the door. "If I were a temporal mage, I might have a vision of, say, Nerio returning with bread and cheese. I would see it like a waking dream. Sight is not the only method — one blind mage reportedly heard the future — but it is most common."

"So you're claiming our lives are already fixed in place," Jonalin said, tying knots in his usual frayed cord. "That we don't choose what we do."

Tiernan smiled wryly. "An age-old theological debate. Do we have free will, or are we subject to fate? If temporal mages make incorrect predictions, were *they* forced by fate to do so?"

"It's a mental rabbit hole," Jorumgard said, cleaning his fingernails with a dagger. "Wise men have wasted away in it."

"There is hope for free will," Tiernan went on. "Scholars' leading theory is that temporal foresight depends on cause and effect. For example, you two agreed to stay, so Nerio offered to bring food. With every action, we prompt a reaction, writing our future in advance. That future is like a letter ready to be mailed. Most likely it will go out that way, but we can still rewrite it."

"So a mage would see Nerio return with bread and cheese because that's most likely?" I said slowly.

Tiernan nodded. "We could go stop him, or destroy the food, or burn down the house, but why would we? Humans are predictable that way. Even the most established plans are not guaranteed, though. Sometimes temporal mages see new visions, or multiple ones, or none. The longer the chain of cause and effect, the less sure a future becomes.

"That is where my research hit a wall — in multiple senses. Temporal magic is restricted to whatever physical space the users can observe with their bodies. Again, if I were a temporal mage, I would not have visions of the kitchen from here because I cannot see through walls. I would need to go there myself. So how does Liet foresee our actions without being near us? Can *he* see through walls? Spying on Halvarind might give us the answer."

"Are you sure Liet's the one doing it?" I asked.

"We're not positive," Jorumgard said. "The Rúonbattai have had other mages. But their uncanny foresight started when Liet took power twenty years ago, and of their old guard, he's the only mage still alive that we know of. Plus, Liet proposed waking the saidu, so we know he's got a uniquely fucked-up approach to magic."

I pressed my fingers to my lips, going over everything I knew about Liet. "He had that makiri of Waredul Rin. What if he made one with his own spirit? Wherever it goes, he can see?"

Tiernan looked surprised. "Perhaps. That still limits him considerably, though."

"He could've made several." Jonalin took a braided cord from his pocket. His keys dangled from it along with a tiny stone falcon. "My grandfather gave makiri to all his kids and grandkids."

"Liet wouldn't have an attuned form," I said. "What animal would he use?"

"The white raven from the Sverbian flag?" Jonalin suggested. "It's already in the Rúonbattai sigil."

As I glanced at him, my gaze dropped. His sleeveless jerkin and tunic exposed his Iyo crest tattoo, a dolphin wreathed by sorrel leaves. I gasped.

"It's the oak crests." I leapt up, grabbed a blank sheet and quill from Parr's desk, and began sketching the oak and lilac design. "Remember I said Liet copied Aikoto crests? He's more loyal to his gods than to Sverba, so he used the sacred oak for his nationality instead of the white raven. Lilacs must represent his family. I bet each crest holds part of his spirit."

Tiernan leaned over the desk, resting on his palms. "That explains why time feels strange around the oaks. This is incredible, Katja."

The door opened, making us jump. Nerio entered and set a tray of bread, cheese, and cured meats on the table. I felt too sick to eat. The cheese seemed like bits of the future packed into pale yellow cubes — or was it the past now?

Tiernan drummed his fingers on the desk, thinking. "To us, Katja, sacred trees seem to be conduits between our world and the shoirdryge. Liet must use his oaks as a conduit between fragments of his spirit. His temporal magic bleeds through just enough for us to sense it."

"Are you sure we're not actually tapping into his power?" I said. "Whenever we find an oak, we see it damaged, then destroy it. Maybe *we're* seeing the future."

"Maybe," he admitted. "Though we never see them damaged in the same way we destroy them, which would make it closer to—"

"Tea leaves and omens," I finished. "In other words, bearshit."

"I see I missed nothing," Nerio said dryly.

"Let's not get ahead of ourselves," Jorumgard said. "Does this makiri-temporal-weirdness fit with the oaks we know about?"

Tiernan went to the wall map and tapped the southern mountains over Brånnheå. "Number one. Liet foresaw the Ombros-méleres' invasion and set a trap underground. It was a devastating battle, but better than facing Suriel in open air. Five years later, Liet foresaw us exploring Brånnheå and sent soldiers after us."

"Why bother?" I asked. "Wouldn't he have seen us win the battle?"

"Yes, and seen Nerio kill an oosoo. Waking a saidu near southern Eremur is exactly what Liet wants. He may have used us to see how dangerous it is. Evidently he decided not to try that method himself, since Ingdanrad's mages and the Kae and Yula nations have not reported any more saidu waking."

I shuddered, not sure what was most horrifying — Liet knowingly sending his soldiers to die, manipulating us into the murder of a sacred animal, or knowing our actions before *we* knew. Jonalin got up and rubbed my shoulder soothingly.

Tiernan pointed high on the map at an island city in Nordmur. "Number two. Mazzina planned an attack on a Hafenaast merchant. The Ombros-méleres are so secretive we did not notice them up north, yet Liet had enough warning to prepare a proper defence."

"And to win," Nerio said. "Mazzina left that part out, but I looked into it. The merchant is still alive and doing business."

I craned my neck to study the dot marking Hafenaast. "If Liet only has nine oaks, why build one at a merchant's home?"

Nerio shrugged. "The rock garden was on a hillside overlooking the coast. It was an excellent vantage point to foresee attacks on the town."

"Then what about number three, the tapestry?" I pointed at Caladsten, a dot on Nordmur's mainland. "What use was it hidden away?"

Tiernan scratched his beard. "Good question. And why was it so easy to steal? Perhaps that relates to the cause and effect theory. I had no cause to care about the tapestry until I recognized the crest, so Liet only saw the theft moments before it happened, by which point it was too late to stop me. His only recourse was sending soldiers after us, prompting me to torch it before I could figure out its power."

"And number four?" Jonalin pointed at Caladheå. "If Liet made all these, he must've been in prison, but those arrested Rúonbattai mages were all murdered."

"Hundreds of people were arrested after the Third Elken War, not always with evidence," Jorumgard said. "The military didn't yet know about Liet, so they might've released him."

"The prison crest fits with cause and effect, too," I said. "Once Jona told me, I was bound to tell Tiernan. Liet would've foreseen him destroy it, but there wasn't enough time to stop him."

"There we have it, then," Tiernan said. "If we are right, Liet still has five oaks to spy through."

Jorumgard frowned at the map. "The prison's not somewhere Halvarind would go often. I'd bet my sword Liet is watching over him through another oak. Between his money and government position, he's probably the Rúonbattai's most valuable ally."

I sank onto the window seat, head in my hands. I wanted no part of this mind-bending bearshit about seeing through time. I wanted to hug my family, kiss Jonalin, and go to work. But thousands of other innocent people hit by this war wanted normal lives, too. They'd lost homes, jobs, families, and lovers, and they would keep losing them. All because the Rúonbattai would sooner burn down the world than accept that any Ferish were worth living with.

"Tiernan's right," I said. "Parr gave us the perfect opportunity."

The men all looked at me.

"If the military investigates Halvarind, everyone will find out. Parr chose me because no one will pay attention to me. If I'm about to take down Halvarind, and the Rúonbattai interfere despite having no reason to spy on me, we've got evidence Liet can see the future."

"He saw you with us in Brånnheå," Nerio pointed out.

"And never came after me again. He probably lost track of me. I got taller, changed my name from Eko Mèrus to Kateiko Leniere, started wearing a dress and pinning up my hair. I look like Nicoletta, not a child of the forest."

Jorumgard chuckled. "True enough, little pint. You've grown up."

Jonalin's mouth twisted. "You've also been working against the Rúonbattai since the war started."

"In secret," I said. "My family declared neutrality and my jouyen supports the Rúonbattai. My uncle *was* one. For all anyone knows, I'm here working at the military hospital, just an ordinary civilian medic. I'm the perfect person to do this."

Tiernan smiled. He looked proud, filling me with an odd sense of warmth.

"I'll need help, though," I said. "People I trust with my life, people trained for war, people ready to do whatever it takes to stop Liet from destroying the land. I need to call on my family in Nettle Ginu."

29.
KIANTA KOLO

That evening, I gathered my family and told them everything. Jonalin helped with my shitty attempt at explaining temporal magic. Dunehein, swearing, cracked a clay mug in his grip. Kirbana seemed on the verge of tears, clutching the fussing Sena, looking at Narun's seagull makiri over the doorway and Kel's toy canoes scattered over the floor. Hanaiko and Samulein pretended to play with Kel in the bedroom, but I saw them eavesdropping.

Dunehein volunteered to travel to Nettle Ginu and recruit our family. As we got up to go home for the night, Jonalin asked me to come to his flat. It'd be empty since Airedain had gone to Toel Ginu for the equinox festival, but Jonalin looked so grim I doubted he was asking what I hoped.

They had a one-room, ground-level brick flat on the Iyo street in Ashtown. The last tenants had left because it leaked, but there'd been so little rain this spring it didn't matter. Jonalin unlocked the building's ash-stained door with one key, then his flat with another. He rummaged around in the dark and lit a lamp. The familiar smell of burning fish oil filled the air.

He and Airedain didn't own much furniture yet, just two mattresses on the floor and a washstand in the corner. On the windowsill were clay pots with herb cuttings from the apothecary. The leaves were wilting from all the sunshine lately. I ran my hand through the air above them, trickling water into the soil, then kicked off my boots and flopped onto Jonalin's bed, a tangle of blankets and fur pelts.

Jonalin built a fire in the iron stove, then sat on the floor next to his bed. "I dunno where to start," he said. "Today's been a fucking mess, and my head will explode if I think about fate and the future anymore. So can we talk about something else?"

"Sure." I studied him. "What's on your mind?"

He twisted a cord, not making any real knots. "You know I'm bad at explaining my feelings, and I've had more today than I can name. But . . . I know one thing for sure. I care about you."

My heart skipped. He'd never said that aloud.

"Which is why I can't go on like this." Jonalin swallowed. "I'm not gonna be like Antoch Parr, pretending to be someone I'm not. I want you honestly or not at all."

I sat up. My voice wavered as I said, "I'm listening."

He sighed. "First, you gotta understand a parole house. It's full of angry, bitter men with wounded pride. Imagine twenty roosters stuffed into a coop, then let out to tear each other apart. My cellmate was a Ferish man who didn't like sleeping near an Iyo. I said stuff I shouldn't have. The next day, he followed me and dragged me into an alley. I was too weak from prison to fight him off. He . . . smashed my fingers with a hammer."

"Oh," I said with faint horror.

Jonalin flexed his left hand. "He threatened to kill me if I talked. I told everyone it was an accident at work, but I knew what to do 'cause I've done it before. When Aire was about fourteen, he kept coming home from school with black eyes. I was older and bigger, so I found the kid who'd been picking fights, and I thrashed him. He never bothered Aire again."

"So with your cellmate . . ."

"I rounded up Aire, Beno, and Hélio, and we jumped him with clubs. It wasn't some schoolyard brawl. We beat the living shit out of him."

I winced. "Did it work? I mean, did he come after you again?"

"Couldn't. He got sent to a parole house in southern Eremur for his safety." Jonalin rubbed his neck. "A few days later, I overdosed. I don't really remember, but . . . I don't think I wanted to die. I just wanted to stop feeling everything, inside and out."

I imagined what Jonalin had suffered. Screaming as his fingers were mutilated, being forced to spend nights in the same cell as his attacker, dreading what would come next. I didn't blame him for defending himself. Still, it was disturbing that in my first days of seeing Jonalin again, he'd tracked down a man to hurt him. Badly. Worse than I could've fixed.

Jonalin heaved himself off the floor. Facing the herbs on the windowsill, he said in a strained voice, "I asked once if you're scared of me. Are you now?"

I debated that with maybe more care than I'd given anything. Over the last year, I'd seen Jonalin be patient while Kel threw tantrums, talk Airedain down from blazing tempers, and pet Luna into a purring stupor. He made *me* calmer, too. I couldn't have gotten through today at Parr Manor without him.

"Did you like it?" I asked. "Hurting that man?"

"Nei. Hated it."

"Have you ever hurt someone out of anger?"

Jonalin shook his head. "I've wanted to, but I can control it."

"Then I'm not scared of you."

He turned back to me, skeptical.

Words wouldn't convince him that I knew what terror could do. I'd nearly let Jorumgard and Nerio die of poison simply because they were soldiers. Fear had been the marrow in my bones, keeping me alive even as it killed me, twisting me into someone different. Maybe we weren't the same people anymore, but Jonalin was still a *good* person. The only way to prove I trusted him was to become vulnerable. To bare the truth of myself, my fears and desires.

My pulse skittered. I stood up and started unbuttoning my dress. Jonalin froze. I pulled the black wool over my head, let my petticoats fall from my waist, and unlaced my corset with shaking hands. Last, I slipped my chemise from my shoulders. The tattoos missing from my skin felt like I was missing part of my body.

"I'm not scared you'll hurt me, Jona," I said. "I'm scared you don't want me the way I want you. You claim to see me as an adult, but you always hold back. So *see* me. Have me honestly or not at all, because I'll probably never get initiated."

Jonalin's mouth hung open in shock. "You think you're the problem?"

I folded my arms over my chest. "What is, then?"

He winced. "Me. I'm staring at a lush, naked girl who wants me, and I dunno what to do. I've never gotten this far."

My arms fell limp. Once again, I'd been too wrapped up in my worries to notice someone else's. Jonalin had spent a year with Téresa, who probably didn't even kiss him since they weren't engaged. Then he'd lost two years of a normal social life to his prison sentence while his sisters, cousins, and friends could spend their nights wherever they wanted, with whomever they wanted.

I stepped toward him, barefoot on the rough floorboards. "I've never done this, either. So we'll figure it out together."

Jonalin tipped my face upward. All at once, he was kissing me, holding me close. I unbuckled his hooded jerkin and pushed it from his shoulders. He pulled off his tunic and tossed it aside. I traced his skin, a sight I'd memorized from swimming last summer — his muscular chest, ridged stomach, the dolphin and sorrel leaves inked on his brawny upper arm.

I pulled out my hairpins. The brown locks tumbled to my hips in waves. Jonalin brushed a strand from my cheek, then hesitantly wove his fingers into my hair. I shivered. I wanted us to know every part of each other, the whole triad — heart, body, and spirit.

But he was only using his intact hand. He'd never touched me with his three-fingered one. When I reached for it, he flinched.

"Does it hurt?" I asked.

Jonalin ducked his head. "Nei. It's not that."

"Then what's wrong?"

"I don't want you to . . . see that hand on your body and . . . always remember that. I don't want you to see me as broken."

"Do you think these make me broken?" I raised my forearm to show him the bite scars.

"Nei." He kissed them gently. "They came from your attuning, part of your gift from the aeldu. That makes them beautiful. My injury's just . . ."

I pulled his hand close, rubbing my thumb over his palm. His life was written here. Thick callouses, shiny knife and burn scars, three ragged fingernails lined with soot, a fresh papercut — the hand of a man working for a better life. I kissed his scarred finger stumps. He gasped, his dark eyelashes fluttering.

"You're perfect how you are," I said. "And the things I've imagined your hands doing would make a sailor blush."

Jonalin gave a strangled laugh. His body was suddenly pressed against mine, warm and hard and shaking. "Well, I'm not a sailor yet."

He was definitely blushing, though. I pulled him toward his bed. As he settled next to me, I glimpsed the herbs on the windowsill and remembered today was the spring equinox. After three tough winters since we first met, we'd made it here to be truly together.

Kianta kolo. I closed my eyes and let the sap flow.

I woke with Jonalin's heavy arm draped over me and blankets tangled around our legs. Brilliant lines of sunshine spilled through the shutters. Since we had today off work, meant to be in Toel Ginu for the equinox festival, we'd stayed up all night learning each other's bodies. Every muscle ached as I slipped out from under his arm.

"Come back," he murmured sleepily.

"Soon." I kissed him and rummaged through my dress pockets.

Of all my medical training, one of my most important lessons had been from Tema. When I was twelve, she'd taught me about bloodweed, a poisonous plant that induced a woman's bloodflow as protection after nights like these. At the time, I'd expected to one day get some from a Rin herbalist and be teased by all my friends and cousins, not to quietly buy some from the Iyo healer.

I opened a cottonspun bag and plucked out a tablet of dried, compressed leaves. It smelled like rotten moss. I called water into a mug and choked the tablet down. Normally, bloodweed poisoning knocked women flat for hours with cramps and cold sweats, but Agata had put together a tincture that should ease the side effects. I'd claimed it was for Rikuja. Agata had just cackled knowingly.

Jonalin sat up and peered into my cottonspun bag. "When did you get this?"

"About a month ago."

"Fuck's sake," he muttered. "So we coulda been making love for a month if I wasn't such a coward?"

I downed my tincture and grinned. "We've got until the bloodweed kicks in to make up for it."

For a second, Jonalin looked floored. Then he grabbed my waist. I yelped. He wrestled me into bed and knelt over me. His shyness was giving way to a hunger that made my body thrum.

The lines of sunlight moved across the floor as we wore ourselves out again. After collapsing, he pulled a grizzly pelt over our naked bodies. We snuggled together with my head on his broad chest, feeling it rise and fall. He twisted a lock of my hair around his finger.

"How often can you actually . . ." Jonalin glanced at my medicinal supplies on the floor.

"I shouldn't use bloodweed often," I said. "But Agata taught me other ways to stay safe. They just take planning. So if this is something we're going to keep doing . . ."

He kissed me. In silence, his lips said what he couldn't. I felt like the stained-glass butterfly in my window at home, sunlight pouring through my body and making the room glow with colour.

The door swung open. I shrieked. Jonalin swore. Airedain lurched in, damp with sea spray and holding a flat deerskin drum under one arm, clearly just off a canoe from Toel Ginu.

He gaped at us, then threw back his head and laughed. "About fucking time, Jona. I *told* you Kateiko kept hinting." He tapped two fingers to his forehead in salute. "Forget I was here. See you lovebirds later."

The moment the door closed, I burst into giggles. Jonalin blushed redder than a raspberry. I kissed him until he calmed down, but our time was up. I dealt with the bloodweed effects while he started cooking flatbread. Not until we were semi-dressed and eating did he speak again.

"I forgot to tell you something last night," he said. "You're kinda . . . distracting."

"Tell me what?"

"After those first weeks at the parole house, I started combat training with another inmate. He's ex-military. Taught me to defend myself. Once he left, I practised by sparring with Aire, Beno, and Hélio."

I paused with bread halfway to my mouth, then touched a bruise on his chest. "That's why you looked so beat up last summer."

Jonalin nodded. "I never bothered taking a combat test to be an Iyo warrior, but I can hold my own in a fight. So I'm gonna help you bring down Councillor Halvarind."

We'd decided to avoid investigating Halvarind until Dunehein returned with help, but it was tougher than expected. Now that I knew about him, he was everywhere. His name kept appearing in newspapers for this Council thing or that charity. Sverbians at the market spoke of him with respect and affectionate jokes. At the spring fair, I saw Halvarind preparing to get on stage and make a speech. He was a smiling man in his fifties with a short white-blond beard and black councillor's robes, checking a gold pocket watch studded with diamonds. I shepherded my cousins away before he noticed us.

To anyone watching, I was a normal girl working and stealing hours with my lover. But in the secrecy of the Iyo gathering place, Yotolein drilled Jonalin and me in combat alongside his regular lessons teaching Hanaiko and Samulein. I was embarrassingly out of practice, and the only proper weapon I owned was the obsidian-handled knife from Brånnheå. I sewed deeper pockets onto my dress so I could carry the sheathed knife in concealment.

Jonalin bought an iron mace to make use of his strength. He started out striking straw-stuffed dummies, then moved onto log segments. They shattered into splinters. At first he seemed uncomfortable holding a weapon again, but Beno and Hélio getting deployed to Nordmur sparked something in him. I watched in awe — his body whirling, muscles flexing, sweat shining on his bare chest. That evening, as our bruised bodies tangled together in his bed, he was more gentle than ever.

Half a month after leaving, Dunehein returned to our flat, grinning. Tema swept me into a hug first, followed by Temal. They'd changed since their visit last spring. Tema was getting wrinkles around her eyes, Temal had grey hairs among his dark ones, and they wore long sleeves to cover their tattoos. They explained that when the war started, everyone in Nettle Ginu started thinking of forming another jouyen to distance themselves from the Rin. With the news about Parr, it had become urgent.

"I was stupid to trust him," I said in anguish. "Temal, you *warned* me to be careful—"

"You can't catch everything," Temal said, ruffling my hair. "Sounds like Parr fooled his friends, too. If giving him Halvarind doesn't make him leave you alone, I'll put his blood in the ground myself. No one messes with my little fireweed."

"We've been preparing for something like this, anyway," Tema said. "Falwen passed on what you learned about Liet's plan to destroy southern Eremur. That's been Aikoto land for thousands of years, ours to protect and preserve. If it means going to war, so be it."

More than twenty people had canoed south to help. Nerio had gotten them into Caladheå on trade permits, here with food, pelts, and medicine for the war effort. Mostly they were Temal's family — my grandparents, two uncles and an aunt, their partners, and all my cousins on that side — but my parents said with sly smiles there were some others. Yotolein and his kids joined us to go meet them at the Iyo gathering place. I was hardly in the door when someone barrelled at me, hair ribbons flying. We collided hard.

"KAKO!" Nili squealed, wrapping me in a hug.

I part-laughed, part-cried. I'd grown half a head taller than her. Her older sister, Aoreli, waved and smiled. They looked nearly identical — round cheeks, dark hair pulled into tails, the muscular arms of archers — but Nili had always been loud enough for them both.

"Your loverboy's here," she said with a wicked grin. "He needs rescuing."

I searched the noisy, smoky, crowded room. My family chatted with Iyo who'd piled in to greet them. Kids tore through the building in a game of tag, skirting brick pillars and ducking into side rooms. I found Malana and my other girl cousins interrogating Jonalin like wolves mauling a caribou. I pulled him out of the throng and gave him a reassuring kiss before taking him to my parents.

Jonalin raised a shaky hand in greeting. "Sohiko, Mikiod. Good to see you again."

Tema greeted him back with a knowing smile. She was matriarch of my family now that we'd split from Isu. No pressure at all.

Temal looked him up and down. "Dunehein's been telling us stories. You spent your first night out of the parole house drinking with our daughter?"

"Temal!" I cried.

Jonalin spluttered. He looked like he was about to pass out.

Temal chuckled and thumped Jonalin's shoulder. "Just teasing, boy. I'm glad you and Kateiko have been there for each other."

"Sorry," I whispered as I dragged Jonalin away.

Shielding him from my family's sense of humour would be next to impossible. I looked for someone easier to talk to. Nili was twirling her hair as she chattered at Airedain, who grinned back. She didn't even come up to his shoulder. Aoreli rolled her eyes and muttered to Malana, their fingers intertwined.

I found myself face to face with Rokiud. Under the hemlock needles tattooed on his arm was a new ring of ink leaves. He'd gotten married. Recently, since he'd only been growing out his hair long enough for it to dust his eyebrows. He and Jonalin grinned and punched each other's arms.

"You know each other?" I demanded.

"We met in Tamun Dael years ago," Jonalin said. "I used to spend summers there with my uncle who married into the Tamu-jouyen."

"And my family traded there every summer, remember," Rokiud said. "Me and Jonalin had canoe races against Tamu kids."

"You mean you *got along*?" I couldn't imagine a shy young Jonalin hanging out with Rokiud, scourge of the seas.

Jonalin shrugged. "We both like boats."

"Unbelievable," I said, shaking my head.

Rokiud's wife was there, too, a cheerful young Dona woman named Ikoya who'd settled in Nettle Ginu. She admitted that at first, she hadn't wanted Rokiud to go aid a former lover, but realized it was stupid to care when so much was at stake. Jonalin's brows furrowed as he listened.

Once the newlyweds moved on, Jonalin said, "You've never mentioned Rokiud."

"We were together one night," I said. "*You* never mentioned being friends with a Rin."

He shrugged.

I crossed my arms. "Don't shut down on me again."

Jonalin squinted one eye shut. "My parents sent me to Tamun 'cause they didn't know what to do with me. I don't like talking about it."

I studied him, frowning. I didn't want another fight. "Fine," I conceded.

One more shock remained. In the back of the gathering place, I found Emehein. My annoyingly perfect, traditional cousin who'd stayed loyal to the Rin was *here*. He saw me and braced himself, shoulders drawing tight. I sent Jonalin off with a whisper. Emehein and I looked at each other a moment, then spoke at the same time.

"I'm so sorry—" he began.

"What the *fuck*—"

Emehein winced. He gestured for me to go ahead.

"You let me think my parents were missing." I couldn't hide the hurt from my voice. "I get why you couldn't tell anyone outside the Rin about the schism, but you should've come to Caladheå and told me and Dune yourself."

"I know—"

"I *trusted* you. Whenever our family fought, you looked after me. But when I'd spent a winter alone and needed help, when I'd lost almost everyone else, you didn't come. You disowned me for something I didn't do! I didn't even know about it!"

Maybe it was saying it aloud, or maybe it was seeing the shame on Emehein's face, but suddenly I was crying all the tears I'd held back when I was fifteen. He wrapped me in his arms. I couldn't remember him ever doing that. It clicked that he was doing what Dunehein would. I'd always thought since Emehein was the oldest, he knew the most. Now I realized he didn't.

"It's no excuse," he said, "but your parents *were* missing. We were trying to track two hundred deserters while the north was in chaos. For all I knew, your parents had been killed. That's why I couldn't face you. You and Dune would've asked why I didn't go with them, how I could lose track of our own family. My answer wasn't good enough."

"What was it?" I asked, my voice muffled by his shoulder.

Emehein pulled back and sighed. "Cowardice. I didn't support the Rúonbattai alliance, but I was afraid to leave in protest. I had two young kids. Aeti Ginu was safe, familiar, the place I always expected to raise my children."

I wiped my eyes. "Then why did you leave?"

"Several reasons." He fingered the long braid he'd started growing when he married his wife. "It wasn't a quick decision. Lohara and I only moved to Nettle Ginu last autumn. Mainly, we decided we had to be better role models for our kids and stand up for our beliefs. You were another of my reasons."

"But I wasn't in Nettle Ginu."

Emehein grimaced. "Exactly. I saw you leave home as a child to protect Hanaiko and Samulein. I heard you stayed in Caladheå with them. My pride couldn't handle telling my children that my teenage cousin was braver than me."

Despite everything, I laughed. I looked across the room. Yotolein and Jonalin were playing marbles with Hanaiko and Samulein, who had balled up like turtles among all these relatives they barely knew. I'd learned a thing or two about proud men.

"Is your family still in Nettle Ginu?" I asked, realizing I hadn't seen them.

"Yes. Lohara's in no shape to travel." Emehein pulled up his left sleeve. Tattooed on his lower arm were four square crosses, linked into a grid. "We have two boys and two girls now, with another coming this summer."

I whistled. "You've been busy."

"Rebuilding a jouyen is hard work, but someone's got to do it."

I was about to say Lohara was doing all the work when I realized Emehein was smiling. My painfully serious cousin had made a joke. About *sex*.

Raising a family changes a man, he'd once told me. For the first time, I believed it.

30.

IVY HOUSE

Gúnnar Halvarind lived in a walled estate known as Ivy House, a short distance northeast of Caladheå on the Roannveldt plain. My uncle Geniod flew over the estate as a bald eagle and found the Rúonbattai oak immediately. In a courtyard behind the house stood a white marble fountain, carved into a leafless tree with water pouring from its nine branches. One branch had red veins in the rock. Marble lilac clusters ringed the fountain's basin.

That would've been enough to arrest Halvarind, but we still had to test Tiernan's theory about temporal magic. My family and friends with bird forms took turns flying over the estate. Aoreli, a dove, was first to see something odd. On a clear evening, Halvarind went into the courtyard, checked his diamond-studded pocket watch, and held up a paper scrap as if showing it to the fountain. Every few evenings, he did it with a different paper, always at seven o'clock.

Jonalin's osprey sight was good enough to read from a distance, but the papers were written in Sverbian, which he'd never learned. Airedain had, and although he wasn't a warrior, I trusted him enough to bring him in as a scout. He got as close as he dared in his bluejay body and read something about Eremur troop movements before Halvarind slipped the paper into his pocket.

It was beyond what we'd guessed. Halvarind wasn't just being watched for his protection. He was passing military secrets *through* the oak. That must've been why the Rúonbattai hid the tapestry in the archives of a Caladsten stavehall. A cleric working as a spy could hold up a document, pretending to examine it while Liet read it from a distance.

But it didn't prove anyone could see the past or future. If anything, Halvarind's precise timing suggested Liet was watching at those exact moments. We couldn't get enough information from the papers to find out whether the Rúonbattai were using the knowledge ahead of time. If a bluejay kept showing up, Halvarind would realize an Aikoto person was spying.

So we formed a plan. Every week on the Sverbian holy day, Halvarind's family and household staff attended religious rites at the Førstown stavehall. While they were there, we'd torch Ivy House. By planning the arson, buying jugs of flammable fish oil, and wrapping arrows and javelins in oil-soaked cloth, we gave Liet all possible cause to have a vision of flames consuming his Caladheå base — but as long as we stayed in front of the house, away from the fountain, he couldn't see who did it. If we found soldiers, barrels of water, or similar defences, we had our evidence that against all odds, he'd predicted the arson.

For good measure, we decided to wait a month before attacking. Liet was probably in Nordmur, so that gave him plenty of time to counter-plan, pull soldiers from somewhere, and send them south.

Nerio had promised to make Parr give *us* plenty of time, too, even though it meant letting Halvarind pass secrets for another month.

The stress of waiting was easier with my family and friends around. I worked so hard to appear like a normal teenage girl that sometimes I forgot I was pretending. Malana, Aoreli, Nili and I visited the markets and made fun of itheran fashion. Nili, fond of tall skinny boys, took a liking to Airedain. I'd seen him go through a few lovers already, but I let Nili have her fun. She didn't want anything permanent, unlike her sister, who we caught gazing into the window of a Ferish bridal shop. Nili bet me five pann Aoreli would propose to Malana. I bet Malana would do it first.

And so the month passed like the flowers blooming outside the apothecary — beautiful, fragile, and gone too soon.

Three days before the arson, nothing had changed at Ivy House. That was the first red flag, but we stuck to the plan and started leaving Caladheå. Dunehein and Temal, who couldn't sneak out in their grizzly bear and mountain cat forms, went south on the pretense of visiting Toel Ginu. Some of Temal's family went east with the fish oil, supposedly to sell it in Crieknaast. Instead, both groups would head to our meeting place on the Roannveldt.

The night before the arson, in cover of darkness, people with aquatic attuned forms slipped into the Stengar. Nili, an otter, and Ikoya, a seal, would have no trouble swimming upriver into the plain. In the morning, everyone with a bird form flew off. That left me and Rokiud, who would've been too obvious surfacing on the river as a blackfin whale.

He had a new seafaring canoe, its prow uncarved until the new jouyen's crest was decided. At the Iyo docks, we loaded his canoe with our custom-made arrows and javelins, then hid them under fishing nets and wicker baskets. Jonalin had offered to help, but I refused to let him smuggle weapons when he'd already been to prison — and I had no better cover for leaving town than going alone with a married man.

The navy had a checkpoint at the river mouth. They waved Rokiud and me by, recognizing me from all my time caring for wounded soldiers. We paddled between Førstown and Shawnaast past people fetching water and scrubbing laundry. At Caladheå's northeast edge, near a stone bridge with a guardhouse, I slipped the Elkhounds a few gold sovereigns to believe that our canoe had been thoroughly searched at the first checkpoint.

Further inland, trees grew along the riverbank, sheltering us from view. Tema stepped out from a copse and flagged us down. We hauled our canoe ashore. Everyone was there, armed and ready — Temal and Yotolein with swords at their hips, Jonalin with his mace over one shoulder, Tema with a knife. Emehein had the double-edged battle axe that once belonged to his father. Temal's mother, my temal-tema, was in command — the eldest of us at sixty-five, grey-braided, and deadly with a bow.

From here, Ivy House was just a short hike away. Malana, who'd been watching the estate in her goldeneye duck body, returned with news. Halvarind's family and staff had gotten in carriages and driven into town, but Halvarind had stayed. That was the second red flag. The third was they'd left the front gates unbarred.

Instantly I knew. "It's a trap," I said. "Just like the Rúonbattai left Brånnhea open to the Ombros-méleres."

"Then there's no way we're going," Temal-tema said.

"Oh, c'mon." Malana tossed a javelin from hand to hand. "So we did all this just to back off?"

"They know we're coming. That's enough evidence—"

"Or they forgot to bar the gates—"

"Wait," I said, understanding how Tiernan felt. "Just wait. I need to think."

I slumped against a hemlock trunk, the bark catching on my dress. It was near impossible for Liet to know Sofia Mazzina had told me about the Brånnheå trap, but *his* knowledge wouldn't impact what he saw. *Ours* did. Cause and effect. What was the trap's most likely result? What new future had Liet written?

The answer surfaced like a shark rising from the ocean depths. My family had drilled caution into me. Since leaving Aeti Ginu, I'd hesitated at every step, from revealing Hanaiko and Samulein's identities to admitting my feelings for Jonalin. Being cautious meant not attacking Ivy House. Liet's new future didn't show us there at all.

"They expect us to back off," I said. "That's what Liet *wants*. It's playing right into his hands."

Temal frowned. "So is walking into a trap."

"There's more than two options," Rokiud cut in.

Everyone looked at him. Not only was he the second-youngest warrior here, but he also had a reputation for being impulsive, the way I had been back when we were together. Maybe we needed some recklessness right now.

He flicked his black hair from his forehead and went on. "We can attack some other way. We just need to act fast, so they don't have time to prepare."

"That might work," I said. "We planned to use the front gate. So that's where their defences will be strongest, right? Instead, we could sneak in the back and smash the oak fountain."

"That's not our job," Tema said. "The military can do it."

"How will that look to Captain Parr?" Emehein asked, leaning on his battle axe. Its steel head sank into a carpet of rotten leaves.

"If we back down, and Parr finds out about the Rin-Rúonbattai alliance, he'll think we're in on it."

Dunehein slung an arm around his brother. "Never thought I'd say it, but I agree with Eme."

"It's impossible to get near the oak without Liet seeing us," Tema argued. "He'll be able to find out who we are."

"It's possible," Yotolein said. "We can hide behind fog. Liet will realize we have antayul, but so does every Aikoto jouyen, plus the Kowichelk and Nuthalha confederacies. We could be any of thousands of people."

Everyone shifted uneasily. I glanced through the tree canopy at the sun high in the sky. We only had so much time before Halvarind's family returned.

"We've got a chance to hit the Rúonbattai *and* get in Parr's good graces," I said. "I won't pass that up. I'm going to Ivy House."

Rokiud grinned. Jonalin squeezed my hand in support. The words were like sparks igniting a flame. It rippled through the group, burning up the future Liet had written.

Temal-tema eyed me, fingering her bow. "What's your strategy, *akesida?*"

I surveyed everyone, thinking fast. "Jonalin's mace will make short work of the fountain. He comes with me and the other antayul to the back gate. Nili covers us. Aoreli scouts on our side, Geniod up front. The rest of you torch the front gates as a distraction."

Temal-tema chuckled. "You've learned from your elders. Good. Let's go."

People began saying hasty goodbyes. Emehein and Dunehein embraced and thumped each other's backs. Aoreli kissed Malana, then she and Geniod took off in their bird forms. Nili came over to me, twirling an arrow and bearing a brave smile.

"All that time we spent sparring back home in Aeti," she said. "Now we're finally going into battle together."

Temal kissed my hair. "Good luck, little fireweed. See you on the other side."

We left the trees and emerged onto the sunny open plain. Shaggy mountain goats grazed in a fenced pasture. Beyond it rose the high stone wall hiding the sprawling grounds of Ivy House. Our two groups separated, going opposite directions around the pasture. Mine crept up to the lichen-speckled back gate where muddy wheel tracks had dried and hardened into ridges.

In the pasture nearby was a reedy pond with goat hoofprints around the shore. We antayul pulled out ribbons of water and evaporated them into dense fog. Dove-Aoreli landed atop the wall, peering inside the grounds, and warbled to signal it was safe.

Tema took out a snare wire and picked the gate lock. "Ready?" she asked.

We nodded. I pulled fog in front of me like a shield, pushed open the gate, and stepped through. Tema, Yotolein, and Emehein followed with their own fog-shields, then we merged them into a misty curtain twice our height. Nili and Jonalin came through last.

A grassy orchard surrounded us. Trees laden with white flowers stirred in a breeze, wafting the scent of apple blossoms toward us. We paced forward on the wheel tracks. I knew the layout, but our fog left us blind to enemies ahead. All I heard was dry mud crunching under our boots — until a bow cracked behind us. Someone groaned.

We whirled. Back near the gate, a man with a blue raven-sigil shield ran at us. Nili loosed an arrow. The man dropped with a *whump*.

"Keep going," Nili said. "I'll bet that first shot was Aoreli's."

We hurried onward up the wheel tracks. Nili kept firing behind us. I heard a burble of running water, then mud and grass gave way to flagstone. I threw out an arm to stop the others. There was that feeling, the sense I'd been here before and would again.

"Jona needs to be totally hidden near the fountain," I whispered. "That means going in blind. I'll guide him and whistle when it's done."

Tema nodded. I stood on my toes and kissed Jonalin's cheek. It felt like our whole relationship had built toward this moment — him trusting me to be his eyes, me trusting him to be my sword and shield.

I linked my arm into his and pulled mist from our curtain, wrapping it tight around us. Dampness kissed my skin. Soon I couldn't see my own hands. I closed my eyes and sank into meditation, seeing the fog as whiteness. The people around me looked like dark, blurry patches where the fog couldn't go, while the flagstone ahead looked black.

Taking a deep breath, I stepped onto the courtyard. Our shroud moved with us. Ahead, a looming black shape solidified into the marble oak. White lines flowed through it — water coursing up the trunk, into nine branches, and out in streams that plummeted into a wide basin.

Abruptly, the lines winked out. I still sensed my fog, but the fountain felt dry. The burbling was replaced by the scrape of dead leaves on marble. I wondered if this was the shoirdryge Tiernan had talked about. I shook off the vision, led Jonalin to the fountain, and placed his hand on the basin's edge.

"Stand back," he said.

Jonalin's blurry figure rolled his shoulders, then lifted his mace and swung. Marble shards hit the flagstone like heavy rain. Water spilled across the ground, soaking my skirt hem. He swung again and again, shattering branches, then felling the whole tree with a tremendous *crash*.

He stepped away, panting. "Did it work?"

We stood still. The strange feeling had faded. The oak's dark magic was gone. Water spurted from its severed trunk, then slowed to a trickle.

I dissipated our shroud, letting us see and be seen. Sweat shone on Jonalin's forehead. On the far side of the courtyard rose Ivy House, an enormous log manor with multiple wings, its high walls cloaked with lush vines. Smoke filled the sky behind it. I folded my hands and blew between my thumbs, making a mournful whistle like a loon.

The curtain of fog at the courtyard's edge dissipated. The others hurried toward us. Moments later, a dove swooped down and shifted in midair. Aoreli landed on the flagstone, bow in hand.

"Nice aim," she said, flicking Nili's tail of hair. "I think we got three Rúonbattai apiece."

"You signalled it was safe," Nili said indignantly. "Where did they come from?"

"The orchard shed. They ran outside when you entered the grounds. I landed behind a tree, shifted to human, and started firing."

Emehein's brows furrowed. "How did they get into a shed? We've been watching this estate for weeks."

An eagle flew down and shifted into Geniod, holding a bloody sword. "There are more in the carriage house, watching the front gates burn. I saw another lurking in a copse and took him down. They're like ants coming out of the earth."

Yotolein's head snapped down. "That's it."

"What?"

"Tunnels. I used to make courier drops in a network under Caladheå. If it extends all the way out here, the Rúonbattai could've snuck into the estate." He paced, staring at the grass. "Which means they can sneak *out*. Halvarind might flee now that the tides have turned."

"Aeldu save us," I muttered. "Let's go through the shed. Geniod, tell the others to breach the carriage house. Watch from the air and pick off anyone who scurries out. Mazzina had the right idea about driving foxes from their holes."

"Her plan led into a trap," Tema pointed out.

I smiled grimly. "That's a risk we have to take."

Geniod flew off. The rest of us ran through the orchard, passing dead Sverbians riddled with arrows. Inside the log shed, we found a trapdoor and climbed down a ladder into a dirt tunnel, only wide enough for single file. A torch flickered in a bracket. Everything was eerily quiet.

Yotolein took the torch and led with his sword drawn. Emehein's and Jonalin's heads brushed against hanging roots. I counted my steps to get an idea of how far we went, but it was hard to match it to the surface. Finally we came across a wooden door. Yotolein leaned close to listen.

"Voices," he whispered. "They're arguing. And . . . I think they're in a cellar. I can sense liquid in casks."

"We can use that," I whispered back. "Jona, we'll need your mace again."

Yotolein kicked the door open. Halvarind and a dozen Rúonbattai whirled. They stood in the shadows of huge wooden casks, stacked to the ceiling in long rows. In seconds, Yotolein and Emehein were upon them, sword and battle axe swinging. Nili and Aoreli took up posts by the wall and started firing.

Jonalin began smashing casks. Golden apple-scented cider spilled out, flowing across the dirt floor. Tema and I pulled it to us and joined the battle. I coiled a cider whip around a soldier's ankle and tripped him, leaving him open to Yotolein's blade.

An arrow hit Halvarind's shoulder. He stumbled and disappeared behind a row of casks. Tema ran after him but got cut off by a soldier. She went one-on-one with him, knife flashing, ribbons of golden cider whirling.

A soldier lunged at me. I leapt backward, but his sword nicked my arm. I snapped my cider whip into his eyes. As he clutched them, Jonalin swung his mace into the soldier's ribs with a horrible *crack*. The man crashed into a cask and dropped, limp.

"Halvarind fled," I panted, pointing.

Jonalin grabbed a lit torch from a bracket. Just then, muffled shouts and clangs came from the far side of the cellar. Someone else was fighting. There must've been other ways in here. If Halvarind escaped in the chaos, there was no telling where he'd surface.

"Nili!" I called.

I led her and Jonalin in the direction Halvarind had gone. Beyond the casks were long rows of shelves lined with preserve jars. We fanned out, each taking an aisle. Jonalin's torch shone through the shelves, glinting off the glass jars. I was nearly at the end when a soldier collided with me. We stumbled apart — and a spear bloomed through his chest. He groaned and dropped to his knees.

Behind him, Rokiud pulled his spear out of the man's back, then blinked at me. "Kateiko? Where'd you come from?"

"Orchard shed. You?"

"Carriage house. We chased a few of the takuran down here. Left a brutal fight behind."

"Kaid," I muttered. The element of surprise could only get us so far. The longer we fought, the more bodies would rack up — and some would be my family and friends.

"You okay over there?" Jonalin said from the next aisle, ducking down to peer through the shelves.

As I turned, I saw dusty liquor bottles behind him. An idea formed. "Hand me one of those bottles," I said.

He passed one through the shelves. The clear liquid inside felt like half alcohol, half water. Probably vodka. He and Nili came around the end of the aisle, looking confused.

"Remember that story Yotolein told us from the Third Elken War?" I said. "When he forced a Ferish lord to surrender?"

"Sure do." Nili drew a flammable arrow she'd prepared for the arson. "But for that, we need Halvarind."

"Look." Jonalin lifted the torch, showing a bloody handprint on a shelf. "He came this way."

We skulked out of the shelves. The cellar opened up into waist-high vegetable bins, giving us a clear view over them. A figure with white-blond hair slumped against a door in the far wall, using his uninjured arm to fumble with a keyring. His jerkin was stained dark around the arrow in his shoulder.

"Halvarind!" I shouted.

His head snapped up. I threw the vodka bottle. It smashed on the wall next to him, dousing him in alcohol. Nili nocked her arrow. As Jonalin ignited it with the torch, Halvarind's expression changed to horror.

"Surrender," I called. "You don't have to die this way."

Halvarind hesitated. "What about my family?" he scraped out. "My household staff? My soldiers?"

"We'll spare their lives. I swear on my aeldu and your gods."

The arrowhead burned hot at my side. After what seemed like eternity, Halvarind dropped the keyring and sank to his knees. Wincing, he lifted both hands into the air. It was over.

31.

HONOUR & HOPE

Brandishing torches at Halvarind, we hustled him along, making him call off his men — first in the cellar, then along a tunnel and up a ladder to the carriage house where blood splattered the log walls. The Rúonbattai dropped their weapons at his command. Our warriors corralled them. Then Temal was at my side, panting and hugging me.

"Take care of the wounded," he said. "I'll handle everything else."

He started giving directions — tie up the captives, search the grounds for escapees, take Halvarind's keys, and secure the tunnels. I moved through the crowd, seeing the damage. Dead Rúonbattai lay wide-eyed and still, their blue shields scattered across the dirt floor. The living soldiers scowled or spat at me. In a pool of sunlight by the open doors was Dunehein, collapsed like a fallen tree, his shirt red and torn over his stomach.

I ran to him. Dropped to my knees at his side, shook him, called his name. If I was too late —

His eyelids slid open. "Easy there, little cousin," he said with a weak smile.

A strangled laugh escaped me. I peeled blood-soaked fabric back from his skin. He needed stitches, and soon. I sent Rokiud back to the Stengar, where I'd brought healing supplies in his canoe, and Nili to raid the cellar for anything useful. Jonalin stayed at my side, helping me gather the wounded, examine them, and reassure them.

The aeldu must've blessed us, since none of our warriors had been killed, but plenty were in bad shape. Malana was found unconscious on the lawn, bleeding from the ear. Geniod dragged himself into the carriage house with a shattered ankle and an arrow in one arm. He'd been shot while flying in his eagle body, fell, and hit the earth hard. I knew from treating Eremur soldiers that we'd be lucky for everyone to survive their injuries.

So when Temal said he was sending messengers to Caladheå — one to summon Nerio, another to tell Rikuja and Kirbana what happened — I asked him to fetch Marijka Riekkanehl from her house in North Iyun Bel. Word had spread around local military hospitals about her extraordinary healing abilities. Magical, some people whispered. I'd try anything to save my family.

For now, all I could do was keep working. I even treated any Rúonbattai who let me. My promise to spare their lives was meaningless if I let them die in my care. As I patched up a Sverbian boy about my age, word came that the military was here. I rinsed my bloody hands and hurried outside. Halvarind and his soldiers were on the lawn, bound to a cottonwood trunk that had been stripped of branches.

Nerio rode through the scorched front gates, longbow strapped to his back, followed by Tiernan, Jorumgard, and twenty black-uniformed soldiers on horseback. One carried a fluttering banner with two rearing red elk. Nerio stopped his horse and gazed down at the captives. The elk pins on his coat glinted in the sun.

"Good afternoon, Councillor," he said coolly. "It seems your reign of betrayal has come to an end."

Halvarind was pale as chalk. He stared in disbelief, then rounded on me. "You fight for the Parrs? Do you know what monsters you are in bed with, girl?"

"Better than the ones in your bed," I snapped. "Liet's messing with magic he should leave alone."

Halvarind laughed, slightly hysterical. "Antoch Parr will torture me for information, then for his own sick pleasure. He'll murder my family and make me watch. Not until his imagination has run dry will he grant me the release of death. You should've burned me alive in the cellar! It would be a kinder end!"

I winced. The pained expression on Nerio's face said it was true. I could make excuses that Halvarind deserved whatever fate Parr gave him, but that's all they were. Excuses. Looking upon a man whom I talked into surrender, whose shoulder I'd bandaged, the pain he faced ahead felt more real than ever.

Tiernan spurred his silver gelding toward Nerio. He leaned in to whisper something. Nerio's brow furrowed, then he straightened up.

"Councillor Gúnnar Halvarind," he said. "I, Lieutenant Nerio Parr of the 1st Royal Eremur Special Forces, acting on behalf of Captain Antoch Parr, sentence you to death for treason. You will be executed here at sunset."

Halvarind's jaw dropped. His face went through a dozen emotions, settling on relief and resignation. Tiernan caught my eye and gave the slightest of nods. *This is the best way*, his kind grey eyes said. I swallowed the bile in my throat and nodded back.

⁂

Only after Tiernan did a sweep of Ivy House and declared it free of dark magic did I feel comfortable moving the wounded inside. We turned a grand hall with log support pillars and stone hearths into a makeshift military hospital. The tall iron-framed windows overlooked a garden in full bloom. Aoreli refused to leave Malana, who kept drifting in and out of consciousness. I was tearing up linen for more bandages when Nerio asked to speak with me. We moved into the dim, quiet hallway.

"I must warn you," he said. "There will be fallout from my decision to execute a councillor. My father will back my decision publicly, though, and I swear to take full blame with him privately. It is my fault you are caught up in this."

I picked at my ragged fingernails. He could say that, but it was my fault, too, for being naive enough to bargain with Captain Parr. For calling on my family instead of cleaning up my own mess. For not being cautious and backing off from a fight.

"What will happen to Halvarind's family?" I asked. "Parr will go after them, won't he?"

Nerio sighed, looking somewhere beyond me. "My men found them at the Førstown stavehall and took them into custody. They will go to trial for aiding and abetting treason. If they are found guilty, which is almost certain, I will suggest they be imprisoned in the southern colonies where my father cannot easily get ahold of them."

I swallowed hard. *Not easily* meant he still could, but it was impossible for Halvarind's wife and fully grown children to have lived on this estate and *not* noticed the magical fountain, unmapped tunnels, or Rúonbattai in their buildings. They'd made their choices. We had to make ours.

"For what it's worth," I said, "I think you're doing the right thing."

"That is worth a great deal." Nerio smiled slightly. "However, there is another issue. Halvarind has asked to see his family. Given the chance, he will undoubtedly tell them who attacked him. If they get word to Liet, you and your people will be in grave danger. It is only fair to let you decide whether to grant his request."

"It's up to my elders, not me."

Nerio bowed his head. "With due respect to them, I value your opinion more."

I rubbed my forehead, exhausted. "I don't think it matters. We exposed ourselves the moment we entered these grounds. If any Rúonbattai escaped, they'll tell Liet everything. The best we can hope is that smashing the fountain bought us time. Liet will have to get his intel the old-fashioned way. So I'll talk to my elders, but I already know what my vote is."

Nerio gave me an hour to come back with a final answer. It took only half that. A couple of my aunts and uncles said we'd shown enough mercy and shouldn't put ourselves at more risk, but Temaltema agreed with me. We'd all known this mission was the start of publicly opposing the Rúonbattai, just as forming a new jouyen would be the start of publicly opposing the Rin.

Halvarind's other request was for a cleric to give his death rites. None of us trusted any cleric he chose, so Jorumgard sent for one from Caladheå along with Halvarind's family. I kept working in the hospital, glad not to see their faces. Smoke from ritual fires drifted past the windows, along with faint, haunting song.

Marijka arrived with tinctures and poultices from her herb garden. She took one look at Dunehein's stitches and asked if he was okay with her using magic. Barely conscious, he said yes. Emehein and I held him down while Marijka pressed her hands to his wound. Dunehein groaned and writhed, but when she pulled back, the gash was sealed. I hardly had time to be awestruck before we moved on. She took longer fixing the bleeding in Malana's ear, concentrating so hard she seemed to be in a trance. She'd just finished fusing Geniod's ankle bones back together when Tema crouched next to me.

"It's sunset," she said. "We should be there when it happens."

"I'm busy," I said, examining Geniod's mended ankle.

"Honouring death is part of being a warrior." Tema brushed stray hair from my face. "This is the future we wrote. We have to own that."

Marijka gave me a gentle smile. "I can handle things here."

I gave in reluctantly. Jonalin came with me, holding my hand. Emehein followed after a long look back at his brother. Tema led us through the house, upstairs, and outside to a balcony. Temal was already there, leaning on the railing with one arm in a sling. The sky was red over the western wall around the grounds. Crickets chirped in the cool, still air.

Below us, Halvarind knelt on the lawn, bare-chested with his bandages removed, wrists tied behind his back. Eremur soldiers stood in a half-circle with Halvarind's family. His wife's face was impassive, but her hands were clutched tightly in front of her skirt. His children wept and covered their young children's eyes.

Nerio had declared he'd perform the execution. I'd expected him to use a blade, but he had his longbow in hand. I wondered if he was showing allegiance to his old regiment, the 5th Royal Eremur Mounted Archers, distancing himself from being a lieutenant in his father's regiment now. He stepped forward from the half-circle. Nocked an arrow. Aimed.

His bow cracked. The arrow pierced Halvarind's chest — a clean shot through the heart.

Halvarind toppled back. He convulsed on the grass, eyes wide. I grit my teeth and forced myself to look. It was over in seconds, but the sound of his daughter wailing would stay with me for life.

I stood in the hospital doorway looking over the rows of patients. My feet wouldn't carry me inside. Aoreli had fallen asleep next to Malana's still, sedated form. Death felt like a presence next to me, trying to creep past. Maybe Marijka and I were too late, or not skilled enough, or . . . maybe saving them today didn't matter. Everyone in this room, Aikoto and Sverbian alike, might die in this war.

"You all right?" Jonalin murmured behind me.

I turned toward him. While his soft voice and kind touch had once soothed me, now I was right back in the Iyo gathering place, watching him overdose and not knowing how to save him. Watching him slip into nothingness. I clamped a hand to my mouth to cover a sob. I couldn't tell him how scared I was, all the time, of losing him. He'd feel so guilty that it might send him back to that place.

"C'mon," he said, pulling me away from the hospital. "I think I smelled food cooking in the kitchen."

I was distantly aware of an Eremur soldier handing me a bowl of stew. I must've eaten it, since the bowl was empty when someone took it from me, but I hadn't tasted a thing. I only remembered patches after that — nodding off against Jonalin, him carrying me, then bundled cloth under my head and smooth parquet floor under my body.

My dreams were full of ivy vines that twisted around my throat. I woke thrashing, tangled in a blanket. Someone stirred nearby and lay a heavy arm over me. I recognized the faint scent of burnt clay. Jonalin held me, strong and soothing, until I drifted back into sleep.

In the morning, we started moving people off the grounds. Nerio took the surviving Rúonbattai to prison, Jorumgard and the cleric went to oversee funerals for Halvarind and the dead Rúonbattai, and Marijka went with our wounded to the Iyo gathering place. Malana, groggy from the sedative, had reported she couldn't hear out of her injured ear.

Temal went to study the smashed fountain. Destroyed makiri kept traces of their spirit fragments, but he found nothing left in the marble. Liet must've used a different form of magic, something not stable or permanent. I went to the courtyard to look myself and found Tiernan examining the fountain.

"Well done," he said. "You dealt a heavy blow against the Rúonbattai. Perhaps most important, you proved my theory."

"So you really believe Liet can see the future?" I asked, nudging a piece of broken marble with my foot.

"Yes, but his visions are not infallible. That is incredible news. I am truly sorry your family and friends suffered to get it, but that means we can beat him. We have *hope* in this war."

"Hope," I echoed dully. "You say we've been seeing a shoird-ryge, not omens, but what if seeing it *is* an omen? Whenever we find one of these oaks, people die."

Tiernan perched on the remains of the fountain basin. "As far as I know, no one died due to me torching the prison crest. Sometimes tragedy is just tragedy."

I eyed him, skeptical.

He smiled gently. "I cannot be sure what you saw. I do know this world is real, alive, and precious. That is worth fighting for."

I sighed and sat next to him. "Then I guess my people are in this war for the long haul."

"Not alone." Tiernan laid a calloused hand on mine. "Our sides may need to band together at some point, your people fighting alongside Eremur's military."

"Alongside Captain Parr?" I said in disbelief.

"I am not asking you to trust him. My friendship with him is dead. However, we are stronger together, and Nerio, Jorum, and I will do our best to keep Parr in check. I only ask that you consider it."

32.
SOMEWHERE SAFE

The more I thought about it, the better the idea of allying with the military seemed. Now that we were exposed and vulnerable, we needed people on our side. A decision like that had to be made by an okorebai, though — which meant the prospect of forming a new jouyen was suddenly very real. We sent a messenger to Nettle Ginu, and two days later, the reply came. As soon as we got our wounded back home, there'd be a vote to choose an okorebai.

Marijka warned me that her magical fixes weren't perfect, and everyone's injuries would have to finish healing naturally, so at least I had time to think. If I wanted to vote, I had to swear allegiance to the new jouyen and be initiated as one of them. I'd be giving up my Rin identity for . . . well, who knew. I'd never even seen Nettle Ginu. I hadn't lived with any of those people for almost three years.

"Your temal and I could take you there now," Tema said as we made the rounds in the Iyo gathering place, changing bandages and handing out painkillers. "The Iyo healer will take over your duties. You'll have time before the vote to get to know everyone again, see what you think of the place."

Come home was her silent plea. *Come somewhere safe*. Ever since the Ivy House battle, we'd all been on edge, checking over our shoulders and jumping if a door closed too hard. Nettle Ginu wasn't my home, but maybe I could make it so, the way I'd built a home here in Caladheå.

The rest of my family wasn't any help. Dunehein said it was up to me. Narun said that although he was proud to be Dona, being part of a small new jouyen meant a lifetime of struggle. Yotolein said he was staying here with his kids and I'd always be welcome in his home, but there was an odd note to his voice that made me suspect he was hiding something. Jonalin said nothing about it. I couldn't tell if it was his usual silence or a something-wrong silence.

"Look at it this way," Nili said one afternoon. We were in the field behind the Iyo flats, picking leaves and bugs from baskets of raspberries. "If Jonalin asked you to marry him and join the Iyo, what would you say?"

"It wouldn't matter," I said. "I need to be eighteen to marry someone from another jouyen."

"Ignoring that. Would you feel ready?"

"Nei. I don't even know if . . ." I ducked my head. "Jona and I haven't even said we love each other."

"Exactly. You care for him, but you're not about to swear your life away for him. It'd mean a bunch of change, right? You'd get a dolphin tattoo, have your fireweed crest carved in the Toel Ginu shrine, be buried on their land. That's permanent. If you're not ready for it with Jonalin, when you've already lived among the Iyo for years, how can you commit to an unknown okorebai for a jouyen that doesn't exist yet?"

I plucked a beetle from my basket and flicked it away into the grass. "That's why I want to vote, so I can have a say in shaping the jouyen. We're at war. People's lives depend on who we choose as okorebai."

"Whoever you vote for might not win," Nili pointed out. "Then you're powerless and sworn to someone you don't support. It's not so bad for me 'cause I'm going back to Nettle Ginu anyway, but what if the new okorebai demands that you move there? Are you gonna break up with Jonalin, abandon your cousins and Kirbana's kids, quit your medical training? People's lives depend on *that*, too. I mean, if you wanna give it all up, fine. But I don't think you do."

"How do you know?"

She rolled her eyes. "Other than being your best friend, I'm tapping your lover's cousin. Airedain saw how messed up you were after Jonalin overdosed. You're spiralling back into guilt, trying to protect everyone, forgetting that *we* all care about *you*. We don't want you to be miserable. So if you don't wanna come to Nettle Ginu with us, don't."

I arched an eyebrow. "You're smarter than you look."

Nili threw a raspberry at me. "One of us has to be."

Jonalin stuck around to help with my evening rounds, then we headed down the street to his flat. I'd been sleeping there so I didn't have to walk back to Shawnaast every night. Warm light spilled from the cracks around the shutters. He was reaching for the door when we heard a shriek inside, followed by Nili's raucous laughter. Airedain's low voice floated out like a purr.

Jonalin backed up. "Wanna go for a walk?" he whispered.

I nodded, muffling my own laughter. We both automatically headed west toward the ocean. Out of earshot, I said, "You won't have to deal with that much longer. Nili's going home soon."

He looked sideways at me. "Are you?"

My smile faded. I slipped my hand into his, thinking. We reached a main road, waited for a horse and cart to clatter past, then crossed into the tangle of warehouses and food stalls in the southern docklands.

"Nei," I finally said. "Nili says I'm trying to protect everyone, but it's impossible. I'd have to be in two places at once. So I want to be wherever I can do the most good. Right now, that's here, learning from Agata, looking after my cousins, and helping Tiernan and the others."

Jonalin didn't reply. I felt a stab of frustration. This happened so often — I'd open up my heart and shake out the broken bits, then I had to poke and pry at his to get anything in return.

"Please don't make me do this again," I said.

"Do what?"

"Drive myself crazy trying to figure out what's going on with you. I thought we were past having secrets, but you're locked up tighter than a clam."

"Sorry. I . . ." Jonalin pulled his hand free from mine. "I thought you were gonna leave Caladheå. Leave me. Then it woulda been easier to tell you."

"Tell me *what*?" I asked with creeping dread.

"At Ivy House, after you fell asleep . . . Nerio and I talked. He said if I still want to work on a ship, I could enlist in the navy."

I stopped on the sidewalk and stared at him. "As a soldier?"

Jonalin's cheeks flushed. "Beno and Hélio are stationed at the siege of Caladsten. Paolo will get drafted soon. Everyone my age at the kilns is gone, and some of 'em have never even been in a fistfight. They're getting shipped north to die. I'm left working with terrified boys who are jealous 'cause viirelei can't get drafted. The older men say if I live here, make money here, I should have to fight. *Coward* is the nicest thing they call me."

"You're *not* a coward. You just fought the Rúonbattai, as bravely as any of us."

"Maybe. But that mission's done, and Tokoda's not gonna bring us into this war. So I've been wondering the same thing as you, where I can do the most good. Maybe it's in the navy. And if I . . . survive the war . . . I'll have my way into working as a sailor. It might be my only way."

"So that's it? You're breaking up with me to enlist?"

"I . . ." He rubbed his jaw. The ocean breeze rippled through his hair.

"Aeldu save us, Jona. Answer the damned question."

"I don't know! I don't fucking know, okay?"

A Ferish woman eyed us through clouds of steam from her noodle stall. I pulled Jonalin into an alley stained with seagull droppings. He dropped onto a cart, making the timbers groan.

"Part of my spirit's still in prison." Jonalin slumped forward, head in his hands. "I need to heal, figure my shit out, get back some self-respect so I'm not so fucking fragile. I dunno if I can do that here. But I can try. I'll stay if you want me to, Kako."

"Oh, Jona," I said softly. My irritation washed away, replaced by guilt for snapping at him. "You can't live your life for me."

"Why not?" he said, sounding defensive.

"Because it's never been enough for you. You once said you'd give up everything to go back and protect those other families in the Customs House. That's why I—" My throat caught. "I admire you. You have the biggest heart of anyone I've ever met."

Jonalin turned away. "You deserve more of it."

I cupped my hands around his face and pulled it back toward me, gazing into his deep brown eyes. "The whole time we've been together, I knew you wanted to be a sailor. I knew you might leave one day. And if I'm going to lose you, I'd rather it be this way, doing what you love and what feels right. Not . . ."

"Not by my own hand," he said so quietly I almost missed it.

I nodded, choking back tears.

He kissed me. When we separated, we noticed an itheran man in a warehouse doorway, smoking a pipe and watching us. We kept walking, uncomfortably aware that the slightest hint of "indecent behaviour" could get us in trouble.

"Nothing's for sure yet," Jonalin said. "Since I've been convicted of assaulting Elkhounds, I have to get assessed to make sure I'm not a threat to our own side. But Nerio says he'll write me a good reference, and from a lieutenant, well, it'll help. A lot."

I bit my lip. "Will Tokoda let you go?"

"Not happily, but yeah. One rogue warrior won't break whatever truce she has with Liet."

"When would you leave?"

"In about a week. I'd go to the naval training camp on Ile vi Dévoye, an island across the bay, for a month. Then I'd come back here, say goodbye, and ship out from Shawnaast."

As if our feet had been drawn there, we wound up at the Iyo docks. My family's unmarked canoes bobbed there among ones with tall seafaring dolphin prows. I thought back to my conversation with Nili about marrying Jonalin, and I wondered if being in his canoe could ever feel like home to me.

"Wanna go out on the bay?" he asked.

I managed a smile. "Yeah. Let's go."

We climbed into his canoe and pushed off from the docks. The temperature dropped as we paddled away from the shoreline.

Golden sunset glittered on the waves. We passed ships moored in the harbour, then stowed our paddles and drifted. Behind us, stars were appearing in the eastern sky, and somewhere ahead lay Ile vi Dévoye, hidden beyond the horizon.

Under his breath, Jonalin sang in Ferish. I caught enough words to know it was a sea shanty. Out here in open water was the only place I'd ever seen him truly happy. His other body was an osprey, but he had a dolphin spirit, and it was trapped by the brick and stone of Caladheå. The kindest thing I could do would be to set him free.

I woke to banging on the door of Jonalin's flat. He stirred next to me, rubbing his eyes. Airedain sat up in his bed, followed by Nili. She stumbled to the door, flung it open, and spoke to someone I couldn't see.

"It's for you," she said, smacking my foot through Jonalin's grizzly-pelt blanket.

Before I could move, Inesa pushed inside. Her eyes were bloodshot and her bonnet hung by its strings down her back. Despite being fourteen and raised with the same iron-clad morals as Matéo and Nicoletta, she either didn't notice or care that two unmarried half-dressed couples had been sharing beds.

"Nica's missing," she said.

"*What?*" I said, jerking upright.

"She—" Inesa's lip trembled. "She went out with Paolo last night but never came back to the apothecary. She's not at his home, or our parents', or any of her friends'."

"Yan taku. Fuck!" I flung off the blanket and sprang up in my thin chemise. "Do you know where Paolo is?"

Inesa shook her head, auburn curls bouncing. "He's gone, too. Grandmera thinks they ran away, or got married so he wouldn't be drafted, or — I don't know. Something stupid."

"Where would they get married? A sancte, right?"

"Right, but all the priests at our sancte know our family. They'd tell us if Nica showed up during the night."

"Good reason to find another one," Nili said, draping Airedain's caribou pelt over her shoulders. "Which one would Nicoletta pick? If she needed to feel safe or hidden?"

"Nen Divinus," I said. "It's like a fortress. I saw priests take my cousins in there, and I thought they'd never come back out."

"Go check," Jonalin said, pulling on his tunic. "I'll try to track down Paolo. Aire and Nili, can you go to the Iyo gathering place and tell Kako's family what's going on?"

They nodded. I yanked on my dress, leaving my corset and petticoats on the floor, pocketed my obsidian-handled knife just in case, then I was out the door with Inesa. I held her small hand as we hurried through Ashtown toward the city square. It was a cool morning with fog filling the streets. It wouldn't have been hard for Nicoletta and Paolo to slip past the city guards and leave town.

The fog hid Nen Divinus's spired towers, making the grey building look smaller than usual. We'd gone up the stone steps and into the portico when I stopped, hit by a realization. "I can't go in there."

Inesa turned her wide green eyes on me, pleading. "Why not?"

"Sorry," I said, abashed. "It's how I was raised. We're not supposed to go into other nations' holy places. Just go inside, find a *padro* or *madro*, and bring them out here. I'll talk to them."

She drew herself up to her full, not-very-impressive height. With all of her older sister's bravado, she pulled open the tall wooden doors and stepped inside. I sat on the top step under cover of the portico, shivering. Down at street level, passersby appeared and disappeared in the fog. Nen Divinus's bell rang from high overhead.

After what felt like ages, the doors reopened. Inesa came out with a middle-aged man in deep blue robes. I sprang to my feet.

"Nica's here," Inesa said, her eyes brimming with tears. "But she won't move, and she won't tell me what happened."

"Is Paolo with her?" I asked.

"The young lady is alone," the priest said with a thick, flowing accent. "She came during the night and asked to pray in the main hall."

"You have to go see her," Inesa begged me. "Please, Kateiko. She told me not to bring Grandmera. You're the only other person Nica listens to."

I buried my face in my hands. Yotolein had told me that I didn't need to follow the customs of a jouyen I didn't live with. And I'd gone inside Brånnhea's stavehall, full of skeletons and dark magic, so a sancte couldn't be any worse. I just had to not think about everything Akohin and my cousins had suffered in the orphanage behind this building.

"Fine," I said, letting my hands drop. "Take me to Nicoletta."

The priest looked me up and down, his lip curling. My hair was a tangled mess, my dress didn't fit right without my corset, and my skirt hung loose without my petticoats. Inesa handed me her long woolen coat. I put it on, and the priest beckoned us inside.

I had the sense of stepping into a hollow mountain. Thick stone pillars ran the length of a great hall, rising to a vaulted ceiling hidden by shadows. The only light came from candelabras whose flames flickered in a draft, and the fog on the other side of the stained-glass windows muted their colours. The silence was so thick it choked me, like I was breathing dust.

A few scattered people sat on long wooden benches arranged in rows facing the far side of the hall. Their heads were uncovered, so it was easy to spot Nicoletta's auburn hair about halfway down the room. My footsteps sounded too loud as I approached her. She sat with her head bowed, hands folded in her lap.

"Nica," I whispered.

"Go away," she muttered, not looking up.

I gathered my skirt and sat next to her. "Are you okay? Did Paolo do something?"

Nicoletta gave a tiny jerk of her head, so slight I wasn't sure if it was a yes or no.

"You can talk to me, Nica. Whatever it is."

She glared at me, her eyes red from crying. "What part of 'go away' don't you understand?"

I held back a sigh. I didn't want to push her into talking, but worst-case scenarios were running through my head. I had to find out what she needed — a medic, an Elkhound, a less judgmental priest. My eyes wandered the room. On the far wall hung the Ferish holy symbol, an enormous three-blossom flower made of wrought iron.

"Look, I'm not supposed to be here," I said. "Can we at least go somewhere else? I'll take you to my flat if you don't want to go home."

"I'm not leaving."

"Then neither am I. And every second I spend in this place, I'm pissing off your god more. Do you want me to get smitten by lightning?"

Nicoletta's small mouth pursed. "What have you done that's so bad?"

"I'm a heathen, remember. Born and raised heathen, blessed by heathen spirits. And I've broken every rule your religion has." I started ticking them off on my fingers. "I've lied, cursed, stolen.

Used magic. Pretended to be a Sverbian goddess and broke into the Sarteres' home—"

"You *what?*" She glanced up at the iron flower in terror.

I kept going, sensing an opportunity. "I brought a pagan warrior into the orphanage where he threatened a priest. Oh, and in the Rúonbattai's stavehall, we stole a knife used for ritual sacrifice. It's in my pocket right now—"

"Stop!" Nicoletta hissed, looking around. "Someone will hear you!"

I raised my voice. "I've kissed three boys I wasn't engaged to. I've thought about kissing girls. I've had sex before marriage, a *lot* of it, sometimes two or three times a night—"

She clamped a hand over my mouth. "Fine! I'll tell you what happened, just *shut up*!"

I lifted my hands in peace.

Nicoletta huffed out a breath and wrapped her arms around her ribs. Her voice trembled as she said, "Paolo turns twenty next week. I've heard of people getting married so they don't get drafted, but . . . he'd never get the courage to ask. And you're always telling me that girls can ask things like that, too."

"So you proposed to Paolo?"

She nodded, sniffling. "He said it wouldn't matter. The military doesn't count marriages that happen after the draft was announced. So I said *that* didn't matter, and I want to marry him anyway before he leaves, and he — he rejected me!"

I winced at the raw pain in her words. "I'm so sorry, Nica."

"He claims it's *because* he loves me," she went on, turning shrill. "What kind of reason is that? He doesn't want me to 'waste my youth worrying.' But I'm going to worry anyway! I'll miss him every single minute! If we can't promise to wait for each other, to fight for each other — then what's the point of love?"

"You can still wait for him. You don't need a wedding ring for that."

"What if he forgets me? Or meets some pretty war nurse? Or gets injured and . . . if he never . . ." Nicoletta wiped her eyes with a handkerchief. "There's no point. I should stay here in the sancte and become a *madro* and swear myself to chastity, because the man I love would rather die alone than marry me and — there's nothing I can do — I can't even kiss him goodbye—"

A sob escaped her. Nothing I could say felt like enough, so I pulled her into a hug, letting her curls brush my cheek. She wailed against my borrowed coat. A few people glanced our way, but they didn't look surprised. Crying in the sancte was probably common these days.

"I'm scared, Kateiko," she gasped. "I'm so, so scared."

Something yanked in my gut. A memory — Akohin, in a snowy mountain pass, noting how hard those words were to say. I was seeing part of Nicoletta she usually hid behind pride and a bad temper, but I'd never shown that part of myself to her. No wonder she'd refused to talk to me. I gently moved her hand onto my loose hair. She didn't notice, and she'd never truly understand anyway, but I wanted her to feel my spirit all the same.

"I'm scared, too," I said. "Jonalin's going to enlist in the navy."

"Why?" Her question was muffled by my shoulder.

"Because that's who he is. And . . ." I closed my eyes. "Because that's who I am. I told him to go."

Nicoletta sat up, apparently shocked out of crying. "You always have to be better than me," she muttered, but there was no heat to it.

"You can still do things for Paolo, you know. Things he'll appreciate more than swearing yourself to chastity."

"Like what?"

"Write him love letters. Write him *lewd* letters. Give him something to hope for, a reason to keep fighting. Learn as much field medicine as you can, so if he turns up here on a stretcher, you can help him. Be brave for him."

Nicoletta was silent for a while. I peered over my shoulder and saw Inesa sitting in the back benches, watching us. I cast her a reassuring smile. She gave a wavering one in response. Nicoletta and I had family here who cared for us, but both our lovers were going off alone. I chewed my lip, thinking.

"What branch will Paolo get assigned to?" I asked.

Nicoletta blinked like she was coming out of a dream. "Infantry, I guess. Riding a draft horse around town hasn't exactly prepared him for the cavalry."

"What if he enlisted in the navy first?"

A crease formed between her eyebrows. "With Jonalin?"

"They'd train together at Ile vi Dévoye. Jona could help teach Paolo sailing and combat, and . . . well, it'll be hard for Jona, being the only Aikoto in a Ferish regiment. He could use someone on his side."

"But they only train for a month, right? Then they'll probably get assigned to different ships."

"Not if I have anything to say about it." I straightened up and adjusted Inesa's coat on my shoulders. "I know a lieutenant in the special forces who's learned how to pull strings, and this time, I'm not going to ask as a favour. I'll ask as a friend."

33.
GOODBYES

The next week was full of goodbyes. My family was first, as I helped our wounded get into canoes. I'd had a few tough partings with my parents — sailing away from them in Caladsten and not knowing when I'd see them again, convincing them I wanted to stay in Caladheå, then convincing them again that I could be happy here after losing Matéo and nearly seeing Jonalin die — but this separation hurt in an entirely new way.

When we saw each other again, whenever that might be, they'd belong to a different jouyen. They'd have new tattoos, a new second name, a new okorebai, a new home where their bodies and spirits would one day rest. I'd still be half Kateiko Rin, half Kateiko Leniere, and no part of their new culture.

"I have something for you," Temal said. "But I need you to understand what it means before you accept it."

He held out a calloused hand. On his palm stood two figurines.

One was a swan with its wings spread, carved from the pale wood of a silver fir. The other was a prowling mountain cat with one paw raised, carved from tawny pine. They were in the same poses as the figurine he gave me at the Caladsten docks, but these ones were separate, the wood carefully chosen for each.

"Are those real makiri?" I asked, astonished. "But you're not allowed to make them—"

"The Rin said I wasn't allowed." Temal smiled wryly. "Things are changing. I've never liked the practice of breaking off bits of people's spirits to put in carvings, but we're at war now, so your tema and I want to leave you with all the protection we can."

"Those are made of heartwood from Nettle Ginu," Tema said, linking her arm into Temal's. "If you ever change your mind, you can come live with us there."

I picked up the makiri. They were warm, maybe from Temal's body heat, maybe from the fragments of my parents' spirits coming to life at my touch.

All around us at the Iyo docks, everyone else was saying goodbye. Rokiud punched Jonalin's shoulder and asked if the navy were brown pigeons or brown waterfowl. Dunehein ignored his still-healing stab wound to pull Emehein into a bear hug. Nili and Airedain were locked together at the mouth. Aoreli pointedly looked away from her younger sister, joining Malana in cooing over Kel and Sena.

Samulein held my hand as we waved, watching the canoes push off. He had a black eye from yet another fight at school. Hanaiko stood apart from us, clutching her rag doll Thymarai. She'd barely spoken in days. I didn't know why, but I knew my place was here taking care of my cousins.

A few days later, Nicoletta and I stood in Shawnaast's crowded docklands, seeing off Paolo and Jonalin. A month without them felt unfathomably long, but at least we'd see them again before they deployed. Jonalin kissed me there on the shore with his hands in my hair. When we pulled apart, I glimpsed the sandstone Customs House across the harbour where we'd first met.

The ship captain called for the recruits to line up and board. Paolo took two steps toward the pier where a white-sailed schooner with Eremur's elken flag was moored, then turned back to Nicoletta. He cupped her face in his hands and kissed her. A stunned smile lit up her face. That alone said more than a thousand songs or stories. For them, it was a promise — an unspoken engagement.

The flowers of spring left, too, leaving my life as muted as the sun-baked plants on the apothecary windowsills. Our one-room flat felt too big without my parents staying there. The Iyo gathering place often just had a few elders cooking, weaving, and looking after their grandchildren. Every Iyo with a day job was busy with the war effort, and everyone else was away harvesting brassroot and berries in South Iyun Bel. The Drunken Otter where Jonalin and I used to meet Beno and Hélio was quiet.

I came home from work one cloudy day and found Hanaiko crying in the alley with her doll. Seeing me, she wiped her eyes and pretended to be fine. I gave her my handkerchief, looked through the window to make sure Samulein was okay, then sat her down on the back steps and coaxed her to talk.

"Everyone's leaving," she wailed. "Auntie Sohiko and Uncle Mikiod and Emehein left, half the Iyo kids left, and now Jonalin's gone."

"*Wala, wala,*" I soothed, rubbing her arm. "We'll see them all again."

"But you were supposed to make Jonalin stay!" Hanaiko sniffled. "Kirbana's making apple cake for my birthday, and I wanted to invite Jona 'cause it's his birthday, too. Temal said he'd make maple sugar bits, eleven for me and twenty-one for Jona. And Jona promised to take Samu and me camping 'cause he's not on parole anymore, and next winter you'd be old enough to get married, and . . . and . . . Doesn't he like us anymore?"

"Oh, Hako." I pulled her into a hug. "Of course he does. But he's a warrior, and sometimes they have to leave to protect us. That's how much they love us."

"Jorum doesn't," she whispered.

"What do you mean?"

"He never visits us." Hanaiko's eyes welled with tears again. "I'm reciting the events of the Brånnveldt Battle at our school exhibition. Jorum fought in it as a Kånehlbattai, so I added things he taught me. I'm working really, really hard, and so is Samu on memorizing his song. It's the only school thing he cares about besides athletics. But Jorum says he's too busy to come see the exhibition."

I swallowed a lump in my throat. My cousins had spent so much of their lives feeling abandoned, from Yotolein sending them away to believing I left them in the orphanage. I hadn't thought what having a relationship with a wanderlust sailor or matchmaking Yotolein with a mercenary would do to them. No wonder Yotolein wanted to keep it secret.

"I'm sure Jorum wishes he could come," I said. "But you've still got your temal and me, Dune and Rija, and Kirbana, Narun, and their kids. And we'll all come to the exhibition, I promise."

*

That weekend, while Dunehein and Rikuja were at the market and Hanaiko and Samulein were at their classmates' house practising for the exhibition, I got back into my still-warm bed. I couldn't remember the last time I'd been able to think alone. My mind kept landing on Jonalin, imagining him swinging a sword on Ile vi Dévoye or reefing the sails on a ship, but my thoughts had a gritty texture that had nothing to do with worry for his safety.

What I hadn't told Nili or Hanaiko was that I didn't know if I'd ever want to marry Jonalin. Maybe that was because we'd gotten together during a war — it seemed pointless to imagine a future when we might not survive to the next day — but that hadn't stopped Nicoletta and Paolo. If anything, the war had brought them closer, forcing them to admit what they'd felt for a long time already.

I cared for Jonalin, and trusted him, and was definitely attracted to him, but I didn't love him in a heart-pounding, body-aching way. I'd been able to let him go. Why was my cousin more upset than me? Why hadn't *I* run away and sobbed to my aeldu that any future without my lover was worthless? Maybe I'd shielded myself all this time, unable to give him my heart because I knew he'd leave one day.

Or maybe we just didn't fit together. It was normal for couples to fight, but this felt deeper. I needed openness he couldn't give. He needed patience I didn't have. The closer we got, scraping at each other's raw spots, the deeper we hurt each other.

Maybe in another world, we'd have been perfect together. If Yotolein's wife, Tove, hadn't been killed, I wouldn't have wound up playing mother to my cousins, growing up feeling obligated to protect everyone and second-guessing every choice. Jonalin wouldn't have gone to prison for us and wound up so strung out and fragile. We could've fallen in love fast and wild, sailed the world until our hearts overflowed, then come back here to our homeland and built a life together.

I was starting to realize in a bone-deep way just how insane and mind-bending Liet's ability to see the future was. If Yotolein and Tove had known the military would raid their village, they could've fled before she got hurt. All our lives would be different. What felt like fundamental parts of my personality, the parts that decided who I loved and where I lived and how I chose to exist in this world, could be *different*.

My head throbbed. I groaned and yanked my pillow over my head. Not until I heard shouting did I lift it again.

"I don't care," Yotolein was saying downstairs. "I don't want to lie anymore!"

I froze. His words were surprisingly clear. I had our window shutters open to give early summer sunshine to my potted herbs, and apparently Yotolein's shutters were also open.

"I'm a danger to your family," came Jorumgard's rumbling voice. "Being a royal deserter draws attention."

"You think you're the worst traitor here?" Yotolein demanded. "I used to be Rúonbattai. *I'm* a danger to my family. If someone comes after us, we'll need a warrior like you at our side."

"There's no reason to put you at more risk—"

"There's every reason!" A slamming sound came from below. "I want to hold your hand in public. I want to tell my children how I feel about you. I'm only thirty-eight, for aeldu's sake. I don't want to spend the rest of my life as a widow!"

I cringed. At least this sounded like a lovers' fight, not political subterfuge, but I really didn't want to overhear it.

Jorumgard's voice dropped low. Briefly I thought I was saved, that he'd noticed how loud they were being with an open window. Then —

"Are you ashamed of me?" Yotolein asked, quiet but clear as dew. "Of being seen with another man? Or with an Aikoto?"

I threw off my blanket, wondering if I could slip outside and leave. Just in time I remembered that the floorboards next to my mattress would creak if I got out of bed. The only thing worse than hearing this argument would be interrupting it.

"No," Jorumgard said, sounding stunned. "Yoto, how could you think that?"

"I'm just trying to figure out why you won't even consider telling people—"

"*I'm* trying to protect Hanaiko and Samulein. But I'm not sure *you* are!"

Something shattered. "You're not their father! How I raise my children isn't up to you!"

After a long pause, Yotolein said thickly, "I'm sorry. I wish you *would* help raise them. My daughter's been crying because she thinks you don't love her. My son's fighting at school and I don't know what to do. But if you won't even go out in public with us, I don't see how you raising them could ever work. I don't see how . . . we . . . can work."

Hard silence.

"Is that it, then?" Jorumgard asked in a choked voice. "You're ending things between us?"

"I don't know, Jorum. I don't know." Muffled footsteps, like Yotolein was pacing. "But . . . I think you should go."

A door scraped open and shut. In the street, I heard Jorumgard swearing.

I waited half an hour or so, marking the time by rainbows from my stained-glass butterfly moving across the floor, before creeping down the iron stairs outside. In his flat, Yotolein was slumped over the table with his head in his hands. He looked up, saw my anxious expression, and sighed.

"You heard," he said.

"I didn't mean to." I held my hand over a pool of cold tea on the floor, evaporating the water, and started sweeping up the shards of a clay mug. The *skritch*, *skritch* of the straw broom filled the air.

Yotolein leaned back in his chair, rubbing his temples. "You probably got the gist of it, then. He doesn't want us caught up in his life."

I scoffed. "It's a little late for that."

"Exactly!" He smacked the table. "I've been giving into Jorum for months, trusting he was right, but now he's just making excuses."

I bit my lip. "Do you want me to talk to him?"

"Nei. This is between him and me, and you've got enough to — oh, kaid." Yotolein ran a hand through his short black hair. "I can't believe you had to listen to all that while you must be missing Jonalin. Is that why you were upstairs alone? Are you okay?"

"Yeah," I tried to say, but the sound stuck in my throat.

He pulled out another chair. "Sit. Talk. I know you're all grown up, but I'm still going to look after you."

I hadn't come down here planning to tell him anything. Unspoken words filled my mouth like wet sand, weighing down my tongue, but knowing that Yotolein was also having romantic trouble made it easier to open up. Dunehein and Rikuja always seemed perfectly happy together, as did Kirbana and Narun. At work, Nicoletta kept switching between crying in the cellar and daydreaming aloud about wedding plans.

So I talked. I told Yotolein all the questions swirling inside my head — if I should've asked Jonalin to stay even though it seemed selfish, if I'd given up on our relationship too easily, if letting him go would really help him. I explained that instead of grief and loneliness and all the things I was supposed to feel, I was . . . numb. That I wasn't sure if I loved Jonalin or ever could. That maybe he deserved better than me.

Yotolein listened with his chair tilted back on two legs and his hands folded in his lap. After I stopped talking, he was quiet for a while, brows furrowed in thought. A seagull squawked outside, got bored, and flew away. Finally he lowered his chair and said, "Have you considered that you're in shock?"

"What?"

"Shock doesn't just come from physical injury. When Tove was killed, I didn't have time to process it. I had to protect our children. It took weeks before I could mourn my wife properly, before it sunk in that she was gone."

"But . . ." I pulled at a loose thread on my skirt. "Jonalin leaving wasn't a surprise. Not really."

"Wounds hurt even when you see them coming." Yotolein smiled wryly. "And you've dealt with a lot of tough stuff lately, Kateiko. It sounds like you're finally getting time to process it all. So whatever you feel — if you need to cry, or scream, or break something — let yourself feel it. I've got a few mugs left you can throw."

I shrugged half-heartedly.

"One other thing." He gazed out the open window at the sunny brick alley. "You said that if Tove had survived, you'd be different now."

"Oh." As I surfaced from my cocoon, my horror grew. "I'm sorry, I shouldn't have said that—"

Yotolein waved away my apology. "Honestly, you're right. My kids and I would be different, too. That's part of being family. But my point is, if you and Jonalin have changed so you don't fit together now . . . isn't it possible you'll change so one day you *do* fit together?"

I blinked at him. Clearly I'd never be cut out for temporal magic. Even having an idea of how it worked, I'd been stuck on the idea of Jonalin and I permanently veering away from each other. I hadn't imagined a future where we veered back toward each other.

*

I didn't quite believe what Yotolein had said about shock. If it hadn't sunk in yet that Jonalin was leaving, I didn't think it ever would. I went alone to our favourite Ferish baker near the docklands. I used his keys to let myself into his flat and water his herbs, not trusting Airedain to remember, and I read his mail to make sure it wasn't anything urgent. All the while I thought, *I knew he'd leave eventually.*

Then one day, leaving the apothecary, I noticed an odd pressure in the air. I couldn't remember the last time I'd felt so much humidity. A cool breeze carried a fresh earthy scent down the back alley. I looked up. Against the blue-black clouds of a storm blowing in from the west, a bird with a white belly and huge mottled wings circled overhead. An osprey.

Jona, I thought breathlessly. He'd come back.

But the bird just circled a few times more, then flew east and out of sight. Jonalin had no reason to continue east. I was here and his family was south, in Ashtown and further down the coast in Toel Ginu. The osprey had been a real one, probably heading inland to take shelter from the storm. Of course Jonalin wouldn't run away from the naval camp, not when enlisting was everything he wanted and needed. Which left me . . . outside his life. Alone and once again outside everyone's relationships, even my own.

It hit me like a kick from a horse. I staggered into the apothecary's brick wall, knocking over a broom that clattered onto the cobblestone. Once Jonalin finished training, he would come back for a night, hardly a blink in the length of our whole lives, and then he'd ship out with the navy. That might well be the last time I ever saw him.

Nicoletta stuck her head out the door just as my knees gave out. She caught me and we sagged into a heap of skirts and petticoats, her clutching me tight, me sobbing onto her shoulder. Raindrops spattered around us, then downpoured until we were soaked to the skin. I didn't know how many had been sent by an anta-saidu with the storm and how many had been building inside me, waiting to burst.

The day Paolo and Jonalin were set to return, Nicoletta and I were too jittery to work, so Agata let us off. We fetched Hanaiko and Samulein from school and waited at Shawnaast's docks along with dozens of women and children. Ferish and Sverbian naval troops both trained on Ile vi Dévoye, so a mix of people had gathered. There was a sense of unity I hadn't expected. A priest in blue robes and a cleric in white ones moved among the crowd, passing out bread and water.

In late afternoon, a schooner drifted into the harbour and docked. Soldiers filed down the gangplank in their dress uniforms — red coats with black braids on the shoulders, black breeches, and polished leather boots. The Ferish recruits had curved swords and the Sverbians had straight ones. Jonalin stood tall above all the others. He'd shaved his head, like the first time I saw him out of prison, but today he was beaming.

The soldiers broke ranks on shore to find their loved ones. Jonalin swept me into his arms and kissed me. He seemed lighter, and I saw a flicker of his osprey body as if he was buoyed high in the air. He looked so confident and handsome in uniform that I nearly cried all over again. It hurt like a fist was squeezing my heart, but this was the proof I'd needed. This was the right path for him.

Paolo and Nicoletta went back to the apothecary while Jonalin, my cousins, and I walked through town to the Iyo gathering place. His whole extended family had come up from Toel Ginu to see off the first person in their family to enlist. Jonalin looked dazed at the attention. I remembered how he'd once seemed jealous of Airedain being first to finish school, but as the two cousins thumped each other's backs, there was nothing but love between them.

Only Jonalin could sound so humble while telling us his good news. He'd done exceptionally well, though he insisted it was because the other recruits were mostly farm boys. Thanks to Nerio's reference letter, the captain of the training camp knew Jonalin was fluent in Aikoto, Ferish, and Coast Trader, could read and navigate, and had spent summers canoeing around Tamun Dael and Nordmur.

The captain had recommended him for a liaison role. Jonalin would serve with the 9th Royal Eremur Naval Forces aboard the *Cavalo via Mèr*, working as a translator and coordinator with Aikoto who lived in the war zone. It was a position with real influence, something that could save lives. I burst with pride for him. All his hard work had paid off — and true to Nerio's promise, Paolo was getting deployed on the same ship.

Late in the evening, we managed to slip away. Airedain had promised to sleep at his tema's place, giving Jonalin and me privacy in their flat. Once we got inside and lit a lamp, though, awkwardness descended between us. Romance wasn't something he'd gotten any practice at while being away. He was still my sweet, gentle, shy Jonalin.

"I spent a lot of time thinking at camp," he began, fiddling with a button on his coat cuff. "We could do the same as Paolo and Nicoletta, writing letters and stuff."

I smiled at the thought of Nicoletta helping me write a love letter to Jonalin. She'd have a heart attack from moral crisis. "I'd like to know you're safe. You can write to me about that. But . . . I don't think a long-distance romance will work for us."

"Why not?"

"Nica and Paolo want to spend their lives together here in Caladheå. Us, though . . ." I looked away at the flickering lamp. "You shouldn't feel obligated to come back here after the war. If you can get work as a sailor, you should. As for me, I'll stay with Hanaiko and Samulein as long as possible, but I can't promise to be here forever."

Jonalin nodded slowly. "I figured you'd say that." He squinted one eye shut, then reached into his breast pocket and pressed something into my palm. "I made you this. To remember me by . . . if you want to."

It was a macramé necklace of tan-coloured ropeweed fibres, knotted into intricate patterns and studded with blue and green sea glass. They looked like tide pools scattered across a sandy beach. It was more beautiful than any gold-and-gemstone jewellery I'd seen in the markets, and I was awestruck that it came from the big, calloused hands of the brawny soldier who stood in front of me.

"I want to remember," I promised him.

Blushing, he moved behind me and fastened it around my neck. The brush of his rough fingers against my skin made me shiver.

I knew by now that I loved him in a way. Maybe I was even in love with him the way stories and songs spoke of. There was no point trying to name it on our last night together. I leaned my head back against his shoulder, pulled his arms around my waist, and we swayed together as if the ocean was singing to us. He pressed his lips to my ear like a whisper.

As my lashes fluttered, the potted herbs on his windowsill caught my gaze. Despite my efforts, they were dying, baked dry from sunshine. Like my memories and feelings, I could abandon them here in this room, or take them home and salvage whatever life was left.

I turned to face him. "I don't want tonight to be sad. I cried enough while you were gone."

"Me, too." He ducked his head. "So . . . what *do* you want?"

"Good memories to take with my necklace." I stood on my toes and kissed him. "We've never been great at talking to each other. Maybe we should just . . ."

His brows furrowed, questioning. Hesitant to ask.

I unbuttoned his naval coat and pushed it off. His muscles showed through his white shirt. I'd meant to keep undressing him to preserve the perfect starch of his uniform, but I wanted him so much it ached. I kissed him again and felt the pressure against my thigh that said he wanted me, too. He made a low sound in his chest that I loved, a quiet groan, and I was completely, utterly undone.

"We have to let each other go," I whispered. "So tonight, let go. Don't hold anything back."

I fumbled at his breeches, unlacing them. Jonalin hiked up my layers of skirts, then scooped me up and pinned me against the wall. My dress caught on the bricks. There, in the same night we were losing each other, hot and breathless and desperate with craving, we truly found each other.

34.
LETTERS

I'd spent my first summer in Caladheå getting my cousins back and my second watching over Jonalin. This one, I spent buried in work. On our lunch breaks at the apothecary, Nicoletta read aloud from Ferish textbooks on field medicine. On the weekends, we volunteered at the Parr Manor military hospital, learning as much as we could firsthand.

Since my cousins were off school for summer, they volunteered with us. Hanaiko read to wounded soldiers and wrote letters they dictated to their loved ones. I didn't want Samulein to see dying men at only eight years old, so Nerio assigned him to the groundskeeper. It was the happiest I'd seen him in months. He fed chickens and gathered eggs for the kitchen, chased crows from the vegetable garden, and admired military horses as he mucked out their stables.

The manor was also the best place for war news. We heard things before the newspapers announced them, like that Captain

Parr's siege on Caladsten worked. He'd trapped the Sverba mercenaries inside the keep, slowly starving them, and razed nearby farms to drive off any Rúonbattai supporters. The mercenaries broke through the siege in one last fight and fled into the wild, leaving Caladsten open to Parr.

Meanwhile, one of Parr's lieutenants had stormed Hafenaast, bolstered by our guess that Liet couldn't foresee an invasion with the rock garden destroyed. The military had recaptured the town, then the rest of the island. Their next target was Thúnveldt, a trading port linking northwest Nordmur to Nokun Bel, the rainforest where the Beru- and Haka-jouyen lived. Gåmelheå, a keep in central Nordmur, was still in the grip of Nyhemur mercenaries.

Nerio, in the spirit of our unexpected alliance against his father, let me read their private letters. I grit my teeth through violent descriptions of what Parr wanted to do to the Rúonbattai and their supporters. He still had suspicions the Rin were involved, but there wasn't enough evidence to act on.

Here in Eremur, Nerio's men had scoured Ivy House, seizing any evidence they could use in the trial of Halvarind's family — property deeds in false names, letters from Sverbian lords and merchants, financial ledgers tampered with to hide thousands of sovereigns vanishing. It was lucky we hadn't torched the house. Halvarind's wife and children went to prison in the southern colonies, and his grandchildren were placed in an orphanage there.

With that wrapped up, Nerio took his soldiers back to Nordmur, worried about how long he'd left his father unchecked. Tiernan stayed to oversee Parr Manor and keep poring over the Ivy House documents for information on the Rúonbattai. Jorumgard was in and out of town, doing any military business that kept him away from Yotolein.

After our volunteer shifts, we stopped by the library. Tiernan was usually seated at Parr's varnished desk with stacks of papers that ranged from torn and yellowed to wet with fresh ink. Sometimes he looked so focused we didn't interrupt. Sometimes he beckoned us in with a tired but kind smile. Hanaiko liked curling up in the corner with dusty atlases, Samulein sprawled on the floor looking at illustrations of exotic animals, and Nicoletta was working through tomes of Ferish poetry. Tiernan and I sat apart from the others and talked over glasses of cold apple cider salvaged from Ivy House's cellars.

The biggest discovery from the estate had been a locked wooden chest containing hundreds of letters, all addressed to *Gúnnar* and written in angular Sverbian symbols. Tiernan felt sure the writer was Liet. He'd started translating and cataloguing the letters, taking detailed notes on anything that might be useful. Whenever we spent an evening together, he read passages aloud from the most interesting ones.

The earliest, dated thirty-two years ago, mentioned Liet had recently met Halvarind while visiting the Førstown stavehall. *I had better not sign my name*, he wrote. *My parents are pleased that I made the acquaintance of someone with your social stature, but from what I know of your family, they will not take a golden view of you corresponding with someone like me*. It was signed instead with a tiny sketch of an oak and a lilac cluster.

From then on, Liet sent a letter every month for more than a decade. At first they were mostly discussions of theology, literature, and politics, speckled with observations about the changing seasons. The details of his life stayed meticulously vague. He called his family and friends by their initials, avoided naming places and instead used descriptions like *the river where we saw that fawn*, and sidestepped topics with *I will tell you more when we next meet*.

Over time, though, the writing grew personal. He confessed to missing his brother, M, who was away serving as a soldier, and his friend, O, who'd left town to care for her sick relative. She might've been more than a friend, but Liet wrote in such a serious, austere manner that it was hard to tell. Most notably, he said he'd started some sort of research project that would get him in serious trouble if he was caught.

"I think he lived in Ingdanrad during these years," Tiernan said one sticky-hot evening, perched on a window seat to catch the breeze. He'd cast aside his jerkin and rolled up his tunic sleeves. "The mage assembly that governs the city has strict laws on experimenting with magic. It would also explain why Liet was concerned with hiding his identity even back then. Halvarind was from an old traditional family, who were likely not fond of mages."

"That fits," I said, sprawled on a couch with my legs draped over the padded arm. The heat had made me sleepy. "It definitely sounds like he was in the Turquoise Mountains, writing about glacial lakes and alpine flowers and stuff."

"I wonder if anyone there could identify him," Tiernan mused. "Not that it would help much. I care more about where he is than who he is."

"We know who he is," I said dryly. "A religious lunatic who thought, *What's the best way to use my incredible talent for seeing the future? Oh, I know. Mass murder.*"

As Liet and Halvarind's friendship had grown, so had their prejudice. Casual slurs against Ferish people turned into admiring the Rúonbattai, then critiquing their tactics. It seemed like Halvarind's family was also starting to support the Rúonbattai, so Liet didn't bother hiding it in his letters. *M has joined the RB*, Liet wrote. *He describes them as gnats biting an elk, all ambition and no vision. We could do so much more.*

From anyone else, it would've sounded like arrogant bluster, but Liet and Halvarind had followed through. Twenty-one years ago, at the start of the Third Elken War, Liet wrote, *Tomorrow I leave to join M at the front. I hope to see you there. O has begged me to stay, but my affection for her is nothing compared to my love for our people. You and M are the only ones who understand the task the gods have placed upon us.*

Agata had told me how that war started. An influenza epidemic tore through Eremur, killing thousands of people, including her teenage daughter. Elkhounds guarded every apothecary, sancte, and stavehall to handle floods of patients begging for help. In the chaos, Ferish rebels tried to overthrow the Caladheå Council, so the Rúonbattai retaliated. Riots filled the streets with blood and flames. Both Agata's sons enlisted in the military. The elder one was killed. Matéo and Nicoletta's father, eighteen at the time, lost a leg in combat. Talking about the war was the only time I'd ever seen Agata tear up.

Parr Manor had been converted to an influenza hospital, then a military hospital. Tiernan showed my cousins, Nicoletta, and me an elk statue in the grounds with a plaque naming every soldier who died here. Another plaque in a rose garden read *Lady Asmalah Parr, née Bitali. 585 — born in Laca vi Rosa, southern Ferland. 603 — immigrated to Caladheå, wedded to Antoch. 604 — gave birth to Nerio, volunteered with ladies' society during Third Elken War. 605 — taken by influenza.*

"Antoch was fighting in southern Eremur when Asmalah died," Tiernan said, brushing fallen rose petals from the plaque. "He has never gotten over it, blaming the Rúonbattai for keeping him from his wife's final days. I wonder if he would be a kinder man if she had survived."

Liet's wartime letters were brief and vaguer than ever. Trying to match them to history was like a macabre game. We worked out that early in the war, his suggestion of waking the saidu made the Iyo withdraw from the alliance. They'd balked at destroying land that bordered Iyo territory. It seemed Liet wasn't as good at predicting and shaping the future back then. Some of his visions must've helped the Rúonbattai, though, because he and M shot up through their ranks. His writing glowed with pride and absolute conviction that they were doing the gods' work.

Hearing the Ingdanrad letters had felt like listening to a made-up story of a secret friendship, but that changed with the wartime letters. They felt real. People I knew were named in them — Captain Parr, Behadul, Tokoda. Liet wrote about battles that Yotolein had fought in. Walking through Caladheå, I passed abandoned lots with burnt chimneys and brick foundations, remnants of the riots. Sometimes the wind sounded like the voices of lost spirits. If the Rin had joined the war, the voices might've belonged to my parents. I might not even exist.

After Liet became the Rúonbattai leader and ended the war, Yotolein had gotten work with them as a courier. He might've carried some of the smoke-stained letters Liet sent from Brånnheå, although Yotolein said he hadn't spent much time in the south and never opened anything he carried. The Rúonbattai's response to getting something with a broken seal was giving broken bones to the courier.

I didn't think hearing the letters could get harder, but then Tiernan read a particular one dated eight years ago. *OR brought his young son to our meeting*, Liet wrote. *The boy put on an admirably brave face for someone of his age.*

He'd written about Fendul. My childhood friend, son of the Okorebai-Rin, a twelve-year-old boy who met a war criminal and had to come back to our plank house and pretend everything was normal. I'd been nine and didn't understand why he wouldn't play with me anymore. My parents had said that's just how things were, that Fendul was growing up and learning to be an adult, but they didn't know what had happened to him, either.

Ever since I found out he'd lied to my face about his family's alliance with the Rúonbattai, blaming Yotolein instead and driving my cousins and me out of Aeti Ginu, fury had smoldered deep inside me like a hot coal. He'd taken away my life. That betrayal had steeped in my mind until it dyed all my memories of him dark. I realized now that he'd been thrust into this as a child, pressured by his family to keep up a secret alliance — but at some point, that excuse didn't work anymore. *I'd* chosen a path different from my parents. Why couldn't Fendul?

I found myself desperate to hear more of Liet's writing, to find another mention of Fendul that would reveal how loyal he really was to the alliance, but there were no answers to be found. The last letter in the wooden chest, dated seven and a half years ago, said, *The Ombros-méleres are coming. If I survive, I will find you again. If I die, do not mourn me. I will meet a warrior's death and feast with the gods. You must carry on without me in this world.*

"There must be more somewhere," Tiernan said with exasperation, running a hand through his hair. "We know Liet survived. Your family overheard the Rin talking about someone very much alive."

I examined the last letter, a yellowed scrap of paper with smudged ink, but the sharp Sverbian symbols meant nothing to me. "Maybe Liet thought it was too risky to keep writing."

"I cannot imagine he would stop. A friendship like that does not simply die out, and after losing nearly all his men in the Brånnheå massacre, he needed all the support he could get."

I didn't reply. These letters had been coming longer than Tiernan or I had been alive, longer than Halvarind had been married or on the Council, longer than Liet had been with the Rúonbattai. A lifelong friendship *had* died, but at Ivy House, not in Brånnheå. I wondered if Liet was mourning. If someone like him could mourn while caring so little for human life.

The military searched every bit of Ivy House again, pulling up floorboards and cutting open pillows, with no luck. They found nothing in the tunnels, other buildings on the grounds, or Halvarind's office at the Colonnium. Soldiers even travelled up the coast and checked properties he'd owned. By early autumn, Tiernan had accepted it was hopeless and was weighing up whether to visit Ingdanrad or go back to Nordmur to fight.

Then one morning, as I arrived at Parr Manor for my volunteer shift, the door guard said Tiernan wanted to see me immediately. I hurried to the library. Tiernan was grinning wider than I'd ever seen. Atop Parr's desk sat an engraved wooden box, open to reveal a stack of folded papers.

"You found them?" I gasped.

"Marijka did. She was at the Førstown stavehall and noticed a new shrub on the back lawn." Tiernan spoke faster than usual, pacing back and forth in short bursts. "She recognized it as a lilac, so she asked the clerics. Halvarind had donated the sapling and planted it while you were investigating him. We dug it up and found the box — buried on the same grounds where he and Liet first met."

"What do the letters say?"

"I have only read a few so far. They are all in chronological order, so I skipped over the letters from the years he was licking his wounds, and I started with the ones from when we first heard about the Rúonbattai's return." He picked up a paper from the desk and read aloud. "'I expect our rumours—'"

“Wait, slow down,” I interrupted. I’d gotten used to his accent, but it grew stronger when he was excited like this.

“Sorry.” Tiernan looked sheepish and started over. “‘I expect our rumours and the resulting chaos to have spread by summer. OR promises he will forbid his people to visit the coast, telling them it is too dangerous, and suggest that they travel into the high mountains instead. Once they arrive, I am sure we can convince them to do some work for the right price.’”

“Work? What kind of work?”

“I hoped you could tell me. What did the Rin do in the mountains three summers ago?”

“My family just traded with goatherds from Nyhemur, the same ones we saw every year. But—” I clapped my hand to my mouth. “Yan taku.”

“What?” he asked sharply.

“That’s when a bunch of Nordmur refugees travelled through Anwen Bel and settled in the Turquoise Mountains. My friend Rokiud and his brothers got work building log cabins for them.”

Tiernan swung toward the wall map. “Show me where.”

I moved next to him and peered at ink lines rising to the ceiling. The flowing gold script was hard to read, but I recognized the shapes of lakes and rivers in northern Anwen Bel. I stood on my toes and used a quill to point at a spot high overhead, where Rin territory turned into the no man’s land of the Turquoise Mountains.

“Somewhere in that region,” I said. “Behadul visited the sanctuary villages a few times, but my family followed him there and never saw any sign of the Rúonbattai, or we would’ve told you when we sold you information. We just thought he was having diplomatic meetings with people living on our border.”

“I believe you.” Tiernan cast me a reassuring smile and began pacing again. "I think I know which villages you mean. The military searched them and also found nothing. If Liet is there, or if he built an oak there, the Rúonbattai would have plenty of warning to hide their presence."

"How much of a presence do you think they have? Like, is everyone there Rúonbattai, or are they hiding among real refugees?"

"I cannot say for sure. However, I suspect their new base is in one of those villages. The area is protected by the difficult terrain and its remoteness. It is a safe place for Liet to command the war from — just like Brånnheå."

I sank into the desk chair, fingers knotted in my skirt, trying to process all my feelings. Discomfort at Liet being so near my homeland, fury at Behadul for lying about yet another thing and manipulating the Rin into working for the Rúonbattai, terror that Captain Parr would find out, worry about whether actual refugees had been caught up in this.

"So . . . what happens now?" I asked.

"That depends." Tiernan turned to me, drumming his fingers on his thigh. "As you said, those villages are on the Rin border. Your people deserve a say in whatever happens. Help me negotiate something before I take the news to Antoch Parr. Perhaps we can lessen the bloodshed on all sides."

Instinctively, I touched my sea glass necklace from Jonalin. Hanaiko had been so upset about him leaving. I wasn't sure she'd forgive me for going, too, but any hope of my cousins growing up safe and happy depended on killing Liet and ending this war for good. Protecting them only left one option. It was time to finally visit Nettle Ginu.

Dunehein and Rikuja had travelled through southern Anwen Bel plenty of times, so they offered to take Tiernan and me. Segowa began sewing me leggings and a shirt in the Aikoto style. Not knowing when I'd be back, I gave my potted herbs to Nicoletta and my swan and mountain cat makiri to Yotolein for safekeeping.

I'd planned my goodbye to Hanaiko and Samulein months ago in case something like this happened. Lituwa had carved white limestone into a tundra wolf howling at the moon. Bracing myself, I went downstairs to Yotolein's flat and sat my cousins down on bark mats. They listened in silence while I explained where I was going and why.

"I know it feels like I'm abandoning you," I said. "But I love you both more than life. If I can't be here, part of my spirit will be instead."

"You mean . . ." Hanaiko said in a wavering voice.

I held out my hand, the makiri balanced on my palm. "Both of you touch it at the same time. It'll come to life and know who to protect."

They each placed a fingertip on the wolf. For a second, the flickering lamplight seemed to make its eyes glow. I set it on a shelf above the stove so it could watch over their home.

"I've got something else for each of you, and one won't wait long." I handed Samulein a wicker basket covered in a handkerchief.

He pulled off the cloth and gasped. A fluffy white kitten blinked sleepily. "Is this one of Luna's?" he cried.

"Sure is. Nica picked the cutest one for you." I lifted the kitten out and placed her in his hands. "Be gentle, okay?"

Samulein kissed her tiny head, ignoring the split lip he'd gotten from a fight soon after going back to school. He'd grown up so much, taller than itherans his age, with messy black hair falling in his eyes, but he was still the sweet boy who loved every animal he met. I hoped caring for something fragile would help him find that part of himself again.

Hanaiko joined him in petting and giggling at the kitten, then looked up. "Can we name her Stjarnå?"

"The Sverbian word for *star*?" Yotolein asked, watching from the table. "Why?"

"'Cause she came from Luna, just like Orebo made the stars from the moon."

"Yeah!" Samulein wriggled, making the kitten squeak in alarm. "*Hanekei*, little Stjarnå!"

Yotolein looked like he didn't know whether to laugh or cry. This was the family we'd raised, a tangle of cultures and languages and love. I wished Jonalin was here to see someone else being guided by the stars.

While Samulein played with Stjarnå, I pulled Hanaiko aside. I'd taken the antlers I once wore as Thymarai and stitched them onto a headband with the deerskin fringe. I settled it onto her head, then untied her twin braids so her black hair hung loose.

"Whenever you feel scared or sad or lonely, put this on," I said. "Remember how strong Thymarai is. Love like she loves her children of the woods, fight like Hafai sending her whales to devour ships, and be as wild and graceful as Hymelai soaring across the sky with her white ravens. Can you do that?"

Hanaiko nodded, the antlers dipping. Her blue eyes peeked out from behind the fringe.

"I don't know how long I'll be gone. You might attune before I get back. If so . . ." I swallowed hard. "When I attuned, I figured out how to shift back because I was determined to rescue you and Samu. Whatever happens, you'll find your way through it."

She flung her arms around me. I heard a sniffle, but when she pulled back, she was smiling.

35.

NETTLE GINU

At the last minute, Jorumgard decided to come with us. Outside our flats, he hugged Hanaiko and Samulein farewell, but hardly looked at Yotolein. They'd barely spoken all summer. It seemed like everything they'd shared might be truly broken.

We set off on foot with wicker carryframes of supplies on our backs. Tiernan had been reluctant to leave Gwmniwyr, but horses couldn't manage the route we were taking. Rikuja led us along narrow dirt paths through the depths of North Iyun Bel. She and her family used to hike this way every spring on trading trips to Aeti Ginu. Without them to cut back the undergrowth, ferns and shrubs had grown wild over the paths.

After our first day, my feet had blisters. It had been months since I'd even left Caladheå. We slept under tents roped to trees, the traditional Rin way. On the fourth day, in the foothills of the Turquoise Mountains, we heard the deep rumbling of rapids. Tiernan and

Jorumgard knew this river as the Holmgar. My family knew it as the border between Iyun Bel and Anwen Bel. There was only one way over it — the sky bridge. The military had a checkpoint on the bridge's south side, with guardhouses and fences among the dense forest. Black-uniformed soldiers examined our identification. Rikuja couldn't hide a grimace. This bridge had once been a shrine to tel-saidu, a sacred space shared by the Rin and Iyo. We didn't use it that way anymore, but it still had history. Itherans had no right to decide who passed over it.

Finally they waved us through. My first glimpse of the river took my breath away. I stood on the edge of an immense canyon, filled with mist from rapids far below. Water churned around boulders in white-capped waves. On the far side, massive trees grew from the soil of Anwen Bel. My homeland.

The bridge itself was high overhead. A pair of immense rioden trees on each bank formed its foundations. We climbed up spiral wooden steps built into one of the trunks, passing ancient crests carved into the weathered auburn bark. At the top, standing in the middle of the timber bridge, I could see over the earth in every direction. Behind us, the rainforest was deep green, but in the distance ahead, the canopy had a rusty tinge.

"Does it always look that dry from up here?" I asked.

"Not that I've ever seen," Rikuja said, frowning.

"The river's low, too." Dunehein pointed at a boulder the size of a shed. "That one's never been so exposed."

On the far side of the bridge, down at ground level, guards from Nettle Ginu recognized Dunehein and me. They greeted us with smiles and invited us into their cabin to share food and news. Their new jouyen had been established. Under the faded Rin tattoos on their arms, they had freshly inked crests of kingfishers — a water bird that was a distant cousin of kinaru, small but tough.

Their chosen name, the Tula-jouyen, meant *people of the gateway*. The sky bridge, a geographical bottleneck, was the gate between the northern and southern halves of the Aikoto Confederacy. Guarding it during a war was an honour and a serious responsibility. The name also referred to Kotula Huin, the lake where legend said that our mother kinaru opened a gate to the spirit world.

"It's a two-handed salute to the Rin," one of the guards said with a smirk. "Just 'cause the lake is in their territory doesn't mean they control our history. We have as much claim to our sacred sites as they do."

For their new okorebai, the Tula had chosen Rokiud's grandmother, Naneko. She was an experienced warrior, a canoe carver who'd travelled the coast and made connections with other jouyen, and she was known for being cautious and fair. If I'd been allowed to vote, she would've been one of my top choices. It also technically meant Rokiud was in line for okorebai, but as the third child of a third child, he was more likely to wind up on the Caladheå Council.

The Tula guards said most people were away at salmon fishing camps, but Naneko and my parents were in Nettle Ginu. They gave us directions and we set off through the forest. Around noon the next day, we reached a mountain marked with a cairn of stacked rocks, and we began climbing. The wooden steps were newer than the crumbling ones rising to Aeti Ginu, and the undergrowth here was far more brambly than I was used to.

The settlement atop the mountain was the same way. The buildings' sod roofs were still growing their moss layers, the rows of huckleberry shrubs were too young to bear fruit, and nettles stubbornly grew everywhere. It was like seeing the sun rise in the west — as if the dawn colours were the same, but the light hit everything wrong, twisting sights into something strange and eerie.

I didn't have time to dwell on it. Emehein and Lohara were here with their five kids, including a newborn boy, and they swept us into a whirlwind of hugs and chatter and excitedly shrieking toddlers. Lohara had heard about Tiernan and Jorumgard and greeted them warmly. Tema overheard the chaos from where she was stretching tanned leather on racks, and Temal hurried down from the shrine where he was doing carpentry.

Since we'd arrived uninvited on a diplomatic visit, etiquette demanded we present ourselves to the okorebai. My parents led us to Naneko's plank house. The grey-braided woman was waiting outside. She wore a set of sheathed knives on her belt and a sleeveless shirt that revealed numerous tattoos, including interlocking lines around her upper right arm, the same okorebai tattoo as in the Rin. Some things hadn't changed. Her eldest son stood at her side, tattooed with the unfinished circle of lines that marked an okoreni.

I didn't know what I was supposed to say. We weren't strangers — I'd spent my childhood hanging out with one of Naneko's grandsons — but I was an outsider now, practically an exile, not even representing another jouyen like Dunehein and Rikuja were. Schisms happened so rarely that there wasn't etiquette for this.

Naneko saved me with a welcoming smile. "It's good to see you safe, Kateiko. Rokiud says you've been doing valuable work for us all. I look forward to hearing more about it." Her words were kind in their briefness, not asking me to explain myself in front of others.

She greeted Dunehein and Rikuja and asked how Yotolein and his kids were doing. Then she fell silent, hands folded. She was waiting again. Testing the itherans who stood in front of her.

Jorumgard stepped forward and raised his hand. "*Hanekei*, Okorebai-Tula, Okoreni-Tula. It's an honour to be in your settlement. I'm Jorumgard Tømasind, and this is my friend and fellow mercenary, Tiernan Heilind."

Tiernan repeated the gesture and the greeting. "We have brought gifts as a promise of goodwill. In return, I hope you will grant us the opportunity to talk with you further. There is much to discuss."

The men laid their offerings on the grass — skeins of fine goat wool and embroidery thread, spices imported from Sverba, medicinal herbs and tinctures from Marijka's garden. They'd chosen well, taking our advice that anything Ferish-made wouldn't be well received. Naneko nodded her acceptance.

"You've travelled a long way," she said. "Eat, rest, and enjoy our hospitality. In time, we will talk."

Itherans meeting the most traditional members of my family didn't go as badly as I'd expected. Emehein and Lohara had loosened up over the years, and Jorumgard was more reserved than usual, like he was trying to make a good impression on Yotolein's family even though they weren't together anymore. We roasted salmon, duck potato, and mushrooms at the outdoor firepits. Tema offered to set up beds in the carpentry workshop, but Tiernan and Jorumgard said they were used to camping and didn't want to intrude.

Well after dark, when the conversation was dying off, my family went to our plank house. I paused in the doorway to look at the carvings on the frame. A kingfisher spread its wings across the lintel, then family crests went down the posts — Temal's fireweed, Tema's silver fir, Emehein's tiger lilies, Lohara's bearberries, and a dozen more. For a second, I imagined seeing Jonalin's sorrel leaves there next to my fireweed.

"We kept a bed ready for you," Tema told me, gesturing at a grass-stuffed mattress on a raised dirt platform. "Any time you want to visit, you're welcome to."

"I might come visit just to get a good night's sleep," Dunehein joked. "It's sure quiet out here compared to living in Shawnaast."

Lohara rolled her eyes. "Wait until tomorrow. You'll get woken up at dawn by toddlers jumping on you."

Dunehein, Rikuja, and I spent the next morning in Naneko's plank house. She wanted to hear our views on the state of things in the south, from the Iyo-jouyen to the Caladheå Council. She asked about my history with the Parrs, too, although she probably knew most of it already. In the afternoon, she called Tiernan and Jorumgard into her home to talk privately, and I went off with my family.

Temal showed me his carpentry work at the shrine. It was designed like Aeti Ginu's, three tiered storeys on the highest point of the mountain. The rioden timbers were so new that their auburn hue hadn't faded. Normally I wouldn't be allowed in the shrine since I wasn't Tula, but it hadn't been blessed as sacred ground yet, so Temal let me go inside while he worked. The golden autumn light and scent of fresh-cut wood was surprisingly calming.

A Tula warrior had snuck into northern Anwen Bel, visited our sacred rioden on the shore of Kotula Huin, and stolen a cone. She'd planted four seeds in pots and placed them inside the shrine. I knelt by the row of green seedlings, wondering if I could channel the power of the original rioden I once saw as black and barren. Without the influence of Liet's temporal magic, maybe I could figure out if my visions showed another world, omens of the future, or both.

I brought it up over dinner with Tiernan, Jorumgard, and my parents. To my surprise, the Tula had been having similar issues. My parents admitted they hadn't told us everything about their new homeland.

"This whole region is . . . odd," Tema said. "A Rin antayul first noticed it when travelling through here six or seven years ago.

Voices on the wind, things looking out of place, water not reacting right. So when we deserted the Rin and were negotiating for land, they offered this region if we promised to look after it."

Jorumgard raised an eyebrow. "You took the deal?"

"Both sides agreed that protecting the land is crucial. Besides, it's a fair price to not end up nomads like the Dona."

"It's getting worse, though," Temal said, tearing flatbread into chunks and handing them out. "We get plenty of rain, but the forest is drying out. You can see the rusty tinge. Some people think it's an omen. Others think we're in the gateway to Aeldu-yan. *That's* caused some arguments, since our land of the dead is supposed to be a lush green rainforest."

"It fits with a shoirdryge," Tiernan said. "Splintered worlds are bound to show some damage."

"We still don't have proof shoirdrygen exist," I countered.

Tema sighed. "I suppose it's our duty to investigate. Kateiko, I'll talk to Emehein and figure out how to help you have another vision."

"The barrier between worlds is thin at sunrise and sunset," Tiernan said. "Katja's first vision was at dawn, so we should try tomorrow morning."

We nodded in agreement. Later, while Emehein's kids swarmed Tiernan and Jorumgard, I moved to sit next to my parents. Temal offered me a bowl of cranberries.

"Why didn't you tell me sooner?" I asked, popping a berry into my mouth.

They looked at each other sheepishly. "We thought it might scare you off," Tema said. "We're still hoping you might move here one day."

"It does kind of freak me out. Being a war medic has put me close enough to the dead."

"Maybe you've been gone too long if you've forgotten our teachings." Temal smiled, the skin around his eyes crinkling. "Imagine standing between two plank houses. One is safe, one is on fire. Which one do you run to?"

I caught myself in time, realizing it was a trick question. "The burning one. I'm an antayul, so I can put out the flames. If I run to the other one, the fire will spread and everything will burn. Ignoring a problem just makes it worse."

He chuckled and flicked my braid. "That's my girl."

"I missed seeing your hair like this." Tema reached out and stroked my braid. "Those pins you used back in Caladheå—"

"Tema," I said, rolling my eyes. "I spend half my time there looking after wounded itherans. I don't want my hair falling into their blood."

She looked horrified at the thought. "All right, then. I won't mention it again. But remember that this war won't last forever, and when you're deciding what to do afterward, we want you to feel like living here is an option. No matter how far you travel or how long we're apart, you'll always be our daughter."

Early the next morning Tema, Emehein, Tiernan, and I entered the cool dark shrine, moved the seedling pots onto the central stage, and sat cross-legged. On Tema's instruction, I closed my eyes and sank into meditation, sensing the water around me. The seasoned timber appeared in dark grey, while a stack of damp wood was light grey. The metal of Temal's saw and axe was black.

"Focus on the seedlings." Tema's soft voice echoed. "Feel the life pulsing within their roots. Feel their slow death. Every leaf will one day fall. Every drop of sap will return to the earth."

I sank my mind into them, finding water in their thin roots and delicate leaves. White lines ran through them.

"These trees are eternal. They're both alive and dead, separate yet connected by their mother tree. Find their power."

The whites and greys of the shrine flickered, then vanished. "Everything went black," I said, stunned.

"Open your eyes."

I found myself floating. I gasped. Stars glittered above me. Far below, a scorched wasteland faded into darkness. On my right were snowy mountains silhouetted against purple sky. A deep rut ran from the mountains across the wasteland to a storm-blue ocean inlet. I described it aloud, my voice sounding hollow.

"Do you recognize anything?" Emehein asked.

I twisted to look behind me. In the distance amid a dark smudge of forest, a bridge rose high over a canyon. "The sky bridge. I think I'm still here, except the ground isn't."

"Can you travel?" came Tiernan's accented voice.

I looked down. My body was gone. "Not physically, but maybe I can use the trees as a conduit."

"Close your eyes again and focus on the seedlings," Tema said. "Follow their connection to the mother tree."

I returned to the blackness, meditating until the white lines returned. I tried threading my mind through them. They flickered. "I can't . . . it's . . ."

A rough hand folded over mine. "Pretend we're meditating at Kotula Huin," said Emehein. "Find the flowing gateway."

I imagined sitting in the lake's shallows. Emehein's deep steady voice during antayul lessons had always helped focus my wandering attention. I pictured the white lines merging together, flowing into the river of Kotula Iren, feeding into the lake.

Whiteness spread across the floor. A grey cloud emerged

above it. I lifted my hand and pulled the cloud aside. The sacred rioden appeared, lines pulsing through its immense branches and sprawling roots.

"I found it," I breathed. "I found the mother tree."

I opened my eyes. The world burst into colour. Turquoise covered the ground, blurring into smudges of deep green and pale pink. Everything rolled like I was somersaulting. Images whirled through my head. Black barren branches, driftwood stacked for a bonfire, canoes with kinaru prows —

Emehein's unseen hand squeezed mine. "Focus. Ground yourself."

The whirling slowed and settled into a foggy lake valley. Down the beach were two cross-legged figures. A teenage girl whittled a figurine, curtains of light brown hair hiding her face. Next to her, a black-haired boy sat with perfect posture, tossing a stone from hand to hand. An okoreni tattoo ringed his arm.

Pain rolled from my skull down through my spine. I cried out. Someone grabbed me as my body contorted.

I came to on the shrine floor, blinking at the high ceiling. Sawdust motes floated in shafts of sunlight. Tema knelt over me, her brows creased with worry.

"It was working," I scraped out. "I saw Fendul and some girl. They're about to do a dawn ceremony. I can try again—"

"No," Tema said sharply. "Once was enough."

She helped me upright. After my head stopped spinning, Tiernan handed me paper and charcoal. I sketched my visions before they faded from memory. Drawing Fendul felt surreal. He'd looked about twenty, the age he would be now, but nothing had marked him as from this world or another.

Emehein studied the wasteland sketch, comparing it to the view from flying over this region in his kingfisher form. "The inlet and snowy mountains match. The rut overlaps Oberu Iren, the river marking our northern border. I suppose it could dry up. But where did *this* mountain go?"

A cold feeling went down my spine. "An edim-saidu could demolish it. You know, if it was pissed off and confused. My other visions lined up with ground level, but that doesn't work when the level changes."

Tiernan sat back, leaning on his hands. "Well, if that is a shoird-ryge, it is terrible for them. Good for us that it is not a vision of our future."

"Unless—" I began.

"I know, I know." He smiled slightly. "Unless seeing that world is an omen."

"Either way," I said, "we'd better kill Liet before he wakes any edim-saidu."

Later, we met Naneko for a war council. Tiernan and Jorumgard had read Liet's recent letters, and based on the way Liet described his location — log cabins, harsh winters, and trading with other Sverbians in nearby valleys — the Tula agreed that he probably was in the sanctuary villages. Tiernan said in good conscience, he couldn't keep that news from Captain Parr, and once he revealed it, there'd be no stopping things. Parr would invade.

The problem was that the easiest route was through Aikoto land, and the Rin would realize what several regiments of soldiers marching toward the villages meant. If they intervened, it'd be a massacre on both sides. Avoiding Aikoto land required looping in huge circles, either south through Dúnravn Pass or north through the tundra, to enter the Turquoise Mountains from the far side. It was a logistical nightmare to haul enough food to sustain hundreds of soldiers and horses on a multi-week trek like that, and they could lose half their force to injury, illness, or desertion. This close to winter, it was practically impossible.

So our only way to protect the Rin was by persuading them to stand down and let the Rúonbattai get attacked. The Iyo might've had enough influence for that, but Tokoda had refused to get involved, even though Liet's letters had implied she opposed the plan to wake the saidu. Telling other jouyen about the Rin-Rúonbattai alliance was almost guaranteed to create backlash against the Rin, which left the Tula as our best hope.

Naneko, true to her reputation, said she needed to gather her advisors from their salmon camps so they could discuss it together. She promised an answer by the autumn equinox, which was a week away. I would've gone crazy if I sat still and waited in Nettle Ginu, so Dunehein, Rikuja, and I canoed northwest with my parents to work at our family's salmon camp. Tiernan and Jorumgard came, too, barely hiding their eagerness to escape Naneko's scrutiny.

A winding creek took us to Oberu Iren. The river had been abandoned for decades until the Tula built fishing weirs across it. My family's new smokehouse was half a league from the inlet, nestled among cottonwoods getting their first hint of yellow foliage. It was beautiful, but I couldn't forget my vision of the dried-up river. I sensed the same oddness as other antayul, hearing voices in the flowing water and feeling like the humidity was wrong.

Being in the salmon camp gave me the same feeling of a sunrise from the wrong direction. When we'd lived in Aeti Ginu far from the ocean, we never went to our old smokehouse until after the equinox, when the salmon had swum far inland. The cottonwoods had always been fully yellow and the undergrowth sparkling with frost each morning. Here it felt too warm, though Tiernan joked it was probably from having a fire mage in our camp.

The work helped me settle in a bit. I knew every step — standing on a footbridge and using a long-handled net to catch salmon trapped by weirs, gutting and filleting them, hanging them from the smokehouse ceiling over pits of damp alder chips. Tiernan and Jorumgard were good students, not minding that a girl half their age was teaching them how to handle a net or measure the right amount of woodchips.

Our first night there, Nili, Aoreli and Malana, and Rokiud and Ikoya came up the river from their camps and had a bonfire with us. Malana's balance was still off since getting injured at Ivy House, and she'd gone permanently deaf in one ear, but she gleefully announced she'd proposed and Aoreli had accepted. Nili begrudgingly paid me five pann. I couldn't remember the last time I smiled so much, watching the pair cuddle and laugh by the fire.

The day before the equinox, we took the last salmon out of the smokehouse and loaded my parents' kingfisher prow canoe. The Tula were returning to Nettle Ginu. Tomorrow, they'd hold their ceremonies in the shrine — blessing it as sacred ground, calling the aeldu there for winter, and performing initiation rites for young Tula who'd attuned recently.

Since we visitors wouldn't be allowed in the shrine after its blessing, there was no point going back yet. Instead, we hiked to a small lake where geese and ducks stopped every year while migrating south for winter. We hoped to bring meat to the equinox feast, which we *were* invited to. Tiernan and Jorumgard weren't trained archers like Nerio, but they'd gotten decent at hunting with shortbows during military campaigns in the wilderness.

When we reached the lake at twilight, though, it was still. Nothing moved among the reedy shallows or on the open green water. Dunehein said the geese were probably late this year because the weather was so warm. Not ready to give up yet, he and I set snares by streams feeding into the lake. The next morning, mine held two cloud weasels and Dunehein's held a hare and a huge thick-furred marsh rat. We walked back to our campsite triumphantly carrying our catch.

"Thank the gods," Jorumgard said, flinging his arm to his forehead dramatically. "I was afraid we'd be eating salmon at the feast. If I never touch one of those scaly bastards again, it'll be too soon."

Everyone laughed, the knowing reaction of people who'd spent so much time handling salmon that we saw them in our dreams. Tiernan cast me a warm smile. I started to smile back, grateful that in the middle of a war threatening to pit his people against mine, we could share a moment like this as friends.

But in the same moment, my antayul senses flared. The lake was changing. Sinking. I could feel water flowing out and going . . . nowhere. It was *disappearing*. I reached out with my mind, trying to pull it back —

The strangest feeling hit me. It was like vertigo and icy water down my spine and the sensation of being watched all at once. I stumbled. The forest vanished, replaced with scorched earth.

I saw myself sitting cross-legged where I'd been a second ago. The other me stared at Tiernan in shock. Her eyes rolled back and she collapsed.

I'm dead, I thought.

I came to on the ground. Ferns tickled my skin. I was several paces away from the lake, lying on the forest's mossy undergrowth. Dunehein crouched over me with a worried expression. I jerked up, searching for Tiernan.

"You—" I stammered. "I saw myself in the wasteland. I — *she* saw you—"

His grey eyes took on an odd look. "Take a moment. Rest."

Rikuja handed me a waterskin, but I couldn't bring myself to drink. The water here wasn't right. This whole forest wasn't right. I shouldn't be having visions without a sacred tree.

Tiernan crouched next to me. "What did she look like? Exactly as you are now?"

I rubbed my aching temples, trying to remember. Her hair had hung loose to her hips, not braided. She had a kinaru and fireweed tattoo from a Rin initiation. "Nei. She was . . . different. And definitely not me in the future, unless she erased these scars." I held up my bitten forearm.

He sighed. "That answers that. You *were* born in the shoirdryge. I suspect the world split six or seven years ago, when your parents said a Rin water-caller first noticed odd things."

"She . . ." I grasped at the fading memory. "I think I saw *her* with Fendul. It seemed like they're still friends. So why is she here now? Why isn't she in Aeti Ginu at the equinox festival?"

Tiernan sank onto the moss. "May I give you some advice?"

I shrugged.

"Forget what you saw. Dwelling on it has driven people to madness. Figure out what you want in this world and fight for it with all your heart. That is all we can do."

36.
THE NORTH

Naneko gave us her answer during the equinox feast. She'd bring thirty Tula warriors north to help the military. As well, she'd send a messenger to the Haka-jouyen in Nokun Bel, who also shared a border with the sanctuary villages. Naneko said they deserved to know that the Rúonbattai were operating out of the villages with the Rin's help. She hoped if she got to the Haka first, she could sway them to our side.

It didn't take long to make up my mind. I'd go north as a war medic. My place was with this alliance I'd helped forge, at what would hopefully be the last battle of the Fourth Elken War. Whatever my life was like in the shoirdryge didn't matter. All that mattered was building a safe world here for my family.

My parents, Rokiud, Ikoya, and my uncle Geniod volunteered to come as well. Emehein said he'd feel too guilty leaving Lohara alone with all their kids again. Nili, apologizing, said she needed to stay with her younger brother. He'd recently attuned to a raven and wasn't handling it well, agonizing over whether a blackbird form meant he belonged with the Rin. Malana reluctantly admitted she wasn't well enough to fight, but promised she and Aoreli would put off their wedding until we returned.

Tiernan and Jorumgard went back to Caladheå to meet with the war council and send word to Captain Parr. As Iyo, Dunehein and Rikuja were forbidden by Tokoda to fight, but they stayed to help us with war preparations — whittling arrows, making camp food, and checking that the Tula's new kingfisher prow canoes were seaworthy. Then we, too, were leaving Nettle Ginu. As much as it hurt to say goodbye to most of my family, I was glad to be leaving this strange rainforest that seemed to be crumbling away. I wasn't sure if it could ever feel like home.

It would've been faster to hike south to Caladheå and leave on a navy ship, but Naneko said we'd enter Rin territory our way. Canoeing down the nearby inlet, around the peninsulas of Anwen Bel, and past Tamun Dael into Nordmur's waters took more than a week. I studied every ship we passed, looking for the *Cavalo via Mèr*'s carved seahorse figurehead, but there was no sign of it. Jonalin had sent his last letter from a naval base in Beru territory further north.

In Caladsten's harbour, we paddled past anchored schooners and galleons with Eremur's naval flag. I stumbled ashore in the docklands, stiff-legged, windswept, exhausted, and crunchy with sea spray. As battered as I felt, though, Caladsten was worse. The military occupation, capture by Sverba mercenaries, and Parr's siege had taken their toll. The surrounding mountains that used to be golden with rye and flax were now charred black.

Hoping to meet some Tamu or Dona and hear news, we stopped by the Aikoto gathering place where I'd met Akohin three years ago, but it was just a heap of splintered wood. We kept our hands near our weapons as we climbed steep hills through town, passing buildings with broken windows and boarded-up doors. Pale faces peered out through shutters. Soldiers patrolled the streets, and the few civilians we saw outside hurried by with their heads down.

The cobblestone gave way to a dirt road winding up the cape. At its peak, Caladsten's main keep rose from blunt cliffs. Its crumbling stone walls had holes patched with boards, mud, and broken bricks, and the wooden gates lay in splinters. A thick rioden log that seemed to have been used as a battering ram lay on the ground near the shattered remains of a catapult.

Guards recognized the kingfisher tattoos on the Tula's arms and waved us through the gates. A young soldier led us past a mix of intact and ruined buildings to the town hall, which the military was using as their northern headquarters. A corner of the roof had caved in, but it was the most impressive structure left standing, three storeys of solid timber and a pair of caribou antlers mounted over the door.

The young soldier showed us into a bright, airy hall with a vaulted ceiling, its tall windows open to let in air that was surprisingly warm for autumn. Men in black or red uniforms sat on benches around a long glossy table. At the far end was Captain Parr, flanked by Nerio and a windburnt naval captain on one side, Tiernan and Jorumgard on the other. They all rose as we entered.

"Welcome," Parr called, spreading his arms. He'd hadn't changed since I'd last seen him this spring, still wearing his black hair pulled back with a ribbon, still clearly strong enough to wield the curved sword at his waist. "I am glad to see you here safe. It must have been a long journey."

The other captains and lieutenants bent their heads close to murmur to each other, eyeing us — our own regiment of warriors with long braids and tattoos on display. Naneko stepped forward, her face cool and impassive, spear straight at her side.

"I know who you are," she said, looking down the table at Parr. "I know *what* you are. You tried to threaten and blackmail my people into capturing Gúnnar Halvarind for you. We did it not because we fear you, nor because we feel the slightest trace of loyalty toward your so-called province, but because we have our own reasons to want Liet and the Rúonbattai eradicated.

"You stand in this hall and welcome the Tula-jouyen as if you own this land. You do not. This always has and always will be the territory of the Aikoto Confederacy. We granted Sverbian civilians permission to live here. When the Rúonbattai are gone, we expect you to vacate this land and return it to the people of Nordmur. That is not a request. It is a condition of this alliance.

"Furthermore, we have agreed to help negotiate your safe passage through Anwen Bel with the sole purpose of giving you access to the Rúonbattai base. Do not count on this route ever being open again. Any intrusion on Aikoto land or violence against any Aikoto person is a crime against our entire confederacy, and we do not forget quickly nor forgive easily. Do I make myself clear?"

The hall was silent. Parr looked taken aback, but he recovered quickly, pasting an equally cool smile on his face. Called out like this in front of other captains, he apparently didn't feel the need to keep up his welcoming façade.

"Entirely clear," he said. "We agree to your terms. Have a seat and join our war council."

The Okorebai-Haka, a middle-aged man named Yunaril, arrived a day later with his advisors. He had a shaved head, a grizzly bear tattooed on his chest, and a mantle of white snowcat fur draped over his broad shoulders. The Haka were always the jouyen we made fun of most, weird northerners whose initiations involved diving into a frozen lake and whose men didn't grow out their hair after marriage, but I was relieved to see them. At least one Aikoto jouyen wanted to stand by the Tula.

After getting Naneko's message, the Haka had sent scouts in bird form to the sanctuary villages. They reported that one village was surrounded by a stakewall and seemed far better defended than the others. The scouts hadn't learned much else spying from the air, but it was enough for the military to know they needed siege weaponry. Yunaril promised that he and his warriors would meet us there.

The rest of us sailed out of Caladsten in a fleet — four transport galleons, a dozen Tula canoes, and two agile schooners to defend us. We headed east up the inlet between Nordmur and Anwen Bel. Gåmelheå, halfway up the inlet, was still held by Nyhemur mercenaries. The Rúonbattai's pale blue flag with a white raven and crossed swords flew boldly in the docklands, but no ships sailed out to attack us. Nyhemur was a landlocked province, not known for producing sailors.

On a cool, rainy afternoon, we spotted our destination — the dock where my parents had once left a Sverbian brigand tied to a mooring post, then torched the ferry house where he attacked us. Now, a group of about ten people waited on shore. We'd seen birds circling overhead for the last day and figured they were Rin scouts. The Tula and I went ahead to meet them, pulling our canoes up onto the rocky beach.

I was on Rin land again, a hundred paces from the ferry house's only remains, a scorched stone chimney. Shrubs and dune grass had grown over the rest of the ruins. I had no time to think about that, though. The waiting people weren't just scouts. Behadul stood with his arms folded, grey braid draped over one shoulder. On his left was his wife, Rumiga, holding an arrow nocked to her bow. On his right was Fendul.

At first, it didn't seem like Fendul had changed. He was full-grown when I'd last seen him in person, and he was still wiry with short black hair and his brows drawn together in a scowl. But something in the way he stood, arms folded exactly like his father, didn't feel like the boy I'd left behind. He glanced over me without a second look. He didn't even recognize me.

"You have a lot of nerve bringing itheran soldiers here, Okorebai-Tula," Behadul said. "Is this an invasion?"

"Not of Anwen Bel," Naneko said. "We only ask for safe passage through your land."

"To where?"

She chuckled dryly. "The sanctuary villages. I'm sure you can figure out why."

"I have no idea what—"

"You used us," Rokiud growled. "You banned us from the coast so we'd build homes for the Rúonbattai. I'd abandon the Rin again if I could."

Behadul's lips thinned into a line. He and Rumiga exchanged a look, seeming to realize there wasn't any point lying anymore. "Who have you told?"

"Only the Haka-jouyen," Naneko replied. "They had a right to know what you've been doing on their border. I promise, though, we have no desire to turn the Aikoto Confederacy against the Rin."

Fendul scoffed. Behadul laid a calloused hand on his son's shoulder, silencing him.

"Then go north through Nokun Bel," Behadul said. "I see no reason to allow hostile itherans to trample through our ancestral land—"

"Oh, come on," Tema cut in. "You've been letting itherans travel through Anwen Bel for years. This isn't about land. Whichever route we take, the question is how hard you'll try to stop us. Are you ready to spill your own people's blood to defend the Rúonbattai?"

Behadul's hand moved to the hilt of his sheathed sword. "The Tula are no longer our people."

"We grew up in the same plank house, Behadul. We've shared meals, we got initiated in the same shrine, we've held each other's children."

"Then you left." Rumiga's soft voice was dangerous, like poisoned water. Raindrops glittered on her black braid. "You turned your back on us. You have a new shrine now, a new name, a new crest."

"I don't," I said.

The Rin swivelled toward me. Fendul's eyes widened with sudden recognition. My hand trembled as I pushed up my sleeve, exposing my untattooed arm. I forced out the words that had been dormant so long, that hot coal of fury searing my insides, stoked by the vision of that other me with a kinaru tattoo. The me who still trusted Fendul.

"*You* turned your back on *us*," I said. "You drove my cousins and me away. Do you have any idea what we suffered? I nearly died alone in Iyun Bel, and I told a tundra wolf to feed on my body and take my spirit back north. That's how much I wanted to go home. And even after I found out everything your family had done, some tiny, stupid, loyal part of me still wanted to come back here!"

The coal inside me was blazing, turning the rain falling around me into steam. I plowed on, my hands clenched into fists. "I was born Rin and I attuned Rin. Even though you've given me every reason to abandon you, I've never been initiated into another jouyen. So if you kill me, you're putting Rin blood in the ground. You're betraying the aeldu who gave me a second body, a second chance at life."

Behadul frowned as if expecting to find some hint it was a ruse. When no one spoke, he said, "We will not harm another Rin. However, we owe no such protection to the itheran soldiers accompanying you."

"Do you know who's on that ship?" Naneko used her spear to point at the largest galleon. "Captain Antoch Parr, the most ruthless and bloodthirsty man I've ever met. He already suspects you're helping the Rúonbattai, and we've worked hard to keep him from getting proof. Every moment we stand here debating makes him more suspicious. Take my advice and stand down."

"I will not be cowed by fear of an itheran—"

"It's not fear, it's common sense," I snapped. "Parr has four hundred soldiers on those ships with thousands more to summon. I know him. He won't give up. How many warriors do *you* have left? What's the point of supporting the Rúonbattai if the Rin-jouyen gets wiped out?"

Behadul, Rumiga, and Fendul lowered their heads to whisper to each other. The other Rin kept their weapons ready. I glanced at the surrounding rainforest and wondered how many warriors they had hidden among the trees. Finally, Behadul straightened up.

"Very well," he said. "You may pass. But do not expect mercy from the Rúonbattai."

Fendul caught my eye for just a second. I had so much left to say, to ask him about meeting Liet, to tell him that I was trying to forgive him and didn't know how — but I didn't get a chance. He shifted into his storm petrel form and shot straight up into the air. All around us on the beach, birds rose through the rain into the sky.

37.

ROLLING THE DIE

Captain Parr had gone all out for this invasion. He'd brought four elite regiments — infantry, cavalry, sappers trained to build things and tear things down, and his own special forces, which included everyone from mercenaries to marksmen. Then there were medics, priests, clerics, and chore boys and girls. *Then* there were wagons loaded with food, weapons, medical supplies, and tools. We couldn't fit everything on the beach at once.

The path to the sanctuary villages had been built over the remains of old Rin traplines. It was forty leagues of dirt track winding through dense rainforest, over hills, into valleys, and up mountains. Travellers had kept the path in decent shape, cutting back the undergrowth and repairing bridges, but for an army, the trip was going to be an ordeal. A spooked horse or broken wagon wheel could hold up the whole procession.

Nerio rode ahead with Tiernan, Jorumgard, and a dozen horsemen to scout and find somewhere for the army to camp. I went along, riding with Jorumgard on his huge white stallion, Skarp, like old times. Tema, Geniod, and a few other Tula flew overhead to keep watch. As we rose in elevation, thick rioden and salt spruce gave way to slender firs and ladder pines. Rain turned to sleet and our breath fogged in the cool air. Frost coated the forest each morning. Our third day of riding, the Tula scouts said they'd spotted the villages.

Sverbians had built five settlements here, scattered throughout different valleys. Each one had a stavehall, granary, mill, and log cabins clustered near a body of water. Three of the villages seemed normal. Their autumn crops had been harvested, the winter rye was sprouting, and shaggy mountain goats with curling horns grazed on hillside pastures. The fourth village looked abandoned. Its fields were overgrown with weeds, its streets empty except for roaming foxes and snowshoe hares. The fifth, on the shore of a glacial lake, was surrounded by a high wall of sharpened stakes. Spearmen guarded the gates.

"That must be the one the Haka described," Jorumgard said. "Doesn't seem suspicious in the *slightest*."

Nerio wanted to learn as much as he could before the army arrived. If any people here were real refugees, he was determined to keep his father from harming them. He sent Sverbian soldiers wearing plain clothes into the normal-looking villages to ask around. They all came back with versions of the same story.

A group of clerics had founded the fifth village, Tjarnnaast. They claimed to have the gods' blessings and offered protection to anyone willing to join them. The clerics hired Rin for all sorts of work — building cabins, digging wells, clearing land for pastures. They also paid good money for Rin food and furs. When the military started searching the region for Rúonbattai, people from other villages flocked to Tjarnnaast, desperate for the gods' protection.

Winters here had been hard, especially for the poorest village. Half its residents starved or froze to death, and the others abandoned it. Tjarnnaast's clerics welcomed them with open arms. The lakeshore settlement had grown to have more than a thousand residents. But last winter, the same time Liet was preparing to launch his uprising, everything changed. The clerics had the people of Tjarnnaast build a wall around their village, then shut their gates to outsiders.

The stories varied about what happened next. Everyone agreed that hundreds of people in Tjarnnaast died in a matter of days — the ringing of their stavehall bell carried throughout the valley, and smoke from funeral pyres filled the sky — but no one could agree on what killed them. A goatherd thought the lake had been poisoned. A farmhand claimed the gods had punished Tjarnnaast for shutting their gates. A blacksmith said the military had massacred them.

Tiernan's theory, based on Liet's letters, was that Rúonbattai clerics had been sowing hatred of the Ferish and turning refugees into soldiers. When Liet revealed himself, most villagers joined him. Others tried to overthrow him. After a brutal fight, Liet had the rebels *dealt with*, as he wrote to Halvarind, so they couldn't sell him out to the military. I hadn't thought he could shock me anymore, but creating the chaos that made his own people flee, then murdering any who didn't fight for him, made me nauseous.

The good part was we could be fairly sure everyone still alive in Tjarnnaast was loyal to the Rúonbattai. That made an invasion simpler. So we got as close as we dared and found a location to make camp, a broad alpine meadow with glacier-fed creeks and plenty of grass for the horses. Then we waited for the army to arrive.

⁂

Tula scouts took turns flying over Tjarnnaast. They saw forges burning night and day, fletchers whittling arrows, labourers shoring up the walls. Kids did practice drills for taking shelter in cellars. The Rúonbattai knew we were coming, though we weren't sure how much they could see of the present or future. None of our scouts had glimpsed Liet or any of his oaks.

"Do you really think Liet's in Tjarnnaast right now?" I asked one chilly evening, huddled in Tiernan and Jorumgard's cramped tent. "He could've fled before we arrived."

"He thought Brånnheå might be his last stand, and he stayed to fight there," Tiernan said. "I believe he will again. He wrote about meeting a warrior's death and feasting with the gods."

"But he told Halvarind to carry on after his death. Now Liet doesn't have anyone left to take his place. In his letters, he said he doesn't think M could lead the Rúonbattai without him."

"Fair point." Tiernan inclined his head. "Either way, in battle, I will be looking for a man with face tattoos and a flaming battle axe."

On a damp grey day, I watched from a hillside as the army arrived and set up camp. Canvas tents sprouted up like enormous mushrooms, smoke and steam from the campfires made a haze over the meadow, and soldiers unloaded wagon after wagon of supplies. Eremur's red elk banner snapped in the wind. It was an impressive sight from up here. No matter how much I disliked Captain Parr, I sure felt glad not to be going against him in combat.

Once I got down into the camp, though, things felt more dismal. Rain, sleet, and thousands of footsteps turned the meadow into ankle-deep mud. The men were exhausted from the march, the reek of sweat and piss was overwhelming, and I kept having to step around piles of horseshit. The other medics and I moved among the soldiers, bandaging blisters and tying up twisted ankles. My only relief was finding Temal in the organized chaos.

"Ai, there's my little fireweed," he said with a grin, wrapping me in a bear hug. "Enjoying your first real war campaign?"

I wrinkled my nose. "It's not as grand and heroic as the songs make it sound."

"Just wait until everyone comes back from battle. There's no stench like someone's guts freshly ripped open."

"Whose guts have *you* smelled?"

Temal's grin faded. "That's a story for another time."

Yunaril and fifty Haka warriors turned up later that day. With their arrival, the war council began planning the invasion. I didn't expect to be invited, but Nerio said they'd relied on my help and knowledge time after time and I deserved to be there. So I wound up in the large tent that served as headquarters, sitting on split logs with uniformed officers and tattooed warriors, all gathered around a map spread across a makeshift table.

Our biggest problem was that the moment we decided on a strategy, Liet would see it. He could defend perfectly, building traps and placing soldiers wherever we intended to breach. So Tiernan made a proposal. During his research, he'd read a historical account from a temporal mage in Sverba who tested her ability to predict a coin toss. She was no better at it than non-magical people because both results, crown and oak, were equally likely.

Tiernan suggested that six people — the captain of each regiment, Naneko, and Yunaril — spend the next day thinking up a strategy. Then he'd assign every person a number and roll a die. Whichever number he rolled was the strategy we'd use. With so many troops under our command, it was the only surefire way of forcing ourselves to be unpredictable. By the time Liet saw our plan, we'd already be riding out.

No matter our strategy, the one thing we were bound to need was siege weapons. The sappers had brought iron parts for trebuchets and were already stripping the abandoned village for readymade boards. Naneko and Yunaril volunteered their woodworkers to help. Temal, Geniod, Rokiud, and the others spent the night in the mouth of the lake valley, constructing the trebuchets as close to Tjarnnaast as possible since they were huge, heavy, and tough to move.

With so many Tula off scouting or building, Ikoya and I were among the few left to help Naneko plan. We came up with using the lake. The autumn rain had raised the water level so much that it reached Tjarnnast's wall. Every Tula and Haka with aquatic bodies, like Rokiud's blackfin whale and Ikoya's seal, could swim up to the lakeside gate, sheltered by the water. Once they broke through the gate, our antayul would open a path through the lake for Eremur's soldiers.

Once that was decided, I headed over to Tiernan and Jorumgard's tent. They wore their cloak hoods up to protect against sleet gusting across the meadow. Their dinner ration of salt pork sizzled over a fire. Tiernan was testing a die he'd whittled, rolling it onto Jorumgard's overturned shield. It kept rolling heavy on three.

I scooped the die up and examined it. He'd used fresh unseasoned wood. It was carved into a perfect cube, but it held moisture that threw off the weight. I pulled out a tiny bit of water and handed it back. After several test rolls, Tiernan grinned.

"I do believe you fixed it," he said.

"I'll check it again tomorrow morning," I said. "In this weather, nothing will stay dry."

"Let's just hope it stays as sleet," Jorumgard said, warming his hands over the fire. "We'll have trouble wheeling those trebuchets through snow."

I grimaced. "If it snows, I guess I'll be on the front lines after all, helping the other antayul melt a path."

"I will be there with you, fire in hand." Tiernan thumped my back. "Do you miss Brånnheå yet?"

"Fuck no," Jorumgard and I said together, and we all laughed.

Tiernan slipped the die into his jerkin pocket and got up. "I should check on our horses. Would you like to come, Katja?"

I followed him to the forest where all the horses were hitched, sheltered by the dense canopy. Gwmniwyr and Skarp had canvas feedbags over their noses, and they'd been groomed and blanketed, so I wasn't sure what more they needed.

"Horses can get skittish before battle," Tiernan explained, rubbing his silver gelding's neck. "They see and hear tension in a camp. They sense fear."

"Jorumgard is right," I said. "You do love horses more than people."

He chuckled. "Horses have simpler loyalties. I feed Gwmniwyr, he lets me ride him. With humans, though . . ."

"It's not simple."

"No." Tiernan looked down at the half-rotten carpet of pine needles. "I wish it was."

I bit my lip. "Do you regret allying with Captain Parr?"

He sighed deeply. "I have no room in my life for regrets. We can never go back on our choices. I am here now, and I know who and what I am fighting for. That will have to be enough."

The next morning dawned frosty but clear. The Tula and I had a breakfast of meat-and-berry slabs, not bothering to light a fire. Temal had dark rings under his eyes from doing woodwork all night, and he'd developed a deep rattling cough, so Naneko assigned him to stay here and help guard the camp.

"You, me, Geniod, a couple Haka, and a whole bunch of itherans," Temal said, slinging his arm over my shoulders. "Maybe we can get a gambling ring going with the clerics."

I tried to smile, but it was starting to sink in that within an hour, everyone else would be marching off to battle. My mother, my friend and once-lover Rokiud, and my newer friends, Tiernan, Jorumgard, and Nerio. I'd be stuck here waiting. Dreading. When the army came back, I would have to stay calm and brave and strong, reassuring wounded soldiers and warriors that they'd be okay. That I'd take care of them. I couldn't get lost in despair like I had at Ivy House.

In a way, it was a blessing that Jonalin wasn't here. I missed him more than ever, the timbre of his deep voice and the gentleness of his calloused hands, but at least he was safer up in Beru territory. I didn't need to dread his still, pale body arriving on a stretcher. My fingertips traced the sea glass in my necklace.

Tema peered at me. "You okay? You've hardly eaten."

I nodded. I'd never told my parents that I might be in love with Jonalin. There hadn't been a point. Even if this was the last battle of the Fourth Elken War and he left the navy, he wasn't coming back to me. He had a different life to lead.

Instead I said, "I just . . . feel guilty staying here with the medics. You and Temal raised me to be a warrior. It feels like I've turned my back on that, too."

"Oh, my love." Tema kissed my hair. "Remember what we taught you. Warriors are measured by how many lives they save, not how many they take."

"You're doing good work," Temal added, squeezing my shoulder. "And we're more proud of you than we ever could've imagined."

I did manage to smile then. Before we could say more, the camp bell rang, summoning us. We crowded into the headquarters tent, shoulder to shoulder with officers. Tiernan had me check the die again, then he began numbering the leaders.

"One, Antoch Parr with the special forces," his voice rang out.

An infantry lieutenant next to me muttered, "We'll see hellfire if it's him."

"Two, Eirik Håskelind with the cavalry. Three, Fedos Valrose with the infantry. Four, Colden Dagind with the sappers."

Murmurs of approval went through the crowd. Sappers knew siege warfare inside and out.

"Five, Naneko with the Tula nation. Six, Yunaril with the Haka nation."

A few itherans sniggered, quickly silenced by glares from all sides.

"The moment I roll this, our plan is set," Tiernan said. "We move out immediately. Every minute we lose is another minute Liet has to prepare his defences. Is everyone ready?"

We all nodded. Tiernan tossed the die onto the table. It landed on one.

I shivered. Tema put her arm around me and stroked my braid.

Parr rose from his seat on a split log. "Very well, then. My plan is simple." He smiled, his lips pressed tight. "Burn everything to the ground."

Parr seriously wanted to burn *everything*. His plan was for antayul to dry the fields around Tjarnnaast, then set them on fire. Burning away the grass and winter rye would expose any traps or secret tunnels. Once our side had a clear path, sappers would roll the trebuchets into the fields, load them with kindling soaked in pine pitch, and fling firebombs at Tjarnnaast. Our soldiers would breach the stakewall, kill any survivors, and raze whatever was left.

It was ruthless, but it played to our strengths. The Rúonbattai had one fire mage and a wall between them and their main water source. We had one fire mage, twenty-some antayul, easy access to the lake, and an entire valley of timber to turn into firebombs. With luck, any of Liet's oaks would burn, too, and the smoke would blind his foresight. If temporal mages couldn't see through walls, they couldn't see through smoke, either.

Our forces marched out of camp in long lines, leaving it strangely quiet. Empty tents fluttered in an icy breeze, campfire coals faded to dark, a lame horse that had been left behind nickered softly. A flock of pigeons, too dumb or stubborn to have flown south yet, pecked at hardtack crumbs in the mud.

Temal, the itheran guards, and I patrolled the edge of camp while Geniod and a Haka scout watched from the air. About forty people were still here. Priests huddled in a circle, murmuring a prayer. Clerics performed some kind of ritual with deer bones. Ferish and Sverbian medics chatted with the lone Haka healer. Chore boys played catch with a leather-bound ball. Around midday, a scrawny girl serving lunch to the priests waved me down. She ladled out a bowl of stew and handed it to me.

"What's this for?" I asked in surprise. The thick steaming stew looked way better than military rations. My stomach growled at the rich smell of rabbit, root vegetables, and beans.

The girl shrugged. "Lieutenant Parr told the *padros* that you's important and we oughta be nice to you. I seen you with him and all the other officers."

I hated questioning a gift, but I had to ask. "Is there animal heart in this?"

"No. Lieutenant Parr said to leave it out." She gave me a wavering smile.

I felt bad for not noticing her before, let alone that she'd talked to Nerio. She looked about fifteen, although she was so tiny it was hard to tell. Her threadbare coat was patched and loose tendrils of black hair fell from her bun. I perched on a supply crate near her campfire as she sliced up bread.

"What's your name?" I asked.

"Lucreza."

A memory flickered, a vision of a girl in a dirty green dress lurking in a courtyard of food stalls, asking if I wanted a meat or fruit pastry. I studied her pinched face. Her nose was crooked. It had been broken — by my elbow.

"We've met before," I said, startled. "Three years ago. I was looking for a stavehall — nei, wait, I said I was looking for a Sverbian market. You offered to take me. Then your brothers jumped me."

Lucreza's eyes went wide. She jerked her head back and forth like a frightened bird, making sure the priests weren't listening.

"It's fine," I said hastily. "I'm not mad. You gave back my carving, and that's the only thing I couldn't replace."

"I—" She gripped her bread knife. "We was street rats. Orphans. We didn't have nothing."

"How'd you get *here*? You can't have been drafted."

Her mouth clamped shut. She held her knife in front of her like a talisman.

I unsheathed my own knives and laid them on the ground. "I swear I don't blame you. I've been scared and desperate, too. I stabbed an Elkhound the same day I ran into you, yet here I am working with the military. Things change."

Lucreza's lips pursed. Slowly, she said, "My big brother joined up when the war broke out. He said he'd send us money, but . . .

I dunno. We ain't heard anything in months. So when me and my little brother, Tonio" — she pointed at a skinny boy playing catch — "heard the sancte was hiring kids to work for military *padros*, we joined up, too. Maybe we'll find our big brother."

My insides wrenched. I remembered the older boy — strong enough to disarm me when I was wounded and half-dead from lung sickness, but probably not enough to beat me in a fair fight. A malnourished teenager with minimal combat training didn't stand a chance in a war. Not that I'd tell Lucreza that.

She finished serving the priests, poured water into the stew pot, and began scrubbing it. She kept glancing up at me, mouth open like she was about to speak, but nothing came out. She reminded me of Hanaiko, terrified but determined to protect her younger brother.

"I should thank you," I said with a wry smile. "You know Tiernan Heilind, that brown-haired mercenary?"

Lucreza's head bobbed. "Everybody knows the fire-caller."

"After your brothers jumped me, Tiernan found me sleeping in a stable. The next spring, I found him in the Turquoise Mountains with Lieutenant Parr and that huge Sverbian mercenary with a braid. I actually told Tiernan that *my* name was Lucreza . . ."

I told her the story of the coal newts and the Brånnheå mission. It sounded like a folk tale, what with the glowing oak, carrion-eating oosoo, and volcanic eruption, but she didn't laugh or scoff, just listened with her mouth slightly agape. After seeing Tula and Haka scouts shapeshift into birds, she seemed willing to believe anything.

When I finished eating, I thanked her and went back to patrolling. Black smoke was rising over the snowy peaks to the northeast. A Haka, flying as a northern tern, returned to camp long enough to report that Tjarnnaast was in flames and our forces were closing in. She'd seen Liet, too — a tattooed man riding through the streets with a cleric, harnessing huge balls of fire and flinging them back over the stakewall.

The news stirred everyone into chatter. By mid-afternoon, though, weariness settled back over the camp. Several people nodded off. Lucreza gave me a mug of black tea to warm me up, and I told her about Matéo tormenting Nicoletta by putting caterpillars in her tea. Lucreza laughed into her coat sleeve, casting furtive glances at the *padros*. I was wondering what story to tell her over dinner, if she'd be as scandalized as Nicoletta about me pretending to be Thymarai, Lady of the Woods, when an eagle screeched overhead.

My head snapped up. The eagle wheeled over camp and landed in its centre. By the time Temal and I reached the headquarters tent, Geniod was ringing the bell. It pealed over and over, filling the meadow, a siren that something had gone horribly wrong.

"What is it?" I cried.

"Riders," he panted. "A hundred or more, carrying the flag of Sverba."

I went cold with horror. "The mercenaries driven out of Caladsten—"

"They're coming. Fast. And they're almost here."

38.

TJARNNAAST

In a single moment, the camp's weary peace shattered. I ran, shouting, shaking people awake. Pigeons flocked into the sky. On and on the bell clanged, piercing my eardrums like a knife.

"Get up!" I screeched. "Get up or die! *Get up!*"

"Everyone run!" Temal bellowed. "Into the woods, *now*!"

I dashed through the clerics' ritual, trampling their deer bones. They scattered in every direction, white robes flying. I glimpsed a smudge of deep blue as the priests fled like a storm cloud soaring out of the meadow.

"Tonio!" came a girl's voice. *"Tonio!"*

I rounded a tent and found Lucreza, wide-eyed and screaming for her younger brother. I grabbed her arm and tried to drag her with me. She slipped in the mud and shrieked at me in Ferish.

"We have to go," I cried. "Tonio's probably running already. Come on!"

I yanked her toward the forest, not thinking of a direction, just knowing we needed cover. An arrow shot past us. It stuck in a tree trunk, vibrating. I whirled. An archer on horseback nocked another arrow —

A dagger whipped through the air and stuck in the archer's chest. He toppled off his horse. I didn't need to look for our rescuer. Temal dropped his throwing arm and drew his sword. He stood alone in the open meadow as a spearman on horseback charged at him.

Jorumgard's lessons kicked in. *Take out the horse*. I swept my arm in an arc, sending ice crackling across the ground. The spearman's horse slid and collapsed, splattering mud everywhere. The spearman flew from the saddle. Temal was on him in seconds, slicing through the man's neck with his sword.

Lucreza shrieked, pointing. Four riders charged at us. I snapped out my arms — downing another horse, coiling a water whip around a rider and yanking him from the saddle, flinging up a wall of ice that a horse slammed into and shattered.

The fourth rider was close. Too close. I glimpsed froth on his horse's coat, a white raven on his blue shield, his spear point aimed at me —

A tawny blur shot into the air, yowling. It struck the spearman and knocked him off his mount. They hit the ground, a tangle of golden fur and flashing metal and enormous paws. The mountain cat ripped into the spearman. Its claws tore through his flesh and rang off his steel breastplate. The cat whirled, crouched, and sprang at another soldier.

Lucreza was screaming. It sounded distant. The cat snarled, thick tail whipping, and tore open a soldier's throat with its fangs. I watched, frozen. Only once, when brigands attacked us at the ferry house, had I seen my father like this — furious, protective, and absolutely lethal.

An arrow hit the cat. Then another. And another.

The cat reeled, hissing. I couldn't move. Couldn't look away. As long as Temal was still in this body, he was okay. Attuned people turned back to their human bodies when they died. But he was still okay. He had to be. I could fix his wounds. I could save him.

The cat swung toward me. Temal's golden eyes looked like two brilliant suns. Blood trickled from the arrows stuck in his tawny hide. *Go*, Temal's eyes urged me. *Run*.

I shook my head. I wouldn't leave him —

His whiskered lips drew back, baring sharp fangs. A shrill scream erupted out of him, making all my hair stand on end. The horses reared. I ran.

Lucreza and I streaked through the forest, swerving around trees, tripping over ferns. I cleaved a gap through a creek, sending icy water flying. Lucreza had to run holding up her skirt. She tried to jump a log and fell, her green dress tangled around her legs. I wheeled back and pulled her up.

"I can't," she panted. "I'm—"

I drew my hunting knife and hacked at her skirt, cutting it off above the knee. We needed a plan, something better than fleeing into the wilderness. I glanced around at the forest. I had no idea where we were. The canopy masked the position of the sun, and dusk would be on us soon.

"I'm going to shift bodies," I said. "If you need help getting down a hill or something, grab onto me for balance."

Lucreza nodded.

I took a deep breath. I'd shown my wolf form to Jonalin and my family, but never a stranger. My bones rearranged and white fur bloomed from my skin. A second later, I stood on four paws on the forest floor. The foliage around us looked grey and washed out.

The hot metallic scent of blood floated from the way we'd come. Ahead was the smell of smoke. Tjarnnaast. If we reached the battle, we could join up with the military and get help. I loped toward the smoke, setting an easier pace for Lucreza. I would hear anyone catching up.

As we reached another creek, exposed to open air, wings rustled in the sky. A black-billed swan swooped toward us. I would've cried with relief if my wolf body could shed tears. Tema arced overhead and led us along the creek. It flowed down a steep hill, spilling over a ridge in a waterfall. I paused atop the ridge and looked out in awe at a hazy valley.

On the shore of a turquoise lake, Tjarnnaast was burning. Flames glowed across its timber buildings and smoke billowed into the sky. The trebuchets stood still in scorched fields. Around the valley, wooded slopes rose into the snow-capped peaks of immense mountains, dyed orange by the setting sun.

I climbed down the ridge first, feeling out a route with my paws. Lucreza followed with one hand gripping the fur on my back, the other grabbing branches and ferns. Pebbles slid from under our feet and clattered away. Finally we reached level ground. The forest opened onto a smoldering pasture. Tema flew low, shifted in midair, and hit the dirt running.

"Tjarnnaast has fallen," she said. "We won. I was flying back to camp to tell everyone when I saw you two running. What happened?"

"Soldiers," Lucreza said shakily. "They stormed the camp."

Tema went pale. She stroked the thick fur on my neck. "Kateiko, go find the captains and tell them. They should be in the village. We'll catch up."

I rubbed my head against her leg, then took off, racing across the scorched fields. Smoke burned my lungs. My wolf nose picked up the stomach-churning scent of seared flesh. Near the village, I started passing dead soldiers riddled with arrows and crossbow bolts.

Guards outside the burnt, collapsed stakewall saw me coming, a patch of white fur against blackened earth. One blew a short blast on a trumpet. By the time I reached the torched front courtyard, Tiernan, Jorumgard, and Nerio were there on horseback to meet me. Soot coated their faces. A tealhead duck landed and shifted into Naneko.

I changed back to my human form and doubled over, coughing. Tiernan slid down from Gwmniwyr's back and handed me his waterskin. I drank gratefully. Once I could speak, I told them about the attack on the camp. Nerio swore and began calling orders to nearby soldiers. A low rumbling horn sounded through the village.

"We'll find your father," Naneko promised me. "He's tough. Don't worry." Then she took off again to round up the Tula and Haka warriors.

"We saw some kind of flare go up from Tjarnnaast at the end of the battle," Jorumgard said. "It looked like a signal, but we didn't know what for. Guess the mercenaries were in the mountains waiting for it."

"Why, though?" Tiernan rubbed his nose, smudging the soot. "Liet was here in Tjarnnaast, so he must have foreseen losing the battle. Why waste skilled mercenaries on a camp of unarmed people?"

I shrugged. "They have our food, medicine, and shelter, and they probably just killed half our medics. All we have now is a razed village—" I stopped short. "Wait. You said Liet *was* here. Did he flee?"

"I have no idea. We lost track of him during the battle. It could take days to sort through this wreckage and find all the corpses. Even then, he may be past recognition. Fire mages are not immune to flames, especially after death."

For the first time, I looked around properly. Ash floated through the air like snow. A pale blue shield with a white raven and crossed swords lay next to a charred body. Arms and legs stuck out from burning rubble. I shuddered to think this was all for nothing if Liet escaped. If he could rebuild the Rúonbattai once again.

The cavalry was gathering outside the stakewall. The low horn blew again, and they rode off, galloping southwest across the fields toward the camp. Birds of all sizes flew with them into the sunset. Parr and the other captains were assembling their remaining soldiers.

"What if *this* was Liet's goal?" I asked. "If he wanted to lure us out of Tjarnnaast? He always writes the future in his favour, right?"

Tiernan frowned. "What would he gain from it? There is nothing here left to salvage. The most anyone could hope for is getting out alive—"

The three of us looked at each other, stunned by the same thought.

"He's still here," Jorumgard said.

"We need scouts—" I swung around, looking for any Tula or Haka left.

Shouts erupted in the distance. Tiernan swung onto Gwmniwyr's back. Jorumgard offered a hand to pull me up onto Skarp, but I was already dropping into my wolf body.

"Nerio!" Tiernan shouted. "We need backup!"

We streaked through the burning streets. Tiernan rode with one hand on the reins, the other sweeping through the air. Fires winked out in front of us. I followed the scent of fresh blood. In a laneway, we found four black-uniformed soldiers, dead on the ground with huge gashes in their chests.

"Antoch's men," Tiernan said hollowly. "We knew them."

All of Captain Parr's men were horseback riders, but their horses were gone. I peered at the ground. Bloody hoofprints led northwest. I started running again, tracking the scent. Gwmniwyr and Skarp galloped in my wake.

The trail led us through the remains of the stakewall, out into smoky fields, and along the lakeshore — or what there was of it. The water level was so high that only a thin strip of mud remained between the lake and the forest. I saw four riders ahead, their horses crashing through the shallows. One rider carried a battle axe. Another wore the white robes of a cleric.

My wolf body was faster than a horse. The second I thought it, flames erupted in front of me. I swerved, howling.

Panic flooded my mind. The lake would protect me, but I couldn't swim fast enough to catch up. Going through the trees could mean running into a forest fire. I tried flinging a wave onto the flames, but I'd never gotten the hang of calling water as a wolf.

Abruptly, the flames vanished. Tiernan must've done something. I took off again, but I couldn't think of any way around this. Catching up to Liet meant leaving Tiernan behind, and Liet would keep fending me off whenever I got close.

A swan trumpeted. Tema split the lake open in front of me, forming a path. I veered into it. Suddenly I was running over wet weeds through a gorge in the lake. Fish darted on either side of me. Tema flew overhead, diving and rolling to dodge fireballs, still cleaving the path for me.

An enormous dark shape appeared to my right. The water distorted it, but I saw white patches near the shape's front. A blackfin whale. Rokiud sped along next to me, keeping pace. We'd nearly caught up. I smelled the horses' sweat, heard the splashing of their hooves —

Tema swung left toward shore. My path swung with her. I glimpsed the riders for just a second before a wall of water struck them. Then I was in the middle of it all, snarling, biting, dodging hooves. The swan called again. I instinctively ran toward the sound.

The blackfin whale shot out of the lake, arcing through the air. It slammed into a horse and rider. They crashed into the forest, splintering trees. Rokiud rolled, shifted, and sprang to his feet with his spear in hand. An inferno erupted, then guttered on the drenched foliage. Heat rolled across me.

A white smudge caught my eye. Somehow the cleric had kept her mount. She looked ghostly. Pale skin, long silver hair, grey eyes staring at me. She loaded a bolt in her crossbow — then Tema soared low and smashed into the cleric's head.

I spun, looking for Liet. There he was. Golden hair, tattoos on his face and hands, braided beard swinging. The head of his battle axe burst into flames. He drew it back to strike at Rokiud.

An arrow struck Liet's shoulder. He reeled. Seizing my chance, I coiled my legs and leaped. We went down in a fury of teeth and claws and fire. He roared and flung me off. I hit something hard and fell, a whine tearing from my throat.

"Katja!" someone cried.

I saw double versions of horses, flames and water whirling, metal flashing. The others had caught up. Nerio shot arrow after arrow. Jorumgard fought Liet, parrying the blazing axe with his sword and shield. Tiernan's hands weaved as he held back a firestorm. Embers swirled around us. Then —

Jorumgard's sword found its mark, in and out of Liet's leather breastplate with a spray of blood. The man's eyes flew wide. His axe hit the ground and he dropped to his knees. The flames around us sputtered out.

"*Fyndestjolv*," Jorumgard growled. "That's what your men called me in Brånnheå. But we all know who the traitor is."

Liet coughed, spitting up blood. "The gods are with me—"

"Then where's your precious cleric?" Jorumgard stepped back, arms wide. "Who's gonna burn your corpse so your spirit passes into Thaerijmur?"

Liet whipped around. The cleric was gone. So were the other two Rúonbattai and the horses, leaving trails of blood and lake muck through the forest.

"Rot in Bøkkhem," Tiernan said through gritted teeth. He swung his sword and opened Liet's throat.

The Rúonbattai leader collapsed, twitching. His grey eyes fixed on the darkening sky. Finally, he went still.

I pushed myself up and shifted to human. The smell of blood faded as colour rushed back into the world. Rokiud stepped forward, clutching his spear. A swan landed in the soaked, trampled foliage.

"Is it over?" I breathed. "He's dead?"

Jorumgard nudged Liet's leg with his boot. "Looks like it—"

The body burst into flame. Jorumgard stumbled back, cursing.

"No!" Tiernan swung out an arm, extinguishing it.

It was too late. The body was charred. Any chance of finding out Liet's identity by his face, tattoos, or anything else was gone — and he'd somehow gotten his last rites.

Tiernan swore loudly. "I have no idea how that happened. Liet's fire magic should have died with him. Maybe he — wait. Do you feel that?" He turned, searching the ruined forest.

I paused. It was a familiar feeling, like I'd been here before and would again. I waded into the lake shallows to get a better look around. Tiernan followed, carrying a fire orb to light up our darkening surroundings.

High overhead, painted on a vertical rock face, was a nine-branched oak with one red branch, wreathed by lilacs. An overhang of soil and trees sheltered the crest. Our bird scouts never would've seen it from the air. It was only visible from down here on the ground.

I sank into meditation, sorting the water around me into a mental picture — white lake, grey forest, black rock. I opened my eyes. The painted crest was gone. So were my companions and all signs of battle. Tjarnnaast had vanished, leaving the twilit valley peaceful and untouched, clear of smoke. I blinked. This world snapped back into place.

"The Rúonbattai never came here in the shoirdryge," I said.

Tiernan nodded. "That other Liet may have died years ago. His crests there seem forgotten and ignored, as if their power was extinguished."

"So shouldn't *this* one have just died?" I asked.

"I think so." He looked worried, and it shocked me how disturbing that felt.

"Then who in bloody hell did we kill?" Nerio asked, staring down at the blackened remains of the tattooed, axe-wielding man.

Tema took off, flapping her wings hard, and rose into the air. She circled around and bobbed in front of the oak, examining it.

A bolt cracked open the silence.

Tema fell. I screamed. She plummeted into the lake, sending up a cascade of water. I cleaved a path and dashed toward her.

A black-billed swan drifted underwater, blood spiralling from the bolt in its chest. I yanked her to the surface. She shifted in my arms, white feathers receding into tanned skin. Her long braid floated around us.

"Tema!" I cried. "Hold on — just hold on—"

"Kateiko," she gasped. "I—"

"You're fine. You'll be fine. Please, you have to!"

"If—" Her dark eyelashes fluttered. "Tell your father — I love you both—"

"Tema, no! I can fix this. *Tema*!"

Her whole body shuddered. "My child," she whispered. "Be brave."

39.

BØKKHEM

I had no memory of leaving the lakeshore. Later, I'd be told that Tiernan had instructed Rokiud to stay with me, then he, Jorumgard, and Nerio scoured the forest, looking for whoever shot the crossbow. All they found was a hidden door in the rock face below the oak painting, sealed with glowing runes. Forced to give up, they lifted Tema's body onto Skarp and took us back to Tjarnnaast.

Night had fallen by the time we arrived. The village was still smouldering, casting ripples of orange and yellow light on the lake. Torches flickered in a dark field where soldiers were gathering the dead. Tula warriors appeared, speaking words that slid past my ears unheard. They laid Tema on the scorched earth next to one of Rokiud's cousins, a young man of about twenty. Rokiud dropped to his knees and took his cousin's limp hand.

Some part of my mind, floating on the surface like a leaf on a pond, understood that my mother was dead. I reached for another thought instead, the only one that could keep from me sinking. I had to find Temal. I had to mend his wounds and tell him what happened. Tell him that Tema loved him.

I kissed her damp hair, whispered that I'd be back, and got up. It felt like moving through a dream, hazy with smoke and strangely muted. My limbs were weightless. Figures ran past in the darkness, spreading the news about Liet, shouting for the military captains.

"Katja," someone called. "Katja!"

It didn't sink in that those sounds were my name. I kept walking toward the road to the camp. Tiernan and Gwmniwyr cantered in front of me, cutting me off.

"Where are you going?" he asked.

I blinked up at him. "Looking for my temal."

"Alone in the dark? In a war zone? Katja, the odds of locating him before morning—"

"I have to find him. He's hurt." I tried to move around Gwmniwyr.

Tiernan reached down and grabbed my shoulder. "Where did you last see him?"

"In the camp. When we got attacked."

"Then I will take you. The road is not safe." He called back to Jorumgard in Sverbian, then reached down to pull me onto Gwmniwyr's back. A fire orb flickered into existence to light our way.

Hardly had we left the lake valley when we heard hoofbeats and the creak of wheels ahead. Tiernan guided Gwmniwyr off the road, hand on his sword, and called out. A voice called back, identifying himself as Håskelind, the cavalry captain, and Tiernan relaxed.

A caravan came down the sloping road. Lanterns swung from horse-drawn wagons. As they rolled past, I saw that the first ones held crates of food and medical supplies. I searched the sky, knowing that Tula birds were probably guarding the caravan. A moment later, a bald eagle dropped from the sky and shifted into Geniod.

"Kateiko," he said, breathless. "Thank the aeldu you're all right."

"Have you seen my temal?" I asked.

Geniod's face crumpled. "He . . . I'm so sorry. There was nothing I could do—"

He pointed at a wagon. This one held a pile of bodies. Flies buzzed around it. I slid off the back of the saddle, hardly aware of my boots hitting mud.

"Stop," I cried. "Stop!"

The driver pulled on the reins and the wagon groaned to a halt. I stood on a wheel spoke and pulled myself up to look over the side of the wagon box. Tiernan rode over with his fire orb, lighting up the bodies and driving back the flies.

Temal's body lay near the top, his legs partly covered by the blue robes of a priest next to him. His hood was up and his braid coiled inside so his hair didn't touch anyone else. Someone had pulled the arrows out of his body, leaving bloody holes in his clothes.

Geniod climbed onto the other wheel and looked down at his older brother. His voice cracked as he said, "I didn't want to move him this way, piled in with itherans, but—"

"Nei," I cut him off. "Temal's not — he can't be. I have to *fix* him!"

"It's too late. Believe me, I wish—"

"It's *not* too late! It's not! I have to tell him — Tema wanted me to—"

My knees gave out. Geniod leapt down from the wheel and caught me. I collapsed on the road, my chest heaving too hard to breathe. Tiernan dismounted, pulled Temal's body out of the wagon, and laid him gently next to me. With a creak of wheels, the caravan moved on.

⁂

When I came back to myself, I was draped over Temal's body. The forest was still dark. Geniod was shaking my arm.

"We can sit here as long as you want," he whispered. "I'll stay with you. But if you feel up to it, there's work to do."

I made some vague, confused sound.

Tiernan crouched next to us. "Several medics were killed in the attack on the camp. We could use your skills."

My parents' words came back to me. *Warriors are measured by how many lives they save*. I wasn't any use here, and it wasn't fair to let other people die. So I hauled myself up, we carried Temal to the field of the dead, and we laid him next to Tema with their hands overlapping and braids intertwined. Then I packed my grief into a little box inside my heart to deal with later.

The familiar scent of camphor led me to another field. A Ferish medic shoved needle and sinew at me and pointed at a soldier's gaping stomach. I got to work with hands that didn't feel like mine. I cleaned wounds, stitched or cauterized them, and bandaged them up, talking patients through the pain. Geniod stayed at my side and helped.

Someone brought my satchel of herbal medicine containing gauze packets of bogmoss and vials of tulanta and willowcloak. Nerio came by to ask if I needed anything else. I had him send soldiers into the forest to collect pine pitch for sealing wounds. Lucreza and her younger brother, Tonio, brought me food that I ate without tasting. Soldiers kept bringing people on stretchers, separating them into the fields of dead and wounded.

Tjarnnaast's fires went out, only for new ones to appear on the horizon. Clerics were sending dead Sverbians onto the lake on burning rafts. Ferish people traditionally got buried, but it would take too long to dig proper graves, so priests were burning the bodies on funeral pyres. Naneko and Yunaril had antayul preserve our dead in ice so we could take them home.

The night seemed endless, and we learned from the military timekeeper that it *was* dragging on. Smoke had settled so thick over the valley that the sky was still black two hours after sunrise, three hours, four hours. Geniod suggested I get some sleep, but if I stopped moving, that box of grief inside my heart would burst open. So I kept working until my vision blurred and my hands shook too much to thread a needle. Geniod handed my tools to another medic and led me to a cluster of tents where I blacked out.

I woke in a cold sweat, feeling no more rested, although my mouth was dry as if I'd been asleep for hours. Pulling back the tent flap revealed yet more darkness. I crawled outside and found Jorumgard sitting by a campfire. He lifted a pot of steaming water from the coals and poured me a mug.

"Military tea," he said. "With enough dirt, it actually has flavour."

I sipped it blearily. "Where's Geniod?"

"Checking in with Naneko. He'll be back soon."

Around us, weary, coughing soldiers slumped by fires outside their tents. The smoke had cleared enough to see the outlines of the trebuchets in the distance, and the sky had patches of deep orange, but it was still too hazy to see the mountains. The scorched fields around us seemed to fade away into nothing. It felt like I'd fallen through a rift into another world. Maybe I was Tula even without being initiated, one of the people of the gateway.

"We're in hell," I said. "Actual hell. This is what the murals of Bøkkhem looked like in the Brånnheå stavehall."

I was mixing Ferish and Sverbian religion, but I didn't care. Both their versions of the land of the dead felt more real than the lush green rainforest of Aeldu-yan. My visions of the shoirdryge's wasteland seemed like an omen of this, a scorched landscape with the forest and mountains erased.

Jorumgard leaned forward, his rope-like braid falling over his shoulder. "I'm so sorry, little pint. I've lost friends in combat, but I can't imagine what you're going through."

I shrugged.

"Geniod and I have been talking, and . . . he wants to take you back to Nettle Ginu tomorrow. It'll take awhile cleaning up this mess. You don't need to stay."

"I came here as a medic. I've got work to do."

"The worst is over. It's just broken bones and whatnot left to patch up. We both think you should be with family right now—"

"What would you know about it?" I cut in. "Family? Parents? *Love*?"

Jorumgard drew back, looking wounded. "What—"

"You didn't even try to fix things with Yotolein. You abandoned Hanaiko and Samulein when they've already lost a parent. Then you sat here with another of my uncles, debating what to do with me? Acting like you have a say in my family?"

"Katja, I—"

"Because you don't!" I shot to my feet. The mug fell from my hand, splashing hot water everywhere. "I had a family, and I wanted you in it, and now it's too late! Everything's broken!"

He rose, towering over me. "Katja—"

"Fuck off!" I shoved him. "I don't want you here!"

Jorumgard stepped back. He tossed away his sword, unbuckled his leather armour, and dropped it on the ground. "You've got every right to be mad at me. I'm an idiot. I've fucked up. So if you need to scream or hit me or whatever, go ahead. I can take it. But I'm not leaving you alone like this."

I hit him. My knuckles throbbed, but I did it again and again, pummelling his chest. He didn't flinch, which made me angrier.

"Come on," he said. "Let me hear you!"

"I — don't — want — you — here!" I struck him with each word.

"You're not loud enough!" Jorumgard crouched down to eye level with me and bellowed. "COME ON!"

"FUCK OFF!" I swung at his face.

His nose cracked. I swung again. Jorumgard blocked my fist and struck my shoulder. I stumbled. He caught me and we collapsed on the ground together.

The impact stunned me. Jorumgard released me and rolled away. A trail of red droplets followed him. He wiped his bleeding, broken nose on his tunic sleeve.

"Why'd you let me do that?" I asked, my throat scraping.

"Because you needed to." He heaved himself into a sitting position. "I know you, Katja, and I know grief. You're pissed off at everyone and everything. It's gotta come out somehow. But your enemies would hit back, and I won't let you hurt yourself."

I looked at my hands. My knuckles were scraped raw, and I'd have bruises soon, but nothing felt broken. Jorumgard had stopped me before I seriously injured either of us.

"Sorry," I said, growing hot with shame. "I shouldn't have—"

"No." He gripped my arm. "Apologize for nothing. Feel what you feel, do what you need to. Maybe I — well, I don't deserve to be part of your family, but I care about you, Katja. I'm here for you."

Wind blew in from the southeast overnight. When I woke again and climbed out of the tent, sunshine warmed my face. The valley was stunningly vibrant — the glittering turquoise lake, deep green forests with yellow veins where alder and cottonwood grew along streams, and snow-capped mountains so white they hurt to look at. I figured the wind was a lucky fluke until I saw a raven circling overhead. Akohin and Ainu-Seru had come to clear away the smoke.

It felt like falling back into the land of the living. My path kept crossing with Akohin's, as if we were birds landing at the same lakes during a long migration. Two orphans who had to figure out where we belonged in the world.

Tiernan stopped by the medics' field to update me on news. He had two theories about Liet's corpse burning up. One was that the cleric or another Rúonbattai was also a fire mage. The other was that Liet's tattoos were actually runes, ensuring his body would burst into flame after death, a safeguard in case the cleric fled or got killed before doing the rite.

He didn't know what to make of the oak crest painted on the rock face, though. Temal had said the oaks' magic seemed fragile and impermanent, so the fragments of Liet's spirit in them shouldn't survive after death the way spirits did in makiri. But Geniod, also a makiri carver, had flown past the painting and felt something still alive. So either the axe-wielding man was an excellent decoy, matching everything we knew about Liet — his fire magic, combat skill, tattoos, golden hair, and braided beard — or someone else had painted the oak. Either way, the Rúonbattai still had a temporal mage on the loose.

I didn't have the time or energy to try to figure it out. The Tula and Haka were going home. There was a taste of snow in the air, and they were building sledges to carry our dead. Naneko said we had come our way and we would all leave our way.

Falling snow marked our last evening there. I slipped away from Geniod, who'd been following me like a shadow, and headed up the lakeshore. I wanted to be alone in the peace that snow always brought. But when Tiernan approached, I let him. He perched next to me on a fallen log covered in lichen. His beard had grown long and his brown hair hung loose around his face. He looked as exhausted as I felt.

"How are you holding up?" he asked.

I shrugged.

He smiled sadly. "The other medics say you have done remarkably well, if that is any consolation."

"Not really." I rolled a vial of laudanum around in my palm. "I don't want to do it anymore. I don't want to be a healer."

"Even in Caladheå? You could go back to the apothecary, or I could ask Marijka—"

"Nei. I don't want to do it at all."

"May I ask why not?"

"Because it's pointless! Everything is! I—" My voice broke. "I couldn't—"

Tiernan's glance flickered to the laudanum in my hand. "Was it pointless to help Jonalin?"

"I don't know! I have no idea if he's still alive! Maybe the Rúonbattai kept going further north into Beru territory, and they'll hurt Jona, and it'll be all my fault because I let him go, and — there's no *point* to anything when my lover and family and friends are all warriors. They're all going to die sooner or later!"

He was quiet a moment, letting me catch my breath. Then he said, "Do the good moments before death count for nothing?"

"They—" I swallowed hard. "They do count. That's the problem."

His brows furrowed, encouraging me to go on.

"I stayed in Caladheå. My parents kept asking if I wanted to move to Nettle Ginu, but I stayed. I missed *years* of good moments with them."

"You have a life there. They understood that."

"I should've at least visited them. I just — always thought I'd have time. I had other people to look after, Akohin and Jona and my cousins and Kirbana's kids, and my parents didn't need my help. But *I* need them. I thought attuning meant I was all grown up, but I don't know how to be an adult. And now they — now—"

I sniffled and tried to pass it off as a cough. Everyone had been coughing for days, even after the smoke cleared.

Tiernan laid his rough hand over mine on the log. "There is no shame in crying, Katja."

"Like you'd know," I muttered.

"I could tell you a dozen stories of losing people I love. My parents, friends, comrades, the woman I wanted to marry. I have cried for them all."

I glanced at him through watery eyes. He'd always been so reluctant to talk about his past that I'd stopped asking. I'd never imagined we had much in common.

"I, ah . . ." Tiernan scratched his beard. "I do not wholly understand the nuances of your culture, but if it would help to . . . know a kindred soul, then . . ."

He bowed his head. I was astonished. After all this time, he was prepared to bare his spirit to me. I slipped the laudanum into my cloak pocket, then hesitantly lifted my hand and touched his tangled hair.

The box in my heart shattered. Grief poured out along with a waterfall of other emotions. I crumbled against him. Tiernan wrapped his arms around me, keeping me upright. I sobbed into his soot-stained jerkin, chest heaving, shoulders shaking. He murmured soothingly in Sverbian.

By the time I could breathe again, snow had covered the shore. Tiernan offered me a rumpled handkerchief. It smelled like smoke.

I wiped my face and sat up, still trembling. He shuffled down the log to give me space, and together we watched snow fall into the turquoise lake.

After a long while, he asked, "Are you going back to Nettle Ginu?"

"For now." I rubbed my eyes. "For my parents' burials and my cousin Malana's wedding, at least. After that . . . I don't know."

Tiernan nodded. "I have no idea where this war will take me, so exchanging letters will be difficult. But if you ever need Jorum or me for anything, a friend to talk to or a shoulder to cry on again . . . look for this tree." He held out a gold coin.

Long ago, I'd told him the story of how Kirbana gave me a rusty tin coin from Sverba and told me to look for the tree if I needed help, which she meant to lead me to a stavehall and instead led me to the Golden Oak. At first I thought this coin was another one from Sverba, but when I looked closer, I saw that the etched oak was in full bloom. Birds nested in its branches and a dog snoozed underneath it, just like the sign outside the Golden Oak.

"Did you make this?" I asked. "I've never seen metalwork this detailed."

Tiernan's mouth edged into a smile. "Enough heat will make anything malleable."

40.
GHOSTS

The Haka set off north in a convoy and the Tula set off west. Six Tula were dead and several were too injured to walk, so the rest of us pulled sledges loaded with people or supplies. Keeping the ice around my parents frozen meant constantly being aware of their motionless forms, but I refused to let another antayul handle it. Halfway to the coast, a seventh Tula succumbed to her wounds. She'd been bleeding internally, beyond what the medics could fix.

At the ferry house ruins, Geniod and I moved my parents into their kingfisher prow canoe. Technically it was mine now, but not being Tula myself, I couldn't very well claim it. I took the bow spot and Geniod took the stern. Sleet followed us on the long journey south. A Tula warrior flew ahead with the news, so by the time we reached the mouth of Oberu Iren, Emehein was there to wrap me in a hug and accompany us back to Nettle Ginu.

I felt like a ghost in my parents' plank house, as if my hand would go through anything I touched. I put Temal's sword on its wall mount and was half-surprised it didn't fall through. A blanket embroidered with the fir branches of Tema's crest covered their bed. I'd inherited that, too, but couldn't bring myself to touch it. I didn't even want to try sleeping in my bed, knowing I'd spend the night looking over at my parents' empty one, listening for their breathing.

My grandmother, Temal-tema, laid out a spare mattress for me in her plank house. Malana lived here with her parents and two siblings, and Geniod still lived there because he'd never married, so I was surrounded by more relatives than ever, but I felt like even more of a ghost here. Family lines didn't work this way. I was supposed to be in my mother's house, not my father's.

People began pouring into Nettle Ginu for the burials. Yotolein and Hanaiko and Samulein, Dunehein and Rikuja, and Kirbana, Narun, Kel, and Sena came from Caladheå. Ranelin and Makinu came from Toel Ginu since Jonalin couldn't be here for me. Dozens of Rin came from Aeti Ginu. Isu didn't, too proud and loyal to the Rin to show up for her dead younger sister.

We buried my parents next to one another, each at the foot of a rioden. Emehein helped me with the rites for Tema. We cut her palms, turned them skyward to receive the earth, and laid a kingfisher feather on each side of her in the grave. Emehein carved a kingfisher in the rioden trunk and I carved Tema's fir crest around it. Temal-tema did the rites for Temal, carving our shared fireweed crest in his tree. Burying her son was the only time I could remember seeing her cry.

After the burials, Yotolein gave me the swan and mountain cat makiri I'd left with him for safekeeping. The warmth they'd held when Temal first gave them to me was gone. He'd never taught me how to handle makiri, to sense spirits in the wood, to talk to them.

I thought about asking Geniod, but Temal was never supposed to have made these. He was the only one of his family to never finish his apprenticeship. I didn't want to start a fight now of all days.

Instead I asked Naneko if I could visit the shrine, and she agreed. It was home to my parents' spirits now, so they could invite me in without offending other Tula aeldu. That night, when I said I wanted to be alone, Geniod looked wary but didn't push it. He'd stopped watching me so closely once we'd arrived in Nettle Ginu.

I climbed a path of packed snow up the slope and through the shrine gate, passing under a lintel carved with a kingfisher and twisting vines. I pushed open the heavy double doors and slipped inside. This late at night, the building was empty and dark, the hearth fires out, shutters closed. Working by feel and the memory of Aeti Ginu's shrine layout, I lit a stone lantern that acted as a beacon to the aeldu. Flickering firelight filled the void between the floor and the ceiling three storeys up. The sacred rioden seedlings were lined up along one wall.

I sat cross-legged on the platform in the middle of the shrine, holding a makiri in each palm, willing them to talk to me. Willing turned to begging. I meditated, sang songs to call the aeldu, held the figurines up to examine them for any change.

"What am I supposed to do?" I asked. "How do I hear you?"

Nothing.

"Why would you do this?" I said, my frustration rising. "All my life, Temal, you said you didn't agree with carving makiri. So why did you finally make these? Why give me something you never taught me to use?"

The lantern just went on flickering.

"I can't put them on a mantelpiece here. Your family will get mad if they find out you made these. Temal-tema will say you didn't have permission, it was risky, the makiri could get corrupted if you did it wrong. So how are your spirits supposed to protect me? I don't even have a home to put you in!"

Silence pressed down, squeezing the air from my lungs. I screamed and threw the makiri. They clattered onto the floor.

Guilt crushed me. I scrambled across the wood planks and seized the makiri, making sure they were okay. I wrapped them up in one hand and clutched them to my chest.

Nowhere was home to me. I couldn't live in this rainforest that was crumbling into the scorched hell I'd just escaped. I couldn't go back to Caladheå and work in the apothecary, watching the war from the sidelines, going to charity socials with Nicoletta and pretending none of this happened. I couldn't marry Jonalin and move to Toel Ginu. I couldn't go back to Aeti Ginu and live with Isu and Fendul and everyone else who'd turned their backs on me.

I fished a vial of laudanum out of my cloak pocket. The red-brown liquid glowed in the lantern light. I'd brought it from Tjarnnaast, telling myself I'd forgotten to return it to the Ferish medics, but I knew the truth. I wanted a way out like Jonalin had. My heart ached so much I wanted it to stop. I wanted everything to stop. And if I could tip myself over the edge into Aeldu-yan, if I could join my parents' spirits here . . .

"Kateiko?" came Yotolein's voice.

My hand snapped shut around the vial. "Are you spying on me?"

He stepped forward into the light. "Geniod was worried, but thought you were getting sick of him. I've been sitting outside the shrine. I heard you scream."

"You're not allowed in here. You're still Rin—"

"I have as much right as you. My sister's spirit lives here, and she doesn't want her daughter to kill herself." Yotolein held out his hand.

Reluctantly, I gave him the vial. "How do you know what it is?"

"I talked to Jonalin's parents after his overdose, and Agata and the Iyo healer. I know what to look for." He crushed the vial under his boot, letting the laudanum spill out among shards of glass, and settled down next to me. "You've gone through an incredible amount of trauma. It would overwhelm anyone."

I flumped back onto the floorboards and covered my face with my arm. "I didn't really want to . . . I mean . . ."

"It hurts. I know. Tove has been gone three years, I've fallen for someone else, and I still miss her every single day. But we have to live *through* that pain. We owe it to the people we've lost. The people who gave us this chance to keep going."

My chest juddered. My body wanted to cry, but I'd shed so many tears during the burials that my body had run dry. "Does it get easier?" I managed to ask.

Yotolein sighed. "It gets . . . duller. I don't know if it ever goes away, but it turns from something that feels like living death into an old wound you're used to." He stroked my hair. "If there's anything you want to talk about, I'm willing to listen."

I shook my head. Suddenly I felt bone-tired. "Do you mind if I just sleep?"

"Here?"

"Yeah."

"Go ahead. My kids are down for the night, so I'll stay with you. And I bet . . ."

Yotolein got up and disappeared through a side door. A moment later, he came back with an armload of canvas covers for ceremonial drums. He bundled one into a pillow and draped another over me as a blanket. With a flick of his hand and a dash of water, the lantern hissed out. Darkness fell over us.

"You know," I said sleepily, "I think Jorumgard wants you back."

⁂

I dreamed of the other me, the girl in the shoirdryge with a kinaru tattoo and arms free of bite scars. She drifted through the shrine as a silvery ghost. Her form blurred like smoke and shifted into Thymarai, Lady of the Woods, dressed in scraps of white leather with deer antlers on her head. She blurred again and shifted into a cleric, pale and furious, silver hair floating around her as if she was underwater. She loaded a crossbow and fired.

I jerked up, gasping. Cold sweat drenched my back. Yotolein stirred in his sleep. The first light of day turned the shrine into a haze of blue shapes.

Legend said Thymarai went everywhere with her *bjørnbattai*, her bodyguards and bear shapeshifters. Jorumgard and Dunehein had acted as mine when we scared the Sarteres into giving back my cousins. They were the muscle, the obvious threat, but Thymarai was always in command. *She* was the truly terrifying one.

I mentally ran through everything Tiernan and I had figured out from Liet's letters. The writer was a mage who once lived in Ingdanrad, was devoted to the gods, had a soldier brother called M, a female friend-maybe-lover called O, and a male friend-maybe-lover in Halvarind. Nothing in the letters explicitly said the writer was a man. Heart thumping, I sifted through pieces of history, putting together a timeline.

Twenty years ago, Liet got chosen as the Rúonbattai's new leader. That was the first time we'd heard mention of a fire mage who kept a cleric at his side. Maybe it had been the same cleric for twenty years. A woman who was blessed by the gods and worked in the shadows, building oak crests, seeing the future, using a man as her bodyguard and decoy. She'd survived Brånnheå, then survived Tjarnnaast by leaving her fire mage for dead. And she still had three oaks out there that we hadn't found.

"Yoto," I hissed, shaking him.

Yotolein lurched upright, the canvas cover falling from his body. Once I assured him there was no danger, he relaxed. He rubbed the sleep from his eyes as I explained.

"Aeldu save us," he muttered. "We should go tell Naneko—"

"Nei, wait. I want to try something. Did you hear about me using the seedlings to have a vision?"

"Dunehein told me. You found the sacred rioden at Kotula and saw yourself with Fendul."

"Right, then I passed out and . . ." A lump filled my throat. "Tema told me not to try again."

Yotolein's brows knit together. "You want to disobey your mother? *Here*, with her spirit watching?"

"Exactly." I held up the swan and mountain cat makiri. "She and Temal promised to protect me. If I tap into the seedlings again, maybe I can find another omen. Some sign of the cleric."

He sighed. "The moment it goes wrong, I'm snapping you out of the vision. Deal?"

I nodded. We moved the seedling pots onto the central stage. I sat cross-legged, a makiri in each hand, canvas draped around my shoulders to stave off the winter chill seeping through the wall. Yotolein sat next to me.

"Want me to talk you through it?" he asked.

"I know the steps already. It helps having a voice to focus on, though. Maybe sing something?"

He thought a moment, then began a Sverbian lullaby he sometimes sang to his kids. I hadn't expected it, but it was the right choice. A Rin song would've felt offensive here in the Tula shrine.

I sank into meditation, building a mental picture of the water around me. White rectangles of frost outlined the shuttered windows among grey timber walls. I focused on white lines pulsing within the seedlings' branches and roots. Yotolein's song guided me, higher and freer than Emehein's steady voice. When everything went black, I opened my eyes.

Once again, I floated in the shoirdryge. Sunlight peeked over the snowy mountains and glittered on the ocean inlet. Huge boulders cast long shadows across the scorched wasteland. I turned to look for the sky bridge and gasped.

A translucent swan hovered in the sky, wings folded. Its outline blurred like smoke. Without thinking, I tried to move toward Tema — and succeeded. It felt like dream-flight, my disembodied self floating as shadows moved far below. All I heard was Yotolein's song.

Tema spread her wings and turned south, leading me beyond the wasteland to the forest around the sky bridge. Snow lay thick on the treetops. We curved west to follow the river canyon. The rapids blurred into whiteness as if they were moving at a different speed.

Near a bend in the canyon, we turned south again and drifted over the dense forest of North Iyun Bel. The creek where I'd first attuned ribboned through the trees. Before we reached it, Tema dropped low and landed in a clearing. I followed. A translucent mountain cat stepped out from the trees, thick tail twitching.

Why are we here? I thought. *What does it mean?*

Temal paced across the clearing, his huge paws leaving no marks on the snow. He passed a rough plank building, paddock, and stable, stopping by a log cabin. I peered through a frosty window.

My other self stood in a cramped kitchen calling water into a kettle. She passed it to someone out of view. I shifted sideways to see. Tiernan, his loose hair brushing his shoulders, placed the kettle in a hearth. He said something I couldn't hear, making the other me laugh. She opened a cupboard and removed a tea tin without looking.

I backed away, unnerved. Tiernan and I had spent plenty of time alone together, but this seemed like they were living together. I didn't want to see more. The Tiernan in my world had told me to forget I saw the other me, so why would my parents bring me here? Why show me living with anyone other than Jonalin, as if *that* would bring me comfort?

"Kako?" came Yotolein's voice. "Kako!"

Fingers latched onto my arm. My head turned inside out. The cabin swirled and faded like I was racing through a tunnel.

I awoke slumped against Yotolein. "What . . ." My throat scraped.

"You stopped breathing." He stroked my hair. "You were in a trance for at least an hour."

"Really?" I blinked at the shrine. Sunshine lit up frosty cracks around the window shutters. I'd travelled leagues away, a journey that would take days on foot, but it had felt like hardly any time at all.

I described my vision haltingly. Yotolein teared up at the mention of his sister appearing as a swan. At the part about the cabin, he sighed deeply and ran a hand through his cropped hair.

"Tiernan's right that dwelling on another world will lead to madness," he said. "Imagine someone's only glimpse of you was living alone as a child of the forest, or dressed as Thymarai to trick the Sarteres, or kissing Matéo. None of those show the full scope of your life, who you are and who you love. So why else would your parents show you this?"

I mulled on that. It would've been simpler, kinder, and more useful to show me where the Rúonbattai cleric or her last three oaks were. The only reason they wouldn't was if they couldn't.

"Sacred trees are a conduit," I said slowly. "They lead somewhere else. You can never see your own eyes, only a reflection. My visions are always of the shoirdryge. And if the Rúonbattai cleric is dead there, my parents can't show me what she's doing now."

Yotolein half-smiled. "Was there anything useful or positive about this vision?"

"I guess . . . that other me is happy? Earlier this autumn she was in the wasteland. Now she's in the forest with someone she trusts."

"If that was an omen, how would you interpret it?"

"That something terrible can lead to something good. Kianta kolo, as Temal always said. Even after a tough winter, the sap will flow — *oh*." I clapped a hand to my mouth. "The Tjarnnaast battle felt like being in the wasteland. Tiernan gave me a gold coin and said to look for the tree if I need help."

Yotolein raised his eyebrows. "What tree?"

I fished through my purse and held out the coin etched with the Golden Oak's leafy nine-branched tree. "I think my parents want me to find Tiernan. To trust him. Maybe together, we can figure out what to do about the Rúonbattai cleric."

"That sounds like good advice."

I paused. "How did you manage that by only asking questions?"

Yotolein chuckled. "I'm pretty sure Hanaiko is smarter than me. I've gotten used to asking things and letting her figure out the answer."

I elbowed him. "You're a better father than you think."

We fell into silence. Beams of sunlight moved across the floor. Down in the settlement, our family would be waking, but I didn't want to shatter this brief moment of peace. It might be the last one I had for a long time to come.

EPILOGUE

Jonalin Tanarem
9th Royal Eremur Naval Forces
Cavalo via Mèr

Autumn equinox + 7 weeks, Year 625

The envelope will probably say this letter is from Shawnaast, since Nettle Ginu doesn't have a post office to mail it from. Hanaiko is writing for me in Trader because I can still only manage Ferish and no one here can help me. She's so worried about missing school that she brought paper, ink, and a quill to keep up with her assignments. I was nowhere near such a good student at age eleven. Emehein once threatened to tie me to a tree during antayul lessons, and he's the most patient person I know.

You've probably heard by now about the Battle of Tjarnnaast, and you've probably heard that the Tula-jouyen fought in it. My parents and I were there, too, but they didn't make it out. My temal was killed during an attack on the military camp. My tema was killed while chasing down Liet. We brought them back to Nettle Ginu and buried them yesterday. That's why Hanaiko is here now, and your parents, too. Samulein brought his kitten Stjarnå. He's tamed her into sleeping on his shoulder. You're not the only one who lives by the stars.

I wish I could tell you I'm okay, but I'm not. Whenever we see each other again, we'll talk — Hanaiko is telling me that eleven is old enough to write about grown-up things. Hanaiko, you're very mature for your age, but nei. Sorry.

Anyway, I'm writing because I won't be in Nettle Ginu much longer. I've figured out something about the ~~Rooon~~ ~~Ruon~~ never mind, Hanaiko can't spell it, which is probably good. I'll stay for Malana's wedding — yeah, she finally proposed to Aoreli — then go back to Caladheå for a bit, then I have no idea what will happen. But if I'm right, and things work out, you'll be able to leave the navy and sail wherever you want.

I've been thinking about things I wish I could tell my parents. I've been thinking about you, too. Just in case I don't get another chance, I want to say that I love you. I know we're over, and our lives have gone different ways, but part of my heart will always be yours.

Yes, Hanaiko is currently giggling and planning flowers for our wedding.

Love, Kateiko

GLOSSARY

etymology: A: Aikoto, F: Ferish, S: Sverbian

antayul: [A. *anta* water, *-yul* caller] viirelei who have learned to control water

attuning: shapeshifting into an animal; a rite of passage for viirelei adolescents

bloodweed: semi-poisonous leaves; used as birth control by viirelei

bogmoss: moss used for dressing wounds; antiseptic and highly absorbent

brånnvin: [S. *brånn* burn, *vin* wine] several varieties of clear rye liquor, including vodka

Coast Trader: a pidgin trade language derived from Aikoto, Sverbian, Ferish, and others duck potato: underwater root of arrowhead plants; ground up for flour by viirelei

Elken Wars: a series of wars fought between Ferish colonists and a Sverbian-Aikoto alliance for control of the coast and its natural resources

fyndestjolv: [S. *fynde* enemy, *stjolv* shield] a traitor

hellseed: a poisonous plant; used in small doses to calm the nerves

irumoi: a wooden rod covered with glowing blue mushrooms; used as a light source

itheran: [S. *ithera* 'out there'] viirelei term for foreign colonists

jouyen: viirelei tribe(s) typically belonging to a confederacy

Kånehlbattai: [S. *kån* royal, *-ehl* female, *battai* guard] Sverbian queensguard

laudanum: tincture made from poppy seeds; used as a painkiller and sedative

madro: a Ferish holy woman

makiri: Aikoto figurines carved in the shape of animals that protect a home or person from cruel spirits

needlemint: evergreen-scented leaves native to Sverba; used as numbing painkiller

okorebai: political, spiritual, and military leader of a jouyen

okoreni: successor to an okorebai, typically passed from parent to child

Ombros-méleres: [F. *ombros* shadow, *mélere* soldier] a secretive Ferish mercenary band

padro: a Ferish priest

pann: a denomination of the sovereign currency; 100 pann to 1 sovereign

plank house: a large building and social unit of the Aikoto, housing up to ten families rioden: massive auburn conifer trees used for dugout canoes, buildings, bark weaving, etc.

Rúonbattai: [S. *rúon* rain, *battai* guard] radical Sverbian militant group who swore to drive off the Ferish but mysteriously vanished several years after the Third Elken War

sancte: Ferish holy building

sovereign: a form of currency introduced by the Sverbian monarchy

stavehall: Sverbian holy building

tulanta: [A. *tularem* a type of plant, *anta* water] hallucinogenic painkiller used by viirelei

viirelei: [A. *vii* they, *rel* of, *leiga* west] colonists' term for coastal Indigenous Peoples, including the Aikoto, Nuthalha, and Kowichelk confederacies

willowcloak: painkiller made from willow bark

GODS, SPIRITS, MYTHOLOGY

AIKOTO

aeldu: spirits of the dead

Aeldu-yan: land of the dead

kinaru: giant waterfowl sacred to tel-saidu and the Rin-jouyen

oosoo: giant salamanders sacred to jinra-saidu and the Kowichelk Confederacy

Orebo: legendary figure who accidentally broke a moonbeam into shards and formed the stars

saidu: spirits that control the weather and maintain balance in nature

ANTA-SAIDU (WATER), EDIM-SAIDU (EARTH AND PLANTS), JINRA-SAIDU (FIRE), TEL-SAIDU (AIR)

FERISH

dios: the god above all

stelos: a star; the aura of god

SVERBIAN

bjørnbattai: [S. *bjørn* bear, *battai* guard] legendary warriors who shapeshift into bears

Bøkkai: a god who steals souls

Bøkkhem: [S. *Bøkkai*, *hem* flatlands] a barren land of the dead

dúnravn: [S. *dún* pale, *ravn* raven] sacred white raven

Hafai: Lady of the Ocean; goddess of ships, swimming, and tides; accompanied by enormous whales

Hymelai: Lady of the Sky; goddess of archery, flight, and moonlight; accompanied by white ravens

shoirdryge: [S. *shoird* shard, *ryge* realm] parallel world that splintered off from other worlds

Thaerijmur: an abundant land of the dead across an ocean

Thymarai: Lady of the Woods; goddess of fertility, love, beauty, and juniper trees; accompanied by *bjørnbattai*

PHRASES, SLANG, PROFANITY

akesida: Aikoto term for *young woman*

cingari tia/sia mera: [F. *cingari* fuck (imperative), *tia/sia* your/his or her, *mera* mother]

Elkhounds: slang for Caladheå city guards

hanekei: [A. 'it is the first time we meet'] formal Aikoto greeting

kaid: any insult to the aeldu, used as strong profanity by the Aikoto

kianta kolo: [A. *ki* golden, *anta* water, *koro* 'to flow'] Mikiod's mantra, lit. *the sap will flow* någva: [S. 'to fuck'] highly versatile Sverbian profanity; adjective form is *någvakt*

pigeon: slur for itherans

sacra flore: mild interjection referring to the Ferish holy flower

sacro dios: strong interjection taking the Ferish god's name in vain

takuran: [A. *taku* shit] highly offensive slur alluding to Aikoto burial rites, referencing someone so foul they must be buried in shit because dirt rejects their blood

tema: Aikoto affectionate term for *mother*

temal: Aikoto affectionate term for *father*

yan taku: [A. *yan* world, *taku* shit] profanity with religious connotations

CULTURES

Aikoto: [A. *ainu* mountain, *ko* flow, *toel* coast] A confederacy of eight jouyen occupying a large region of coastal rainforest.

Ferish: Colonists from Ferland who landed on the west coast of the Aikoto's continent. Later, a mass exodus from Ferland of famine victims caused a population boom in Aikoto lands.

INDUSTRIES: wheat farming, manufacturing, naval trading.

RELIGION: monotheist.

Kowichelk: A confederacy of jouyen in the rainforest south of the Aikoto. Largely wiped out from disease brought by foreign colonists.

INDUSTRIES: fishing, textiles, jade carving.

RELIGION: animist.

Nuthalha: A confederacy of jouyen in the tundra north of the Aikoto. Largely isolated.

INDUSTRIES: whaling, trapping, bone carving.

RELIGION: animist.

Sverbians: Settlers from Sverba who landed on the east coast of the Aikoto's continent, migrated west, and later allied with the Aikoto against the Ferish.

INDUSTRIES: rye farming, goat herding, logging.

RELIGION: polytheist.

AIKOTO JOUYEN: NORTH

Beru-jouyen: *People of the sea.* Live in Meira Dael on the coast of Nokun Bel.

CREST: grey whale.

INDUSTRIES: whaling, soapstone-carving.

Dona-jouyen: *Nomad people.* Live in Anwen Bel and on the ocean. Formed when members of the Rin and Iyo split off.

CREST: white seagull.

INDUSTRIES: fishing, transient labour.

Haka-jouyen: *People of the frost.* Live inland in Nokun Bel.

CREST: brown grizzly bear.

INDUSTRIES: fur trapping, tanning.

Rin-jouyen: *People of the lakeshore.* Live in Aeti Ginu in central Anwen Bel. Oldest jouyen in the Aikoto with significant territory and influence.

CREST: white or black kinaru.

INDUSTRIES: woodcarving, embroidery, fur trapping.

Tamu-jouyen: *People of the peninsulas.* Live in Tamun Dael on the coast of Anwen Bel.

CREST: orange shark.

INDUSTRIES: fishing, boatcraft.

AIKOTO JOUYEN: SOUTH

Iyo-jouyen: *People of the surrounds*. Live in Toel Ginu and Caladheå on the coast of Iyun Bel. Largest and second-most powerful jouyen in the Aikoto. Historic allies with the Rin.

CREST: blue dolphin.

INDUSTRIES: stone carving, textiles.

Kae-jouyen: *People of the inlet*. Live on the coast of Ukan Bel alongside Burren Inlet.

CREST: green heron.

INDUSTRIES: fishing.

Yula-jouyen: *People of the valley*. Live inland in Ukan Bel in a network of river valleys.

CREST: copper fox.

INDUSTRIES: weaving.

A BRIEF HISTORY OF EREMUR AND SURROUNDING LANDS

WRITTEN BY HANAIKO KIRBANEHL

-200 The Rin-jouyen constructs a shrine in Aeti Ginu, one of the oldest surviving buildings in the Aikoto Confederacy.

-60 Sverbian sailors land on the east coast of the Aikoto's continent and begin migrating west.

1 The Sverbian monarchy introduces a new calendar, marking the birth of an empire.

428 Sverba founds the province of Nyhemur across the mountains from Aikoto lands. The two groups begin trading.

487 Ferish sailors land in Aikoto territory. They clash violently with Aikoto and Sverbians over trade routes and natural resources.

492 Gustos Dévoye, a Ferish naval captain, builds a trading post on an island in Iyo-jouyen territory. He names the island Ile vi Dévoye. The post fails to last the winter.

513 Barros Sanguero, lord of the New Ferland Trading Company, builds the Colonnium stronghold in Iyo territory. He quickly dominates regional trade.

530 Dévoye's son, Gustos II, builds a stone keep on the peninsula north of Tamun Dael, taking advantage of local unrest caused by a historic land dispute between the surrounding Rin, Tamu, Beru, and Haka-jouyen.

533 FIRST ELKEN WAR

Sanguero and Gustos II join forces, prompting Sverbians and Aikoto to ally against them. Some Rin and Iyo refuse to go to war and instead split off to form the nomadic Dona-jouyen.

In the south, the Sverbian-Aikoto alliance kills Sanguero and captures the Colonnium. Iyo, Rin, and Sverbian settlers build a fort around it to ensure Ferish soldiers cannot retake it. They name the fort Caladheå.

In the north, the Sverbian-Aikoto alliance kills Gustos II and captures his keep, which they name Caladsten. The Rin, Tamu, Beru, and Haka let Sverbians occupy the disputed region on the condition they protect it from the Ferish. The Sverbians name the region Nordmur.

535 Imarein Rin, traumatized from the war, abandons his jouyen. He climbs Se Ji Ainu and swears devotion to the air spirit Ainu-Seru, known by itherans as Suriel.

545 Sverba founds the province of Eremur in southern Aikoto territory, declares Caladheå the capital, and establishes a local military. The Aikoto Confederacy refuses to recognize these actions.

547 Famine hits Ferland. Thousands of Ferish immigrants flee overseas to Eremur and nearby lands. Caladheå blooms into an international trading port. Construction begins on a new district, Ashtown, to house Ferish refugees.

557–8 SECOND ELKEN WAR

Mardos Goyero, a Ferish naval captain, attempts to retake the Colonnium and claim land for new immigrants. The Sverbian-Aikoto alliance nearly defeats Goyero — until his soldiers raze Bronnoi Ridge, the Aikoto district in Caladheå. The Rin abandon the city and return north.

Sverba agrees to share control of Eremur with Ferland via an elected council. The Iyo surrender Bronnoi Ridge in exchange for land and housing in the Ashtown slums. Sverbian dissenters form the Rúonbattai, a radical militant group, and vow to drive out the Ferish.

559 The war treaties prompt another immigration wave from Ferland. Wealthy settlers take over Bronnoi Ridge and the nearby town of Shawnaast, which later merges with Caladheå.

563 The Rúonbattai construct a hidden colony, Brånnheå.

604–5 THIRD ELKEN WAR

An influenza epidemic ravages Eremur, killing thousands. Ferish rebels, angry about treaties from the previous war, take advantage of the weakened military and stage a coup. The Rúonbattai have a resurgence of support and retaliate against the Ferish rebels.

The war-torn Rin and other northern jouyen refuse to come south and fight, breaking the Aikoto alliance. The Iyo temporarily abandon Caladheå.

The Rúonbattai leader is killed in combat. Their new leader, Liet, retreats and ends the war. The Caladheå Council regains control of the city.

606 Several Sverbian mages, accused of helping the Rúonbattai massacre Ferish immigrants, are murdered in Council custody. The mage city Ingdanrad cuts diplomatic ties to Eremur.

614 Antoch Parr is promoted to captain of the 2nd Royal Eremur Cavalry. He recruits Jorumgard Tømasind and Tiernan Heilind, immigrant mercenaries from Sverba, to fight the Rúonbattai.

618 The Rúonbattai vanish without a trace.

622 Rumours emerge that the Rúonbattai have reappeared in Nordmur. Captain Parr coordinates with Eremur's navy and storms the north in search of them, causing thousands of Sverbians and Aikoto to flee.

ACKNOWLEDGEMENTS

My gratitude to the following:

Rob Masson, my life partner, for your endless love, support, and patience during my rambles about everything from character arcs to interreligious theology. If thousands of worlds do exist, I'm glad to be in this one with you.

Jen Albert, my editor, for your insight and expertise, challenging me to delve deeper and taking the plunge into this new world with me. Susan Renouf, my former editor, for your lasting influence on how I navigate storytelling. Jessica Albert, my art director, for developing another stunning cover (not to mention everything else you do). Tania Blokhuis, my former publicist, for all your help over the years, even while we're on different continents. Anita Ragunathan, my new publicist, for your work on this book. Everyone else at ECW Press whose skill and hard work helped this book come to fruition.

Simon Carr, my cover illustrator, and Tiffany Munro, my cartographer, for your beautiful and attentive artwork. Sera-Lys McArthur of the Nakota, not just for your vivid, powerful narration of the *Flight* and *Veil* audiobooks, but for all your work as an actor and activist, teaching by example how to portray Indigenous characters and stories.

All my wonderful writer groups. Squid Squad: Roy Leon (THALL), Rochelle Jardine, Shannon O'Donovan, Lilah Souza, and Bo Jones for writing memes and kraken gifs. Cythera Crew: special thanks to Jessica Smith #453 for your unwavering support. CRLiterature: special thanks to Jay Knioum, my Texas skeleton friend. Australian Speculative Fiction: special thanks to David Myers for welcoming me into the fold at Supanova Expo.

Kathleen and Douglas, my parents; Fletcher and Nic, my brothers. Writing a book about separated families, especially during a pandemic that keeps us on opposite sides of the world, made me miss you more than ever. Shawna, my future sister-in-law, for inspiring Jonalin's love of macramé.

Jackson 2bears of the Kanien'kehaka (Mohawk) and Luke Parnell of the Haida and Nisga'a, my former art instructors, for teaching me how to blend old and new culture. Dr. Rob Budde, my former CanLit instructor, for being an ongoing role model of allyship.

Many, many First Nations, Inuit, and Métis creative folk whose work I've learned from. Of particular note from the literary sphere: Eden Robinson, Alicia Elliott, Waubgeshig Rice, Jesse Thistle, Cherie Dimaline, and the late Gregory Younging.

The Wurundjeri, in whose territory this novel was written; and the nations of the Northwest Coast of North America, in whose territory it's set.